COPPER RIVER

ALSO BY WILLIAM KENT KRUEGER

Mercy Falls
Blood Hollow
The Devil's Bed
Purgatory Ridge
Boundary Waters
Iron Lake

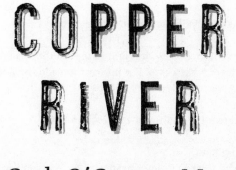

COPPER RIVER

A Cork O'Connor Mystery

WILLIAM KENT KRUEGER

ATRIA BOOKS
New York   London   Toronto   Sydney

ATRIA BOOKS
1230 Avenue of the Americas
New York, NY 10020

Library of Congress Cataloging-in-Publication Data

Krueger, William Kent.
  Copper River : a Cork O'Connor mystery / by William Kent Krueger.—
1st Atria Books hardcover ed.
    p. cm.
  1. O'Connor, Cork (Fictitious character)—Fiction. 2. Private investigators—Minnesota—Fiction. 3. Minnesota—Fiction. I. Title.

PS3561.R766C67 2006
813'.54—dc22   2006042717

ISBN-13: 978-0-7432-7840-9
ISBN-10:   0-7432-7840-2

First Atria Books hardcover edition August 2006

10 9 8 7 6 5 4 3 2 1

ATRIA BOOKS is a trademark of Simon & Schuster, Inc.

Manufactured in the United States of America

For information regarding special discounts for bulk purchases, please contact Simon & Schuster Special Sales at 1-800-456-6798 or business@simonandschuster.com

To my grandson Aiden Alan Buchholz,
with the hope that life smiles on him kindly.

ACKNOWLEDGMENTS

For all the help I'm given when writing a book, a simple thank-you never seems enough, but I'm hoping it will do.

To Michelle Basham I offer not only my thanks for her guidance in understanding the tragic situation of the lost and forgotten children alone on America's streets, but also my profound admiration for her own unselfish efforts to establish Avenues for Homeless Youth (formerly Project Foundation).

Thanks to Barbara Klick of the University of Minnesota Veterinary Medical Clinic, who gave me a lot of wonderful information and insight into the working life and ethics of veterinarians.

Thank you to the people of Marquette and Big Bay, Michigan, who told me stories only the locals know.

As always, I owe a huge debt to the members of Crème de la Crime for their support, encouragement, camaraderie, and critique. You guys are the best.

Finally, should you ever find yourself in St. Paul, Minnesota, be sure to stop by the St. Clair Broiler, where this and every book that bears my name has been written. Beneath the historic neon flame you'll find good coffee, great food, and the comfort that comes from the company of truly fine folks.

1

*H*enry Meloux, the old Ojibwe Mide, might tell the story this way.

He might begin by saying that the earth is alive, that all things on it—water, air, plants, rocks, even dead trees—have spirit. In the absence of wind, the grass still trembles. On days when the clouds are dense as gray wool, flowers still understand how to track the sun. Trees, when they bend, whisper to one another. In such a community of spirits, nothing goes unnoticed. Would not the forest, therefore, know that a child is about to die?

She is fourteen years, nine months, twenty-seven days old. She has never had a period, never had a boyfriend, never even had a real date. She has never eaten in a restaurant more formal than McDonald's. She has never seen a city larger than Marquette, Michigan.

She cannot remember a night when she wasn't awakened by nightmares, some dreamed, many horribly real. She cannot remember a day she was happy, although she has always been hopeful that she might find happiness, discover it like a diamond in the dust at her feet. Through all the horror of her life, she has, miraculously, held to that hope.

Until now.

Now, though she is only fourteen, she is about to die. And she knows it.

Somewhere among the trees below her, the man she calls Scorpio is coming for her.

She cringes behind a pile of brush in the middle of a clear-cut hillside studded with stumps like gravestones. The morning sun has just climbed above the tops of the poplar trees that outline the clearing. The chill bite of autumn is in the air. From where she crouches high on the hill, she can see the gleam of Lake Superior miles to the north. The great inland sea beckons, and she imagines sailing away on all that empty blue, alone on a boat taking her toward a place where someone waits for her and worries, a place she has never been.

She shivers violently. Before fleeing, she grabbed a thin brown blanket, which she wrapped around her shoulders. Her feet are bare, gone numb in the long, cold night. They bleed, wounded during her flight through the woods, but she no longer feels any pain. They've become stones at the end of her ankles.

In the trees far below, a dog barks, cracking the morning calm. The girl focuses on a place two hundred yards distant where, half an hour earlier, she'd emerged from the forest and started to climb the logged-over hillside. An hour after dawn, Scorpio's dog had begun baying. When she heard the hungry sound, she knew he'd got hold of her scent. What little hope she'd held to melted instantly. After that, it was a frantic run trying to stay ahead.

Scorpio steps from the shadow of the trees. He's like a whip, thin and cruel and electric in the sunlight. She can see the glint off the blue barrel of the rifle he cradles. Snatch, his black and tan German shepherd, pads before him, nose to the earth, tracking her through the graveyard of stumps. Scorpio scans the hillside above. She thinks she can see him smile, a gash of white.

There is no sense in hiding now. In a few minutes, Scorpio will be on her. Grasshopper quick, she pops from the blind of brush and sprints toward the hilltop. Her senseless feet thud against the hard earth. She lets the blanket fall to the ground, leaves it behind her. Starved for sunlight, the skin of her face and arms looks bleached. Beneath her thin, dirty T-shirt her breasts are barely formed, but the small, fleshy mounds rise and fall dramatically as she sucks air in desperate gasps. Behind her, the dog begins a furious barking. He has seen the prey.

She crests the hill and comes to a dead end. Before her the ground falls away, a sheer drop two hundred feet to a river that's a rush of white water between jagged rocks. There is no place left to run. She casts a frenzied eye back. Scorpio lopes toward her with Snatch in the lead. To her left and right, there is only the ragged lip of the cut across the hill.

Only one way for her to go now: down.

The face of the cliff below is a rugged profile offering hand-holds and small ledges. There are also tufts of brush that cling tenaciously to the stone, rooted in tiny fissures. She spies a shelf ten feet below, barely wider than her foot, but it is enough. She kneels and lowers herself over the edge. Clinging to the brush and the rough knobs of stone that punctuate the cliff, she begins her descent.

The rock scrapes her skin, leaves her arms bleeding. Her toes stretch for a foothold but, numbed, feel almost nothing. Weakened by an ordeal that has gone on longer than she can remember, her strength threatens to fail her, but she does not give up. She has never given up. Whatever the horror in front of her, she has always faced it and pushed ahead. This moment is no different. She wills a place to stand. Her feet find support, a few inches of flat rock on which she eases herself down.

"Come on, sweet thing. Come on back up."

Scorpio's voice is reasonable, almost comforting. She lifts her face. He's smiling, bone-white teeth between thin, bloodless lips. Beside him, the dog snarls and snaps, foam dripping from his purple gums.

"Hush!" Scorpio orders. "Sit."

Snatch obeys.

"Come on, now. Time to end this foolishness."

He lays down his rifle, bends low, and offers his hand.

In the quiet while she considers, she presses herself to the cliff where the stone still holds the cold of night. She can hear far below the hiss and roiling of the white water.

"We'll go back to the cabin," Scorpio says. "Have a little breakfast. Bet you're hungry. Now, doesn't that sound better than running over these woods, ruining those pretty little feet, freezing your ass off?"

He bends lower. His outstretched hand pushes nearer, a hand that has offered only humiliation and pain. On his wrist is a tattoo, a large black scorpion, the reason for the name she has given him in her thinking. She eyes his hairy knuckles, then looks into his face, which at the moment appears deceptively human.

"Think about it. You find a place to perch on that cliff, then what? It's not so bad out here right now. Sun's up, air's calm. But tonight it'll be close to freezing. That means you, too. You want to freeze to death? Hell, it doesn't matter anyway. I'll just leave old Snatch here to make sure you don't climb back up, go get me some rope, and come down there to get you. But I guarantee if I have to do that, I won't be in a forgiving mood. So what do you say?"

Not taking her eyes off him, she seeks a foothold farther down, somewhere out of his reach, but she cannot feel her toes. Finally, she risks a glance below her. In that instant, Scorpio's hand locks around her wrist.

"Got you."

He's strong, his grip powerful. He drags her kicking up the face of the rock. She struggles, screams as he wraps his arms around her. The dog dances back from the edge, barking crazily. Scorpio's breath smells of tobacco and coffee, but there's another smell coming off him, familiar and revolting. The musk odor of his sex.

"Oh, little darling," he croons, "am I going to make you pay."

She puts all her desperation, all her remaining strength, into one last effort, a violent twist that breaks her loose, sends her tumbling backward over the cliff.

The world spins. First there is blue sky, then white water, then blue sky again. She closes her eyes and spreads her arms. Suddenly she isn't falling but flying. The wind streams across her skin. Her held breath fills her like a smooth balloon. She is weightless.

For one glorious moment in her short, unhappy life, she is absolutely free.

* * *

Meloux would finish gently, pointing out, perhaps, that the fall of the smallest robin is known to the spirits of the earth, that no death goes unnoticed or unmourned, that the river has simply been waiting, and like a mother she has opened wide her arms.

2

*R*enoir DuBois kept his heart in his bedroom closet, hidden in a Nike shoe box.

There was an agate he'd found on the shore of Lake Superior when he was very young, the image of a wolf so clear on its smooth surface that it seemed etched by a purposeful hand. In the totemic system of the Anishinaabeg, Ren was Ma'iingan, Wolf Clan, and he believed the stone was a sign of some kind whose full meaning he would someday understand.

In the box there was also an eagle feather given to him by his great-grandfather, who told him this story: A certain man spent his whole life searching in vain for an eagle feather, which would signify his great wisdom. He paid no heed to the needs of his family or relatives or other people. Finally he gave up and said to the Great Spirit, "I have wasted my life searching for the eagle feather. Now I will spend my time helping others." As soon as he said this, a beautiful eagle flew overhead and a feather gently drifted down.

There was a small figure of the Marvel Comics character Silver Surfer, one of Ren's all-time favorite superheroes. His best friend, Charlie, had spotted it at a swap meet in Marquette and had given it to him for Christmas.

There was the skull of a vole, small, delicate, perfect, that Ren had discovered in the meadow south of the cabins one summer afternoon. Only the skull, no other bones. So that it would not be crushed by his other treasures, he kept it in a tiny box that had once held one of his mother's necklaces. Sometimes he opened the necklace box and spent hours drawing the skull in minute detail, imagining as he did so what kind of world such a small brain and perspective would see.

There was a newspaper article, which his mother did not know he had, cut from the *Billings Gazette,* about the murder of his father, and also the long, celebratory obituary that had been printed in the *Marquette County Courier.*

The most precious item in the box was a drawing his father had given him, done on a plain sheet of notepad paper, the kind kept by the phone to write messages. It had been created on a good day, Ren recalled, an August day. They'd spent the morning putting a new toilet in one of the cabins, and his father had talked while he worked, offering Ren his understanding about Kitchimanidoo, the Great Spirit, about life, about art. He'd said, as he put the wax ring in the flush hole and settled the porcelain bowl on top, that life was a reflection of the Great Spirit, and that art was a reflection of life. All of them were simpler than people imagined. At lunch in the main cabin, which was called Thor's Lodge, he'd illustrated his point with a pen-and-ink drawing—two long arcs, a few easy loops. "What is it?" he'd asked Ren. Though nothing connected in a way that completed the image, Ren saw it was a bear. "There aren't many clear connections in life. God, Kitchimanidoo, they're pretty sketchy when you come right down to it. But you don't need everything spelled out for you, son. Here"— and he touched Ren's chest above his heart—"here is where it all comes together." A week later, his father was dead.

All the treasures in his box Ren loved and in loving them found the connections simple and unseen that ran from the outside world deep into the world of his heart, just as his father had promised.

That afternoon, fourteen-year-old Ren was at work on something that would eventually find its way into his box. He had no idea at the moment of the enormity of the events that would put it there.

"On your knees with your nose in the dirt. Dude, that's so lame, but so *you.*"

7

Ren looked up from his work, startled. Charlie Miller stood above him, her face a narrow mask of disgust. Her real name was Charlene, but she preferred Charlie. A lot about her besides her name belied her gender. She looked like a boy, dressed like a boy, and was the fastest runner in the eighth grade at Bodine Area Middle School. Her hair was shaved close to her scalp and from a distance appeared to be no more than a dusting of charcoal. Her left nostril and her lower lip were pierced and sported small silver rings. She was taller than Ren, more slender, and moved with the quickness and grace of a forest animal. Also the wariness.

"Get bent," Ren said, and returned to his work.

Charlie knelt beside him. Ren could smell that she needed a bath.

"What's up?" she said.

"Cougar track."

"Bullshit."

Two nights before, rain had turned the ground around the cabins soft. Ren hadn't discovered the track until the next afternoon; as soon as he did, he set about preserving it. He was used to seeing tracks in the vicinity of the resort cabins. Raccoon, bear, even an occasional bobcat. They came nosing around the trash bins, which Ren's mother kept locked. At first he'd thought the track was a large bobcat, but when he got out his copy of Peterson's *A Field Guide to Animal Tracks,* he realized it was not. He'd heard stories of cougars still roaming the woods of the U.P., but he never thought he'd find the evidence. Using an old paintbrush with soft bristles, he'd gently cleaned debris from the imprint, then sprayed it with clear lacquer. When that dried, he mixed up a batch of plaster of Paris in an empty Folger's coffee can, and he'd been pouring this into the track when Charlie startled him.

"How do you know it's a cougar?" Charlie asked.

"I looked it up."

"I never heard of a cougar around here."

"They used to be all over the place, but people killed most of them and drove the others away. I heard there might not be more than twenty on the whole U.P."

"Dude, you're worse than *National Geographic.*"

She hit him hard on the arm and he dropped the coffee can.

"Goddamn it, Charlie, quit screwing around. This is important."

"Yeah? So's this." She hit him again.

Ren launched into her and they rolled over in the soft dirt. Charlie easily got the upper hand, straddled him, and pinned him to the ground.

"Say it," she commanded.

"Bite me."

She slapped the side of his head lightly. "Say it."

"You suck."

She lifted her butt and bounced hard on his stomach so that he grunted.

"Say it."

"All right. I give."

She sprang off him, raised her hands above her head, and did a victory dance. Ren got back on his knees and crawled to the cougar track.

Charlie knelt beside him again. "Cougar. No shit."

"No shit."

"Sweet," she said.

Ren heard the scrape of pine wood. He glanced up as the door to the nearest cabin opened.

The man with the wounded leg stood at the threshold, looking stunned, as if the beautiful afternoon, the evergreen-scented air, the blue autumn sky, the warm sunshine were the most amazing things he'd ever seen. Or maybe it was just the fact that he was still alive. After a moment, he fell forward, tumbled down the steps, and lay sprawled facedown in the dirt.

"Jesus." Ren sprang to his feet and sprinted to the fallen man.

"What happened to him?"

"Somebody shot him yesterday."

The man's pants were bloodstained. The left leg had been cut off near the crotch, revealing two wounds, one on the outside of his thigh where the bullet had entered and another on the inside where it exited. The exit wound was larger and open, fitted with a tube and drainage bag that were held in place with surgical tape. The entrance wound had been stitched, but the stitches were broken and the wound was bleeding. The man's eyes were closed. His face had gone slack.

"Is he dead?" Charlie asked.

"God, I hope not. I was supposed to be watching him." Ren felt the man's neck. "He's got a pulse. We've got to get him back inside. You take his left arm, I'll take his right. Let's see if we can lift him."

"Unh-uh." Charlie backed away a step. "I've tried dragging my old man into bed when he was passed out. You might as well try lifting a dead horse."

"Come on, damn it, give me a hand."

"All right, but I'm telling you, you're better off just getting a blanket and letting him lie there."

She grasped his arm as Ren had instructed and they tried in vain to bring the man to his feet.

"Like a dead horse, I told you." Charlie grunted as she dropped the arm.

Ren pushed himself up. "Don't leave him."

"Where are you going?"

He bounded up the steps and ran inside Cabin 3. The bedding lay on the floor where the man had thrown it. Ren grabbed the blanket, then another from the closet, and raced back outside. Charlie was bent over, examining the man's wounds.

"He's been bleeding pretty bad," she said.

Ren spread out one of the blankets on the ground next to the man.

"Could he, like, bleed to death?"

"Mom says it looks worse than it is."

"She sewed him up?"

"Yeah. Help me here."

Together they rolled him so that he was on the blanket. Ren stood up.

"I'll be right back."

He made for Thor's Lodge, took the steps in a single bound, shoved open the door, and grabbed the telephone. He dialed the animal clinic where his mother worked. Dawn, the receptionist, told him she was out on a call. He tried her cell phone, got her after three rings. Her signal was breaking up, but not so badly she didn't understand. She told him what to do and that she'd be there as soon as she could.

After he hung up, he went to the closet in his mother's bedroom and took her medical bag from the shelf. He returned to where Charlie sat beside the man.

"You were gone a long time," she said.

"I talked to my mom. She'll get here as soon as she can."

He checked the tube and bag taped to the man's thigh.

"What *is* that?" Charlie asked.

"It's called a Penrose drain. It helps the wound stay clean while it heals." Ren dug into the medical bag, brought out a pair of latex gloves and Betadine scrub. He put on the gloves. "Hold his leg."

Ren cleaned the area around the second wound where the stitches were broken. The fast flow of blood had subsided into a steady ooze. He reached into the medical bag again and pulled out a sterile pad, a roll of gauze, tape, and a pair of scissors. He pressed the pad to the wound, bound it in place by wrapping the gauze tightly several times around the man's thigh, and secured it with the surgical tape.

Charlie watched in silent fascination. When Ren finished, she looked at him with admiration. "That was pretty sweet."

"Yeah, well."

"Who is he?"

"Family. My mom's cousin."

"Has he got a name?"

Charlie pulled off the gloves and began to put away the medical things. He considered a moment before answering her.

"Yeah," he said. "It's Cork."

3

A mile outside Bodine, Jewell DuBois turned off the main highway and bounced up the rutted road toward the old cabins. She was not happy. She'd been on an emergency call, a horse whose symptoms made her suspect tetanus. The last thing she wanted to hear that afternoon was that Cork O'Connor needed her.

She pulled her Blazer to a stop on the lane that ran between the guest cabins, grabbed her medical bag, and hopped out. Ren and Charlie were with him, sitting on the ground on either side. They didn't seem upset. A good thing.

Cork was awake.

"Hope you don't charge much for a cabin," he said weakly. "The ground out here's more comfortable than that bunk you had me in."

Jewell addressed her son as she went down on her knees, asking sternly, "What happened?"

"He just opened the door and fell down the steps, Mom."

"Where were you?"

"Out here," Ren said.

"What were you doing out here? Why weren't you with him like I told you?"

"Not his fault," Cork broke in. "My own stupidity."

Jewell drew the blanket back and examined the work her son had done. "Good job, Ren." Then to Cork: "Why did you get up?"

"Seemed like a good idea at the time." Cork smiled faintly. "The truth is I forgot where I was and panicked. Then I fainted."

The sun was low in the sky, the afternoon going cool. Where the sun sliced between the trees that backed the cabins, the ground was still warm, but with sunset everything would chill quickly.

"Orthostatic shock, probably," Jewell said.

Cork looked confused. "Orthostatic?"

"You got up too fast," Ren said.

"Nothing to worry about. Your brain just needed more blood than it had at the moment," Jewell explained. "Happens some-times when people have been lying down for a while and stand up too quickly. We need to get you inside. Can you help us?"

"I'll try."

"Ren, Charlie, take that side. I'll help over here." To Cork she said, "Don't put weight on that leg if you can help it."

"Whatever you say, Doc."

They positioned themselves and he sat up, then they helped him to his feet. Cork grunted as he came upright, and his pasty face went even whiter, but he didn't buckle.

"Up the steps, one at a time," Jewell instructed.

They mounted slowly. Cork struggled not to lean on his bum leg. By the time they got him inside and laid him on his bunk, they were all breathing hard and Cork was soaked with sweat.

A bag with a drip tube hung from the curtain rod on the window next to the bunk. "I see you pulled out your IV," she said.

He shrugged. "Don't remember."

"Ren, get my bag."

Her son scurried out and came back a moment later with the medical bag and the blankets. He handed her the bag and laid the cleaner of the two blankets over Cork.

Jewell pulled the blanket back enough to expose the wounded leg. She cracked open her medical bag, took out a pair of bandage scissors, and cut away the gauze binding Ren had put on. "I need to sew it closed again. I'll be here awhile. You guys hungry?"

"Yeah," Charlie said quickly.

"My purse is in the car. Get what you need for a couple of burgers in town or whatever you want. Charlie, you can't talk about this, you understand?"

"Yes, ma'am."

"Not to your father, not to anybody."

"I won't."

"Good." She thought about Charlie and about something else. "It's Saturday. You want to stay here tonight?"

Charlie shook her head. "I'll be all right."

"That changes, you come on over, you hear?"

"Thanks."

"And, Charlie?"

"Yeah?"

"When you go home tonight, do yourself a favor: take a good long shower, plenty of soap."

"Whatever."

"I mean it."

"Right." Charlie looked down.

Jewell watched the kids walk out the cabin door, then she turned back to her patient.

"Good kid, Ren," Cork said. "Sure he won't say anything?"

"I'm sure."

"What about the other boy?"

She reached into her medical bag. "Charlie? Not a boy."

"Could've fooled me."

"She fools most everybody."

He eyed the syringe she held.

"Local anesthetic," she explained, and stuck him. "I should have put you in Thor's Lodge with us last night so we could keep an eye on you better."

"I'll be fine here. Promise not to go wandering again." He laid his hand gently on her arm. "I'm sorry about this. I didn't know where else to go."

"A hospital, for starters."

"I told you last night. I can't do a hospital right now. They'd have to report the gunshot wound, and I'd end up a sitting duck for the people trying to kill me."

"Who are they?"

"Professionals."

"You mean like hit men."

"Yeah, like that."

"Why do they want you dead?"

"They'll be paid handsomely for it."

"Who put up the money?"

"A man who believes I killed his son."

"Did you?"

"No."

"Why does he think that?"

"Circumstances."

"You couldn't just talk to him?"

"I tried. He wouldn't listen. It's complicated."

"So what now?"

"There are people trying to prove I'm innocent."

"That could take a while?"

"I don't know. Look, as soon as I can, I'll leave."

She put on latex gloves, pulled an Ethilon nylon suture pack from her bag, tore it open, took out the curved needle and black thread.

"I don't hear from you in forever, then you show up on my doorstep, shot, bleeding all over everything, expecting me to take you in. Christ, that's just like a man."

"You've cut your hair," he said.

"Easier to keep out of my way while I'm working."

When her hand, which held the needle, descended toward the entrance wound on the outside of his thigh, he looked away. "How are you doing?"

"How am I doing?" She squinted over her work. "I go to the clinic in the morning, come home late, fix dinner, help Ren with his homework, do laundry and what I can around the house, try to go to bed so tired I don't have to think about anything. So I guess, all things considered, I'm doing pretty shitty."

"Long time to be grieving."

"What do you know about grief? Damn." She shook her head at something she'd done. Cork didn't look and was glad she'd numbed the area first. "I still miss him. Every minute of every day. You want to know the worst part? Sometimes I hate him. Sometimes I don't know if I'm grieving or just royally pissed at him. There." She clipped the thread.

"I didn't feel a thing."

"Because I'm good. Hungry?"

"A little."

"I'll fix something that'll go down easy." She closed her bag, stood up, and headed for the door.

"Jewell, thank you."

She paused before stepping outside. "You can thank me best by getting better and getting out of here without bringing any more trouble around."

"As long as no one knows I'm here, you and Ren are okay, I promise."

"Good. I've had enough of people I care about dying."

In the late afternoon air outside Cabin 3, she stood a moment, breathing out her anger, her despair, still feeling the hurt of a wound that hadn't healed. In the cabin at her back, Cork O'Connor coughed.

Men, Jewell thought. All they'd ever brought her was trouble.

4

*B*odine, Michigan, was the end of the line. It lay near the terminus of thirty miles of poorly maintained county road that ran northwest out of Marquette along the shore of Lake Superior. It was *Anatomy of a Murder* territory, a place that despite its beauty was probably best filmed in black and white. For decades Bodine had been fighting a slow death.

To the south and west rose the Huron Mountains, thick with timber. Beyond that lay the Copper Country where the red-brown native ore leached out of the Keweenaw Peninsula and spread its veins through much of the western U.P. Stretching north all the way to the horizon was the vast blue of Lake Superior, which became, somewhere far out of sight, part of Canada. On good, clear days, you could see the Keweenaw curling out of the west, protecting Bodine from the worst of the gales that swept across the lake in late fall, storms that had spelled doom for generations of sailors. Looking east from Bodine, you could almost see the spot where the water had swallowed the *Edmund Fitzgerald*.

On this late Saturday afternoon, Bodine, population 1,207, was quiet as usual. Ren straddled the ATV his father had purchased for the old resort, and Charlie held on tight behind. For nearly a mile, he drove along the drainage ditch at the side of the road. Then he came onto the asphalt, crossed the iron bridge over the Copper River, and entered town. Legally, he

17

couldn't drive on a roadway, but in Bodine, a place used to ATVs and snowmobiles and anything else that would lure the tourists, no one paid much attention to that detail. He passed the Superior Inn, a lodge and restaurant of lacquered yellow pine logs, and the Supervalu market, where the parking lot was almost empty, and pulled to a stop in front of Kitty's Café. Charlie sprang off the seat with the flourish of a gymnast and bounced to the café door.

"Jesus, you're like a slug or something," she called to Ren, and disappeared inside.

They sat at the counter and ordered pasties, chocolate shakes, and fries. Pasties were small pies consisting of meat, vegetables, and gravy completely enclosed in a flaky crust. They were a local favorite, an import brought by Cornish immigrants who'd come to that part of Michigan in the late 1800's to work the copper and iron mines. While they ate, Charlie made fun of the other customers, some of them locals, some tourists come for the fall colors. The customers, for their part, eyed Charlie—her buzzed head, her piercings, her dirty clothing—as if she were an animal who'd wandered out of the woods.

When they finished, Ren pulled out the money he'd taken from his mother's purse and paid the bill.

Outside, the sun had settled on the tops of the distant Huron Mountains and the air was cooling fast with the approach of evening. Ren knew he should head back to the resort to help his mother with the man in Cabin 3, but he'd already wasted most of the day sitting by the man's bed, and he wasn't eager to return.

At that opportune moment Stash appeared.

"Hey," he called out, and skateboarded across the street toward the café. Stash was never without his skateboard. Taller than Charlie and Ren, older by a year, he wore his dark hair long. He was dressed as usual in baggy jeans that rode low on his butt, a black T-shirt a couple of sizes too large, and Doc Martens. A long, thin chain connected to a belt loop hung against his thigh and disappeared into his back pocket where he kept his wallet.

"Dudes, I was looking for you. I'm heading to the river, thinking of smoking a little weed. Want to come?"

"I'm there," Charlie said.

"Yeah, okay," Ren agreed. "Hop on," he said, indicating his ATV. "You can ride behind Charlie."

Before they could mount up, three teenagers rounded the corner beyond the café and made straight for Ren and his friends.

"Circus must be in town," the boy in the lead said. "Check out the freaks."

"Ah, shit," Stash said. "Greenway and his Nazis."

"Be cool," Ren said.

Charlie ignored him. "Make like a bee," she said to Greenway, "and buzz off."

The big kid smiled. Goose Jablonski and Kenny Merkin smiled, too. They all wore gold and blue Bodine Bobcats letterman jackets.

"Yeah, and who's going to make us?" Greenway said.

"Bite me," Stash said under his breath.

Greenway turned to him. "What did you say?"

"Nothing," Stash said.

Charlie stepped forward. "He said fuck off."

"Whoa. The junior dyke's flexing her muscles. What do you think?" Greenway said, addressing his buddies. "Maybe she really was born with balls."

"Leave her alone," Ren said.

"Shut your hole, Pocahontas. You'll end up with your head split open just like your old man."

Ren threw himself at Greenway with all the fury his small body contained. The larger boy stumbled back a step, then held his ground. He wrapped Ren in a powerful hug, flung him to the ground, and sat on him. He gave Ren a couple of hard open-handed slaps before Charlie kicked him in the ribs. Greenway toppled over, holding his side. Goose grabbed Charlie and gripped her in a headlock before she could dance away. He squeezed until her face turned red.

"Let her go, shithead." Ren tried to get up, only to have Merkin pounce and pin him to the ground.

"Help her, Stash," Ren hollered.

Stash stood frozen.

"Hey, hey, hey, break it up here." Gary Johnson trotted up, waving his hands. He was an adult and built like a bulldozer. Johnson latched an enormous hand onto Goose's shoulder. "Let her go, Goose."

The kid complied, but unhappily.

"Get off him, Kenny," Johnson said to Merkin.

Merkin lifted himself off Ren.

Johnson stared down at Greenway, who was still on the ground holding his ribs. "I'm more than a little disappointed, Dan. Big guys like you picking on kids, and a girl yet."

"Bitch kicked me," Greenway said.

Johnson shoved his ball cap back showing a high forehead. "Big deal. You get kicked all the time on the football field, and by guys with cleats, eh." He turned to Ren. "That lip's going to be puffy for a while. Better go on home and put some ice on it."

"I'm okay."

Johnson faced the three lettermen. "I've a good mind to talk to your fathers."

"Screw off," Greenway said.

"Or how about this, Dan? How 'bout I talk to Coach Soames, tell him what a big man you are, how you and Goose and Kenny here like beating on girls? I could get you yanked from that starting position faster 'n you could say Brett Favre. I'll do it."

In addition to being the publisher and editor of the *Marquette County Courier*, Johnson covered all area high school sports. That carried a lot of weight in Bodine.

Greenway and the others exchanged surly glances but said nothing.

"Now go on." Johnson gestured down the street. "I'm sure there are cats somewhere need torturing, eh."

When the boys had gone, Ren said, "Thanks."

Charlie said, "We were doing fine."

Johnson laughed. "That's exactly what Custer said, Charlie." He turned his attention back to Ren. "Like I said, have your mom look at that lip. How is she, by the way? Haven't seen her in a while."

"Busy," Ren said. "You know."

"Sure. Tell her I said hello, eh."

Ren nodded.

"Charlie, I swear I'm going to see you in the Olympics some-day." Johnson gave her a smile, then strolled away.

"Come on," Stash said, stowing his skateboard under his arm. "Let's get high."

5

A hundred yards from where the Copper River spilled into Lake Superior, perched on a small rise among a stand of red maples on the west bank, stood an old stone picnic shelter. The shelter was part of the Big Cascade Wayside, a little park named for the stair step of rocks and churning water it overlooked. The shelter had been built during the Depression as a CCC project but wasn't used much anymore. The locals and tourists preferred Dunning Park on the lakefront. More often than not, Ren and his friends had the place to themselves.

By the time they reached the river, the sun had set. The water as it dipped and swirled over the rocks was a reflection of a golden sky. Ren parked the ATV and the three kids stepped inside the shelter. The corners were littered with fallen leaves. A blackened fireplace dominated the back wall. The place smelled of old burn, dusty stone, rotting leaves, and faintly of piss. Stash stood on one of the two concrete picnic tables, reached up to a low rafter, and pulled down a cigar box bound with a thick rubber band. He sat down, slipped the band off, and lifted the lid to reveal a dime bag of weed, a package of Zig-Zag rolling papers, and a Bic lighter. His real name was Stuart, but Ren and Charlie had dubbed him Stash because he kept small caches of weed hidden in a number of places around Bodine. A hole in a tree in Dunning Park on the lake. Taped under the bleachers at the ballpark. In a disconnected downspout in the alley behind Linder's

Garage. He didn't like to carry anything on him. He'd been stopped too many times and ripped off, he claimed, by the deputy constable.

As Stash sat on the table and rolled a joint, Ren eyed the inside of the box lid. Printed in bold magic marker: PROPERTY OF STUART GULLICKSON.

"You're crazy, man," he told Stash. "That'll get you sent to juvie for sure."

"So I get picked up. The old man springs me, gives me a lecture on disappointment and shame, yells about military school again. Only problem is there aren't any I haven't already been kicked out of." He licked the seam to seal the joint. "Besides, it's a rush whenever I think somebody might find it and turn me in. Walking the edge. You down with that?"

"Yeah, dude," Charlie said. "You walk the edge real good. Showed us that back there in town with Greenway and his two turds."

Ren laughed. "Yeah, man, you were a real Captain America the way you tore into those guys."

"Hey, I was just about to kick their asses when Johnson showed up."

Charlie said, "Dude, I've seen lawn ornaments move faster than you."

She and Ren slapped hands.

"Fuck you guys." Stash stood up and started to leave the shelter.

"We're just funning with you," Ren called to him. "Come on back, man, and fire up that doobie."

Stash returned and sat on the picnic table. He lit the joint, took a hit, passed it to Ren, who took a hit and passed it to Charlie.

"I still think," Ren said, after he'd held the smoke in his lungs awhile, "that putting your name in the box is a stupid idea."

"'Live fast, die young, leave a beautiful corpse.' John Derek. *Knock on Any Door.*"

"Who?" Charlie asked.

Stints at private schools had taken Stash away from Bodine for long periods of time, and although Ren and Charlie often

23

hung with him, they weren't what Ren would have called tight. Stash's family had money. His father was president of a paper company in Marquette. They lived in a restored Victorian home, huge and elegant, that overlooked the lake. Stash's older brother was an athlete—football, basketball, baseball—but sports held no interest for Stash. In his bedroom, he had a television with a thirty-two-inch screen. He also had an extensive library of DVDs and videotapes. For some reason, he loved gangster movies, especially the old black and whites. When he wasn't skateboarding, he spent hours in that shaded room, watching a dark world filled with characters Ren didn't know played by actors he'd never heard of.

"Don't you watch *any* good movies?" Stash asked.

"Dude, you don't watch good movies. You watch, like, ancient history." Charlie shook her head. "John Dork."

"Derek."

"Whatever."

"It's called noir, ass wipe. And it isn't ancient history. When I get sprung from Bodine for good, I'm hitting Hollywood, man. I'm going to be—"

"The next Tarantino," Ren and Charlie finished in unison.

"The hell with you guys." Stash pushed off the table again and strode outside.

"Hey, don't take the joint," Ren called.

"My weed," Stash threw back over his shoulder.

"No problem," Charlie said, grabbing the cigar box. "We'll roll our own."

Stash said nothing, just stood on the riverbank getting high by himself.

Charlie rolled a tight number. "Toss me the lighter, dude," she called to Stash.

"Light it between your legs."

"Wait, I got a match." From her pocket, she dug a matchbook she'd picked up at Kitty's Café. She lit up and for a few minutes they smoked in silence.

"Dude, know what I heard?"

"What?" Ren said. He was looking out the shelter toward the golden water and the far bank lined with birch trees whose autumn leaves were like drops of the river splashed over the branches. He didn't know if it was the weed or the moment, but he wasn't sure he'd ever seen anything as beautiful.

"I heard Amber Kennedy likes you."

"Right."

"No shit. And don't tell me you haven't looked at those tits of hers when you pass her in the hallway. Dude, the way she pushes them out, it's totally grotesque. Like *Alien,* you know. I keep thinking something really scary is going to pop out of there."

Ren slid off the picnic table, went to the fireplace, and picked up the remains of a burned piece of wood. He walked back and began to doodle in charcoal on the tabletop. Charlie watched him for a while.

"What is it?" she asked.

"Can't you tell?"

"I don't know. Looks like mountains or something."

Ren drew a few more strokes.

"Jesus, that's Amber Kennedy, and those are her tits." Charlie laughed and gave Ren a playful shove.

"Hey, guys. Guys. You gotta see this. Quick." Stash frantically waved them over to the riverbank.

They moved slowly, not just because of the weed but because Stash sometimes got worked up over stupid things.

"Look. See it? Do you see it?"

Stash pointed at something in the water, sweeping downriver in and out of the troughs of the cascades. Ren couldn't, in fact, see it clearly because the light was so poor now, and the river had become a dark gloss of black and pale silver. Also, the fast water quickly carried away whatever it was that Stash had seen.

"It was a body," Stash said.

"Bullshit," Charlie said. "It was just a log or something."

"I'm telling you it was a body. I saw it when it went by."

"You mean like a dead person?" Ren said.

"Yeah, man, a dead body."

Charlie shook her head. "Naw, if it was a body it had to be, like, a deer or something."

Stash turned on her angrily. "If you weren't so goddamned slow you'd have seen it."

"Slow? Me?" Her fist exploded forward and caught Stash hard in the arm.

"Owww. Damn it."

"That's from my movie. *Charlie Kills Stash*."

Stash rubbed his arm. "I'm telling you guys it was a body."

"You've been watching too many old gangster movies, dude. It's screwing with your head."

"That or the weed," Ren threw in.

"I'm going down there to find it."

"You do, and you're walking home, Stash. I've got to split for the cabins. You want a ride, you come with me now."

"It was a body," Stash said sullenly.

"Yeah, well, now it's in the lake, and you know what they say about Superior: it never gives up its dead. So whatever it was, it's gone."

Stash stood looking downstream where a hundred yards away the pale river water met the deep blue of the great lake. "'Oil and water are the same as wind and air when you're dead,'" he said.

Ren and Charlie stared at him and waited.

"Humphrey Bogart. *The Big Sleep*," Stash said, disappointed. "Let's go."

6

Cork heard the boy enter and quietly close the cabin door.

"I'm awake," he said.

Ren paused and looked at him without emotion. Very Ojibwe, Cork thought. The blood of The People was evident in his fine black hair, high cheeks, dark eyes, latte-shaded skin. Ren said nothing but continued to the kitchen area, turned on the light, and sat down at the table. Carefully, he laid out the things he'd been carrying. A stack of comic books, a sketch pad, a box of colored pencils, a hard white lump that Cork couldn't identify.

"What time is it?" Cork asked.

"Nine."

The boy opened one of the comic books, then flipped back a page of the sketchbook. He selected a pencil, paused a moment, and began to draw.

"Where's your mom?"

"She got a call. An elk ranch west of Marquette. Some kind of emergency."

"And she asked you to sit with me again, is that it? Thanks."

The boy remained intent on his drawing.

"What are you doing?" Cork asked.

"Nothing."

"How do you know when you're finished?"

The boy hesitated, thought that over, decided to smile.

"Did your mom tell you about me?"

"Not much."

"You've got questions, I imagine."

The boy finally looked up.

"You deserve answers," Cork said.

Ren tapped the pencil top on the table a few times. "Who are you?"

"Your mother's cousin. You visited my house in Minnesota once with your folks. You must have been seven or eight then. Do you remember?"

"I remember you arrested Dad."

"I thought you might."

"Made Mom mad, but it was a story Dad used to like to tell." He thought a moment. "I remember two girls, older than me. One was blond and really pretty."

"That would be Jenny."

"The other one could play baseball as good as Charlie."

"And that would be Anne. They're both in high school. You probably don't remember Stevie. He was just a baby. He's seven now."

The boy looked unsatisfied. "That's not exactly what I meant."

"You meant who am I that somebody would want me dead?"

"Yeah, that."

Cork worked on sitting up. Despite the painkiller Jewell had given him, his leg throbbed. He edged his way upright with his back against the wall. Finally he could look at the boy eye to eye.

"I'm Corcoran Liam O'Connor, sheriff of Tamarack County, Minnesota."

"Oh. A cop." As if, of course, that was all he needed to write Cork off.

Cork went on. "I was shot because a rich man has put a bounty on my head. Half a million dollars, as I understand it."

Ren's eyes opened like a couple of sunflowers. "Why?"

"He thinks I killed his son."

"Did you?"

"No."

"Will he come looking for you here?" He seemed less worried than curious.

Cork shifted his position a little, hoping to ease the pain in his leg. It didn't work. "Men like him don't soil their hands with the actual dirty work. That's the reason for the bounty."

Ren worked this over in his thinking, then his face went slack again. "So you're the police."

"You hold that against me?"

"You know how my father died?"

"I know."

"The police murdered him."

"Most police aren't like that." He tried to judge how the boy received his words, but Ren was a blank slate. "It's hard for you, I know. I lost my father when I was your age."

Again, a flicker of interest in Ren's dark eyes. "Yeah?"

"He was the sheriff of Tamarack County, too. He was killed doing his duty, protecting people."

"How?"

"Some men tried to rob the bank in town. My dad and two deputies responded. There was shooting. In the middle of it, a deaf old woman walked onto the street right into the line of fire. My father ran out to pull her to safety, took a bullet that probably would have hit her. He died on the operating table."

"You're trying to tell me all cops aren't bad."

"No. Just telling you about my father and me. I still miss him."

Ren studied the sketch he'd begun in his pad. "What do you do when you miss him?"

"Try to remember that he's never completely gone. He's here." Cork touched his head. "And he's here." He touched his heart. "Sometimes when I'm not sure what's right, I find myself thinking, *What would Dad have done?*"

"Me, too," Ren said.

"What do you do when you miss him?"

"What he taught me to do. Draw."

"You're an artist, too?"

"Not like him."

"What are you working on?"

"It's just a comic book."

29

"You like comic books?"

Ren nodded.

"Me, too."

"Yeah?"

"I used to anyway. I always knew when the new issues were due to arrive at the drug store and I'd head there right after school. I was a Marvel fan. The Fantastic Four were my favorites. They still around?"

"Yes."

"Who do you like?"

"The Silver Surfer's pretty awesome. I like Hellboy, too."

"The comic book you're working on, does it have a super-hero?"

"His name's Jack Little Wolf. But he's really the reincarnation of a famous warrior named White Eagle."

"What's he like?"

"Jack's an artist, kind of a quiet guy. White Eagle's this awesome dude. He calls up the forces of nature. You know, wind and lightning, that stuff. Also animals. He's, like, very psychic with animals. But he doesn't realize he does all this. He has these blackouts and he doesn't remember."

"Disconnected from who he really is?"

"Right."

"What triggers the blackouts?"

"Evil. He can sense it. He, you know, begins to tingle and stuff."

"Lucky him. Been times I could have used that myself. May I see?"

"I don't really show it to anybody."

"That's cool." Cork nodded toward Ren's left. "What's the white thing?"

Ren held up the hard lump. "A plaster cast of a cougar track I found outside."

"A cougar? Here? You're sure? Maybe it's a bobcat."

Ren stood and brought the casting to the bunk. "Too big for a bobcat. This one's almost four inches across. And see the second toe, how it's longer than the others? That's like our index finger. It's one of the characteristics of the cougar's forepaw. I looked it up."

"You have a dog, Ren?"

"No."

"Cats?"

"No. I had a pet raccoon once, but I had to let him go."

Although the idea of a cougar seemed pretty far-fetched to Cork, he wondered if he should be concerned. Most wild animals were careful to avoid humans. It would be very unusual for a predator as large and cautious as a cougar to prowl so near a dwelling, especially one without pets or small livestock to attract it. Still, if it was desperately hungry . . .

"Have you told your mom?"

"No."

"Let her know, okay?"

"Sure."

Cork, knowing boys, wondered if he actually would. He made a mental note to mention it to Jewell himself.

"What happened to your lip?" Cork asked.

Ren reached up and touched the puffed area. "Got into a fight. It's okay."

He started back to the table. Cork called after him. "Could you do me a favor?"

"What?"

"I need to call someone. My cell phone is still in my car, in the glove compartment. Could you get it?"

"Sure."

Ren put the casting on the table and headed toward the door.

"Maybe you should take a poker, just in case you meet the cougar."

Ren smiled big, then seemed to understand that Cork wasn't kidding.

"I'll be all right," he said.

Cork was sure he would be, but he knew from his own mistakes that it paid to be careful.

Outside, a wind bullied its way through the pine trees, and a cloud scarred the face of the rising moon. Around the cabins, everything was dark. There was a yard light on a pole near Thor's Lodge. When they'd had guests, Ren's father kept the light burning until ten p.m. After that, he turned it off, believing that dark was one of the things people sought when they fled the city. Now the yard light was always off because the bulb had burned out and neither Ren nor his mother had bothered to put up a ladder to change it. The dark didn't worry Ren anymore, but he used to be afraid at night. His father had tried to explain that the woods—the animals and trees and rocks and rivers and lakes—were family, Ren's family, and that the wind was the breath of manidoog, spirits that watched over him and guided him. Ren liked hearing that, but he didn't believe it, not in a way that dissolved his fear. He knew from the stories his great-grandfather told him that there were other spirits in the woods not particularly inclined to look kindly on him. The Windigo, for example, a horrible cannibal with a heart of ice.

After his father's death, Ren had determined not to be afraid anymore. It was something that he wanted to do for his father. So he went out alone one night, far from the cabins, far from anyone who could come if he called out. He didn't build a fire. He wanted to see the true face of the dark. It had been a night like this with a restless feel in the wind and strange sounds in the forest. He'd been afraid at first, terrified. But gradually he understood that the noises were simply the nocturnal prowling of small, harmless critters. Eventually the sky filled with the aurora borealis. Ren finally fell asleep on a bed of pine needles under a canopy of lights with the music of the woods all around him. He dreamed of a white eagle that night, dreamed the great bird carried him on a flight that left him breathless, and when he woke, he woke free of many burdens.

Ren stopped in Thor's Lodge for a flashlight, and also for a walkie-talkie his mother had asked him to give to Cork so he could call them if he needed anything. Then he headed to the equipment shed. His mother had parked the man's car behind the shed, hiding it from sight should anyone come calling. Ren hadn't taken much notice of the car except that it was old and a yellow-green that reminded him of the color his urine turned whenever he ate asparagus. He tried the passenger side door. It was locked. When he went around the driver's side, he saw the pocking of bullet holes, four in all. He gingerly lifted the handle, released the door. A smell rushed out at him, raw and unpleasant, like old meat. The dome light didn't come on, so Ren used his flashlight. The beam fell across a massive black stain on the upholstery. The carpet was stained, too. The man's blood, he realized.

Not *the man,* he told himself. Cork. It was Cork's blood. Ren suddenly wanted to know how it felt to be shot, and wondered if it would be impolite to ask.

To get to the glove compartment, he would have to crawl across the bloodstain. The idea didn't appeal to him. He opened the back door, climbed in, and slid to the other side. He reached over the passenger seat and popped open the glove compartment. He saw the cell phone immediately, and also saw that it was broken, a hole smashed through the middle. A bullet, Ren figured. Something else in the glove compartment caught his eye. A gun. A small stainless steel pistol with a beautiful polished wood grip. Sometimes the hunters who used to come to the cabins carried handguns along with their rifles, but they were ugly-looking things. Ren had never before seen a pistol so carefully crafted. He couldn't resist touching it. The metal was cold against his fingertips. He was tempted to pick it up but thought better of it. He closed the compartment and started back.

When he handed Cork the cell phone, the man seemed disappointed. "Looks like it got hit by a bullet," Ren told him. "But here, you can use ours." He handed Cork the phone he'd taken from Thor's Lodge on his way back and also a walkie-talkie.

"What's with this?" Cork asked, looking at the little Motorola unit.

"Mom wanted you to have one of the walkie-talkies. None of the guest cabins have phones, so if you need us in the night or something, just use that." Ren started to turn away but held up a moment. "The people who shot at you, did you shoot back at them?"

"No." Cork studied the pad on the cell phone, his finger poised to dial.

"Why not?"

"I'd have been firing on the fly. My shots might have gone wild. Somebody innocent could have been hurt. It was a better idea just to get the hell out of there."

"Have you ever shot anybody?"

Cork hesitated before answering. "Yes."

"Did you kill them?"

He hesitated even longer. "Yes."

Cork didn't look like a man who killed people. He wasn't tall or menacing or grim. He didn't even look like a cop, really. Maybe it was his eyes. There was something kind in them.

Ren took a chance. "Did it hurt when they shot you?"

Cork closed the phone and put it in his lap. "Not at first. At first, I was too scared."

"Scared?"

"Somebody shoots at you, Ren, believe me, you're scared. You know about adrenaline, right?"

"Sure."

"One of the effects of adrenaline is to mask pain."

"So, did it hurt later?"

"A lot. What scared me most was losing blood and the chance of going into shock." He waited, but at the moment Ren didn't have anything more to ask. "Mind if I make my call?"

"Oh, sure. Go ahead."

Ren went back to his sketch pad on the table and pretended to be drawing while Cork talked.

"Dina? It's Cork." He closed his eyes. "Safe at the moment. I screwed up, though. Somebody almost collected on that bounty. They put a bullet in my leg before I got away." He shook his head. "No, no hospital. I don't want to be a sitting duck. Look, is there any chance your phone's been tapped? You're absolutely certain? Okay, I'm in Bodine, Michigan, forty miles northwest of Marquette. I'm staying with my cousin and her son. A resort called Copper Country Cabins, about a mile west of town on County Road Eighteen." He laughed quietly. "God was smiling on me. Jewell's a veterinarian. Patched me up, gave me some painkillers, and put her son, Ren, to work as my personal assistant and bodyguard." He winked at Ren, who'd looked up at the mention of his name, then turned serious again. "No, don't call Jo. I'm sure her line's been tapped. They may even have bugged the duplex. I don't want her or the kids or anyone else down there jeopardized." He gave a final nod. "Fine. I'll see you in the morning. And, Dina? Thanks."

He broke the connection and laid his head back against his pillow in a tired way.

"Dina?" Ren asked.

"A friend. She's saved my life on a couple of occasions."

"You could have used her yesterday."

Cork grinned. "I'm all right, Ren. You don't have to stay. I have my bedpan. And the walkie-talkie if I need you."

"Mom asked me to stay. I don't mind."

"Suit yourself."

Ren went back to his sketching. He was working on White Eagle, but he hadn't been able to get the features to his liking. The guy was supposed to be Indian, yet every time Ren tried for that look, he failed. White Eagle had all the muscle you'd expect on a superhero, but his face looked too, well, white. When he forced himself consciously to draw Indian, it felt exaggerated and artificial.

His father had taught him to draw from life. Looking around him, Ren saw no model. As far as Indians went, in Bodine he and his mother were it. And his mother had never been big on being Indian.

He heard Cork snoring softly and he considered him. There didn't seem anything imposing about the guy, especially laid out on the bunk with a bedpan in easy reach.

A cop in the family.

Who would have thought?

7

*H*e wasn't given to nightmares, but this night he dreamed a doozy.

His father with his head split open, scratching at the window.

Ren jerked awake. Although sleep still dragged at his senses, he was certain something had been there. He sat upright and glanced toward the window glass that glowed with moonlight. An eerie evanescence invaded his room. It gave the familiar contours—his desk, chair and computer, his shelves of books, his plaster castings and plastic models and wall poster of Spider-Man—an unfamiliar sense of menace. He listened, heard nothing for a full minute. Thought *wind*. Thought *branches*. Thought *nightmare*. Still, there was a nudging certainty behind his thinking that told him *something*.

He didn't think of himself as brave. His fifth-grade teacher had once told him that he was bright and reasonable, and that had sounded fine to Ren, though he hoped *brave* might be added someday. He was curious, however, and finally his curiosity overwhelmed his fear. He inched the covers back and slid his bare feet onto the cool floorboards. He crept to the window, stepped into the spill of moonlight, and peered out.

His room was at the back of Thor's Lodge and the windows opened toward the forest that ran almost unbroken from the old resort all the way to the Huron Mountains in the west. Tall hemlocks shattered the fall of moonlight, and a quilt of silver splashes spread over the deep bed of evergreen needles that covered the ground. On that soft bed, anything could approach without a sound.

He pressed his nose to the cold glass. His eyes shifted left, right, trying to pierce the night and the shadows. The fog of his breath obscured the windowpane for a moment. He drew back, wiped the glass with the arm of his pajama top.

In that instant, he caught a glimpse of motion, a blur among the trees. He leaned forward so quickly his nose bumped the glass and his eyes blinked shut. When he opened them, the blur was gone.

It was an animal, he was sure. A coyote, maybe even a wolf. Yet, there was something about it that was not like any coyote or wolf he'd ever seen. The swiftness. There, gone. And a sense—okay, maybe he was imagining this, he admitted—of power barely contained.

The cougar?

He stood at the window for a few minutes more, but nothing moved.

Ren knew he should go back to bed, and he knew he would not. The thrill of the possibility of what was out there was far too attractive. He felt afraid and excited at the same time. He pulled on his pants and a hooded sweatshirt, slipped into socks and his sneakers. As a last thought, he grabbed the baseball bat from his closet.

In the kitchen, he took the Coleman flashlight from its charging cradle, then he stepped outside.

A clear fall night. Breathing the air was like sucking frost. The careless hand of the wind off Lake Superior brushed the tops of the pines, which rocked back and forth easily. Ren held the flashlight in his left hand, the beam turned off. In his right, he gripped the bat. He crept to the side of the cabin, pressed against the sturdy logs, and peered around the corner. He scanned the clear area with the chopping block in the center where his father used to split wood for the cabins' stoves.

Quiet as a spider, he stole along the wall to the back. He poked his head around that corner, too, and saw no more than he'd seen from his window: the woods empty except for all that silver light and shadow. He held his breath and listened.

He thought of turning on the flashlight, but if there was something there, something magnificent and cautious, he didn't want to scare it away.

A thump on the ground behind him made him spin. In the dark, his eyes darted around desperately. He edged backward, finally hit the switch on the flashlight, illuminating a big pinecone the wind had nudged loose from a branch.

He padded to his bedroom window and ran the beam of the flashlight along the wall. Beneath his window frame, long scratches cut parallel lines down the logs. Ren had never seen those marks before. He knelt and brushed his hand over one of the gouges. From the exposed bone-white wood at the heart and from the curl of the shavings along the edges, he knew they were new. Very new.

A low growl preceded the impact. Ren was slammed against the cabin wall. He didn't even have time to scream before he hit the ground with the animal on top of him.

Then the animal laughed and said, "You're dead meat, dude."

"Get the hell off me, Charlie. Goddamn it, get off."

He struggled, awash in adrenaline and a killing rage. Charlie, usually about as sensitive as a brick, seemed to realize the depth of his anger. She jumped off him and stepped back.

"Dude, I'm sorry. I was just joking with you."

Ren bounded to his feet, his hands fisted. He was on the verge of laying into her, held back from throwing blows by the thinnest of threads.

Charlie had been in more fights than she could probably remember, but she didn't lift a finger to defend herself. "Ren, I'm sorry. I'm really sorry."

In the moonlight, her face became a silver mask of pain and Ren was caught by surprise, as startling in its way as Charlie's ambush had been. She was the most fearless, pigheaded person he knew, and she never apologized.

"Come on, Ren. Please don't be mad at me."

He understood that it wasn't just an apology. It was a plea. Charlie needed him. His anger vanished and he lowered his hands.

"Your old man on a bender?" he asked.

"No worse than usual. He'll drink himself to sleep in a while."

"Want to sleep here?"

"Naw. I'm going to look for Stash's dead body."

"The one he saw in the river?"

"You catch on quick, Einstein."

"You told him you didn't think there even was a body."

"You coming or not?"

He was so wide awake now, it would take him forever to get back to sleep. Besides, the truth was that the idea of looking for a dead body in the middle of the night appealed to him.

"All right, sure." He bent and picked up the flashlight and the baseball bat. When he straightened up, Charlie was grinning at him.

"What?" he asked.

"You were going to try to kill me with that bat? Dude, I've played baseball with you. You've got the lamest swing in the whole world."

She turned from him, laughing, and led the way through the dark.

From the shed where the now unused resort equipment was stored, they took two mountain bikes. They followed the lane to the county road, navigating by moonlight. It was almost a mile to the picnic shelter overlooking the Copper River. Because the cold had already driven away the crickets and the tree frogs, they biked in a silence broken only by their heavy breathing and the rattle of the bike chains.

They left the bikes at the shelter and walked a hundred yards down a tree-lined path that led to the mouth of the river, where the fast water seemed to have no impact at all on the vast, deep stillness of the lake. On either side of the river mouth lay small beaches of smooth, rounded stones. After big storms, Ren loved to walk the shoreline searching for agates washed up by the waves. There were also large boulders that had tumbled down the river over aeons and come to rest on Superior's shore. That night the lake was peaceful. The sky was a sweep of stars melting into the glow of a gibbous moon. There was plenty of light for Ren and Charlie to see their way without a flashlight. Ren preferred it that way. He liked the eerie feel of the moonlit scene. Although he didn't believe they'd find a body, he'd let himself open up to the thrill of an expedition with such a dark purpose, and he was glad Charlie wanted him along. In a way, it was like telling a ghost story. He didn't believe it, but he loved the creepy feel and the grim distant voice in his head that said *Maybe* . . .

The water lapped at their feet. After a while, they sat on two boulders that gave a view of the river mouth and the scattering of lights to the east that was Bodine.

Charlie had been unusually quiet. Ren wondered if she was still upset because he'd been mad at her. For as long as he could remember, they'd been best friends. There'd been times when they'd been royally pissed at each other, but it had never been a big deal. Lately, however, Charlie was different. Things seemed to bother her more. Moods held her a long time in their grip. Sometimes she was distant, and Ren wondered where she'd gone.

Charlie had never had an easy life. Everyone in Bodine knew it. Just about the time she was learning to walk, her mother had run off with a logger named Vernon Atwater, and nobody'd ever heard from either of them again. Charlie's father raised her alone. He was moody and had a lazy eye that never quite looked at you straight on. Summers he worked for a nursery this side of Marquette. Winters he bolted a plow onto the front of his pickup and cleared snow. He wasn't a mean man, exactly, but neither was he affectionate. Saturday nights he drank too much, and then he got loud and angry. He'd rant about how he ended up consigned to life's craphouse, and he'd blame everybody from his bastard old man to the lying sons of bitches in Washington for his misery. Somewhere along the way, he'd usually include Charlie. Which might have been somewhat tolerable if he'd only taken out his disappointment verbally.

When she was eleven, Charlie was sent to live with a foster family in Marquette while her father, under court order, got himself on more stable footing. When she finally returned to Bodine, she wouldn't talk about her experience. The one thing she would say, and said adamantly, was that she'd never go to a foster home again. Even drunk, her old man was better.

Now when things got too bad, she'd run off for a while. Sometimes she showed up on Ren's doorstep and his mother let her stay in the guest room. Sometimes she needed to get away completely and she hitched to a safe house for homeless teens in Marquette. Eventually she'd return to Bodine. She told Ren that whenever she was gone she could always tell that her father was happy to see her again. Even his lazy eye, for a short while, would focus entirely on her.

"Maybe it's on the other side." Ren pointed toward the rock beach on the far side of the river mouth.

"What?" Charlie asked.

"The body."

"Oh," Charlie said. "Yeah, maybe."

Ren realized she wasn't even thinking about the body now. Probably she'd never even believed in it, but looking was better than being home.

"You want to go back?" he asked.

"Not yet."

She reached down, picked up a rock, threw it far out into the lake. Ren saw a burst of silver.

"Careful," he said. "You'll wake up Pressie."

"Who?"

"Not who. What. The Presque Isle Monster. The monster of the lake."

"Bullshit."

"No, really. I can't believe you've lived here your whole life and never heard of it. You know, like Nessie, the Loch Ness monster. It's that kind of thing. The big ore boats have seen it for years. Every once in a while a boat disappears out there without a trace. Nobody knows why or where. I heard that one time the Coast Guard got a radio transmission from a fishing boat a few miles off Marquette saying their nets were caught on something that was pulling them under. That was it. The boat was never heard from again. If the lake weren't so cold and people actually swam in it, I bet there'd be lots of folks who ended up dinner for Pressie and everybody would know about it."

She was stone silent and her face turned from Ren toward the lake that was a great, flat plate of pale reflected moonlight.

"You're so full of shit," she said, although she didn't sound convinced.

He could see that Charlie was intrigued, which was good. He wanted to coax her out of the quiet dark into which she'd slipped.

"Think so? Look, here it comes."

His finger directed her attention to a long black shape sliding along the surface of the lake, following the shoreline on the far side of the river mouth. It moved slowly, silently rippling the moonlit water.

"What is it?" Charlie whispered.

"I told you. Pressie."

Charlie watched a while longer. "It's just a boat," she said hopefully.

"Where are the running lights? And if it's a boat, what's it doing out here now?"

"Fishing, probably."

"It's Pressie. You woke it up with that rock you threw." Ren made his voice sound afraid.

There was something about fear that was like fire in dry grass. It spread easily. Ren could feel Charlie tense up as the black silhouette crept nearer.

Then a spotlight popped on, the long beam sweeping the surface of the lake.

"Asshole," she said, and slugged Ren's arm.

They could hear the low thrum of the engine now, idling as the boat sat in the water with the beam poking at the rocks on the shore.

"What are they doing?" Charlie asked.

"Who knows?"

She watched a minute, then turned to Ren. Even in the dark, he could see the devil in her eyes.

"Let's moon 'em."

"Let's not."

"Come on, dude. It'll be totally awesome."

"Go ahead if you want to. Me, no way I'm going to freeze my butt."

"You don't think I'll do it, do you?"

Ren said, "Dare you."

Charlie stood up. "Hey," she yelled. "Hey, over here."

Ren thought, *Oh, shit,* and hid behind the boulder he'd been sitting on.

The beam swung toward Charlie and suddenly she was on fire in the light.

"You looking for a dead body? How about looking at this."

She turned her back to the spotlight and in a few swift, graceful motions, bent, tugged her jeans down, and waggled her bare ass at the boat. Hunkered down, Ren couldn't see it all clearly, but he caught the look on Charlie's face, which was pure delight.

Suddenly the boat engine roared and Ren heard the craft cut toward them.

"Run," he shouted.

Charlie hiked her pants into place and leaped ahead of him toward the path back to the shelter, zipping and buttoning as she went. She was also laughing hysterically.

At the shelter, they finally stopped, breathless.

"Dude, what did I tell you? Totally awesome." She hit his arm with her fist, hard. "You are such a wuss. Know what? I feel like getting high."

She grabbed the flashlight from Ren and leaped onto the picnic table in the shelter. She shined the light along the rafter and pulled down the cigar box bound with a rubber band.

"Here." She handed the box to Ren. "Roll a spliff. I'm too electric."

Ren sat down on the cement table and opened the box. He took out the Baggie of weed and the papers.

"Dude, what do you think was up down there?" She paced, as if walking off the rush.

"I told you. It was Pressie. That was his eye of fire. You better be careful. He's seen you. He knows you. He'll come for you."

Charlie howled, not a laugh but an actual howl like a wolf. She was full of the old Charlie energy, and Ren was glad to see it. He became intent on the work of his hands.

"Dude, kill the light."

The quiet intensity of her voice made Ren look up. Charlie stood still, facing downriver toward the lake.

"Turn the light off," she said, a little desperately this time.

Ren obeyed. He stared where she stared, and then he saw what she saw. A beam of light scanning its way up the path they'd just followed.

"Jesus, you really pissed somebody off."

"Pressie?" There was still a touch of devilment in her voice.

"Let's get out of here," Ren said.

"I hear you."

He threw everything back into the cigar box, slipped the rubber band in place, and stood on the tabletop, reaching toward the rafter. He thought he had it in place, but when he let go, the box fell to the ground.

"Come on," Charlie growled.

The light was less than fifty yards down the path. Ren kicked the box under a pile of leaves in a corner of the shelter and ran for his bike. Charlie was already mounted.

They heard the heavy footfall of boots pounding rapidly toward them on the path. They shot off, pedaling hard for the main road. When they reached the bridge, they finally risked a look back. The light was gone.

"Guess nobody ever mooned them before," Ren said.

"Screw 'em if they can't take a joke."

"Want to come home with me?"

"Naw, my old man's probably asleep by now. I'll be okay."

"Take the bike."

"Okay." She didn't move. "Ren?"

"Yeah?"

"Thanks for . . . you know."

"Sure."

He watched her head into town, and felt something immeasurably sad in seeing her go, knowing what she was heading home to.

Ren's father was dead, but despite what people said, he'd never been a drunk, nor had he ever laid a hand on his son. Even in death, he'd left something precious behind for Ren.

If Charlie's old man were to die, all he'd leave behind was an empty bottle and a huge sigh of relief.

8

Jewell woke early and lay in bed, staring at the ceiling while big tears rolled down the sides of her face. Sunday mornings were still hard, maybe always would be. Often on Sunday mornings, she'd awakened to Daniel slipping quietly from the bed. He would go to the bathroom, shave, brush his teeth, run a comb through his long black hair, and come back to bed smelling of aftershave. He'd press himself gently against her, nuzzle the nape of her neck, cup her breast. Usually she was already awake, but she liked to pretend she was still sleeping, let him believe he had to wake her, coax her to his pleasure. But, oh, it was her pleasure, too. She looked forward to those mornings that began with lovemaking. She adored being loved by her husband, and she loved him fiercely in return.

She had never much considered the other side of love, thinking vaguely that if love were gone, what was left was sadness or perhaps simply emptiness. It surprised her to find there was no emptiness, that many emotions rushed in to fill her heart along with the sadness. Self-pity. Bitterness. Anger. Sometimes even hate.

Sunday mornings, it was often loneliness, and that's what held her in its grip as she lay crying silently, dreading the day.

At last she drew back the covers and planted her feet on the floor. Once summer was past, the floorboards were cold. Her father, who'd built all the cabins himself, didn't believe in carpeting. Although many rooms had an area rug, hand-loomed or -braided, to add a splash of color, mostly the floors were left bare to show off the beautiful grain of the polished maple.

In the kitchen, she began coffee dripping, then sat down at the table and lit a cigarette. She'd given up smoking when she was pregnant with Ren; she'd gone back to it after Daniel was murdered. Mornings, she often sat like this, alone with a cigarette and her coffee, waiting for the dawn.

She'd always been an early riser, but it seemed that no matter how early she got up Daniel was up before her, the coffee made, the good aroma filling the cabin along with her husband's whistling, which was generally cheerful and a little off-key. She'd find him in the kitchen at work on breakfast making blueberry pancakes or waffles, of which he was duly proud. His specialty, though, was omelets with wild rice and Gouda cheese.

Now breakfasts were usually cold cereal and juice.

The walkie-talkie on the kitchen counter crackled to life.

"This is Cork. Anybody there?"

Jewell held off for a few seconds, taking her time putting out her cigarette, savoring just a bit longer the feel of her aloneness before picking up the unit to reply. "Go ahead."

"Sorry to bother you, Jewell. I saw a light on. This is a little embarrassing but my bedpan's full."

"I'll be right there."

She threw on a robe and slippers, picked up her medical bag, and headed to Cabin 3. Cork was sitting up, the curtains above his bunk opened to the gray light of early morning.

"I'd have emptied it myself," he said, "but I'm plugged into this damned IV."

"If you think you can walk a little, I'll put you on an oral antibiotic." She emptied the bedpan, washed her hands, then removed the IV needle. She took his pulse and checked the bag that collected the drainage from the wound in his thigh.

"You seem to be healing nicely," she said.

"My saving grace: I heal good."

"Hungry?"

"As a matter of fact, I am."

"I'll bring you some breakfast." She looked down at him and made no move to leave. "But first I want to know exactly what's going on. I want to know names: who shot you and why. And at the end, I want to be convinced that there's no way Ren and I could be in any danger."

"It's complicated," Cork said.

"Give it a try."

"Pull up a chair then."

When she was seated next to the bunk, she said, "Go ahead."

"It began ten days ago," Cork told her. "Someone ambushed me on the Iron Lake Reservation outside Aurora. I lost a piece of my earlobe. One of my deputies was badly wounded. A couple of days later a businessman from Chicago was brutally murdered at a place called Mercy Falls, not far from town. His name was Eddie Jacoby, and he was not a good man. The Jacoby family turned out to be wealthy and powerful, and headed by one hell of a bastard named Lou.

"Lou Jacoby had a second son. His name was Ben. A long time ago Ben Jacoby had been in love with my wife."

"With Jo? How long ago?"

"Back in law school," Cork replied. "As I began to uncover more and more truths about the incidents in Aurora, I became more and more convinced Ben Jacoby was responsible for the ambush on the rez."

"He wanted Jo? And—what?—he was willing to kill you to get her?"

"That's how it looked to me. Then someone planted a bomb in my car that could have killed me or anyone else in the family, so I sent Jo and the kids away. They went to Evanston, Illinois, to stay with Jo's sister, Rose. Turned out that was just a hop, skip, and jump from Ben Jacoby's home in Winnetka."

"Coincidence?"

"I've never been a believer in coincidence."

"So naturally you thought this Ben Jacoby was responsible for the bomb."

"It seemed like a reasonable conclusion at the time. Then Jo disappeared. She went to meet Ben Jacoby and never came back. I drove to Evanston as fast as I could."

"You found her?"

"Yes, but not before she was raped."

"Oh Jesus, Cork. I'm sorry. Was it Ben Jacoby?"

"No. But I'm sure he had a hand in covering up for the son of a bitch who did it. He was murdered before I could talk to him."

"And now you're a suspect?"

"Mostly in the mind of Lou Jacoby."

"Who hired the men who tried to kill you."

"That's it."

"Do you know who killed Ben Jacoby?"

"I'm pretty sure it was the same people who murdered his brother, Eddie."

"And that would be?"

"Eddie's wife, a woman named Gabriella. And her brother, Tony Salguero. I think they killed Eddie because he was an abusive husband. He was also rich. And they killed Ben because he knew they did it."

"How do you prove any of this?"

"I hope the police are pretty well on their way to doing that for me. If they do, I'm hoping it will bring Lou Jacoby to his senses. Until that happens—*if* it happens—I need to be careful. Lou's probably got more than a few cops in his pocket, so it's best I stay off the law enforcement radar, even up here. With this bounty on my head and Lou's hired guns beating the bushes looking for me, it's probably wisest just to lie low and let this leg mend."

Jewell realized she'd been at the edge of her seat. She relaxed and sat back. "They found you in Kenosha. What makes you think they can't find you here?"

"I made a mistake in Kenosha. I called Jo at her sister's place. Jacoby's people must have tapped the line. I won't make that mistake again. Until this is over, I'm not contacting my family at all. I don't want them dragged into this."

"You'll just leave them in the dark wondering whether you're alive or lying dead somewhere?" She folded her arms as if she were cold. "You weren't happy running a burger stand. You had to go and put on a badge again. And now look at you, lying there lucky to be alive while you're family worries themselves sick over you. Men. You only think about yourselves."

Cork spoke quietly. "Are you talking about me now, or about Daniel? He put himself at risk and died because of it. The hell with his family. Is that it?"

"He died because of bastard cops."

"Like me? You think I'm that kind of cop? That kind of man?"

"I don't know who you are."

"I'm family, Jewell."

"You lay a lot on that."

"Family holds weight."

"Don't count on it." She stood up, prepared to leave. "I'm on at the clinic today. Ren will be here if you need anything."

"He doesn't have to stay close. I'm feeling better."

"You're still in no shape to move."

She started for the door.

"Jewell, there's something else you should know. Someone's coming here today, a woman named Dina Willner. A friend. To help me."

She looked back at him, angry. "Someone knows you're here?"

"I trust her. Twice in the last week she saved my life."

Jewell shook her head fast. "I don't care. Somebody knows where you are. I don't like that. I don't like any of this."

"It'll be over soon, I promise."

She eyed him coldly. "That's exactly what Daniel said the last time I saw him alive."

"Jewell, I left my family because I knew they'd be in danger if I stayed. If I thought you or Ren were in danger, I wouldn't be here, either."

"If your thinking has been so good, how come you're lying there with a bullet hole in your leg?"

"This woman who's coming, I trust her with my life."

"And mine. And Ren's."

"If you want me gone, I'll leave now."

"I should take you up on that, but with that leg you wouldn't get far." She'd talked enough, argued enough. She didn't have the stomach for it anymore. Turning her back to him, she said, "I'll have Ren bring you something to eat."

* * *

She showered and dressed, got herself ready for the clinic. After that, she began bacon frying and pulled eggs from the refrigerator. She was mixing batter in a bowl when Ren appeared, coming from his room with his hair wild and his eyes still a little glazed.

"I thought I smelled food," he said.

"Hungry?"

"Yeah."

"Sit down. I'll fix you something." She watched him shuffle to the table, looking in so many ways like his father. "How about blueberry pancakes?"

"Really?"

"Really."

"That'd be great."

While she worked at the stove, she spoke to him over her shoulder. "I thought I heard you moving around last night."

"Remember that cougar track I told you about? I thought I heard him outside."

"The wind, probably."

"Something scratched the cabin wall, Mom."

She turned from the griddle where the pancake batter had just started to bubble. "And you went outside to check?"

"I was curious."

She pointed her spatula at him. "Ren, I don't know if that animal is a cougar or bobcat or what, but I don't want you going out in the middle of the night to find out. At least, don't do it alone. Wake me up if you're really scared."

"I wasn't scared."

"Okay, curious. But wake me up. We'll go together. Promise?"

"Yeah."

"Good. I've got to take off for the clinic pretty soon, so after you eat your breakfast, I'd like you to take a tray to Cork. And keep an eye on him for me, okay? If he wants to put a little weight on that leg, let him, but nothing strenuous."

She served him the blueberry pancakes and bacon. While he ate she finished getting herself ready. She kissed the top of his head on her way out. "Call if you need me."

"I will."

He looked up and smiled. Smiled so like his father that she flashed on Daniel in a way that felt like a hard blow to her heart.

"You okay, Mom?"

"Fine, Ren." She gathered herself and turned to the door. "Be good. Be careful."

"Always am."

With a stab of fear she could do nothing about, she thought, *Not always.*

9

Cork stared at the exposed rafters above his bunk, solid pine logs honey-colored and varnished. They made him think of Jewell's father, who'd built the cabins himself. He'd been a strong man, straightforward, with a comforting, easy humor that Cork would have thought of as Ojibwe, except that neither of Jewell's parents was eager to acknowledge that part of their heritage. Both were of mixed blood—Irish on her mother's side, Swedish on her father's. They grew up in a time when being Indian only invited problems, so they put forward the white in their blood and turned away from Indian associations. It had been a bit of a sore point between Cork's mother, who was proud of her Ojibwe heritage, and Jewell's mother, who was not, but that didn't keep them from loving each other as sisters should. Across a lot of summers, he'd visited the resort with his mother, creating history. It occurred to him, lying there nearly helpless, that that was much of what family was about. History. And from history came community. And community was something that spread out beyond itself, resulting in towns and nations. But it all began with family.

Family was why he was lying there with a hole in his leg. Because of the Jacobys, a family unraveled, and his own, a family he was trying desperately to protect. If he'd stayed in Evanston with Jo and the children, they would surely have been in harm's way. Jacoby had put a half-million-dollar bounty on his head. Five hundred large. For that kind of money, there was a kind of man who wouldn't hesitate to take out Cork's whole family to get to him. Leaving them was the smart thing to do.

Wasn't it?

An eye for an eye. That was the last thing Jacoby had said to him. The man was old, but he was the most dangerous kind of adversary: a guy with nothing to lose. His sons had been murdered and all his money could not change that. No telling the lengths he'd go to in his hunger for vengeance. The idea of a hit, Cork could handle. What worried him most was that Jacoby, in his craziness, might turn his anger toward Jo or the children. In which case, abandoning them might turn out to be the worst thing he could have done.

Cork hammered his fist against the mattress. Damn, what he wouldn't give to be in the same room with the son of a bitch. Didn't matter that Jacoby was old: Cork would have loved the chance to beat some sense into him. Instead he lay there helpless, battling two enemies he couldn't lay a finger on: uncertainty and rage.

Christ, how fucked was that?

The door creaked. He glanced over, expecting Ren with breakfast. It wasn't.

"Dina," he said.

The woman who had saved his life on two separate occasions was not very tall. She stood five-four on tiptoe, weighed maybe 120 pounds. She had light brown hair, green eyes, and a face no less lovely than the best Hollywood had to offer. Her name was Dina Willner. She called herself a security consultant, a term that covered a lot of ground.

"Where'd you come from?" he asked. "I didn't hear a car."

She looked the cabin over carefully, stepped inside. "I parked in town and walked through the woods. Didn't want anyone to see me coming here. Also, I wanted to be able to reconnoiter a little first." She crossed to his bunk, looked down at him, shook her head. "Can't leave you alone for a minute, can I? How's the leg?"

"Healing. Or so my cousin, the vet, says."

"Were you a good patient, and did you get a doggie biscuit?" Her eyes flicked toward the door. "I saw a woman drive away. Her?"

"Jewell, yeah."

"Who else is here?"

"Her son."

"Guests?"

"They don't rent out the cabins anymore."

"Shame. Nice place." She went to the table, grabbed a chair, and placed it next to Cork's bunk. "So, what's the story?"

"I screwed up."

"I figured. How?"

"After you left me in Evanston, I hitched a ride north, went up to Kenosha, Wisconsin. I wanted to make sure I was clear of any kind of net that Jacoby's goons had thrown around the North Shore of Chicago. I checked into a fleabag motel there, place called the Lake Inn. First thing I did was use some of the money you gave me to get a set of wheels."

"The shot-up, piss-colored Dart behind the shed?"

"That would be the one."

"How'd it get shot up?"

"I'm coming to that." He shifted and grimaced from the pain it caused his leg. "I called Jo at her sister's place."

"Big mistake."

"I know. The phone must've been tapped."

"I could have told you that."

"Next time I'll be sure to ask."

"How long before the goons showed up?"

"They waited until dark. I'd gone out to get some dinner. They tried the hit as soon as I came back and got out of the car."

"The motel lot?"

"Yeah, pretty public. The car got the worst of it, but I took a bullet in my leg."

She shook her head. "Amateurs. But with half a million on your head, even my grandmother would be tempted." She gave an admiring look. "You drove all the way here with a bullet hole through your leg? That's a good eight hours."

"I used my sweatshirt as a compress to stop the bleeding. After that it was a matter of gritting my teeth and hoping shock didn't set in. Amazing what you can do when you're motivated. Like running for your life."

"Why didn't you head back to Minnesota?"

"I figured they'd be watching for me there."

"You're probably right. Lucky you had family to fall back on up here."

"My cousin doesn't think so."

"How soon before you can move?"

"I can move now, just not very far or very fast."

"On my way into town, I saw a sign: *Home of the Bobcats. 1980 Class C State Football Champions.* A place like this is dead center in the middle of nowhere. You're four hundred miles from Chicago. Who would think to look for you here? You might as well stay put."

Cork wasn't a hundred percent convinced. "With his money, Jacoby can throw a big net," he said. "Tell me about Lou."

"The Winnetka police are keeping a lid on everything about Ben's murder, so I don't know."

The door opened. Cork had never seen anybody move as fast as Dina. She was out of her chair and had spun around before he could blink.

Ren was obviously startled by her presence, but he looked even more surprised by the gun that had materialized in her hand from nowhere.

"Easy, Dina," Cork said. "It's Ren. He's family."

She was a woman like the cougar Ren had imagined. Her hair was that color, her movement that swift, her eyes that focused, knowing, and hungry. She was probably the size of the cougar, too, should the animal stand on its hind legs. She looked every bit as dangerous.

"Close the door," she said.

Cork saw the boy's wariness and wanted to put him at ease as quickly as possible. "Come over here, Ren. I want to introduce you."

Ren had a tray in his hand that held a covered plate of eggs and bacon, a small glass of orange juice, and a cup of coffee. He went to the table, put the tray down, then walked to the bunk. His heart beat against his chest like a boxer working a bag. His eyes never left the gun and the woman who held it.

"You're making a horrible first impression, Dina," Cork said. "Put your gun away."

She looked Ren over a moment longer, then as quickly as she'd produced the gun she flashed a smile. The Glock slid into a holster under her sweatshirt, and the same hand that had threatened Ren was held toward him, open and empty.

"How do you do? I'm Dina Willner."

He shook her hand warily. It felt strong as a man's, but different, too.

"Ren DuBois," Cork said, because Ren, who was still trying to put everything together, hadn't replied. "Dina's the friend I called last night."

"Oh." Ren nodded slowly.

"Are you always this talkative?" Dina asked.

"Huh?" Then he got it. A joke. He smiled.

"Sorry about the gun." She patted the place where it was holstered. "You surprised me."

Ren wondered if he'd surprised her any more, would he be dead?

"Mom asked me to bring Cork's breakfast." It sounded apologetic, a little pathetic, and he didn't like that. He stood straight and as tall as he could. Even so, his eyes were not quite level with the woman's. "I didn't see your car. I didn't even hear you drive up."

She took the chair she'd been sitting in, flipped it around, and sat down again with her arms folded over the back. She continued to study him with her green, catlike eyes.

"I came through the woods," she said.

"You should be careful. There's a cougar out there."

"What I carry would stop a bear."

"You wouldn't shoot him," Ren objected.

"I've never harmed a thing that wasn't trying to harm me. If I run into this cougar, what do you suggest I do?"

Ren glanced at Cork, who was enjoying the conversation immensely.

"First, you never turn your back on a wild animal," Ren said seriously. "You should stand as tall as you can, get up on a tree stump or something to make yourself look even bigger. It sometimes helps to wave your arms and shout. Usually, unless you're threatening its young, it will leave you alone."

"You've had that experience?"

"It's what I've read."

He stood awkwardly, aware that he'd interrupted something and should probably go, but he wasn't sure. Adults weren't easy to figure.

Dina's stomach let out a long growl. "Sorry," she apologized. "I haven't eaten this morning."

"I could fix you something," Ren offered.

She laughed. "The last time I had a man fix me breakfast, it turned out to be beer and corn dogs. What I'd really like is a latte."

"Do you like *kolaches*?"

"Do you make *kolaches*?"

"No, but the Taylors do. In town. Really good ones. And they have espresso and stuff."

"Long walk for coffee," Dina said.

"I'll take the ATV. I was thinking of going anyway. I have a friend and I was going to take her some breakfast."

"Charlie?" Cork said.

"Yeah. Sometimes there's not a lot of food in her house. I could drop a *kolache* off at her place and be back here in half an hour."

"Or I could just share whatever's on that tray you brought," Dina said.

"I don't mind going."

"Ren," Cork said, sounding as gravely serious as he possibly could, "if you go into town, you have to promise not to say anything about me or Dina."

"I won't, I promise."

"And make sure, absolutely sure, that Charlie doesn't, either."

"I can do that."

"All right. Why don't you head into Bodine, then," Cork said, thinking it would give him a chance to talk to Dina alone. "I'm starved and I'll be damned if I'm giving up my breakfast."

"Here." Dina pulled a wallet from her back pocket and took out a twenty-dollar bill. "A vanilla latte and a *kolache* for me. And get whatever you want for yourself and for your friend. How about you, Cork?"

"I'm fine."

"Thank you, Ren," Dina said. "This is quite nice."

"'S okay." He gave a nonchalant shrug, but the glow on his face was obvious. He went to the door and just before leaving glanced back at Dina. His eyes lingered a hair too long for mere curiosity. Dina smiled at him. The boy blushed and hurried out.

"Nice kid," she said to Cork. "But can we trust him to keep his mouth shut?"

"Unless you want to shoot him, we don't have much choice."

10

Ren loved Bodine. And he hated it. The town circumscribed his life, defined him in many ways. It gave him a place to belong, offered him a stable center from which to view the world in order to make some sense of it. On the other hand, it was small, suffocating, and sometimes cruel. There were days when he felt like a prisoner. He knew every street, every shop, every shop owner, and they knew him. They called hello when he passed. They made him feel part of a large family. Like any family, however, they always had their noses in his business, and in his mother's. When his father died a little over a year ago, there'd been an outpouring of sympathy, but there'd also been a vein of censure that ran through the sentiments, the feeling—occasionally voiced—that Ren's father had somehow got what he deserved, that his business should have been minding the resort cabins and taking care of his family, not stirring up trouble in other places. This bothered Ren. What bothered him more was that he knew there was a dark voice inside his mother that sometimes spoke to her in the same way.

Harbor Avenue, Bodine's main street, ran due north off the county road straight to the lake. Shops lined the street in the block before the harbor. The commercial buildings were mostly brick, built simple and sturdy to withstand the gale winds that often blew off Lake Superior.

In the sixth grade, Ren had done a long project about the history of the town. He learned that over the years, Bodine had seen good times and bad, though for a long time they'd been mostly bad. It had begun as a lumber town, taking the fine hardwoods of the southern Hurons and turning them into planks prized for their solid grain and durability. Henry Ford had been so struck by the quality of the wood that he'd purchased vast tracts of forestland and used the timber for paneling in his early automobiles. But the lumber didn't last.

In 1881, the Cyril Mine opened fifteen miles southwest of Bodine, tapping into a solitary vein of native copper, a long splash of ore as rich as any on the Keweenaw. That had brought prosperity in many forms until the copper finally petered out in the late 1950's. When the mine closed, jobs vanished and people with them.

Both the lumber and copper industries had resulted in the development of Bodine's harbor, which was small but deep enough to accommodate the heavy freighters of the day. Early on, Bodine had become a modest terminal for lake traffic. In 1890, an entrepreneur named Edward Farber, who'd made decent money in shipping and who'd fallen in love with the beautiful Huron Mountains, built a fine hotel overlooking the picturesque little harbor. In its day, the Farber House was reputed to serve the best food between New York City and the Mississippi River, and for a while it attracted a rich clientele who considered the Upper Peninsula an exotic destination.

For most of the wealthy, however, the U.P. turned out to be a passing fancy, and eventually they found other places to play. By the early 1920's, the writing was on the wall, and Farber, an old man by then, let things slide. The advent of the Great Depression seemed to nail the coffin shut on his beautiful hotel.

In the years since, the Farber House had gone through a number of incarnations. It had served as temporary housing for the Civilian Conservation Corps, which carried out numerous public works projects in the area, like the picnic shelter on the Copper River. During World War Two, it housed a group of Canadians and Americans who worked on breaking codes. For three decades after that, it had been a nursing home. Finally, it had simply been abandoned.

In 1998, it was purchased by a couple, Ken and Sue Taylor, who invested their life savings into making it once again a fine inn. They'd captured much of the old charm, and they called it by its proper name: the Farber House.

The parking lot was full that Sunday morning, and Ren left his ATV on the street in front. As soon as he entered the lobby, he smelled coffee and pastries. Both were freshly made and available in a small bistro area opposite the front desk. On the far side of the hotel was a large dining room with windows that opened toward the deep, placid blue of the lake. Most of the tables were occupied. Leaf peepers, Ren figured.

Ren went to the bistro, where Barb Klish was wiping crumbs from the top of the glass case that held the pastries. A tall blonde with a broad smile, she taught home economics at the high school, worked at the Farber House on weekends, and had recently begun trading over the Internet on eBay. She liked to call herself a broker.

"Hey, there, Rennie," Barb said. She was the only person who ever called him Rennie, but he liked it. "I know what you want. A *kolache,* right? What kind?"

"Ham and cheese. Two, please."

"Really hungry, eh?"

"One's for Charlie," he said.

"What a good friend you are." She slid open the case.

"And I'd like a vanilla latte, too."

She eyed him through the glass as she bent for the *kolaches.* "Since when do you drink coffee?"

"It's not for me."

"Charlie?"

"No. A friend who's staying at the resort."

This was one of the problems with Bodine. No question was a simple one. They led one to another until you found yourself caught in a web from which it was impossible to escape.

"Oh? Friend of your mom's?"

"Yes."

"How's she doing? Your mom, I mean. I can't remember the last time we talked."

"She's fine."

"I'll just put these *kolaches* in a bag and then whip up that latte for you."

He heard the elevator doors slide open at his back.

61

"Well, look what the north wind blew in. Renoir!"

He turned as the Taylors swept into the lobby. They were in their early sixties, but always seemed full of more energy than people half their age. With his towering stature and brilliant red hair, Mr. Taylor reminded Ren of a maple tree in fall. Mrs. Taylor was half his size. That morning she wore a dark blue dress and heels. Her husband wore a suit and tie.

Church, Ren thought.

"Don't move," Mr. Taylor said. "I've got something for you. Wait right there." He vanished into the office behind the front desk.

"We haven't seen you in a while, Ren," said Mrs. Taylor. She snared his shoulders and gave him a squeeze.

"I've been around," Ren said.

"Not around here. How's your mother?"

"Fine. She's just fine."

"We're on our way to church, and I do so miss her voice in the choir. Will you tell her that?"

"Yes, ma'am."

Mr. Taylor returned carrying a white cardboard box, which he handed over to Ren. "Go ahead and open it."

Ren found it packed with dozens of comic books, all Marvel and DC, that seemed to cover many of the classic superheroes he knew and appreciated: Green Lantern, Batman, Superman, Blackhawk, the Fantastic Four, Dr. Strange, Thor.

"Wow," he said. "Thanks."

"We knew you had a birthday coming up—when is it?"

"Next week."

"Right, so we had Barb do a little horse-trading for us on eBay."

"Some of those issues are rare, Ren," Barb said behind him. "Real collector's items. I struck some good bargains."

"This is great," Ren told them. "Let me take these outside. And I'll bring back something I want you to see."

He carried the box to his ATV and took from the storage compartment his own small box. He brought it inside and handed it to Mr. Taylor, who opened it and removed the contents.

"What have we here? Looks like a big-cat track." He studied the plaster cast further. His hands quivered, a slight tremor that had affected him his whole life. He'd told Ren that people made all kinds of harsh erroneous judgments about him based on that insignificant detail. Ren, who was part Ojibwe, and small for his age, understood. "A bobcat?" Mr. Taylor asked.

Ren shook his head. In his estimation, Mr. Taylor was the smartest man in Bodine and seemed to know something about everything. Ren knew he'd appreciate the significance of the cast.

"Not a bobcat, eh? Well, it couldn't be a cougar, could it?"

"It is," Ren said.

"You made this cast? Where'd you find the track?"

"Near one of our cabins."

"A cougar that close to human habitation? Interesting. Ren, do you mind if I keep this for a while? I have a friend who's a zoologist at Northern Michigan down in Marquette. I'd like him to have a look at it."

"Sure."

"Wonderful. I'll have it back to you in a few days." He disappeared into the office again, came out with his hands empty, and took his wife's arm. "If we don't want to be late for church, Sue, we'd best be moving. Good to see you, Ren. Say hello to your mother for us."

When they'd gone, Ren paid for the *kolaches* and the coffee, then he headed off on his ATV, making for Charlie's place. He followed Lake Street, where the finest houses in town had been built, old Victorian places. The people who lived there now were professionals—doctors, lawyers, executives—most of whom worked in Marquette but had been lured to Bodine by the beauty of the place and the stunning old houses they could buy for a song. A lot of the homes had been refurbished over the last few years. Stash's family lived there. So did Amber Kennedy's.

Ever since the day before when Charlie told him that Amber liked him, the girl had occupied much of his thinking. She was pretty, with long gold hair that always seemed to flip in just the right way over her delicate shoulders. She wore braces on her teeth, and when she smiled she usually covered her mouth. For some reason, that made Ren like her more. In truth, he'd been thinking less about her prettiness or long gold hair or smile than about her breasts, which over the past summer seemed to have erupted and now pushed up like a couple of active volcanoes under her sweater.

He didn't linger when he reached her house, not wanting her to think, should she see him pass, that he'd come that way just because of her. He did cast a quick glance in that direction, but was disappointed to see no one at the front windows.

He turned west. Near the edge of town, the pavement gave way to gravel. He bumped along beyond the last of the small ranch houses and entered an area of failed commerce. He passed Zeke's Small Engine Repair, now abandoned, a small pasture where a man named Fry Ahearn still sometimes kept a few goats, and finally the Huron Lumber Company, which had given up the ghost years ago and now sat idle behind a tall Cyclone fence.

Charlie lived with her father in a beat-up green trailer home set on a cinder-block foundation a quarter mile south of the abandoned lumberyard. There were two red maples in front and between them a big patch of raggedy grass that was usually long overdue for mowing. In back a sea of weeds swamped the empty frame of a swing set, a couple of rusted barrels, an old gas stove, a claw-foot bathtub, and a hundred other smaller items with so many jagged or broken edges that Charlie and Ren no longer set foot there.

Because he didn't want to risk waking Charlie's father, who would probably be battling a mammoth hangover, Ren pulled to the side of the road a good distance from the trailer, killed the engine, and walked the rest of the way. Far from town, everything was quiet. The maples were a deep red and shedding. Their fallen leaves lay embedded in the tall grass of the front yard like rubies. Ren knew better than to knock. He crept to a side window, which was closed, the blinds inside lowered. He tapped at the glass, waited, tapped again. He put his lips to the window pane and called softly, "Charlie?"

Nothing.

Which was understandable. It had been a late night for them both. He walked around to the front, saw that the door was open. He climbed the crumbling set of concrete steps and peeked through the screen.

He'd been inside hundreds of times over the years and the place was always a mess. This morning it looked even worse than usual. Way worse. As if Charlie's father had gone on a drunken rampage and tried to break everything he hadn't already broken. Christ, how could Charlie stand it?

Ren didn't like the idea of disturbing Mr. Miller, but the place looked so bad, he was worried about Charlie. If she'd come home while her old man was going crazy . . .

"Hello?" Ren called timidly. "Mr. Miller? Charlie?"

The day was sunny and still. The clarity of the Huron Mountains in the distance was softened by a blue haze. Ren watched a stray dog squeeze through a hole in the lumberyard fence, look his way, then trot off in the other direction. This was all so normal, yet Ren sensed that something wasn't right.

A long moment of uncertainty passed, then he decided.

He eased the door open and stepped inside. Immediately, his nose was assaulted by the same raw odor that had hit him when he opened the door of the car where Cork O'Connor had bled heavily after he was shot. Ren would have turned around and got the hell out of there except he was afraid for Charlie.

Although the trailer was full of broken debris, it felt empty. Ren made his way toward Charlie's bedroom. As he approached the threshold, part of the room was revealed and what he saw stopped him cold.

Charlie's walls were powder blue. The wall that Ren could see was splashed with a different color. As he stood there, unable to make himself move ahead, the artist in him tried to find form in what he saw. Numbly he thought that the splatter resembled a jellyfish with many long tentacles.

A big red jellyfish.

11

Cork offered to share his breakfast with Dina. She accepted a bit of his coffee and a piece of toast. She sat at the cabin table, hunched over her half-filled coffee cup. She'd removed the forest green jacket she'd been wearing. Underneath was a tan sweater. Below were khakis and hiking boots.

"For a city girl who never learned much about the woods, you look pretty good here. Pretty natural," Cork said, speaking from his bunk.

With her thumb she flicked a crumb from the corner of her mouth. "Deep-cover training."

"You haven't talked to Jo, right?"

"That's what you wanted, wasn't it?"

It was, but he was dying to know how they were doing, to be assured that they were fine. And he wanted them to know they shouldn't be worried about him.

"The less they know, the safer they are. They're of no use to Jacoby," he said.

Dina used Cork's butter knife to brush some char from her toast. "You know, I never believed cops and families were a good idea. You get hurt, killed, it's not just you who suffers."

"If cops didn't have families, where would little cops come from?" He smiled. She didn't. "Is that the reason you don't have a boyfriend?"

She leveled her green eyes on him and said dourly, "Boy-

66

friend?" She picked up her coffee with both hands. "I haven't had a boyfriend since high school. I have lovers."

"Anyone special?"

"Special gets complicated and leads to things like families." She gave her attention to the coffee.

Cork lifted the tray on which Ren had delivered breakfast. He tried to move it out of his way, twisted his leg, and grunted in pain. Dina got up, came over, took the tray from him, and carried it to the table. She came back, lifted the sheet, and looked at his wounds.

"Hurt much?"

"Only when the drugs wear off. Or I think about it. Ever been shot?"

"That's a pleasure I've missed." Her eyes moved from his leg to his face, then slid away quickly. "You were lucky."

"I know."

She let the sheet drop. "Is this really the kind of thing you want to put your family through?"

"Maybe when all this is over I'll go back to running the hamburger stand. Except I got shot doing that, too."

"Maybe guys like you just attract trouble."

"What about people like you?"

"Like me?"

"Who make a living pulling other people's keisters out of the fire."

"I'm not making a nickel off you."

He laughed softly. "You can use me as a reference." He reached out and took her hand. "Thanks for coming, Dina."

She glanced at her fingers, small in his palm. "What was I going to do? Leave you to the wolves?"

"Some would."

"In my shoes, what would you do?"

"Deep down, we're the same kind of people, you know. Except with you, it comes in a nicer package." He laughed easily, jesting.

"And with you, it comes with a family." She slid her hand from his easy grip, walked back to the table, and sat down with her coffee.

"I didn't mean it that way," he said.

"Forget it."

"Look, all I meant was—"

"I said forget it, okay?"

"No. I want to get this straight."

"It couldn't be any straighter. You're married. Happily. The perfect family. End of story. I get it."

For a while it was quiet in the cabin. Cork stared out the window at the square of sky and tree branch he could see from the bunk. "Wish I knew how the investigations are going."

"Like I said, the Winnetka police are playing dumb. Won't answer any of my questions. Maybe your people in Aurora know something."

"Got a cell phone I can use?"

"What happened to yours?"

Cork grabbed his shattered unit from the windowsill and held it up. "Took a bullet in the parking lot in Kenosha."

Dina finally smiled, then something seemed to dawn on her. "When you talked to Jo before the goons ambushed you at the motel, did you tell her where you were staying?"

"I didn't think so, but I must have. How else would they have known where I was?"

"Did you pay for the room with a credit card?"

"Cash, from the roll you gave me."

"But you used the cell phone to call her?"

"Yeah."

"Let me see it."

Cork handed it over.

"When did you buy this?"

"Couple of months ago. Replacement for the one that got broken when we busted a meth lab near Yellow Lake."

She popped the face off the phone, studied the guts, and said, "Uh-huh."

"What?"

"I think I know how they found you. E911 capable."

E911. Cork understood. Many new cell phones were equipped with a chip that, when the unit was turned on, broadcast a continuous GPS signal that was accessible if you knew the phone's unique chip code. This allowed emergency personnel to locate someone who either didn't know where they were or couldn't relay that information. It had other, less publicized uses. It was possible for law enforcement to track suspects or known criminals using the chip's signal. Also, some cell phone companies documented their customers' activities on a continuous basis, logging information that might be of interest to a corporation wanting to know, for example, how many Starbucks someone hit in the course of a normal week. Anyone with the right money and proper connections would have had no trouble at all tracking Cork to a dingy motel in Kenosha, Wisconsin.

"Christ, why didn't I think of that?"

"Have you used the phone up here at all?" Dina asked.

He shook his head. "The bullet killed it."

"Good."

She tossed it to him and he set it back on the windowsill. "Here." She took a cell from the pocket of her jacket and gave it to him. "Use this."

"This one can't be tracked?"

"Whenever I buy a cell phone for myself or my operatives, the first thing I do is disable the chip."

"Thanks," Cork said. He punched in the number for Captain Ed Larson's office at the Aurora County Sheriff's Department. "Ed, it's Cork."

"Where the hell are you?" Larson's voice faded in and out over the phone, the connection tenuous.

"Best you don't know, Ed. Jacoby's put a price on my head."

"I heard. I talked with Jo a little bit ago. You should call her. She's worried sick."

"I called her once and it turned out bad. I won't call her again. If these guys know I'm in touch with her, I'm afraid they might try using her to get to me, understand?"

"Yeah. Look, I think you've got trouble here, too. We got a call last night from one of your neighbors. Someone was sneaking around your house. Dispatched a cruiser and the guy ran. Somebody thinking you came back to Aurora to hide, maybe?"

"That's my guess. Jesus, these guys are everywhere."

"How are you doing?"

"Hanging in there. Dina Willner's with me, so I've got backup."

"That's good."

"We've been talking things over, trying to figure our next move, but we're working in the dark. Tell me what's going on with the Jacoby murders."

"We've had a couple of breaks. First off, we picked up some teenagers joyriding in a car they admitted stealing. It matches the description of the vehicle at Mercy Falls the night Eddie Jacoby was murdered. The kids claimed they took it from a small airfield near Biwabik where it had been parked for several days. Turned out to be a rental. Under the front seat, we found lip gloss manufactured in Argentina."

"Gabriella Jacoby is from Argentina."

"Bingo. We're checking the prints against the ones she submitted when she applied for citizenship here. If they match, we may be able to prove she was in Minnesota when she claimed to be sailing on Lake Michigan with her brother Tony."

"Who rented the vehicle?"

"It came from an agency at the Duluth airport three days before Jacoby was murdered. A phony ID and credit card were used, but the rental agent, a young woman apparently much impressed with Tony Salguero's swarthy Latin American ways, identified him from a photo. Salguero used the same credit card to purchase a round-trip airline ticket from Chicago to Duluth."

"He set it up ahead of time, flew out with Gabriella in his private plane; they killed Eddie and flew back in time to be on their boat next morning," Cork said. "Probably planned to return the car when things settled down, only the kids got there first."

"Everything points in that direction. We have motive—the insurance and inheritance money—and opportunity. And don't forget we have Arlo Knuth, who'll testify about the Spanish-speaking couple he saw at Mercy Falls the night Eddie was stabbed. We don't have every nail in place yet, but we're getting there, Cork."

"What about Ben Jacoby's murder?"

"Winnetka PD tells me they've got a shoe print. When Ben Jacoby was shot in his pool, you and Dina were covering the front of the estate. The only way for the killer to make a get-away was through the back gate down to the lakeshore. There was a heavy dew that morning, made the sand wet and compact. It held tracks. The only tracks on the beach that early in the morning came from a sport shoe. Fila, size ten and a half. Coincidentally, Salguero's shoe size. Winnetka's working on a warrant right now to search his place for a shoe that matches the prints."

"All good news," Cork said. "But still nothing that pins them solid. Look, Ed, I'd bet it was Salguero who did the actual killings. Gabriella has children, two young sons. That makes her vulnerable. What if Winnetka PD brought her in and sweated her. She might be inclined to roll over on Salguero in exchange for a deal that wouldn't keep her away from her boys forever."

"I'll talk to them about it."

"Thanks, Ed. All this is good to hear. If you need to get in touch with me, call Dina's cell phone number." He gave it to Larson and ended the call.

"Well?" she said.

He explained what he'd learned.

Dina slipped the phone back into her jacket pocket. "Even if they arrest Gabriella, Lou might not call off the hit. I've worked a lot of jobs for him over the years, and Lou's one stubborn son of a bitch. No matter what the evidence, he might decide not to believe his darling daughter-in-law had a hand in killing his sons." Dina yawned and stretched. "I need a shower. And a good cup of coffee. Where the hell is Ren? How long does it take to get a latte and get back here?"

"You know kids. They dawdle."

Dina flipped on the light switch in the bathroom and glanced around. "As a matter of fact, I don't know kids. They scare me. They're like something I see at the zoo. And as long as they stay on their side of the bars, I do fine. Okay if I use your shower?"

Before Cork could answer, he heard the growl of the engine as the ATV bounced up the lane from the county road. "Speak of the devil."

"Latte and a *kolache*," Dina said eagerly.

She went to the front door and opened it. Cork felt a cool draft of late morning air rush into the cabin.

The ATV stopped outside. Dina stepped back abruptly, and Ren stumbled past her looking as if he'd been chased by a monster. He spoke in gasps.

"He's . . . he's . . . dead."

"Whoa," Dina said. "Who's dead?"

Ren's eyes swung from Cork to Dina then back to Cork. They were wide and wet-looking. "Charlie's . . . father."

"How do you know?" Cork asked. He pushed himself into a sitting position.

"I saw him."

Dina came around Ren so that she could look into his face, too. "Where?"

"At their trailer. I was just there. Somebody beat his head in."

Cork swung his legs off the bunk, ignoring the pain of his wounds. "Where's Charlie?"

"I don't know. She wasn't there."

Cork stood up and limped to the boy. With some difficulty, he knelt and put his hands gently on Ren's shoulders. "Take a deep breath. Okay, another. Now, tell me everything from the beginning."

Ren told it all, from his stop at the Farber House to the red jellyfish on the wall of Charlie's bedroom to the dead man lying on the floor with his head beat to mush.

"The baseball bat was right beside him," Ren said, choking a little on the words. "It was Charlie's bat. It was, like, the nicest present her dad ever gave her."

"You're sure he was dead, Ren?" Dina asked.

"His head . . . I could see his brains sticking out." He squeezed his eyes shut, as if that would block the image.

Cork said, "We need to tell the police, Ren. And we need to call your mother. She should be with you. Okay?"

The boy nodded.

"Give me your cell phone, Dina. What's her number at the clinic, Ren?"

Cork spoke with someone who told him Jewell was out on a call. Ren gave him her cell phone number and he tried that, but she was out of the service area. He handed the phone back to Dina.

"We shouldn't wait," she said.

"I know."

"I'll go with him," Dina volunteered. "Would that be all right, Ren?"

He considered her a moment. "Okay."

Cork said, "Is there a police department in Bodine?"

"Yeah. There's the constable. Ned Hodder."

Dina put her hand on Ren's shoulder. "Let's start with him."

"Wait," Cork said. "This is risky. You're a stranger here. That'll raise questions."

Dina thought a moment. "What if I were a relative? Mind having an aunt Donna, Ren?"

"Donna?" Ren said.

"For a little while, I'll be Donna Walport. It's a name I use sometimes when I don't want people to know my real name. I have a few of those."

"Like an alias?"

"I prefer to think of it as a cover name."

"Aunt Donna," Ren said, trying it out. "That's all right with me."

Cork wasn't thrilled, but he didn't see another way. "Stay close to her, Ren, and follow her lead. And be careful what you say."

"I will," the boy promised.

"Don't worry," Dina said. "We'll be fine."

But he did worry. He watched them go knowing there was a great gulf between what Ren bravely believed he was capable of and what the reality of the situation might force on him. The boy would have to walk a tough line, holding to the truth here, embracing a lie there, all under the cold eye of people with badges and uniforms. It was a lot to ask. Not many adults could pull it off.

Except that Ren had something most others did not. He had Aunt Donna.

12

The constable's office was on Harbor Avenue, sandwiched between the Ace Hardware store and Kitty's Café. An old, narrow, redbrick one-story, it had a desk area up front and two holding cells in back accessed through a heavy metal door. Ren had been in the jail area before. His mother and Constable Ned Hodder were old friends, and Ned had once locked Ren in one of the cells to give him a sense of what it was like to be incarcerated. Ren was just a kid; it had been a kick. That was before his father was murdered and cops became the enemy. Ren wasn't even certain his mother had spoken to Ned Hodder since his father's death.

They parked Ren's ATV in front of the building and walked inside. The constable was at his desk, writing in a small lined notebook. As soon as the door swung open, he shut the notebook and put it away in the top desk drawer. When he saw Ren, a big smile dawned on his face.

"And here I thought it was going to be just another boring Sunday." He stood up.

In his video collection, Stash had a movie called *Anatomy of a Murder* that Ren had watched with him one rainy Saturday. The movie was pretty good. It had been filmed not far from Bodine and starred a guy named James Stewart, apparently a big-deal actor in his day. The constable reminded Ren of that guy. Ned Hodder was more than six feet tall and lean. For an adult—and a cop on top of it—he had an easygoing approach to most things. He was straight when he spoke to you, though he sometimes stumbled around for the right words. And every feature of his plain face seemed to tell you that he wouldn't lie to you even if his life depended on it.

Every year Hodder confiscated the illegal fireworks that folks brought with them when they came up from Wisconsin, where such things were legal. He stored them in a locker in the basement beneath his office. Every Fourth of July, just after sunset, he enlisted the help of the town fire marshal and, in Dunning Park right on the lake, set off all those pyrotechnics to the delight of most everybody in Bodine.

Last summer, he'd arrested two members of a band playing at the Logjam Saloon for urinating in public. They were young musicians without a lot of money, so he'd offered them a deal. In lieu of a night in the city jail, the band put on a free concert in Dunning Park. It turned out they knew a lot of old swing tunes, and folks ended up dancing on the grass and having a fine time. Ren was there with his mother, and it was one of the few instances since his father died that he'd seen her look happy.

Hodder came from behind his desk and extended his hand toward Dina. "Don't believe I know you. I'm Ned Hodder. How do you do?"

"Fine, thanks. I'm Ren's aunt. Donna Walport. Ren here has something pretty awful he needs to tell you."

"That so?" Hodder bent a little in Ren's direction and looked serious. "What is it?"

"Charlie's father," Ren blurted. "He's dead."

"Max? Dead?" The constable straightened up. "What makes you think so?"

"I saw him."

"Where?"

"At their trailer, a little while ago."

"How do you know he's dead?"

Ren began to shiver. "Somebody, like, smashed his head in."

"Where's Charlie?"

"I don't know. She wasn't there." He went on shivering. He couldn't stop.

"A little while ago, you say. How long?"

"Half an hour."

Hodder put a large comforting hand on Ren's shoulder. "You mind going back there with me?"

Ren didn't like the idea at all, but he said, "I won't go inside."

"I won't make you, I promise."

"All right."

Hodder looked at Dina again. "Ren's aunt, you said. I don't believe I've ever seen you here before."

"My dad's sister," Ren put in quickly. "She lives in San Francisco. I never get to see her. She's visiting us for a few days."

"Ren's mom is at work," Dina went on smoothly. "I didn't think he should come here alone. If you don't mind, I'd like to go with you. Be there for Ren, you know?"

Hodder thought it over briefly, finally shrugged. "I guess that would be all right."

They took the constable's black Cherokee, which looked to be quite a few miles past warranty. Ren sat huddled in back. He didn't want to be going where they were going, but he hoped it might help Charlie somehow. Hodder asked him some questions on the way: why he'd been at the trailer, how he'd got inside, if he had any idea where Charlie might be. He pulled into the weedy gravel drive and parked behind the old Toyota pickup that belonged to Charlie's father. He turned off the engine and said, "Wait here."

"Constable?"

He turned to Dina.

"Do you ever carry a weapon?" She nodded toward his empty belt.

"Not generally. I keep a shotgun in the trunk, but honestly I've never had occasion to use it. I carry a pocketknife that comes in handy once in a while."

"Uh-huh." She raised an eyebrow and nodded, as if she found his approach rather quaint. "Have you ever been at a murder scene?"

"How do you know it's murder?"

"You think he bashed his own head in?"

"I've never been at a murder scene," he admitted.

Hodder got out and approached the trailer with caution, turning his head as he scanned each window in front, looking, Ren supposed, for some movement out of place in a trailer home with only a dead man inside. He mounted the steps and reached for the screen door.

"Constable," Dina called from the Cherokee. "You might want to put on gloves before you touch anything. At least, that's what they do in the movies."

Hodder glanced at his bare hands, then at the door handle. He pulled his pocketknife from the pouch that hung on his belt and unfolded the blade, which he used to open the door. He disappeared inside.

"Andy Griffith," Dina said with a shake of her head.

"Who?" Ren asked.

"Forget it."

He looked at her thoughtfully. "Have you ever been to a murder scene? I mean in your work and stuff?"

"I'll let you in on a secret, Ren. I used to be with the FBI."

"FBI?"

"Yep."

"But not anymore."

"Nope."

"Why?"

"Long story." She'd been staring intently at the trailer, but now her intense green eyes settled on Ren, and he felt himself grow warm under their scrutiny. "Why don't we talk about it over a beer sometime."

It took a moment for the smile to grow on her lips, and then he understood it was a joke and he smiled, too.

"I'll buy," he said, feeling good, feeling special.

Then he looked back at the trailer and stopped smiling.

"Have you seen people who were murdered?" he asked.

"Yes. And it's always ugly and upsetting, even for cops."

Hodder came back out and walked to Dina's side of the Cherokee. "Ms. Walport, there's a cell phone in my glove box there. Would you mind handing it to me?" He took it and punched in 911. "This is Constable Hodder in Bodine. I've got what appears to be a homicide on my hands." He gave the address, listened a moment, and said, "I'll be here."

* * *

Detective Sergeant Terry Olafsson of the Marquette County Sheriff's office had a wide, ruddy face. He was sandy-haired, not much taller than Dina Willner, but with a broad chest. He wore a red windbreaker with the sleeves pulled up to his elbows. Veins ran across the hard muscles of his forearms like thin ropes against smooth wood.

After the introductions were made, Dina said, "I'd like to stay with Ren while you interview him."

"You an attorney?"

"Like I said, his aunt. I'm just concerned."

Olafsson said, "Where's his folks?"

"My father's dead," Ren jumped in, irked that the detective was ignoring him. "And my mother's a veterinarian. She's out on a call and we can't reach her."

Olafsson looked toward Constable Hodder for confirmation.

Hodder nodded. "Just like Ren says."

They stood beside the constable's Cherokee. Marquette Sheriff's people went in and out of the trailer home. "Crime scene technicians, right?" Ren asked Dina.

She winked at him and gave a nod. Then she added, "See that guy?"

A tall, balding man wearing a white shirt and black slacks and carrying a medical bag stepped from a blue sedan and walked toward the trailer.

"Coroner?" Ren guessed.

"Or medical examiner," she replied.

Ren was grateful for Dina's observations. They kept him from thinking too much about what was inside the trailer or what might have become of Charlie.

"Any reason the boy needs an adult with him while we talk?" Olafsson said.

"Any reason he can't have one?" Dina replied.

With a slight nod, Olafsson gave in. "All right." He took out a small notepad and focused on Ren. "How'd you find the body, son?"

"I just walked in and there it was."

"Walked in? The door was open?"

"Yes."

"Both doors?"

"The inside one was already open. I just opened the screen."

"Anyone tell you to come in?"

"No."

"Is it your custom to walk into a house uninvited?"

"I was worried about Charlie."

"Charlie?"

"Charlene Miller," Hodder clarified. "The dead man's daughter."

"And why were you worried about her, son?"

"Her father drinks sometimes. When he does he gets scary. He was drinking last night."

"And you know that how?"

"Charlie told me."

"You saw her last night?"

"Yes."

"Give me a time."

"I don't know. A little after midnight, maybe."

"Where?"

"We were down at the lake."

"What were you doing at the lake at midnight?"

"Charlie's dad was drinking and she didn't want to go home until she was sure he'd passed out. We were just hanging."

"She went home when?"

"Like I said, a little after midnight." Ren thought a moment. "That's when she left me, anyway. I guess I don't know for sure that she went home."

"Did she seem upset, angry?"

"Not when she left."

"What time did you get here this morning?"

"Around ten."

"Why'd you come?"

"I had a *kolache* for her. Sometimes she doesn't eat right." Ren looked down at the gravel under his feet. "The truth is I just wanted to make sure she was okay."

"You opened the screen door and went in. Then what?"

"Everything was a mess, worse than usual. I went back to her room and I saw, like, this stuff on the wall. The blood and all. I was afraid it was Charlie. I thought he'd hurt her. Then I saw him on the floor."

"What did you do then?"

"I got out of there as fast as I could."

"And went straight to the constable?"

"No. I went home first."

"Why home and not to Constable Hodder?"

"I don't know. I guess I wasn't thinking."

"Do you know where Charlene—Charlie—is?"

"No."

"Do you have any idea where she might be?"

Ren hesitated. "No."

"But you do know the girl pretty well?"

"We're friends."

"I don't know Charlie myself, but I just got off the phone with some folks in the juvenile division who do, son," Olafsson said. "One thing they told me about Charlie, she has a temper. And they told me about her father and how he treated her sometimes."

"So?" Ren didn't like the feel of the detective's words.

"You saw the baseball bat beside the body?"

"Yeah."

"Do you know who the bat belongs to?"

"It's Charlie's."

"That's right. Charlie's. I want to ask you something, son, and I want you to answer me as honestly as you can. Will you do that?"

"I'll try."

"Do you think Charlie could have done this to her father?"

Dina stepped in. Ren appreciated how firm and cool she seemed. "I don't think that's an appropriate question, Detective."

"I'm just asking for an informed opinion."

"Of a fourteen-year-old boy? About a murder? That's low and you know it."

"It's okay," Ren said quickly. He looked at Detective Sergeant Olafsson steadily. "She couldn't. He was a bastard sometimes, but she loved him. She wouldn't do something like . . . like in there."

Olafsson nodded, scowled a little. "I understand you live in the woods, a resort, with your mother. That right?"

"Yes."

"You ever see a small animal, a rabbit, say, trapped in a corner? Even a rabbit can get vicious when it's threatened."

Dina said, "He's not the jury, Detective. And you're not the prosecutor. No need to convince him of anything."

Olafsson looked at her, and Ren saw his jaw tighten. "You certainly seem to think you know your way around the law, Ms. Walport. What is it you do?"

"I watch a lot of television. Cop shows. You'd be surprised what you can pick up."

Although a smile played briefly across the detective's lips, it didn't seem friendly. The way he started to look at Dina, as if she were a steak sizzling on a grill, didn't sit well with Ren, either.

Olafsson returned his attention to Ren. "Did you touch anything or move anything while you were in the trailer, son?"

"No."

"You're sure about that?"

"I'm sure."

Olafsson seemed to be waiting for Ren to reconsider. With his silence, Ren held his ground.

"All right, then. I guess that's it for now."

Hodder said, "Okay if I take these folks back to town?"

"I suppose. We may want to talk to the boy later." He glowered at Ren. "No trips out of town for a while, okay?"

Ren nodded.

"I want you back here right away, Ned," Olafsson added. "We need to go over the vic's friends, acquaintances, drinking buddies, girlfriends. Whatever you can tell me."

"I'll be back in ten."

Olafsson strode toward the trailer home.

They piled into the Cherokee. Hodder backed out and headed north into town.

Dina spoke toward the windshield. "You know Olafsson?"

"I've worked with him before. Never a murder investigation. He's not what I'd call a warm man, but he's thorough. And fair."

Ren said, "He sounded like he thought Charlie did it."

"He's got to consider that possibility," Hodder replied. He turned onto Lake Street. Lake Superior stretched away on the right, the great old homes of Bodine rose on the left. "Everybody knows Charlie's a firecracker. When she goes off, well . . ."

Hodder sounded like a policeman now, and Ren didn't like it.

"I'd like to talk to your mother about all this. When she gets home today, have her give me a call, okay?"

Ren held off answering.

"Okay?"

"Okay," he mumbled.

"How're you doing?" Hodder asked, sounding more like a normal guy. A guy who might actually care about what had happened to Charlie.

"I'm fine."

"I hope it goes without saying, Ren, that if you hear from Charlie, you'll let me know."

Ren stared out the window at the houses sweeping by. They were just coming up on Amber Kennedy's place. He thought about the shining feeling he'd had when he rode past on his way to Charlie's. How was it possible to feel that good and this lousy in the same morning?

13

Cork lived in an old, well-kept two-story clapboard house. The front porch had a swing. A huge elm that was older than Cork shaded the front yard. The house was on Gooseberry Lane in Aurora, Minnesota. He'd grown up in that town and had chosen it as the place to raise his family. Its rhythms were as natural to him as the pulse of his own blood.

Aurora was hundreds of miles away. At the moment it seemed even farther, on the other side of a barrier that was more than just miles. It was a barrier of experience, the result of monstrous events that could not be undone or forgotten.

He lay on the bunk in his cabin, helpless against despair.

His wife had been drugged by Lou Jacoby's grandson, an angry young man who then raped her. Cork pictured Jo with her ice-blond hair all wild as it had been the morning after that terrible night. He saw again her dazed face, her eyes blinking like fireflies as she stared at the gun in his hand, then at the water of a swimming pool turned red with a dead man's blood.

In Cork's anguished thinking, the whole earth was a vast hunting ground, and you were either predator or prey. Killing was the answer. Killing the man who'd spilled his rage into Jo. Killing the men who'd put a bullet through his leg. Killing Lou Jacoby, the son of a bitch who'd set it all in motion.

"Damn!" He realized that the Beretta that Dina had given him in Evanston was still in the glove box of his car. If the men who'd attacked him in Kenosha showed up now, he had no way to protect himself.

He pulled the sheet away and swung his legs off the bunk. He gathered himself, stood, and took a step.

"Oh, shit," he groaned, then took another.

His shoes sat beside the door. They were brown Rockports, the left one stained dark with blood. He gritted his teeth, knelt, and scooped them up. Outside, he plopped down on the cabin steps and tugged them onto his sockless feet. He looked toward the end of the lane where his car was parked behind the big shed. It seemed like a long way.

In addition to Thor's Lodge, the resort had six rental cabins staggered along either side of a central dirt access with enough room between each cabin to allow a vehicle to park. They were all the same design, one large square central room that functioned as a sitting area, kitchen, and sleeping quarters. Each cabin also had a small bathroom with a shower stall. The cabins had bunks and were typically rented by hikers or hunters or snowmobilers. Summers when Cork had visited with his mother, the cabins had been well maintained by Jewell's father. Now there were signs of neglect. Spiderwebs in the window wells. Fallen branches and evergreen cones littering the ground. Brittle weeds creeping around the cabin steps. In such an environment, the wild things—coons and squirrels and snakes—would eventually make their homes.

So much had been left undone because Jewell didn't care, and because Ren, for all his fine qualities, was yet a boy. The work had been his father's, and his father was gone for good.

Cork picked up a long, thick branch that had fallen to the ground next to his cabin. Although a little crooked, it seemed sturdy enough for a walking stick. He started for the shed.

The sky was a flawless blue, the air dead still, the late morning only just now crawling out from under the chill of the night before. The hardwoods were in full autumn glory and the Huron Mountains were like a stormy sea caught fire.

Getting to the shed took a toll. The makeshift walking stick helped a little, but the torture of his leg sucked at Cork's strength, gobbled his energy. Twice he stopped to rest on the steps of other cabins.

During the second rest he heard a scream break from the woods south of the cabins. He scanned the tree line but saw nothing unusual. The scream came again, farther west. This time Cork realized exactly what it was. The cry of a big cat. Ren's cougar. Circling.

Cork had lived in the Northwoods most of his life. He understood the behavior of many of the animals of that habitat. Although he knew very little about cougars specifically, he was pretty certain of one thing: Like most wild animals, they were loath to approach humans or the dwellings of humans. Yet, here was a cat, a fierce hunter, deep in the territory of men.

"So what are you doing here?" he whispered toward the woods.

He put his weight on the walking stick and pushed himself up. Keeping an eye to the trees, he gimped his way to the shot-up Dart and reached for the door handle. He was startled to see recent scratches on the finish, four lines that ran from the driver's side window down the door, spaced just right to have been put there by the claws of a big wild cat. He opened the door, and the smell of the blood poured out: his blood. He clicked the glove box latch and snatched the Beretta Tomcat. As he popped the clip to check the cartridges, the cougar screamed again.

With the rosewood grip of the pistol solidly in his palm, he felt less vulnerable. That didn't mean safe. Was it the smell of the blood that had attracted the wild cat? What did it take to stop a hungry cougar? He wasn't just concerned about his own safety. He was also thinking what a tragedy it would be if he were, in fact, forced to shoot the animal.

He started back to his cabin. As he neared Thor's Lodge he heard the phone ring inside, and he thought maybe Jewell had finally got the message to call. He limped up the stairs, found the door unlocked, and went in. By the time he reached the phone, the ringing had stopped. Caller ID informed him that it had, in fact, been Jewell calling from her cell phone. He punched in her number.

"Ren?" she answered.

"It's Cork."

"Where's Ren? I got a message there was an emergency of some kind." Her voice came to him across a sea of static.

"He's all right, Jewell. It's Charlie. Or rather her father. He's dead."

"Max dead? How?"

"According to Ren, he was beat to death."

"How would Ren know that?"

Cork explained. Every so often, because of the poor reception, he had to repeat himself. While he spoke, he gradually became aware of a sound from the rear of the cabin. A scratching.

"I'm on my way now," Jewell said. "I'm heading to Max Miller's place."

"If they show up back here, I'll call you."

He set the phone in the cradle and listened carefully. The sound had stopped. Quietly he hobbled toward the back rooms. He hadn't been inside Thor's Lodge in decades. It seemed more modern than he remembered—new appliances, fixtures—but it held the same feel of a place built with careful hands, an eye to the beauty of small detail, and a respect for the spirit of each rock in the foundation and every log in the walls and rafters. The two bedrooms in back were separated by a bathroom. To the right was Ren's room, easy to tell from the Spider-Man poster on the wall. The room on the left had been the guest room where Cork's mother stayed. Upstairs was a master bedroom and a large loft area where Cork, when he visited all those years ago, had slept on a cot.

Standing in the narrow hallway, he heard it again, the scratching. It came from the back wall of Ren's room. Cork had left his walking stick on the porch. Using the bureau, the desk, and finally the post of Ren's bed to support himself, he laboriously made his way to the window where the curtains were closed. As he'd started across the room, he'd stepped on a board that gave a sharp creak, announcing his presence, and the scratching abruptly died. Now he stood at the window, the Beretta tight in his grasp, his ear cocked toward the wall as he listened intently for a sound that didn't return. He reached out with his empty hand and slowly parted the curtains.

A red squirrel clinging to the screen glared at him belligerently. After the bravado of a Mexican standoff, the little creature broke his stare, leaped to the ground, scampered to the nearest tree, and scrambled up the trunk.

14

Ren returned on his ATV in a cloud of dust and with the engine roaring, enough racket, Cork figured, to scare off even a hungry cougar. The boy stopped in front of the cabin and dismounted. He climbed the steps, his face heavy with so much concern for one so young.

Cork stood at the door. "Where's Dina?"

"Coming in her own car."

Ren stepped past him into the cabin.

"Your mother called," Cork told him. "She's on her way to Bodine. Why don't you let her know you're here?"

The boy nodded. He didn't seem eager to talk. As Ren picked up the phone, Cork heard another engine, much quieter than that of the ATV. He stepped outside. His leg throbbed, and he sat down and watched as Dina pulled up in a red Pathfinder.

"How'd it go?" he asked.

She sat beside him on the steps. "He was dead all right. Marquette County Sheriff's people are working the scene."

"What happened? Any way to tell?"

Dina rubbed her eyes in a tired way. "Hodder found him lying on Charlie's bedroom floor. Like Ren said, somebody had bashed his head in with a ball bat. The bat belongs to Charlie."

"Where is she?"

"AWOL."

"They think she did it?"

"At the moment, they don't have another suspect."

"Ren's pretty quiet."

"A lot to process."

"Jewell's on her way."

"I could use some coffee and a bite to eat. Think your cousin would care if I helped myself to something inside?"

"Are you kidding? You just guided Ren through a tough situation. I don't imagine she'd begrudge you anything. But then, I'm not exactly on her good side at the moment."

"I'll risk it."

Ren had gone to his room and closed the door. Dina found the coffee and started some dripping. She opened the refrigerator, pulled out a block of cheddar and what was left of a carton of eggs. Cork sat at the table, took the weight off his bum leg, and watched her prepare to scramble eggs and cheese in a small frying pan.

While she worked, she asked, "What's between you and this cousin of yours? Jewell."

Cork stretched his leg and grimaced. "We haven't been on speaking terms for quite a while."

Dina opened a couple of kitchen drawers, located a grater, and began to shred the cheddar onto a plate. "Why's that?"

"I arrested her husband."

"No kidding? What for?"

"Trespassing and disturbing the peace."

"A troublemaker?"

"Not exactly. It's kind of a long story."

"I'm not going anywhere."

Cork settled back. "Daniel was adopted, but it wasn't a pleasant childhood. He didn't know anything about his real parents. All you had to do was look at him to know there was a lot of Indian in him. After he and Jewell got married, he tried to find his mother. Turned out she was a Shinnob."

"Anishinaabe. Ojibwe, right?"

"Same thing. She was from L'Anse, the reservation on the Keweenaw just the other side of the Huron Mountains. She'd passed away by then, but Daniel got in touch with her people. Not long after that, his grandfather, an old guy named Jacob

Harker, came here to live with him and the family for a couple of years. Daniel told me it was a kind of watershed experience. He discovered a way of looking at things that made sense to him. The problem was that he'd found something Jewell didn't have any interest in sharing. I gather it was a sore point in their marriage."

"What about the arrest?"

"Seven, eight years ago, not long after Daniel's grandfather passed away, they came for a visit to Aurora. Daniel was a quiet guy. I liked him. While they were visiting, a situation developed. A group of Shinnobs from the Iron Lake Reservation blocked access to a stand of virgin white pines scheduled to be cut by a logging company. The Anishinaabeg called the trees Ninishoomisag, which means 'Our Grandfathers,' and considered them sacred. Daniel joined the protestors."

"And you arrested him for that?"

"Not for that. And not just him. A fight broke out between some of the Ojibwe and some of the loggers. That's when I made the arrests."

"On both sides?"

"Both sides."

"You say this Daniel wasn't a hothead?"

"Not at all. It was just the circumstances. But after that he became more and more involved in the wider Indian community and concerns, and in exploring his own Indian identity. I used to think Jewell resented the fact that I arrested her husband. Now I think it was because the arrest sent him in a direction she didn't want to follow."

Dina put the pan over a low flame on the stove and dropped in a pat of butter. She cracked the eggs into a bowl, and added water, salt, and pepper. "How'd he die?" she asked. She began to beat the mixture with a fork.

He watched her work, admiring how she suddenly seemed as at home in the kitchen as she'd been in the deep wilderness only a few days earlier, sighting her rifle on the heart of a man intent on murdering him.

"He'd become a pretty well-known artist with his photography and painting," Cork said. "A few years ago, there was a brouhaha down in Wisconsin over tribal hunting and fishing activities. Whites felt the Ojibwe had overstepped their bounds. The Ojibwe believed they were exercising their rights under the terms of treaties the government had signed. There were some violent confrontations. We had pretty much the same situation in Minnesota."

"Seems to me I remember reading about it in the papers."

"Daniel documented the confrontations, took some pretty damning photos that captured the anger and violence, especially on the part of the whites involved. Got national exposure. After that, he received requests from a lot of tribes all over the country who were deep in conflicts of one kind or another. He traveled a good deal, helping wherever he could. Another huge issue between him and Jewell.

"A little over a year ago, he agreed to document a standoff that had developed between the Shoshone in Montana and a mining company, something to do with coal reserves that ran under tribal land. He flew to Billings and was met at the airport by one of the tribal members who was supposed to drive him to the site. It was getting dark. On the way, a red and white begins to flash behind them. They pull over. Four men in khaki uniforms approach, ask them to step from the vehicle, then proceed to beat the crap out of them. The Shoshone survived. I understand he has a metal plate in his head. Daniel was in a coma for several weeks. Never came out of it. Jewell finally made the decision to pull the plug. The men responsible were never identified."

"That's pretty tough."

"Jewell's still taking it hard. Ren seems to have rebounded better."

Dina put the eggs in the pan on the stove and began to work them with a spatula. "For a guy who hasn't seen his cousin in several years, you know a lot."

"It was in all the papers. And I keep abreast in other ways, through relatives."

A couple of minutes later, Dina transferred the eggs to a plate. She poured herself a cup of coffee and joined Cork at the table. She'd just seated herself when Ren stepped from his bedroom.

"Oh," he said, sounding disappointed. "Your *kolache* and latte. They're still out in the ATV. I'm sorry."

"Forget it. I'm fine." She gave him a bright smile.

"Thanks," Ren said.

"For what?"

"Being there with me. You know. At Charlie's. With the police and all."

"Glad I could help."

Cork said, "Ren, your cougar's back."

The boy's eyes grew big, like dark mushroom buttons. "You saw it?"

"No, I heard it. I had a sense it was circling the resort."

Dina looked up from the forkful of eggs about to disappear into her mouth. "Circling? As in stalking?"

"I don't know cougars," Cork replied. "What I know about most wild creatures, really wild, who've had any exposure to humans is that they'll do their best to stay clear of us."

"Why wouldn't the cougar?" Dina asked.

"Hunger would be my first guess."

Ren shook his head thoughtfully. "I don't think it would have any trouble finding food in the Hurons."

Cork shrugged. "Then maybe its environment's been invaded or threatened."

Dina sipped her coffee. "What animal would threaten a cougar?"

"Us. Humans," Ren said. "Boy, a cougar. That would be something to see."

"Unless it was coming at your throat," Dina pointed out.

"I don't think anyone should wander far from the cabins," Cork said.

Ren nodded vaguely, but Cork saw the boy's eyes stray to the window and wistfully study the distant wooded hills.

The rattle of suspension came from the resort road, and a minute later Jewell pulled her Blazer to a stop behind Dina's Pathfinder. Through the screen door, Cork watched her leap out and bound up the steps to the cabin. She came in, went straight to Ren, took his head in her hands and looked deeply into his face.

"Are you all right?"

"Yeah."

She hugged him and kissed the top of his head. Ren glanced

at Cork, then Dina. His face flushed from embarrassment at his mother's display of concern.

"Where's Charlie?" Jewell asked. She released him from her embrace and held him at arm's length.

"I don't know. She wasn't there."

"Providence House, you think?"

"Maybe."

"Providence House?" Dina said.

Jewell seemed to notice her for the first time, and not with pleasure. "You're Cork's friend."

"Dina Willner."

"Mom," Ren said as he edged between Jewell and Dina, "she, like, went with me and talked to the police and all. She was great."

Jewell's dark Ojibwe eyes held for an icy moment on the other woman. "Thank you."

"This Providence House. What is it?" Dina asked.

Ren leaped in. "A place where Charlie sometimes stays. It's in Marquette."

Dina sipped her coffee. "You neglected to mention that to the police, Ren."

"If Charlie's there, I didn't want them finding her. I mean, Jesus, they think she killed her dad." Ren looked up at his mother. "Could we see if she's there? You know, call or something?"

Jewell put a light, protective hand on her son's shoulder. "I'm sure they won't give out information over the phone, Ren. But maybe if we went in person."

"Could we?"

Jewell glanced at Cork, and he realized that she was seeking his advice.

"If she's there, she's safe," Cork offered. "Once you know that, you can decide the best course of action. And maybe help her decide, too. I'd recommend she talk to the sheriff's people, but that's up to her."

Ren seemed momentarily troubled. "But if she doesn't want to talk to them, that's okay, right?"

"She could be what's called a material witness," Cork told him. "That makes it tough. If you know where she is and you don't tell the police, they could charge you with a crime. Me, I'd find out if she's there. Wouldn't you like to know she's safe? Then you can decide what to do."

"Mom," Ren said. "We've got to go."

"All right. Wait for me in the Blazer."

Ren darted out without saying good-bye. Jewell delayed her own departure.

"You've been walking on that leg?"

"Yeah. Too much probably."

"If you want a cane, I'll get you one."

"Thanks."

She went to the guest room and came back with a wooden cane, the handle carved in the shape of a wolf's head. "Daniel made this."

Cork gratefully took the cane. "I know I promised I'd be gone. We'll leave soon."

Jewell studied him, then spent a moment looking Dina over. A smell came off his cousin that Cork suddenly realized was the strong clean scent of Phisohex, the soap she probably used to clean herself after she'd spent time with an animal. The knees of her jeans carried soiled ovals where she'd knelt in the dirt, doing her work. She gave her head a single faint shake.

"I'd rather you stayed." On a softer note she added, "If you're willing."

15

*R*en sat on the far side of the Blazer's front seat, staring straight ahead. Jewell drove for a while in silence, not sure what to say to him, wondering, a little desperately and sadly, if she really knew her son.

He'd always been quiet. Like his father. Daniel was a contemplative man. When he talked with Jewell, it was usually about common things—what needed fixing around the resort, the weather, Ren. When he spoke out in public, which was seldom, his words were chosen carefully and his views well considered. Until he became identified as a troublemaker, an Indian troublemaker, he'd been respected in Bodine.

That they were Ojibwe, the only Indians in the town, had never been an issue. Jewell's family had never acted Indian, and those residents of Bodine who knew of their mixed heritage didn't seem to care. Daniel's involvement with the Indian causes, and especially his brutal death, had changed that, branded the DuBois in an unhappy way. Being Ojibwe hadn't always been a burden for Ren, but it seemed so now. Occasionally, when she was particularly concerned, Jewell considered moving closer to the reservation near L'Anse, where many of Daniel's relatives lived. If they were going to be thought of as Indian, they might was well be among those who'd understand. She'd said nothing about this to Ren, and she realized now that there was much in her own mind she hadn't said to her son. She'd thought the silence that sometimes came between them was Ren's choice, a sinking into himself as he dealt with his father's death. But she considered now that perhaps the silence was really her choice.

"You okay?" she asked.

His head jerked toward her, as if her speaking surprised him. "Yeah. I guess. I'm, like, scared for Charlie. You know?"

"I understand. But I can't think of anyone who can take care of herself as well as Charlie. Except maybe you."

He nodded, twice, seriously.

"Mom, he was . . ." His voice stretched out as he sought the words to finish his thought. Apparently he didn't find them.

"*He*? You mean Max?"

"Yeah. He was, you know, all messed up."

She wondered if he was referring to the man's mental state or his physical condition at death.

Ren looked at her, imploring. "But Charlie didn't do it. She couldn't have, Mom. Not like that."

Jewell wanted to tell him that he was right, that Charlie would never do anything so brutal. She wished she could say that despite his faults, Max loved his daughter so much that even drunk he'd never do something threatening enough to drive Charlie to such an extreme response. But the truth was that when he was drinking, Max Miller generally turned belligerent and the potential for violence was always there, lurking in that cramped, messy trailer like a vicious pit bull.

"We'll find Charlie," she said. "And then we'll find out the truth."

It wasn't exactly comforting, but neither would it give him false hope.

The day had warmed, low fifties, and was holding bright. A strong and steady wind had risen, sweeping out of the northwest over the high ground of the Keweenaw Peninsula, whipping the lake into a frenzy. Whenever Superior came into view, Jewell saw whitecaps leaping across the water.

They entered Marquette and drove south on Presque Isle Avenue past Northern Michigan University's Superior Dome. She wove her way to Ridge Street and turned left, which took her past the Landmark Inn where scenes from *Anatomy of a Murder* had been filmed.

Providence House stood on the corner a block past the inn. It was a sturdy three-story built of red stone. Originally, it had been one of the many fine houses on Ridge, constructed around the turn of the century on a hilltop with a million-dollar view of the harbor. Somewhere along the way, it had taken a more utilitarian turn and been converted into apartments. Most recently, a non-profit organization called Children First had bought the property and turned it into a shelter for runaways and homeless youth. Several programs operated within its walls, providing everything from simple short-term shelter to more extensive, long-term support for teens who were chronically homeless. The wealthy neighbors weren't fond of the house or its mission, and constantly threatened legal action. Jewell knew these things because once she'd learned that Charlie used the place as shelter, she'd done a thorough investigation. As a result, Providence House had become one of the nonprofit organizations to which she donated.

She parked the Blazer on the street in front and said to Ren, "Wait here."

"Unh-uh." Ren shook his head vigorously. "I'm coming, too." He didn't wait for Jewell to respond before popping his door open and sliding out.

The rear of the property ran down a long, grassy slope to a line of trees through which the blue of the harbor flashed in luminous patches. An old carriage house stood half hidden behind the big main building. Marigolds still bloomed along the sidewalk that led to the front steps. A fresh coat of white paint brightened the window frames. Jewell knew that because the neighbors weren't happy to have a program like Providence House so near, those responsible for the shelter worked hard to keep the place looking good.

Jewell opened the front door and stepped in, Ren right behind her. Inside, the place was quiet and felt empty. To the left was a living room furnished with a brown area rug, a couple of end tables, a sofa, and several chairs, none of which matched and all of which faced the television. Through French doors to the right, she could see a long, scratched dining table around which sat ten chairs. Directly ahead was an uncarpeted stairway. Beside the stairs ran a hallway that led toward darkness at the back of the building where the murmur of voices could be heard.

"Hello," Jewell called.

"Wait right there." It was a command, not a request.

Jewell had driven past Providence House on several occasions, assessing it from the street, but she'd never been inside before. Charlie, when she stayed, always got there on her own and, when she was ready, found her own way back to Bodine. She'd never asked for Jewell's help.

Ren said quietly, "It's not so bad."

"What did you expect?"

"I don't know. Like, mattresses on the floor or something."

Jewell found this interesting. Charlie had never talked to her about Providence House, which she assumed was because she was as an adult. She'd supposed, however, that as her best friend Ren had probably been taken into her confidence. Apparently Charlie hadn't spoken to him about it, either.

Sunlight flowed through a window beside the door and fell across the floor. The latticework of the leaded-glass panes created a pattern of shadow on the scuffed boards that suggested a spider's web. A woman emerged from the dark hallway and stopped just short of the web. Midfifties, Jewell speculated. Gray hair cut sensibly short. She wasn't tall—a few inches over five feet—but she had a solid quality to her. She wore black jeans, a red turtleneck, white canvas slip-ons. She looked at her visitors suspiciously.

"Yes?"

"Hi. I'm Jewell DuBois." She stepped forward and offered her hand, which was accepted without enthusiasm. "This is my son, Ren."

The woman blinked at them both and waited.

"We're looking for a young woman who may be staying here."

"I can't give out information about our clients."

"And you would be?"

"Mary Hilfiker. I'm the director here."

"She's disappeared and we'd like to be certain she's all right, Mary," Jewell went on. "She's stayed here before. Her name is Charlene Miller. Charlie."

The woman's face didn't change. "As I told you, I can't give you information."

"Not even just to confirm she's okay?"

"Not even that."

"Look, I can understand the need for privacy, but her father's been murdered and we're going out of our minds with worry."

"Oh, my." Mary Hilfiker looked very hard at her face and at Ren's, as if trying to find a crack in their sincerity. Jewell saw something change in her aspect. She relaxed just a little and kindness softened her eyes.

"If I told you she was okay, it would be a tacit admission that she's here, and that's privileged information. Do you see?"

Ren said, "It's awful quiet. Is anybody here?"

The thread of a smile appeared as she glanced down at him. "Although we operate what is essentially a residential program, our clients are required to leave every morning. They're gone to jobs or school all day. They return for dinner and a bed."

"All of them leave?" Jewell asked.

"Yes."

"But they can't all have jobs or be going to school."

"No, not all."

"And the others?"

"They go where kids without homes go to hang out."

"Back on the streets."

"Generally, yes."

"Do you know where Charlie hangs out?" Ren inquired hopefully.

"No."

"If she were to come back this evening, what time would she be here?"

The woman seemed to weigh her response, then said, "I'm not going to tell you that."

"I'm not trying to be difficult," Jewell said with a prickle of irritation. "I'm just worried."

"I understand. And I hope you understand my position. People come here all the time looking for children they've abused. They're sorry for what they've done, genuinely sorry. More contrite people you can't imagine. But the fact is that those who've abused will generally continue to do so. Or they come insisting they're concerned relatives or friends, looking for children who, in actuality, they've recruited as prostitutes

98

or runners or whatever." Her hands finally moved from her side and she held them out, empty and entreating. "You seem respectable, concerned, but put yourself in my shoes. Would you want to take the risk of delivering a child into the hands of someone who'd mistreat her?"

"Can't you tell us anything?" Ren said. "She's my best friend."

"I'm sorry—Ren, is it? Honestly, my hands are tied. Especially now, in light of what you've told me about her father."

"Would you do us a favor?" Jewell said. "If you see Charlie, just let her know that Jewell and Ren came by and that we're concerned. Could you do that?"

"If I see her, I will."

"Thank you."

Jewell took her hand and this time felt a strong grip in return.

Outside, Ren said, "That's it?"

They stood in the sun on the sidewalk, between the blooming marigolds. Late in the season as it was, honeybees still buzzed around the blossoms. They were weightless insects, yet the strong wind didn't seem to affect them as they went about their careful, important business. In her son's face, Jewell saw frustration and fear. Where was Charlie?

"Let's try something else. Follow me," she said.

She led the way to the sloping backyard and walked across the grass to the carriage house.

"What are you doing?" Ren asked.

"Delmar Bell lives here."

"He's one of the guys who's always drinking beer with Charlie's dad. I thought he was a trucker or something."

"He used to be. The company went bankrupt. Now he's the caretaker for Providence House. Keeps the grounds and building in order."

"I don't like him," Ren said.

"The truth is, neither do I, Ren. But maybe he can help us out here."

She didn't know much about Charlie's interactions with Providence House, but she knew that it began as a result of Delmar Bell. He'd done some running himself when he was a kid, trying to escape a father who never spoke to him in anything but anger and never offered his hand in anything but a fist. There were rumors of even worse things going on at the Bell house. Delmar had always been a little scary, but he'd never been in any serious trouble. He'd been the one who suggested to Charlie that when Max was hitting the booze and things seemed shaky at the trailer in Bodine, she might try the shelter. Max Miller had told Jewell this with a full measure of gratitude toward Bell, because when he was sober he appreciated the idea that Charlie had someplace to go when he wasn't.

The door opened quickly to her knock and Bell stuck his head into the sunlight. Jewell remembered that as a kid he'd had fine yellow hair like a dandelion, but he'd long ago gone mostly bald. Now he kept his head shaved, showing a skull rusty with freckles. His eyes were the earthy brown-green of dead moss. He looked surprised to see Jewell, and then he saw Ren and looked confused as well.

"Hey, Del," Jewell said brightly.

He stepped fully into the doorway and the sun struck him hard. He was small, but strong in the way of someone who'd spent long hours in a gym grunting under weights. He wore a white sleeveless T-shirt, faded jeans, and a pair of Adidas stained green from the yard grass.

"What are you doing here?" he asked.

"Looking for Charlie."

"Oh." He nodded in a knowing way. "Max on the sauce again?"

"It's a little more complicated than that, Del. He's dead."

"Naw." Delmar grinned as if it were a joke. Then he saw she wasn't kidding. "Jesus. How?"

"Somebody broke his head open with a baseball bat."

"When?"

"Last night. Charlie's missing. We were wondering if she came here."

His fine, feathery eyebrows dipped together. "I can't tell you that."

"Del, I just want to know if she's okay, that's all."

His dead moss eyes flicked toward the back of Providence House. "Check up there."

"We did. They wouldn't tell us anything. But they don't know me."

"Christ, Jewell."

"Just a yes or no, Del. Was she here last night?"

He sucked in a breath and puffed out his cheeks. He eyed the house again, then offered reluctantly, "As far as I know, she hasn't been here. And I'd know because I see all the kids at breakfast before they leave."

"Would you do me a favor?"

"What?"

"If she comes tonight, give me a call."

"I can't. No. Absolutely not. If they found out, they'd can my ass in a New York minute. I like this job, Jewell. Hell, I need this job."

"What time do they open the door to the kids?"

"Four-thirty. Look, you gotta go." He cast a fearful glance toward the house and shut his door.

Jewell walked away not wanting to cause Delmar trouble if she could help it. Ren followed her to the Blazer and they got in. She slid the key into the ignition and heard in her son's silence unspoken censure.

"I don't know what else to do," she said.

"We could look for her?"

"Where? I'm open to ideas, kiddo."

Ren tapped his chin with his index finger, a gesture Jewell was sure he was unaware of but one he often employed when thinking deeply. It was a Daniel thing, something Ren had unconsciously copied from his father. At last he gave a hopeless shrug. "I don't know."

"We could spend all day in Marquette and still not find her. What if we head home and come back at four-thirty to see if she shows up at Providence House?"

She could tell from the scowl on his face that it wasn't what he'd prefer, and she gave him time to consider an alternative to offer. Finally he said, "Okay."

In the Blazer, Jewell turned them toward Bodine.

Ren dropped his hands to his lap, hunched his shoulders, and climbed back into himself and his silence.

16

*D*ina said, "Someone's coming."

Cork looked up from the table where he'd been making notes on a small tablet. "Can you see who?"

She stood at the door of Thor's Lodge, looking through the screen toward the resort road. "Not yet. Too many trees. It doesn't sound like the Blazer."

"Close the door."

She did, and walked to the window where she drew the curtain slightly aside. Cork came out of his chair and hobbled up beside her. She'd taken a shower and smelled of soap and lavender shampoo. They watched a mud-spattered Jeep pull into the lane between the cabins and stop. The man who eased himself from behind the wheel was wide and powerful looking, a refrigerator wearing Nikes. He had on a blue windbreaker with the Northern Michigan University crest on the front, and a blue and silver ball cap with LIONS above the bill. His jaw line was thick with black stubble like a heavy smear of ash. He eyed Dina's car, then approached Jewell's cabin. Dina carefully let the curtain drop into place and they waited silently while the big man knocked at the door.

"Jewell?" he called. "Ren? Anybody home, eh?"

Dina tossed a glance at Cork, asking if they should answer the door. He shook his head. They heard the porch creaking under the man's weight, then the groan of each wooden step as he descended.

With her finger, Dina carefully parted the curtains again. A thin, bright blade of light cut across her face as she peeked out. Cork watched her eyes track to the left.

"He's standing in the road," she reported in a whisper. "Scratching his jaw, looking around. Now he's walking again."

"To his Jeep?"

"No." She watched. "Toward the shed."

"My car," Cork said.

"I'm on it." She moved quickly to the door and was out before Cork could respond.

The plates on the Jeep were Michigan. The spattered mud around the wheel wells and the patina of back-road dust that coated the finish seemed to indicate a local. That and the fact that the man had called Jewell and Ren by name. Cork didn't think he was on Lou Jacoby's payroll, but he didn't want to be careless. Except for the fact that the tube and bag taped to his leg would have been hard to explain, he would have preferred to be out there with Dina.

He limped to the guest room. In the closet he found boxes that held men's clothing, Daniel's probably. Cork located a pair of folded jeans and checked the size tag: 36 x 32. His waist was a 34, but the length was right. He sat on the quilt-covered bed and pulled his shoes off, then undid his bloody khakis. He slipped the belt free and let his pants slide to the floor. Gingerly maneuvering the left pant leg over the tube and bag, he eased himself into Daniel's jeans. He buttoned, zipped, and belted himself, then put his shoes back on. All this he did with great discomfort, endured with a stream of muffled groans.

He decided to leave the cane Jewell had given him earlier. He would do his best to walk normally. By the time he stepped onto the cabin porch, however, he was already breathing heavily. In the sunlight near the shed, Dina was in conversation with the visitor. They both looked his way, squinting into the sun as he came. The wind was up, strong, and it pushed at his back, making him work even harder to walk normally. He took his time, a man on vacation, perhaps, with a tight but cordial smile glued to his lips.

"Morning," he said brightly.

"Howdy," the big man said.

"What can we do for you?" Cork asked.

Cork saw immediately that the big man noticed details. Most people focused on faces and missed other things, but the man's eyes had already traveled the length of Cork's body, lingering a moment over the unnatural lump on the inside of his pant leg. With luck, the guy would think he was simply well endowed.

"I was just telling Mr. Johnson that we're visiting awhile with Jewell," Dina said. She crossed her arms as if the wind were chilling her.

"Call me Gary, please. And you said *you* were visiting. Didn't say anything about this fella, eh."

Cork kept the smile on his face, though his leg was killing him. "Looking for Jewell?"

"Ren actually. I just came from the Miller place, from talking with Ned Hodder."

"You a cop?" Cork asked, thinking that would explain the eyes that didn't miss much.

"A newspaperman. I publish the *Marquette County Courier*. Old friend of Jewell's. Like you. You know, I still haven't caught any names here."

"We haven't thrown any," Dina replied.

"I'll bet you're Ren's aunt. Donna Walport, right?"

"If I am?"

He offered a smile that seemed genuine. "Ned said you were there with Ren, helpful, like you were his lawyer or something."

"If it's Ren you want to talk to, Gary, he's not here."

He ran a huge knuckle over the stubble of his cheek. The wind pulled at his hair. "He's okay, though, right? I mean, it must've been awful, what he saw. Look, I'm not just asking as a newspaperman. Like I said, old friend of the family."

"I'd rather not say anything without Ren or Jewell here. You understand."

He held up his hands in surrender. They looked like they could pulverize bricks. "This is all off the record, eh. You have my promise."

"I hope you'll forgive me, Gary," Dina said evenly, "but I don't know you well enough to know the quality of that statement. And I hope you understand that as friends of the DuBois family ourselves we're reluctant to say anything that might cause them any trouble."

Johnson shifted his focus toward Cork, who simply smiled and shrugged.

"Are they looking for Charlie?" Johnson asked. "Is that where they've gone?"

"We can't comment on that," Dina said.

For a very brief moment, the man looked perplexed, balanced at the edge of irritation. Then a broad smile cracked his face and his great cheeks drew back and he barked out a laugh.

"I can see you've dealt with reporters before, eh. I swear, everybody should have a relative like you."

"Mind if I ask you a couple of questions, Gary?" Dina smiled, with just a hint of the coquette. *Oh boy, here it comes,* Cork thought. "Do you know Charlie Miller?"

"In a small town, everyone knows everyone."

"The Marquette sheriff's people consider her a suspect."

"That's because they don't know Charlie," Johnson said.

"He liked to drink, I understand. When he did, Charlie had to make herself scarce."

"That's true."

"Anyone ever intervene?"

"Charlie took care of herself, eh."

"Right. And good neighbors don't interfere."

The bitterness in her voice was acid. About her own life, the early years especially, Cork knew little. She'd once let slip that she left home young and never looked back. Cork realized that although she didn't know Charlie, she might understand her quite well.

Johnson's broad face twitched in an uncomfortable way. "Look, any idea when they'll be back?"

"None," Dina said.

He pulled a hand-tooled leather wallet from his back pocket and plucked out a business card. "I'd appreciate it if you'd let Jewell know I was here and that I'd like to talk with Ren as soon as possible. And just a heads-up, eh. I'm only the first. The *Mining Journal,* Marquette's newspaper, will be sending out reporters, too, I'm sure."

"We'll keep that in mind," Dina said.

They stood in the wind while Gary Johnson lumbered back to his Jeep, turned the vehicle around, and headed away, waving to them briefly as he passed.

When the Jeep was out of sight, Dina turned to Cork. Her eyes had darkened to a green the color of an angry sky before hail. "What the hell were you thinking? That I couldn't handle some hick reporter by myself? Just how dumb are you, limping out here like a wounded I-don't-know-what? What if he turned out to be somebody on Jacoby's nickel? Think he wouldn't know exactly what you look like? And now he'd know exactly where you are. That was stupid on so many levels, I don't even know where to begin."

"I think you've made a good start," Cork said. "I've got to sit down. My leg is killing me."

As he turned to the cabin, his leg gave out and he faltered. Dina slipped under his arm, and he leaned into her for support.

"He wasn't one of Jacoby's people," Cork said.

"How can you be sure?"

"He's definitely local. A lot of ways to tell a Yooper. Speech, for one. You pick up on that 'eh' of his?"

"Canadian, I thought."

"Yooper, too."

"He's a reporter, and reporters are usually trouble," Dina grumbled.

Cork limped a few steps with Dina nestled in the crook of his arm, the bone of her shoulders his good support. "Anybody ever tell you you're pretty when you're mad?"

"Just shut up," she said, "and keep walking."

17

*T*hey drove into Bodine from the south, the way they always came from Marquette. Ren stared out the window, his eyes sliding over Wyler's Greenhouse, Pruitt's Antiques, and Superior Lanes, the town's bowling alley. It was all familiar territory. The same place it had always been. The geography hadn't changed, but something had.

As they crossed Calumet Street, he looked automatically to the west. Not far away stood the small trailer where, over the years, he had watched hours of television, played a lot of Risk, built a go-kart from the junk in the backyard, and straddled his bike under the maple trees while he talked with Charlie before hitting the long road home. And where that morning he'd found a man dead.

As they skirted the harbor area, his mother said, "Lots of folks down near the pier. Is something special going on today, Ren?"

He didn't know and told her so.

"You've been quiet the whole way back," she said.

"Just thinking."

"We'll find her, Ren. She's somewhere and she's fine." She smiled encouragement.

Which was something Ren couldn't remember coming from her in a long time. This was his old mom, the one who'd been around before his father died, who'd taught him silly songs— *It was a one-eyed, one-horned flying purple people eater*—who'd dressed like a werewolf one Halloween with a furry face and fake fangs and won first prize at the community center party, and who, while Ren watched, had once pulled a lamb, wet and quivering, from the body of a dead ewe and cradled it gently in her arms as if it were her own child.

Cork and Dina Willner were still in Thor's Lodge. Ren could see that Dina had showered: her hair was still damp. She was on her cell phone when they came in, but she hung up quickly.

"Did you find her?" Cork asked.

"No," Ren said. "We're going back later."

His mother walked into the kitchen. "Anyone hungry?"

"I could eat," Cork said. "By the way, someone came looking for Ren. A guy name of Johnson."

"Gary Johnson?" Jewell craned her neck around the refrigerator door. "What did he want?"

"To talk to Ren about this morning at the Miller place. Said he was an old friend."

"You grow up in a small town, everybody's an old friend."

"He wanted you to call. He also said he thought other reporters might be dropping by."

"You think that will happen?" she asked, looking worried.

"In my experience, reporters would dive into an outhouse hole if they thought there was a story down there."

Dina said, "I'd be glad to help you handle them. One of the many things I'm paid to do."

Ren saw his mother's eyes hold on her for a moment, as if she were trying to decide how she felt about the other woman's presence. Then she smiled cordially. "Thank you. I appreciate your help."

For some reason, it made Ren feel good that his mother was being polite to Dina.

"Tuna sandwiches okay?"

"Great," Cork responded. "What did you find out in Marquette?"

Ren stood near Cork. He ran his index finger over the table-top, tracing the grain of the wood beneath the varnish. "Charlie didn't go to the shelter last night. They open the doors again at four-thirty, so we'll go back and see if she shows up."

"Do the police know she uses the shelter?" Dina asked.

She'd put her phone in the pocket of her jacket and had come close to Ren. He liked her being that near, but it made him nervous, too.

"I don't know," he said.

His mother was at the counter, opening a can of tuna. "I don't know why they would. She's only been using it for a year or so, and I don't believe she's been in any trouble that's involved the police lately."

Dina nodded and laid her hand on Ren's shoulder. Her touch surprised him, but he didn't move away. It was like something warm leaked from her fingers and soaked into him.

She said, "Then maybe you have a good shot at getting to her before the police do."

The wind outside shifted suddenly and the screen door banged. Dina's hand slid away.

"What if she doesn't show up?" Ren asked.

"If she's hiding in Bodine, do you have any idea where that might be, Ren?" Cork asked.

"I've been thinking about it," Ren said. "But nothing makes sense."

"Does she have any other friends? Any relatives she might be with?"

As far as he knew, there wasn't any family. No one close enough that Charlie had ever talked about anyway. And friends? Everybody in Bodine knew Charlie, but she wasn't one of the popular kids. She was like him, considered odd. "I don't think so," he said.

"Her family's scattered," his mother offered. She'd pulled out mayonnaise and was stirring things in a bowl. "Nobody left in these parts. Nobody close enough to be of immediate help."

Or help, period, Ren thought. He realized that if he were in her situation, he'd head over the Hurons and stay with his relatives in L'Anse—people who would welcome him and be glad he was there. He was lucky. He had family. Charlie had no one.

"I'm not hungry right now," he said to his mother. "I'm going outside."

He went to his bedroom, grabbed his sketchpad and a charcoal pencil, and left the cabin. The wind was strong. Clouds raced across the sky, their shadows like dark hands scraping the ground. He found a sheltered spot in the lee of the last cabin and sat down in the dirt. He opened his pad. The most recent drawing had been a sketch of White Eagle in pen and ink, a careful line rendering of the hero in a loincloth, the muscles of his chest and arms and calves flexed mightily, a single eagle feather set in his long black hair.

The idea of White Eagle had come to Ren from his greatgrandfather, a man named Jacob Harker. He was old, moved slowly, spoke with a fragile voice, and had skin that was thin, brittle, and spotted. His eyes were not old, though. There was something sharp and fine in them, and often funny. For a man who seemed to be cheating the grave day by day, he had a remarkably generous view of time. He shared a lot of what he had left of it with Ren. He told the boy about his young days at a government school, how he ran away, mined copper on the Keweenaw. He told stories of his people, the L'Anse Band of Ojibwe, whose blood was in Ren. He was Ma'iingan, he said proudly. Wolf clan.

Once, late at night, when Jacob Harker lay snoring in the guest room, Ren heard his parents talking heatedly upstairs.

"But we're *not* Indian, Dan," his mother said. "It's like a lion that's been bred and raised in a zoo claiming it's from Africa."

"Not the same at all, Jewell. And this is important for me. I never had a real family."

"You do now. Me and Ren. And we're not Indian. I'm not going to wear a jingle dress and I don't want you beating a drum at a powwow, all right?"

It left Ren wondering who they were, who he was.

Not long after, Jacob Harker died in his sleep. He wasn't in Ren's life very long, but in many ways, he changed its course.

Ren studied the drawing of White Eagle, the legendary warrior who Jacob Harker had said was Wolf clan, too. His feet were suspended in midair, as if he'd just dropped from the sky and was about to land somewhere. Although the details of his face were still uncertain, one thing was for sure: in every drawing Ren had done, the warrior was in motion, in the midst of action. He wished he were White Eagle, that instead of sitting, he knew exactly what to do to save Charlie.

Cork found the boy sitting against the wall of Cabin 6, the sketch pad open on his lap.

"Sorry to break in on you, Ren, but your mother insisted I bring you a sandwich."

Ren didn't seem to mind. "Thanks."

"Okay if I sit down?"

"Go ahead."

Cork handed him the paper plate that contained a cut tuna sandwich, a handful of potato chips, some grapes, and an Oreo cookie. He'd had a tough time keeping it all together in the wind. Supporting himself with the wooden cane, he eased down beside the boy.

Cork stared into the woods where that morning the cougar had screamed at him. Through the shifting branches of some birch trees he could see the flaming crests of the Hurons in the west.

"You know, it occurs to me you're very lucky," he said.

Ren, who'd just bit into his sandwich, paused with crumbs on his lips and gave Cork a quizzical look.

"You always have a place to go, that place in your head where your art comes from. Seems to me it must be a place where things come together for you. *Miziweyaa*. Know what that means?"

Ren shook his head.

"It's an Ojibwe word. It's when everything comes together, all of a piece." Cork kept his eyes on the mountains, careful not to look at Ren's drawing, which would have been a trespass. "You're Ma'iingan. There's a lot of power in your blood. Did you know that?"

Ren looked down at his plate. "Mostly it makes me weird here."

"You get a lot of flak?"

"It didn't used to be a big deal, not until my dad died. Then everybody was like, 'Hey, Tonto.'"

"What do you do when they give you a hard time?"

"I say *Screw you* in my head and try to ignore 'em."

"Sounds reasonable."

The wind shifted for a moment and the papers on the sketch pad riffled wildly. Ren held them down.

"Mom's not big on being Indian," he said.

"I know."

"Ever since Dad died she's seemed kind of mad all the time."

"At you?"

"Not me, but everything else. Mostly Dad, because of what he was doing and that it got him killed."

"How do you feel about it?"

He looked up at Cork. He seemed taken by surprise, as if no one had ever asked him that. "He was doing what he thought was right. I guess I understand."

Cork put his arm around the boy. "It may take your mom a little longer to get there, Ren."

"If those men who shot you had killed you, would your wife understand or your kids?"

"I hope they would."

"But you're a cop. That's pretty dangerous."

"I never thought about it in terms of the danger. I always thought more about trying to do what's right."

Ren nodded thoughtfully.

A dab of tuna fell onto Ren's sketch pad and the boy wiped it off. Without thinking, Cork glanced down and saw a greasy smear across a sketch of a cougar. The drawing was quite good and seemed accurate, except for one thing: the face was feminine and lovely and belonged to Dina Willner.

"I've been thinking about Charlie," Ren said. "She didn't come here. She didn't go to the shelter."

"And?"

Ren's chest rose with a deep breath. "Whoever killed her dad, maybe . . ." He looked at Cork, his dark eyes fearful. "Maybe they took her."

Cork said, "All right. Let's think about that. Why would they take her?"

"I don't know. She saw something?"

"What would she see?"

"They killed her dad."

"So she's a witness?"

"Yeah."

"And they wanted to keep her silent?"

"Right."

"Why wouldn't they have killed her right there, like her dad?"

"I don't know."

"I don't, either. But that's what would have made the most sense. What also makes sense is that she understood the danger and she ran. I think you're right, though. I think she knows exactly what happened in that trailer, and she's hiding."

Ren looked as if he wanted to believe this, but something stood in his way. "Why didn't she come here?"

"She has a good reason. When we find her, we'll ask. Okay?"

Ren let it roll around in his head a moment, then he gave a sober nod. "Okay."

"I'm heading back in."

Ren said, "Me, too."

Cork worked his way to his feet while Ren gathered up his things. They started back together.

The phone was ringing as they came through the cabin doorway. Jewell answered. "Hello?" She nodded. "Yes, Sue." Cork, as he hobbled to a chair, saw her face go ashen. "Thanks, Sue." She hung up.

She stared at the floor a moment, then raised her eyes, but avoided looking at anyone directly.

"Sue Taylor," she said. "She and her husband own a hotel that overlooks the harbor. Ren and I saw a commotion down that way as we came into town."

Ren had stopped in the middle of the room, his sketch pad wedged under his arm, his paper plate in his hand. Dina sat in a rocker near the fireplace. She stopped rocking.

"Sue thought we ought to know." Jewell ran a hand, thoughtless and swift, through her hair.

Ren stood rigid as a stick of chalk. "Know what, Mom?"

She said the last of it in a breathless rush and Cork heard the heartbreak in every word. "The police pulled a body from the water. Sue didn't know much except that—I'm sorry, Ren—it was a teenage girl."

18

You live in a place your whole life. You know it. It's as familiar as the mole on your left wrist or the flatness of your nose or the way your tongue rests in your mouth. You stop noticing.

Then something happens, and it all changes. You step through some unexpected looking glass of tragedy—the murder of your husband, say—and although everything around you appears the same, nothing really is, not at all, not ever. You wait for a day that feels normal, when the sun is a reason to smile, when the sight of a couple holding hands doesn't make you want to cry, when you walk without dragging a coffin behind you.

You pray for even a moment of letting go. But it never comes.

She shook her head, clearing those thoughts, preparing for death again and wishing there was a way to prepare Ren, who'd insisted on going with her into Bodine. He sat pressed against the passenger door, cringing like a dog that had been kicked and was waiting to be kicked again.

God, you bastard, if that girl is dead . . .

She let it go. What good was railing at the deaf?

The Taylors stood on the steps in front of the Farber House. They both wore jackets. Sue had her arms crossed. Ken, tall and angular, looked a little like a dead tree leaning in the wind. They stared across the street at the pier where the remnants of a crowd still lingered. Jewell parked in an open space in front of a yellow fire hydrant. She and Ren got out.

"Where is she?" Jewell called above the rush of the wind off the lake.

"They took the body away a few minutes ago," Sue replied.

Ren walked to the Taylors. His hands were buried in his pockets and his eyes were deep beneath a furrowed brow. "Was it Charlie?"

"We don't know, son," Ken answered. "It was hard to see. They kept people back."

"How do you know it was a girl?" Ren demanded.

"People who got a closer look told us," Sue replied gently. She clasped her hands; her small fingers flushed red. "Ren, we heard about what happened after you left this morning. We're so sorry you had to see something like that." Her eyes were wet as she looked to Jewell. "We heard Charlie was missing, then they pulled this poor girl from the lake, and we thought . . . well, we thought you'd want to know."

"Thank you, Sue," Jewell said. She moved next to Ren and put her arm around his shoulders.

She looked toward the long pier. It had been a commercial enterprise for decades, a place for big ships. Now it was a tourist walk lined with planters, a place for a stroll on a beautiful day, a spot for snapshots to remember. There was a breakwater a quarter mile out, but the wind was strong enough to push the normally calm water of the harbor into high waves that crashed against the pier pilings and the rocks along the shoreline in eruptions of white spray. The clouds had thickened. Where their shadows fell on the lake the water had a dark, brooding look. Normally on a Sunday afternoon, the bay would be full of sailboats and cruisers, but the strong wind and the whitecaps had driven them in and the lake was deserted. There were two Marquette County Sheriff's cars parked at the pier entrance. Several deputies stood near them, talking.

"I don't see Ned Hodder," Jewell said.

"I saw him go back to his office." Ken Taylor leaned into the wind and seemed ready to curse the lake. "What a tragic day. I can't remember one like this since . . ." He thought a second. "Well, since that whole Tom Messinger thing."

"In a town like this . . ." Sue said, making it sound unthinkable and immeasurably sad.

Jewell and Ren hiked up the street to the constable's office. She noted how rigidly Ren moved, like an old man stiff with arthritis. Ned Hodder sat inside, his long left arm poised above his desktop, his right hand gripping the phone. He was making notes on a pad, and when he saw them enter he used the pencil to wave them toward chairs.

"Uh-huh," he said. "That's right. Charlene. *C-H-A-R-L-E-N-E*. Last name Miller. Want me to spell that one? All right. Thanks, Sam." He put the phone in its cradle.

Jewell tried to keep her voice even. "Was it Charlie?"

He swiveled in his chair to face them. Jewell had always thought that he had a boyish look to him, a big kid who'd never quite grown up. Now he looked every bit as grim as any grownup she'd ever seen.

"What did you hear?" he asked.

"That it was a teenage girl," Jewell replied. "That's all."

His eyes shifted to Ren, and a look of deep sympathy softened every feature. Jewell wanted to save her son from what was about to happen, from this great, heartbreaking fall.

"You can relax, Ren. It wasn't Charlie."

Jewell heard a deep, quivering breath from Ren. Or had it come from her?

"It was a young girl, yes. Early teens. It may have been a suicide."

"Do you know who?" Jewell asked.

"Unidentified at the moment. The sheriff's people will be working on that."

"Not from Bodine?"

"I'd know her if she was. I'd know that tattoo for sure."

"Tattoo?"

"A long snake down her arm. Huge for such a small girl. Kids." He shook his head. "It wasn't Charlie, though. It definitely was not Charlie." A can of Dr Pepper sat on his desk. He took a drink, finished it off, and dropped the can in the wastebasket next to his chair. "Ren, I wonder if I could talk to your mom alone for a few minutes."

Ren shrugged. "Okay." He glanced at Jewell. "I'll wait outside. Like on the sidewalk or something."

He ambled out.

Ned sat back and let out a deep sigh. "Two bodies in the same day. That's a little more than I'm used to."

Jewell wondered coolly if he was looking for sympathy. She'd known him forever. In high school, they'd dated for a while. She'd gone to college, met Daniel. Ned had gone into the Marines, where he'd been an MP. Afterward, he used his educational benefit to attend MSU in Lansing. He'd married a girl from Okemos who died a few years later of leukemia. No children. He'd returned to Bodine, where, for the last seven years, he'd been the town constable. People liked him. These days, Jewell avoided him.

She reached into her purse and pulled out a pack of Newports and a lighter. "Mind?"

"I thought you quit."

"Yeah, well, sometimes a cigarette is the only thing that relaxes me."

He nodded as if he understood. "How's Ren holding up?"

She lit up and dropped the cigarettes and lighter back in her purse. "He's scared for Charlie."

"We all are. She's a good kid."

"Who you think killed her father."

"They've already run the prints on that baseball bat. There were only two sets. Hers and Max's. And Max didn't kill himself."

"So it had to be Charlie?"

"I didn't say that. It just doesn't look good for her." He threw his hands up uselessly. "I've never worked a homicide investigation. The most I've ever been involved with here are a couple of suicides, and that's different. I mean, things like this just don't happen in Bodine."

"No? What about Tom Messinger?"

"That was twenty years ago. But I get your point. The unthinkable can happen anywhere, anytime, to anyone. Right?"

She saw it in his eyes, the unspoken *Daniel*.

After her husband's murder, when the allegations arose that law enforcement officers were responsible, something happened in Jewell's thinking. Police—all of them, every one— became deadly snakes to be watched for and avoided. The sight of the uniform itself was enough to send her anger spiking. She understood how irrational this was, but that's how she felt.

She looked for a place to tap the ash from her cigarette. Ned dug into his wastebasket and handed her the empty Dr Pepper can.

"You know Charlie didn't kill her father," she said.

"I don't. And neither do you."

"If she did, she had a good reason."

"That may be. The important thing is to find her. If you or Ren hear from her, you need to let me know. I'll deal with the sheriff's people." He leaned toward her again and his voice had an odd edge to it, sharp but not vicious. "Jewell, this is a case of murder. If you know where Charlie is, or if you find out and don't say anything, it could get you into a lot of trouble. I'm serious."

"I'm sure you are." She glanced outside and saw that Ren had been joined by one of his friends. "Why suicide?"

"What?"

"Why do the sheriff's people think the girl in the lake was a suicide?"

"For one thing, she wasn't dressed for the weather. No shoes, no coat. So probably not accidental. Also she had no identification. I guess that's something suicides do, remove anything that might identify them. And she's a teenager with piercings everywhere and tattoos."

"What's that got to do with anything?"

"Seems to matter to Olafsson."

"Any marks on her body?"

"The waves battered her pretty badly against the rocks. The ME'll be able to determine if any of the damage came before her death. Why does this interest you?"

"Just curious how a cop's mind works. Me, I deal with horses and cows. Simpler creatures."

"And smarter?" He tried a smile, but gave up quickly. "It feels good to be talking to you again, Jewell." He waited in a silence that got long and awkward.

"Are we done?" she finally said.

She saw the flicker of disappointment in his face, but she didn't care.

"Yeah, pretty much."

She dropped the butt of her cigarette into the Dr Pepper can, handed it to him, and left.

Outside on the sidewalk, Ren had run into Stash, who was carrying his skateboard under his arm.

"Dude, I heard about Charlie's old man. That must've been, like, seriously fucked. You hear from Charlie yet?"

"No," Ren said. "Nothing."

"This sucks royally. I heard they pulled somebody out of the lake. I heard it was a chick."

"It wasn't Charlie."

"Man, that's a relief. Hey, what about that body we saw in the river?"

"You saw."

"Maybe it was the same body."

Ren hadn't really believed in what Stash claimed to have seen. Now he wasn't so sure. "Maybe," he said.

"Shouldn't you tell the flatfoot?"

"The what?"

"The constable."

"I don't know. I'll think about it. Right now all I can think about is Charlie."

"Something else, dude. Some douche bag stole my weed from the picnic shelter."

Ren remembered the previous night when he'd kicked the cigar box under the leaves before he and Charlie fled.

"Probably the wind," he told Stash. "Maybe it fell. Did you check under the leaves?"

"I checked everywhere. Zippo." He squeezed his eyes together as if he'd felt a sudden pain. "My name was on that box."

Ren considered pointing out how many times he'd told Stash it was a stupid thing to do, but it didn't seem worthwhile. He also felt responsible for the loss and wanted to get off the subject as soon as possible.

"You've got more."

"I was just thinking of going over to Dunning Park, make sure I've still got weed there. Want to come?"

"No, thanks. My mom's inside." He tilted his head toward the constable's office.

"'I killed him for the money and the woman. I didn't get the money and I didn't get the woman.' Fred McMurray, *Double Indemnity*. Catch you later, dude." Stash dropped his skateboard, gave it a push with the Doc Marten on his right foot, and rolled off toward Dunning Park.

In a minute, Ren's mother came from Ned Hodder's office. Even though she knew that it wasn't Charlie's body the police had pulled from the lake, she still looked plenty worried.

"Let's go," she said.

"Where?"

She looked at her watch. "Let's see if we catch Charlie at Providence House."

19

Jewell called to let Cork know the dead girl wasn't Charlie and to say she and Ren were headed back to Marquette.

Cork hobbled from the phone to the sofa. He caught sight of Ren's sketchbook sitting on an end table where the boy in his haste had dropped it.

"He likes you, you know," he said, easing himself onto a cushion.

Dina turned from the window where she'd been watching what blew past the cabin on the wind. "Who?"

"Ren."

"He's a nice kid."

"No, I mean he's quite fetched with you."

"'Fetched?'"

"In my neck of the woods we still use that word. Means—"

"I know what it means. You're crazy, though. To him, I'm an old lady."

"I don't think so."

"Great. All the good men are gay, married, or under fifteen." She swept a few strands of hair from her face. The day had been so busy that she hadn't had a chance to do much with it, but she still looked good. "I need some coffee. Want some?"

"I'd take a cup if you made it."

He sat back and listened to the wind sweep around the cabin like a great flood around a small island. He felt marooned, out of touch with the world beyond the old resort. He also felt help-less. Although he'd proved to himself that he could get around despite his wounded leg, the reality was that he had nowhere to go, no way to move toward resolving everything that threat-ened.

Which got him to thinking about the issues that were unresolved. Not all of them looked hopeless. His people, the Tamarack County Sheriff's Department, were closing in on Lou Jacoby's daughter-in-law, Gabriella, and her brother, Tony Salguero, for the murder of Gabriella's husband. The case wasn't nailed down yet, but everything was in place. The Winnetka police had good leads connecting Salguero with the murder of the other Jacoby son, Ben. Not enough for an arrest, but they were pushing hard in that direction. These were positive things.

There was another issue, however, that was nothing but a deep well of rage. Cork had worked at keeping himself from thinking about it, because whenever he did, he started to go ballistic.

The man who'd raped Jo.

Man? Hardly that. An angry rich kid who'd assumed Jo was something she wasn't—Ben Jacoby's lover. He'd used Jo to lash out at the man he hated—his father. Cork had that much fig-ured, but knowing the motivation didn't blunt the horror of the act or its effect. He couldn't think about the young man, whom he'd never seen, without imagining his fists breaking the bones of the rich kid's face, his knuckles covered in the rich kid's blood.

"You okay?"

At the feel of Dina's hand on his arm, he looked up.

"I've been talking but you haven't heard a word, Cork. For a minute there you looked like you were staring down a cobra. Are you all right?"

He heard the wind again, felt the soft cushion of the sofa, the lingering touch of her hand, smelled the aroma of the freshly ground coffee beans, and he came back to the moment.

"I don't like this waiting," he said.

She smiled. "You'd make a terrible PI."

"What time is it?"

"Four-ten. Fifteen minutes later than the last time you asked." She headed back to the kitchen. "You ask me, you need to talk to your family."

"I'd love to hear their voices, but until this thing with Lou Jacoby is settled I won't risk it. 'An eye for an eye,' he said to me. I don't want him even thinking about my family. I'm afraid if he knows I'm in communication with them in any way, he might use them as leverage."

"Threaten them?"

"Exactly." He laid his head against the sofa back. "Maybe I should just head down there and kill him, eliminate the risk."

He heard the clatter of cups on the countertop, the gurgle of coffee being poured. Dina came to his side a moment later and handed him a full cup.

"Go down there?" she said. "With that leg? I doubt it. And let me clue you in to something else. You're a lot of things that probably aren't good, but a cold-blooded killer you're not."

She went back to the kitchen for her own cup, then returned to the window.

"What things?" Cork said.

"Huh?"

"You said I was a lot of things that aren't good. What things?"

She looked back at him and rolled her eyes.

Later, she stood at the open door. Beyond her the sky was going dark. The wind blew straight out of the north now, and a cool breeze came through the door screen. Dina was working on her third cup of coffee. She'd be up all night, Cork figured.

"Mind if I ask you a question?" he said.

She kept her back to him and shrugged.

"What was your childhood like?"

She glanced over her shoulder. "Why do you want to know?"

"Something you said this afternoon made me wonder."

She turned back to the darkening sky. "I didn't have a childhood. My mother was an alcoholic. I took care of her. Until I wised up and left."

"When was that?"

"When I got tired of everything, including her boyfriends pawing at me. About Charlie's age."

"Where'd you go?"

"Relatives first. It didn't take me long to realize where my mother's problems came from. Then I was on the streets for a while."

"Harsh," he said.

"Reality check."

"And you got yourself together?"

"Not without help. A social worker. Marcia Kaufmann. A smart woman with a dry sense of humor and a big heart. She helped me get a place to live, finish school. She worked with me until I was off to college. Sometimes you're born into the wrong people's lives. If you're lucky, you stumble into the right ones."

Cork heard the sound of Jewell's Blazer.

"Here they come," Dina said.

A couple of minutes later, Ren walked in. His mother was a few steps behind.

"Well?" Cork asked.

The boy shook his head and looked down at the floor. "She wasn't there."

20

*D*eath visited Ren that night. It came in the form of a girl with a body blue as lake ice. Her hair drifted behind her, lifting just a little now and then as if caught in a dreamy current. She opened her mouth and spoke to him, words that later he wouldn't recall. She pointed at him in an accusing way, and the tattooed snake on her arm came alive. It crawled down her skin and hung from her wrist for a second before dropping to the ground, where it slithered toward him. He tried to back away, but his feet were sunk deep in black mud, cemented there. Broad, chestnut-colored bands marked the snake, and Ren thought, *Copperhead,* and panicked because he knew it was deadly. Thinking, too, in the middle of his fear, *Odd,* because there were no copperheads in the U.P. of Michigan. Thinking finally as the snake wriggled across the surface of the mud and coiled to strike, *Dreaming* . . .

And he woke.

It was raining, a steady downpour. The wind was still up and drove the rain against the windows so that the panes, as Ren stared at them from his bed, seemed to weep.

Although he'd dreamed of the dead girl in the lake, it was Charlie on his mind when he woke.

"Dead," he whispered, out loud and hopelessly. "Oh Jesus, she's dead."

He stared at the ceiling and he wondered what that meant, to be dead.

His father had been murdered fifteen hundred miles away. He was just gone. He became the emptiness of the cabin, and that's how Ren had thought of death. Emptiness. A grabbing at air. A conversation stopped in mid-sentence. A body from which the soul had simply departed. He'd learned in church that the soul could go to different places: heaven, hell, purgatory, limbo. His grandfather had told him the Ojibwe believed the dead traveled west on the Path of Souls to a beautiful place.

But that was after. What about the slide into death? What about the dying?

Until he saw Charlie's father on the floor in a puddle of blood and brain, he'd never before thought about what his own father might have felt. His father, he realized, must have died in much the same way. Did he know what was happening? Did it hurt? Was he scared?

The girl in the lake, what did she feel? She was just a kid, like Ren. He'd been in the lake before, but only for moments at a time because the water was so cold, so painfully cold. Suicide, the constable had said. That seemed terribly lonely, to feel all that pain, to sink alone into the darkness with the light still above you, to know that you were about to die.

And Charlie? What about her?

He'd begun to cry, softly, because he didn't want his mother to hear. He didn't mind crying when he was alone. It felt good. Sometimes it was the only way to let out everything that he kept squeezed inside.

A thump at his window startled him. Something had hit the screen. A pinecone blown by the wind? He waited. The thump came again, sharp and deliberate.

The night and the rain made everything outside impenetrable. He threw the covers back and crept across the room. He reached the window just as a fist came out of the dark and rapped on the screen. He lifted the pane.

"Charlie?" he called hopefully.

He received no response.

Then Charlie's voice: "Let me in, asshole. I'm freezing."

He hurried through the dark cabin to the front door and opened it. He stood on the porch waiting for Charlie to appear.

Finally she slipped around the corner of the cabin and dashed toward Ren.

As she reached the first porch step, a flashlight beam burst over her. The source came from somewhere behind Ren, from the direction of the other cabins. Charlie tried to stop, to halt her momentum in mid-stride and backpedal. Her feet slid in the mud. She managed a difficult spin and began to sprint toward the trees that marked the boundary of the woods that edged the resort. The flashlight followed at a dead run.

Ren leaped from the porch and brought up the rear of the chase.

Shit. Someone had been waiting, someone who knew that Charlie would eventually come to the old resort as she'd often done in the past. Ren's heart galloped. His feet were bare, and although the cold of the ground penetrated his soles like icy needles, he hardly noticed. The rain instantly soaked his pajamas and the material clung to his skin. He held to one hope: that Charlie, the fastest runner in Bodine Middle School, would not be caught.

His hope collapsed when he saw the flashlight hit the ground as Charlie was tackled twenty yards ahead of him. He lowered his head to run faster, not knowing at all what he'd do to help his friend, knowing only that he had to try.

Then he heard a familiar voice come from the black shape that sat on top of Charlie, pinning her to the ground.

"Charlene Miller," Dina Willner said. "Or am I crazy?"

When Dina brought her in, the girl smelled like roadkill. Jewell ran a hot bath and gave her a sweatshirt and sweatpants to wear afterward. Charlie sat on the sofa near the leaping flames of the fire Ren had laid in the fireplace. The flare and shadow that the fire created on her face gave her a restless, jumpy appearance. She drank hot chocolate and refused to look at Dina.

Jewell fixed her a ham sandwich and gave her some Fritos. Charlie tore into the food.

Ren, who'd put on jeans and a flannel shirt, sat beside her on the sofa. Cork could see the boy's eyes were shining with delight. Every so often, Ren floated his hand toward Charlie as if to touch her, to be certain she was real, but he always drew up shy.

While the girl was bathing, Ren had asked Dina how she knew Charlie would come.

Dina had put on dry clothes—a lime green sweater and dark jeans—and she stood near the fire as it spread across the logs. "People are pretty predictable, Ren. I figured she was hiding and hungry and you were her best hope for food and safety. If she was afraid of being seen, she'd come at night. I just posted myself to watch your cabin and I waited."

Cork thought about all the coffee she'd drunk that afternoon. He realized she'd been planning her stakeout even then.

"How did you know she was alive?" Ren asked.

"I wanted her to be, Ren. That's all."

She'd smiled at him across the room and Cork saw a flush of the boy's face that had nothing to do with the heat of the fire.

When she'd eaten her fill, Charlie stared at the flames leaping toward the chimney. It was Jewell who eventually began the asking. She spoke gently, as if coaxing a skittish animal.

"Where have you been, Charlie?"

The girl didn't answer.

"Can you tell us what happened?"

She gripped her cup of hot chocolate and a visible quiver ran the length of her body. "They killed him," she said.

"Yes, Charlie, we know."

Outside, the wind and rain pummeled the cabin, but in that room except for the pop and crackle of the fire, it was quiet.

Charlie leaned forward. The sofa creaked. "I saw him. I saw him and I ran away."

The sullen look had vanished, and her face had gone slack, dazed.

"Did you see who did it, Charlie?"

She gave a faint shake of her head. "I got home. He was still awake, still drinking. I didn't want to be there with him, so I told him I was going to spend the night in the truck. I do that sometimes when he's drunk. I went out there and went to sleep. Then somebody came. I heard car doors closing, and when I peeked out, some guys were heading toward the front door. I figured they were, you know, drinking buddies. A little bit later I heard them all yelling. I got out and went to one of the windows and listened. I didn't even want to go in there."

"Sure, Charlie. Of course."

"I heard stuff breaking and some more yelling. I couldn't hear a lot of what they were saying but it sounded like they wanted him to tell where something was and he wouldn't. Then it got real still. A minute later the front door opened. I hid in the bushes and waited until they drove off."

Her gaze shifted from the hot chocolate to the fire. Jewell didn't press her. In a minute, Charlie continued.

"I went in. Everything was a mess. I didn't see him. I went to my bedroom. The light was on. I saw his feet. I thought at first he was drunk, passed out. Then I saw the rest of him."

Her shoulders began to quake and in a moment her whole body was shaking. Jewell crossed to her quickly, took the cup from her hand and set it on the floor. She put her arms around Charlie and let the girl weep into her shoulder.

Jewell whispered, "Why didn't you come here?"

"I was afraid."

"Where were you, Charlie?"

The girl shook her head and wouldn't say.

Cork said quietly, "Did you hear what it was the men wanted?"

"No."

Jewell pulled back from the girl slightly and looked into Charlie's face. "You're safe here, okay? Totally safe. Oh, sweetheart, you look so tired. I'll make up the bed in the guest room for you. Ren, will you get some clean linen?"

Ren nodded obediently. His eyes never left his friend.

When everything was settled—Charlie and Ren in bed—Cork, Jewell, and Dina stepped onto the front porch so they could talk without being overheard. The wind was strong around them, and a cold spray of rain occasionally blew over them.

"Those men wanted something," Cork said. "They wanted it badly enough to kill Charlie's father. Do you have any idea what it might have been, Jewell? Was Max Miller into drugs? Using? Selling? Or heavy into gambling, maybe?"

Jewell wore a hooded gray sweatshirt. Though it was lined with fleece, she hugged herself against the damp cold. "I don't know. He drank, but that's all I was aware of."

Cork leaned against the wall to give his leg a rest. "It could simply have been drunks arguing and things got out of hand. I've seen it before. People die over stupid things, kill for something as simple as the refusal to share a bottle of booze." He waited a beat, then offered what he suspected would be an unpopular opinion. "She needs to talk to the sheriff's people."

"No way am I going to turn that girl over to the police," Jewell snapped.

"Look, Jewell, if you keep her here and they find out, you could be charged with interfering in a felony investigation. That's serious."

"That's a chance I'm willing to take."

"I agree," Dina said. "She's in no shape to talk to anyone right now. And, Cork, you know what they'll do."

Jewell looked from Dina to Cork. "What?"

"It's not a sure thing, but they'll probably take her into custody," Cork said. "Just to hold on to her. She ran once. They'll view her as a flight risk."

"I absolutely won't allow that," Jewell declared.

Cork shrugged. "Even if you let her stay here, there's no guarantee she won't bolt."

"I think right now she'll sleep. She needs it."

"All right," Cork said. "It's your decision. But there's one more thing to consider."

A gust of wind hit him so hard he almost fell over.

"What if it wasn't drunks arguing?" he went on. "If they were after something they thought Charlie's father had, they may wonder if Charlie knows where it is, and they'll be looking for her. If it was important enough to kill a man over, they probably wouldn't balk at killing a girl. Or anyone who stands in their way, for that matter."

Although he couldn't see her face clearly in the dark, Jewell's silence told him much.

"We'll talk about it some more tomorrow," she said at last. "I'm tired."

Dina said, "It might be a good idea if I slept on your couch tonight, Jewell. Just to be on the safe side."

"Fine. I'll get the linen and see you inside."

Jewell opened the door and a wedge of warm light cut into the rainy night. Then it was gone.

"I hate being the voice of reason," Cork said, speaking mostly to himself.

Dina put a hand on his shoulder. "You're a good cop, Cork, but sometimes it gets in the way of being a compassionate human being. Good night."

She turned and went back into the warm cabin.

Cork stood alone in the cold wind, wondering if his was really the voice of reason, or simply the rumble of a grumpy old man.

21

"Ren?"

He woke up, groggy. "Huh?"

"You asleep?"

He tried to focus and through a drowsy murk saw Charlie standing next to his bed, dressed in the blue sweatsuit his mother had given her. He rubbed his eyes. When he looked at her again, even in the dark he could see the worry on her face.

She sat on the bed and shoved him with her hip so that he made room. They both sat with their backs against the headboard.

"I can't sleep," she said. "Whenever I close my eyes I see him."

"Who?" Then he understood. "Oh."

She drew her legs up and hugged them, as if protecting herself.

Ren said, "I saw him, too, Charlie. I went looking for you at your place and I found him. I was really scared that something had happened to you, too. Where'd you go?"

"The old mine."

Of course. Why hadn't he thought of it? Two summers ago, while they were hiking along the Copper River a couple of miles outside of town, they stumbled onto an old mine dug into a steep, rocky ridge overlooking the river. They'd been picking blackberries and had felt an unusually cool pocket of air that seemed to have its source somewhere behind the thicket. Charlie scaled the ridge and dropped behind the vines, then hollered for Ren to do the same. He found her standing at the mouth of an excavation, a hole not much taller than they but wide enough for both of them to fit in together. Sunlight penetrated the tunnel, revealing a collapsed ceiling a dozen feet beyond the entrance, which blocked further access. The beams that had been used to shore up the opening were still in place and seemed solid. That whole summer they'd used the old mine—which Ren suspected had been the work of one of the early gold prospectors—as a hideout. Mornings, they'd head off with a packed lunch, swim in the river where the water pooled below the ridge, then hike to the cave and eat in the cool shade it provided. From there, unseen, they watched fishermen and canoeists and kayakers, and once saw a couple of teenagers swim naked in the same stretch of water they'd just enjoyed.

"You stayed there this whole time?"

"Uh-huh."

"You should have told me or something. I was going crazy. I thought you were . . ." He didn't finish, didn't want say the word *dead*.

"I freaked. I wasn't thinking." She put her chin on her knees and stared at the window, which was streaked with rain. "Not really."

"Huh?"

"I mean, I *was* thinking. And one of the things I thought was that I knew it was going to happen."

"Like, psychic?"

"No, just that someday because of his drinking he'd be dead like that. Just like that."

She grabbed the pillow from behind her back and put it close to her face and spoke at it angrily.

"I wanted to yell at him, Ren. I wanted to kick him and yell at him and tell him, 'I told you so, you total screwup. You and your drunk buddies. Why couldn't you just stop?'" She buried her face in the pillow.

A moment passed, then Ren ventured quietly, "Alcohol's like that. It doesn't let you go."

"Other people stop. Why couldn't he?" She threw the pillow across the room. It hit Ren's desk and something toppled to the floor. "Sorry."

"It was just my Hellboy model."

"Sounded like I broke it."

"A little glue, it'll be okay."

"Ren?" Her voice got soft. "What if I'd been in there?"

"You weren't."

"I could've been."

"But you weren't, and I'm glad."

"Maybe everything would be better if I had."

"Don't say that."

"What am I going to do? I'm, like, an orphan."

Orphan. It was an odd word to Ren, archaic somehow, from a different era. It made him think of that comic-strip character with orange frizzy hair. But Charlie was right. That's exactly what she was.

"You can stay with us," he said.

"Oh yeah, like those social service freakazoids are going to let that happen."

"I mean it. We'll figure a way."

Lightning flashed somewhere in the distance, an instant of blue light that filled the room and made Charlie a bright, solid presence in his bed.

"I thought for a while you were dead," he said.

She turned her head, her face dark, unreadable. "Why?"

"They pulled a dead girl from the lake today. We heard she was a teenager. I thought at first it was going to be you."

"Who was it?"

"They don't know."

"Ren." She drew in a sudden breath. "Maybe it was the same body Stash saw in the river."

"I was thinking that, too."

"Was she from around here?"

"Constable Hodder said he didn't think he'd ever seen her before. He said he would have remembered because she had this weird tattoo on her arm."

"What kind of tattoo?"

"A snake or something."

He felt Charlie stiffen.

"Which arm?" she asked.

"I don't know."

"Left?"

"Maybe. I don't know."

She turned to face him, tucking her legs under her. "Did he say anything else?"

"Like what?"

"How big was she? Small like you?"

"I'm not small."

"You know what I mean."

"Why are you asking all these questions?"

"I might know her. There's this girl at Providence House. She's there all the time. Her name's Sara Wolf. She has a big—I mean really big—snake tattoo on her left arm."

Ren thought back to that afternoon and remembered something. "The constable said it was big for such a small girl. He also said she had lots of piercings."

"Oh shit." Charlie sank back. "How?"

"They think suicide."

"Bullshit. That's bullshit."

"*Shhh*. Keep your voice down."

"No way she'd off herself."

"Don't get mad at me. I'm just telling you what they said."

Another flash of lightning, so far away the sound of the thunder took forever to reach them. In the long quiet, Ren heard Charlie crying. Charlie never cried. He wasn't sure what to do. Awkwardly he reached an arm around her shoulders. She laid her head against his chest, and he felt her shaking.

"The world is fucked, Ren. Totally, screamingly fucked," she sobbed.

After a minute, she pulled away and wiped her nose on the sleeve of her borrowed sweatshirt. She lay down next to Ren and rolled over so that her back was to him. He gently nudged his pillow under her head. In a little while, he could tell from her breathing that she'd gone to sleep.

Ren lay a long time staring up at the ceiling, listening to the sound of the storm outside, thinking Charlie was probably right about the state of the world.

Totally, screamingly fucked.

22

Cork didn't sleep well. The pain in his thigh kept him uncomfortable and he had fevered dreams: that his house in Aurora was full of mud and his children were sinking into it and he couldn't find Jo anywhere; that he was driving a car and couldn't get the brakes to work no matter how hard he pressed the pedal; a brief one in which instead of bullets he was loading wads of toilet paper into the cylinder of his revolver.

He woke up and the first thought he had was about what Dina Willner had said to him the night before: that sometimes he wasn't a very compassionate human being. She might have been talking about recent events, but Cork suspected it went a bit further back.

She'd entered his life as a consultant hired by Lou Jacoby to see to it that Cork didn't screw up the investigation of Eddie Jacoby's murder. Dina had made it clear early on that she found him seriously attractive. Cork, devoted family man though he was, had found himself sorely tempted in return. He'd held back from acting on that temptation, but in the end he'd used Dina's feelings against her. Briefly he'd led her to believe that she'd charmed him into submission and in doing so had laid a trap she'd stepped into. His motive had been understandable—to unravel the tangle of misdirection the Jacobys had looped around the case and to get to the truth of Dina's involvement—but he'd hurt her badly and he knew it.

Although the situation probably justified his actions, he wasn't proud of his behavior. Especially considering all that Dina had done since to help him.

So sometimes he lacked compassion. Big deal. Hell, what did she expect? What could anyone expect of him now? It had been a tough couple of weeks. Three times someone had tried to kill him. He'd been suspended as sheriff, suspected of murder, was on the run from people trying to fit him into a coffin, and because of his wounded leg he was useless to everyone who needed him. To top it off, his family didn't have the slightest idea of his current situation, whether he was alive or dead.

The wind had stopped and he couldn't hear the rain anymore. Birds were just beginning to sing, and he knew dawn wasn't far away. He thought about getting up, but instead lay there thinking about being a good cop.

A good cop. It was something that had been important to him, the line he followed to get through a lot of tough situations. He was a cop largely because his father, whom he'd loved fiercely, had been one.

He was still tired. He closed his eyes.

And his father walked out of the dark across four decades and stood beside him. He wore a tan chamois shirt, dungarees, and Converse high-top tennis shoes. He was tall and clean-shaven. His hair had recently been cut. He held a football in his big hands.

Day off? Cork asked.

Thought we'd toss the pigskin. His father smiled, displaying an incisor outlined in silver.

Cork loved Saturday afternoons in the fall when the leaves were like drops of butter and brown syrup on the grass, and the chores were done, and for an hour before supper his father directed him on passing routes in the backyard—down and out, post, buttonhook—floating the ball into Cork's hands. "Little fingers together," his father would call out. "And bring the ball into your body. Cradle it into your body."

I can't play today, Cork said. *Bum leg.*

His father tossed the ball straight up a couple of feet, giving it a twist so that the laces spun. He caught it with a soft slap of leather against his palms.

I screwed up, Cork said.

You think so?

I should be with Jo and the kids. I should be protecting them.

I thought you were. Isn't that what this is about?

Did I do the right thing?

I can't answer that for you.

There's a girl here. She ought to be talking to the police.

Isn't that you?

Out of my jurisdiction.

Doesn't stop you from helping.

I've missed you, Cork said.

He could smell the leather of the old football, the scent of raked leaves clinging to the chamois shirt, the bay rum his father used every morning as aftershave.

Then it was gone.

An instant later he was aware of a pounding at his door that brought him awake in the faint light of early dawn.

"Cork?" It was Jewell.

"Yeah?"

"We need you. Something's happened."

He hobbled into Jewell's cabin dressed in the jeans he'd borrowed the day before and a clean shirt that Jewell had given him that had also been Daniel's. Everyone else had already gathered around the dining room table. Cork could smell coffee brewing.

Gary Johnson, the newspaperman, had called early and given Jewell some bad news. A friend of Ren's, a kid named Stuart Gullickson, had been hit by a car the night before and was in critical condition at a Marquette hospital. Johnson thought Ren would want to know.

Jewell poured coffee for Cork and topped off what was already in Dina Willner's cup. Ren and Charlie were drinking orange juice.

"I'm taking Ren to Marquette to see Stuart," Jewell said.

"I'm going, too," Charlie said. From her stubborn tone, Cork gathered it wasn't the first time she'd put forward that proposition.

"I've told you, Charlie, it's too great a risk," Jewell replied.

"If someone sees you, we could have the police here in no time."

Charlie gripped her juice with both hands as if she were trying to strangle the glass. "He's my friend, too."

"I understand," Jewell said. "But you'll just need to be patient until Ren and I get back. I doubt they're letting anybody but family see him anyway."

Charlie sat back hard and crossed her arms defiantly. "We're family, Ren and me."

"They won't see it that way, Charlie. You're not going."

Ren said to her, "I'll call you from the hospital."

Charlie stared at the table with stone eyes.

"Cork," Jewell said. She gave a nod toward the front door.

He stepped onto the porch with her. The morning was cool and wet from the night storm. Leaves stripped from the trees littered the ground, and the bare patches of dirt had been turned to black mud. The sky was a promising blue, however, and honey-colored sunlight already dripped over the tops of the Huron Mountains.

"You'll need to watch her," Jewell said. "I'm afraid she might try to get to Marquette on her own."

"I'll put Dina on it. She already ran Charlie down once." He gave her a reassuring smile. "We'll feed her breakfast and do our best to keep her mind off things. She'll be fine until you get back."

Jewell looked tired. It had been at least a couple of nights since she'd had an uninterrupted sleep. With all the grief she carried, Cork figured it might have been even longer. Her eyes were dark circled and her black hair needed a good brushing. Yet, there was a strength in her voice, a determined sense about her actions that Cork admired.

"If what Gary told us yesterday is true, we might get other reporters out here," she said.

"We'll handle them," Cork replied. "You and Ren do what you have to do."

She took a deep breath. "Okay. How's the leg this morning?"

"All this activity actually seems to help."

"I'll take a look at it when I come back."

"Deal."

She turned toward the door and started inside, then hesitated. "Cork, I'm sorry."

"What for?"

"I've been hard on you. But I'm glad you're here."

He smiled and shrugged. "Family," he said.

23

*T*hings did not go well.

From the start, it was clear that Charlie resented being left behind, that in her mind Cork had no authority over her, and that she'd just as soon spit on Dina. She slumped on the sofa with her arms locked across her chest and refused to be coaxed or cajoled into civility.

"How about some breakfast?" Dina offered cheerfully from behind the kitchen counter. "What do you guys want? Eggs? I make a mean omelet."

"I'm fine with cereal and juice," Cork said.

"Come on, let me impress you. How about you, Charlie?" She pointed a long-handled wooden spoon at the girl. "I don't know where you were hiding, but I'm willing to bet it wasn't a bed-and-breakfast. What'll you have? I can make almost anything."

Charlie kept her back to Dina and addressed the front door. "You wouldn't have caught me except I slipped in the mud."

"That was last night. This is this morning, a whole new day. Let's start over. What do you say?"

"I could beat you in a race any day."

Cork watched Dina as she assessed the back of Charlie's head and flipped through the whole registry of possible responses. Her eyes became hard green pellets.

"You're fast, Charlie," she said, "but not as fast as me."

"Right. You're, like, what? A hundred years old?"

"It doesn't matter how old I am. You run, I'll catch you."

"Fine," Charlie snapped. "Race me."

Dina left the kitchen, still holding the wooden spoon. She walked purposefully across the floor until she stood directly in Charlie's dour line of vision. Charlie lifted her eyes, which were full of defiant fire.

"I'm not going to race you, Charlie. We've already been there. The thing that's important for you to understand now is there's no reason to run. You're safe. We're not going to let anything happen to you."

"Safe? Because of you two? Grandma Moses and"—she cast a desultory look at Cork—"the gimp? If I believed that, I'd be *so* screwed."

Dina paused, giving a few moments of weight to the girl's words, evidence that she'd heard. Then she said, "One of the things I'm sometimes paid to do is protect people. I'm very good at it."

"Yeah? Bite me."

Dina tossed the spoon toward Cork, who managed a decent catch. "Stand up," she said to the girl.

Charlie stayed firmly rooted on the sofa.

"Stand up and hit me."

Surprise replaced the girl's glare. "What?"

"You've been in fights before?"

"Sure. Lots."

"Ever hit anybody?"

"Of course."

"Then stand up and hit me."

"You think I won't?"

"I think you can't."

Charlie launched herself from the sofa. She went straight at Dina, who nimbly sidestepped. Charlie spun, her right fist in a fast, angry sweep. Dina caught her arm, twisted, and sent Charlie down. The girl was so fast, she seemed to be back on her feet even before she'd hit the floor. This time she attacked with a kick. Dina danced back and the girl's foot connected with air. Charlie's own inertia caused her to lose her balance and she fell squarely on her butt. This time she sat there, breathing hard and staring at the floor.

"So," Dina said dryly above her, "how about a little breakfast after that workout?"

"I'm not hungry." Charlie picked herself up and stomped toward the guest room at the back of the cabin.

After he heard the door slam, Cork said, "You didn't exactly win her heart."

Dina grabbed the wooden spoon from him. "All right, maybe it was a little over the top, but she pissed me off, okay. I didn't like her attitude. The important thing is that if the shit ever hits the fan, she'll understand I can handle it. By the way, how's the leg this morning, gimp?"

"Let's just hope the shit doesn't hit the fan. I'd be *so* screwed."

"How about that omelet now?" She headed toward the kitchen.

"If I said no, would you beat me up?"

"Don't test me."

He watched her work in the kitchen, such an everyday kind of thing. Chopping mushrooms and onions, grating cheese, beating eggs. By the end whatever irritation she'd felt as a result of Charlie seemed to have vanished and she hummed softly to herself. The omelet she made, with additional hints of garlic and basil, was marvelous.

"Thanks," he said as he finished his last bite.

"For the gourmet meal? You're welcome."

"And for coming." He wiped his mouth with his napkin. "And for being willing to forgo Jacoby's money. After all, I'm worth half a million dead, no questions asked."

She scooped the final bit of omelet onto her fork. "Don't think it's not tempting."

"I owe you an apology. In Minnesota, I misjudged you, then I used you."

"You had your reasons. Good ones. If I had a family like yours, I'd do whatever it took to keep them safe." She finished eating and dabbed the napkin to her lips. "More coffee?"

"No, thanks. Let me do the dishes?"

"With that leg? Dude, you'd be *so* screwed. I'll take care of things. You just sit."

"Sitting is all I've been doing. But I could sure use a shower."

"Go on. I'll keep an eye on Charlie."

Outside, the day felt good. The storm had washed the air clean, and the sunlight and meditative quiet gave the morning a hopeful feel. The ground was littered with leaves and small branches torn from the trees. Rainwater filled every depression. Cork made his way toward Cabin 3, the tip of his cane leaving small perfect circles beside his deep shoe prints. As he came to the steps of his cabin, he paused and studied the wet ground. He knelt, moved aside a big russet oak leaf, and saw clearly what had been partially obscured. A paw print, one that had not been there the day before.

The cougar had returned.

Cork followed the tracks, easily done because the muddy ground held the impressions well. The animal had circled his cabin. It had also visited the locked trash bin, where scratches indicated the big cat had tried to claw its way in. He picked up the trail again at Thor's Lodge and followed the tracks to the shed where his car was parked. The hood of the yellow-green Dart was covered with muddy paw prints, as were the windows. The cat had been very interested in the car. Cork wondered if it had smelled the blood that soaked the seat inside.

One hungry animal, he figured.

Although the presence of the wild cat was a concern, Cork discovered something else that was far more disturbing: boot prints. They were all around the Dart, particularly deep on the side that was pocked with bullet holes. Cork studied the waffle pattern of the prints, which had been made by boots much too large to belong to anyone at Jewell's place. Unlike the cougar's prints, they weren't filled with rainwater. They'd been made sometime after the rain had stopped. The tracks ended at the edge of the shed, a vantage from which the cabins could be easily observed. They were even deeper there than beside the car. Whoever it was, he'd spent a while standing, sinking into the ground, watching.

Cork followed the boot prints away from the resort into the trees and found a trail that led south through the woods. Whoever had been interested in the car and the cabins had come and gone along this trail.

Cork leaned on his cane. His leg throbbed from the effort he'd put into the tracking. A hungry animal he could understand. A man in boots was something else.

24

Stash's family was a mystery to Ren. He'd been to their house a few times but mostly he hung out in his friend's big bedroom with the blinds drawn, watching tapes or DVDs or playing video games. Stash's mother was a slender blonde with nails painted a shiny red like drops of blood at the ends of her fingers. She wore a lot of makeup. Whenever Ren visited, she was cordial but a little tense and seemed to watch them both with uncomfortable concern. His father was like a telephone pole in a suit, tall and silent, and he never laughed. He bent and shook Ren's hand every time they met, his grip strong and purposeful. Stash didn't talk about his parents much, and when he did it wasn't with great affection. Stash had an older brother, Martin, who was seventeen and an athlete. He played for the Bobcats and had lettered in a bunch of sports. Stash sometimes called him Jack Armstrong, All-American Boy, a reference that had something to do with an old radio program Ren had never heard of. To Ren, Stash's family seemed just fine, but he didn't have to live with them. That always made a difference.

Stash was in the Intensive Care Unit and not allowed visitors other than his immediate family. There was a waiting room down the hall and Stash's brother sat there, staring toward the windows that opened onto a vista of Marquette and a sky full of promising morning sunlight. Ren and Jewell were about to step into the room when Stash's mother emerged from the ICU and came toward them. She looked exhausted.

"April," Jewell said, "I'm so sorry."

The woman's eyes were red, and Ren figured she'd been doing a lot of crying.

"They say he's stable now," she said. "All we can do is wait and pray."

Tears rimmed her eyelids and Ren's mother took her in her arms. Ren slipped into the waiting room. Martin looked his way.

"Hey," he said to Ren.

"Hi, Marty."

Stash's brother hadn't shaved. His face was a drawn landscape of sparse stubble and teenage blemish. The television in the corner was on, tuned to CNN, but the volume was turned to a low, unintelligible drone. Ren stood with his hands in his pockets.

"What happened?" he asked.

Marty wore his hair in a buzz cut, like a Marine. He ran his hand over the bristle. "He was on his skateboard, going down Ruby Hill. A car hit him from behind, didn't stop. He'd probably be dead except some guy was walking his dog and saw it happen. Jesus. That skateboard. I've been telling him it's dangerous. I've been trying to get him into a real sport." He balled his fist, but there was nothing to hit. "Jesus."

"Do they know who hit him?"

"No. A car, that's all. It was almost dark. He shouldn't have been skateboarding so late." He looked across the room again. The light from the early morning sun washed orange over his face. "I'd love to get my hands on the guy behind the wheel, the son of a bitch who didn't have the guts to stop."

Ren glanced at the television, where CNN was running images of damage being done by a tropical storm in Florida: a mobile home with the roof peeling away, a downed power line popping sparks.

"Have you talked to him?" he asked.

"He's still out. Dad's with him. He hasn't left the room. God, it's killing him."

"Ren?" his mother called to him from the doorway.

"Gotta go," he said to Marty.

"Yeah."

"He's good," Ren said, before he left. "He's really good."

Marty looked at him, his tired face blank of understanding.

"On his skateboard, I mean. He's awesome to watch. He's way better than anybody I've ever seen."

Marty considered this and nodded thoughtfully.

"When he's awake, tell him I said hi." Ren turned to leave.

"Ren, come back to see him. He doesn't have a lot of buddies."

"Sure."

In the hall, Ren's mother put her arm around his shoulders. Stash's mother was just vanishing back into the ICU.

"I can't see him at all?" Ren said.

"You can't go in. But I suppose there wouldn't be any harm in taking a look from the hallway."

They went together and stood outside Intensive Care. In a small room on the far side of the nurses' station, Ren saw Stash's parents standing beside a bed, looking down at a lump of linen. All he could see of Stash was a bare arm with an IV tube attached to it. Stash's father put a hand down, and Ren could tell from the way his arm moved that he was stroking his son's hair. It was such a gentle gesture from a man Ren had always viewed as being as caring as a chain saw.

"Let's go," he said, and turned away, thinking that if he ever heard Stash dis his father again, he'd let him have it but good.

25

"What do you think?" Cork said.

Dina's keen green eyes followed the boot prints as they disappeared down the path through the woods.

"Where does this trail lead?" she asked.

"Damned if I know. But Charlie might."

Inside Thor's Lodge, Dina knocked on the door to Charlie's temporary bedroom.

"What?" came the girl's surly reply.

"We need your help," Dina said.

"Bite me."

Dina opened the door. Charlie lay sprawled on the bed, a comic book in her hands. Her eyes cut into Dina like razor blades.

"Get out," she spat.

"Normally I would, Charlie, but the circumstances aren't normal right now."

"What do you want?"

"There's a trail just west of the resort," Cork said, moving in next to Dina. "Do you know what it is?"

"The Killbelly Marsh Trail. It's part of the Copper River Trail system. Hiking, snowmobiling, that kind of thing."

"Where does it go?"

"Loops around the marsh and connects with the main trail along the river."

"Is it heavily used?"

"Heavily?" She rolled her eyes, as if having to think about it was an incredible imposition. "It's fall. A lot of trolls come up here for the color. The trail's popular."

"'Trolls'?" Dina asked.

"People from the lower peninsula," Cork clarified. "Below the Mackinac Bridge, get it?"

"'Trolls,'" Dina said.

Charlie put down her comic book and sat up. "Why do you want to know this stuff?"

"Just curious," Cork told her.

"So, is that it?"

"Yes, thanks."

He turned to head out, but Dina held back.

"Hungry yet?" she asked the girl.

"No."

"Suit yourself."

Dina joined Cork and closed the door behind her.

In the kitchen, they spoke quietly. Cork leaned on his cane; Dina crossed her arms and leaned against the counter.

"A troll?" Cork said. "Just some curious hiker?"

"It's possible, I suppose. Someone who stumbled across the cougar tracks and followed them."

"Or someone who thought the girl would show up here eventually and dropped by to check it out."

"Or," Dina added, "someone looking for you."

Cork shook his head. "He'd have picked me off the moment I stepped out the door. Has Charlie been outside this morning?"

"Not since we've been up."

"Let's keep her in the cabin."

Dina nodded. "Maybe I should reconnoiter."

Cork did a quick appraisal of her outfit: a white sweater, black jeans, white Reeboks. "You'd look like a zebra prancing through the woods."

"It was my intention," she said evenly, "to change into something more fitting. And to arm myself appropriately."

"What are you packing?"

"In addition to my Glock, I've got a Colt .45 with a suppressor. Or I could opt for the Ruger .44 carbine still in my trunk. How about you?"

"Just the Tomcat you gave me. It's in my cabin."

"Maybe you should get it," Dina said.

"You go on and change. I'll stay and let Charlie know what's up, then get the gun."

Dina headed to the door.

"You'll be careful?" Cork said.

"At what I do," she replied without looking back, "I'm the best."

Cork moved to the front door. He watched her enter Cabin 2, which Jewell had given her to store her things. For ten minutes he stood waiting for her to come out. She never did. It dawned on him that she'd probably left in a way that would be unobserved. A bathroom window maybe.

She *was* good.

"Where's the old lady?"

Cork turned around to find Charlie standing near the kitchen counter. His leg was killing him. He sat down at the table and hung the cane on the chair back.

"The lady's out there right now, making sure you're safe."

"I didn't ask for her help."

She went into the kitchen, opened a cupboard door, and hauled out a bowl. She opened another door and plucked out a box of Cap'n Crunch. From the refrigerator, she got a carton of milk. In another minute, she was sitting at the table across from Cork, greedily eating her breakfast. She slumped in her chair, her face six inches from the bowl. Cork didn't know if this was her normal eating habit or done simply to keep her from having to look at him.

"She saved my life on a couple of occasions," he told her.

"Big deal," Charlie said through a mouthful of cereal.

"It is to me."

Charlie wiped her mouth with the back of her hand. "So she's, like, what? Your girlfriend?"

"She's a friend to me in the same way you're a friend to Ren."

It was a while before she spoke again. "Do you think she's pretty?"

"Yes."

"Is that why you like her?"

"No."

"Right."

"Charlie—"

Cork's comment was cut off by the sound of a gunshot outside. It didn't come from a handgun. Something heavier. Shotgun, probably. He grabbed the cane and pushed himself from the chair just as another report smacked the morning air. He hobbled to the door and scanned the grounds outside where nothing moved.

"Charlie, get into your room. Hide under the bed or in the closet. Just stay out of sight until I come back. Okay?"

She stared at him.

"Move," he said sharply.

She stood up and turned.

He threw the screen door open and hurried down the steps. Dina hadn't said anything to him about a shotgun, so he figured it wasn't hers. The gunfire had come from a distance. He hoped that meant there was time to get to his cabin, where he'd stowed the Beretta. He berated himself for not having grabbed his weapon earlier. He felt exposed, vulnerable, stupid.

The .32 Tomcat was under his pillow. For safety, should Ren find the weapon, Cork had removed the clip and slipped it under the mattress. He pulled them both from their hiding places and slapped the clip home.

As he started back to Thor's Lodge, he felt the intense, unsettling quiet of the woods in the wake of the gunshots. Two reports, then nothing. Why hadn't Dina returned fire? He didn't want to dwell on that one. He scanned the trees as he limped across the wet ground, leaves sticking to his soles like leeches. Nothing moved. However, a man with a shotgun, a heavy slug, and good scope wouldn't need to move much to keep the crosshairs on Cork's chest.

He made the steps, the porch, then stumbled inside. With his back to the wall beside the door, he caught his breath. He risked a look through the doorway, a limited field of vision that revealed nothing. He hobbled to the back room.

"Charlie, I'm here now."

There was no answer.

With difficulty, he knelt and checked under the bed, then tried the closet. The girl wasn't there.

"Charlie?" he said again, louder this time. "Charlie?"

How long had he been gone? Three minutes, maybe four? Long enough for whoever wanted her to have taken her?

He limped back to the main room where he bellowed, "Charlie!"

The porch steps squealed under the weight of quickly mounting feet. Cork swung around, the Beretta leveled on the center of the doorway.

Dina stepped into view, saw the weapon in his hand, and spun back instantly out of sight.

"It's me, damn it," she hollered.

He lowered the Beretta. "You okay?"

She peered tentatively around the corner of the doorway, her face dark beyond the screen. "Yeah."

"The gunshots?"

"A hunter. Some guy with his dog shooting at birds, whatever the hell is in season." She opened the screen door and came in. "Everything okay here?"

"Not exactly," Cork replied. "I seem to have lost Charlie."

26

*T*o reconnoiter, Dina had changed into camouflage fatigues of muted autumn gold and brown. She would have blended easily into the woods. Cork was a little amazed at the foresight required to have such an outfit on hand.

He explained what had happened—Charlie's disappearance—and near the end, he heard the rattle of heavy suspension on the gravel road that led to the resort. They stepped outside onto the porch and watched as Jewell's Blazer pulled up and parked in the sunshine. Jewell got out, and a moment later Ren followed. Both looked concerned at the firearms that Cork and Dina held. On the steps of the cabin, Cork told them the situation.

"The man with the dog," Jewell asked, shading her eyes against the morning sun, "was he kind of tall? And was the dog a golden retriever?"

"Yes," Dina said.

Ren jumped in. "Bill Pothen. He hunts partridge. He's okay." His eyes darted around the resort as if he hoped to spot his friend lurking somewhere.

Dina glanced toward Cabin 3. "Is it possible someone came while you were gone?"

"Possible," Cork said, "but not probable. I was away for three, maybe four minutes at most. I think Charlie would have yelled her head off if anybody tried anything."

"If she was able," Dina said. "Maybe she was surprised and didn't have the chance."

"Surprised by whom?" Jewell asked.

Ren climbed the steps and put his face to the screen. "Did you look all over inside?"

"I called plenty loud enough that she'd hear me," Cork replied.

"Charlie!" Ren hollered. "Charlie, it's me, Ren."

A brief moment of silence followed, then a distant voice came from inside the cabin: "I'm here."

Ren flung the screen door open and flew inside. The others were right behind him.

"Where are you?" he called.

"In here." The words came from the kitchen.

Cork followed the others who moved faster than he.

"Here." This time it was clear her voice had come from behind the cabinet door below the sink.

They found her contorted around the plumbing. She slowly extricated herself, limb by limb. When she was fully out, she began to twist and stretch her cramped muscles.

"Why didn't you answer when I called?" Cork asked.

She arched her back. "I didn't know if someone was, like, holding a gun to your head or what."

Dina smiled. "Smart."

Charlie bent low, lithe enough to press her forehead to her shins. "What were the shots all about?"

"A hunter," Cork said.

"Pothen," Ren replied.

"Gorgeous George with him?"

"The dog," Jewell explained to Cork and Dina.

The girl straightened and faced Ren. "So how was Stash?"

"Unconscious," Ren replied. "His family's with him."

"Not all of us," Charlie said, obviously still resentful.

Ren punched her shoulder lightly. "We'll go back when he's awake."

"It's a school day, Ren," Jewell reminded him.

"Not today, Mom. Please. I mean, everything's so crazy. And I don't want to leave Charlie. *Please*."

She gave in quickly. "All right. I'll call." She walked to the phone.

"Could I talk to Charlie for a little while alone?" Ren's eyes went to Cork and then to Dina.

"Sure," Dina said. "Why not?"

The two teenagers headed toward Ren's room.

After Jewell made her call, she came into the kitchen where Dina was making fresh coffee.

"Mind?" Dina asked.

"My kitchen is yours," Jewell replied. She glanced toward the hallway where Ren and Charlie had disappeared. "How's she doing?"

Dina began to fill the coffeepot in the sink. "If dinosaurs had that kind of survival instinct, they'd still be around, eating us for breakfast. She's tough."

"She's had to be. Any reporters?"

"No," Cork said. "I'm thinking the sheriff's people haven't released Charlie's name. That's a good thing. But we need to talk about those boot prints behind the shed."

"And we ought to figure what to do about that damn cougar," Dina added as she poured the water into the coffeemaker.

"Boot prints behind the shed?" Jewell looked confused, and Cork explained to her what he'd discovered near the Dart.

Jewell said, "I don't like the idea of any animal creeping around out there, human or otherwise."

Cork hobbled to the dining table and sat down. The bowl from which Charlie had eaten her cereal sat directly across from him. Soggy pieces of Cap'n Crunch floated in the milk. He idly tapped the tabletop with his cane.

"We could contact the Department of Natural Resources," he said. "They might have the wherewithal to deal with a cougar. But we'd end up with a lot of strangers mucking around. I don't think that's such a good idea right now. You know how to handle a firearm, Jewell?"

"I've been around hunters all my life. I'm fine with a rifle."

"Okay, how about this? None of us goes out without a firearm. And Ren and Charlie don't go out unescorted."

"Oh, they'll love that," Dina said, hitting the brew switch.

"They'd rather deal with a hungry cougar alone?"

Jewell pulled clean mugs from the cupboard. "I'll talk to them. They'll be okay. What about those boot prints?"

"It could be simply a curious troll, but we should probably assume the worst," Cork said.

Jewell set the mugs on the counter near the coffeemaker. "The worst, you mean, being that the guys who murdered Charlie's father are looking for Charlie?"

"That would be it."

"Could it be someone who's after you, Cork?" Jewell asked.

"If they knew I was here, I'd be dead already."

"So okay, it's about Charlie." Jewell frowned. "What are they after?"

The coffeemaker burbled. Dina folded her arms and stared at the floor. Cork tapped the tabletop with the tip of his cane. No one had a word to offer in answer.

Charlie threw herself onto Ren's unmade bed and rammed a pillow over her face. "Those guys are such assholes."

"Charlie."

She lifted the pillow and saw his expression. "Dude, you look like somebody just threatened to cut off your 'nads."

"I don't think Stash's accident was an accident."

"Huh?"

He began to pace, moving from the door to his desk to the window, then retracing his steps as he spelled out the connections.

"I've been thinking about it all the way back from Marquette. I think somebody hit Stash on purpose. I think they were trying to kill him."

"Stash?" She looked at him as if he were crazy. "What for?"

"Because they thought he was me."

"Dude, are you tripping?"

"Just shut up and listen." He stopped, and his hands formed a frame as if creating a window for her to see through clearly. "We spot this body floating down the Copper River, right? That night you and me go looking for it. There's a boat down there and the people on it are looking for something, too. Then you, in your brilliance, holler at it, and they get a good look at you."

"My butt."

"You, too. You even said something about the body, remember?"

"Yeah."

"Next thing we know, they're chasing us. At the shelter, when I was rolling the spliff, I left the cigar box on the ground with Stash's name in it. That same night they came to your place looking for you, but your dad wouldn't tell them anything. They . . . you know." He paused a moment, then rushed on. "The next day they go after Stash, thinking he was the one with you that night. Charlie, they're afraid because they think we saw the body."

"That's what this is all about?"

"I think so."

Charlie stared at him, then a deep sadness came into her eyes. "Ren."

"What?"

"My father. He knew I was sleeping in the truck outside, but he wouldn't tell them. Oh Jesus." She looked away.

"Yeah," Ren said, understanding. "He sure had his problems, Charlie, but he loved you."

She was quiet awhile. "What do we do?"

Ren chewed on his lip, then shrugged and nodded toward the bedroom door. "We should tell them."

Charlie looked skeptical. "What can they do?"

"We have to trust somebody." He looked from her to the door. "And, Charlie, they have guns."

27

Jewell had an eclectic collection of mugs. The one she held was white, with TOWANDA! printed across it in red. Dina drank from a blue *Best Mom In The World* cup. Cork had a red mug with *The older I get the better I was* emblazoned in gold. He looked up when Ren and Charlie marched in. From their deliberate stride he could tell that they had something important to say.

Ren stood in front with Charlie to his left. He squared his shoulders. Charlie buried her hands in her pockets, and her eyes seemed interested in everything except the adults.

Ren said, "There's something we should tell you."

Jewell nodded seriously. "We're listening."

Ren proceeded to lay out to them a bizarre-sounding scenario that included a body floating down the Copper River, a midnight search along the lakeshore, a mysterious boat, a childish mooning, followed by a pursuit up the trail along the river. The story ended with a cigar box containing marijuana left where it might easily have been discovered.

"You get high?" Jewell asked at the end.

"Sometimes," Ren admitted.

"Oh Jesus."

"I'm sorry, Mom."

"How long?"

Ren shrugged, then shook his head. "A while."

"Jewell, I know it's an important issue and you and Ren

158

need to talk about it," Cork said, "but there's a more pressing concern here. Is someone trying to kill these kids, and if they are, why?"

Jewell drilled her son with her dark eyes. "We *will* talk." She transferred her stern look to Charlie. "And you, too."

They sat at the dining table, and Cork walked Ren through everything again, double-checking each point with Charlie to be certain they were in agreement about the circumstances.

"You saw the body?" Cork said.

"No," Ren replied. "Stash—I mean Stuart—did. We kidded him, but he was sure."

"Did you actually see anything?"

"Maybe. But I thought it was, like, a log or something, you know?"

"Charlie?"

The girl shook her head. "I didn't see anything."

"You were high? All of you?"

They nodded together.

"All right, tell me about this boat."

Ren and Charlie exchanged a blank look. "It was just a boat," the boy said.

"How big?"

"Not very."

"Thirty feet? Twenty? Ten?"

"Maybe twenty."

"Charlie?"

"Yeah, I guess," she said.

"Think."

For ten seconds the girl stared at the empty fireplace. "It was just a regular powerboat, nothing special. A good engine, though. Maybe ninety horse."

"You know engines?"

"I know a lot of things."

"Did your father know anybody with a boat? Fishing buddies, maybe?"

"They all fish. A lot of 'em have boats."

"Can you give us some names?"

She looked irritated, as if it were a pain to have to think. "I don't know. Joe Otto. Skip Hakala. Calvin Stokely sometimes borrows his brother's boat. Then there's Pat Murphy. There's Roadkill—"

"Roadkill?"

"His name's Rodney, but they call him Roadkill."

"Sounds like he had a lot of friends."

"Duh. He lived here his whole life."

Cork looked at Jewell. "You know any of these guys?"

"Most of them."

"Anyone who might be the kind of guy who'd do what someone did to Charlie's father?"

"When they're drunk, all of 'em," Charlie spit out.

Jewell said, "Max wasn't particular about the company he kept. But I'd have to say that of them all, Calvin Stokely's always been the scariest. When we were kids, anything particularly cruel happened around here without knowing exactly who did it, Calvin Stokely's name popped pretty quick to people's lips. His folks lived off the grid."

"Off the grid?" Ren said. "What's that, Mom?"

"It's when someone tries to live a life that's not documented by the government. No Social Security, no taxes, that kind of thing."

"Like survivalists?" Ren said.

"Not exactly. But they were hard people. Hard on their kids for sure: Calvin and his brother, Isaac. Isaac's older. He went off to the Army young. When he came back on leave, he found Calvin and his mother beat up pretty bad and got into a fight with his father, who tried to shoot him with a shotgun. I guess Isaac's military training tipped the scales in his favor. It was the father they buried. Court ruled it a justifiable homicide and Isaac went back to the service. Calvin stayed, but it would have been fine with me if he hadn't. I know he's not to blame for what happened to him when he was a kid, but honestly, when I see him in town I try to avoid him. Even after all these years he still gives me the creeps."

Dina leaned on the table and cupped her coffee mug with both hands. "The men who killed Charlie's father weren't necessarily his buddies. I'm willing to bet a lot of people in Bodine know who Charlie is. She doesn't exactly blend into the woodwork."

"But we're all thinking it's somebody local, right?" Cork said.

"Local," Dina concurred.

"If it is about the body in the river, what is it about the body?" Cork went on. "Why go after kids who may have seen it?"

Jewell sat back, turning her mug slowly in her hand. "The body in the river, it's probably the same one that washed up in Bodine?"

"Hard to believe there'd be two corpses," Cork replied.

Dina frowned, thinking. "What could it be about the dead girl that would make someone come after Charlie and Stuart?"

Cork said, "It would be helpful if we knew who she was."

Ren looked at Charlie.

"We do," he said. "Tell them, Charlie."

Cork listened along with the others as Charlie told them about Sara Wolf, the girl from Providence House. When she was finished, he said, "It's time you talked to the sheriff's people."

"No." Charlie backed away. "I'll run away. I will."

Cork spoke quietly but firmly. "Somebody killed your father. The same people may have killed this girl. And they're probably responsible for your friend lying all torn up in a hospital bed. If that's true, they're after you, too. The sooner the investigators know all this, the better the chances of identifying these guys and putting them away."

She spoke over Ren's shoulder. "I don't like police. I won't talk to them."

Cork looked to his cousin for help. "Jewell?"

Jewell took a breath and tried. "Charlie—"

"No!"

"I think Charlie's right," Dina said. "What we have are a series of events, none of which are connected except by proximity, circumstance, and speculation. At the moment, the sheriff's people strongly suspect that Charlie might be responsible for her father's death. If she goes to them with the story she's told us, they're going to hold her, question her, and because she ran once already, they'll probably find a way to keep her in custody." She eyeballed Jewell, then Cork. "You want that for her?"

"The dead girl may have family who are worried," Cork said.

"Yeah, and monkeys fly out my butt," Charlie tossed in. "She was in a homeless shelter. You think she'd be there if she had a choice? You think anybody would?"

"The police need to know who she is," Cork persisted.

Dina shrugged. "Maybe they already do." She glanced at Jewell. "That constable friend of yours. You think you could find out from him?"

"I can try."

"Ned, it's Jewell DuBois."

"Jewell." He sounded surprised and pleased. He also sounded distant and fuzzy.

"Are you in your office?" she asked.

"No. I'm at Fry Ahearn's place. Goats got out again. We're rounding them up. When I'm out of the office, I forward the calls to my cell. What's up?"

"Ren and I just came back from Marquette. We went to see Stuart Gullickson at the hospital."

"How's he doing?"

"He's not out of the woods yet."

"Poor kid." There was a disturbance, a grunt, the clunk of heavy wood. "Sorry, Jewell. Just putting the gate back in place." He was breathing hard. "You know, I do an assembly every year at their school, talking to them about safety issues. Skateboarding in the street in the dark. Jesus. I might as well have been talking to the wall."

"Ned, Ren's pretty upset about all this. Charlie's father dead, Charlie gone, Stuart in the hospital from a hit-and-run. Then there's that girl they pulled from the lake. Have they identified her yet?"

"Yeah, they have."

"Really? Who is she?"

"I can't tell you that, Jewell."

"Would the Marquette sheriff's people tell me?"

"I doubt it. Last I heard, they were still working on notifying next of kin. Why would you need to know anyway?"

"Just concerned, Ned. Is it somebody I would recognize, or Ren?"

"It's nobody from around here, I can tell you that much." He was quiet a moment. Jewell could hear the bleat of goats in the background. "Say, you haven't heard from Charlie, have you?"

"No," she replied.

"And you'd tell me if you had?"

"Thanks for your help, Ned."

She ended the call and turned to the others. "They know who she is."

Charlie looked relieved. "So I don't have to talk to them?"

"Not yet, anyway," Dina said.

"She's still a material witness," Cork pointed out.

Dina gave a brief nod. "Before she talks to Olafsson—"

"Olafsson?" Jewell asked.

"The sheriff's investigator," Dina clarified. "Before she talks to him, it would be helpful to know how a girl from Providence House ended up in the Copper River. What's the connection? If they understand that, they'd be more inclined to believe Charlie and less likely to put her in custody."

"There's no guarantee," Cork said.

"We play the odds. What do you say?"

"Let me guess," Cork said. "You have a strategy for this."

Dina smiled demurely. "As a matter of fact, I have. How's that leg?"

28

Jewell drove with Dina beside her and Charlie in back. They left Bodine and took the potholed county highway toward Marquette. The road was still wet from the rain the night before. In those stretches where the old asphalt tunneled through stands of deciduous trees, russet and gold leaves spattered the road. Jewell kept her eye on Charlie in the rearview mirror. The girl hunkered down in her seat, quiet, staring out the window as sunlight and shadow exploded against her face. Occasionally she brought her hand up and idly fingered the line of rings and studs that marked the piercings of her left ear, or she scratched the stubble on her head, the emerging ghost of her lost hair.

Charlie had shaved her head over football. When classes began in September, she sought a spot on the eighth-grade flag football team. She was firmly told that football was a boys' sport. Her response—"Bullshit. Girls can compete just as good"—had earned her a reprimand from the principal. To prove her point, she'd goaded the coach, Mr. Morrow, who also taught earth science, into pitting her against his fastest players in a forty-yard dash. She'd beaten them all by a mile, after which Mr. Morrow explained once again that the issue wasn't her ability but her gender. If she'd had money or connections, she might have filed some kind of discrimination suit. Instead, she'd protested in her own way: sacrificing her hair. She'd done it with Ren's help. In his defense afterward,

Ren had explained to Jewell that Charlie was hell-bent on doing it anyway and more than willing to go it alone. He'd helped only because he didn't want her to hurt herself with the razor.

Her protest got her suspended for two days. For a while the whole incident was a hot topic of conversation in Bodine. Gary Johnson had written a fine editorial supporting Charlie's position, but it didn't change a thing.

Although Jewell often worried about the young woman, she also knew that there was an extraordinary depth to Charlie's strength, which was good because coming into this world she'd been given little else to help her along.

Dina Willner was busy writing in a small notepad.

"What are you doing?" Jewell asked.

"Preparing an interview, making notes on the questions I want to be sure to ask. I can fly by the seat of my pants when I have to, but I prefer to go in prepared."

Jewell nodded, liking the way this woman operated. "How is it you know my cousin?"

Dina glanced up from the page. Jewell saw that her green eyes held a guarded look. "We worked on a case together in Minnesota."

"The Jacoby murder, right? The one in Aurora."

"That's the one."

"He trusts you."

From the rear, Charlie said, "He likes you."

Dina twisted around in her seat. "What?"

Charlie kept her eyes on the scenery out the window and spoke in a matter-of-fact way, as if it were something anybody could see and probably everybody had. "The way he looks at you. And the way you look at him, it's the same. You like him back."

"He's married."

"Big whoop." The girl crossed her arms, then said more darkly, "Ren likes you, too. Must be the boobs."

"That's enough, Charlie," Jewell snapped.

"I'm just trying to figure why guys like her."

"There are lots of reasons to like people of the opposite sex besides physical attraction."

"Yeah?" Charlie leveled her gaze on Dina, who was still turned toward her. "So what is it you like about the gimp?"

Dina replied calmly, "This is not a conversation I'm going to have with you."

"Fine." Under her breath, Charlie whispered, "*Bitch.*"

Jewell braked and pulled to the side of the road. "That calls for an apology. Now."

Charlie stared out the window and offered a grumbled "Sorry."

"If you're going to do this with us, Charlie, you're going to be civil, understood?" Jewell said.

"Yeah."

"What?"

"Yes, ma'am."

"That's better."

The rest of the way into Marquette, Charlie didn't say a word. They drove past Providence House and parked on a side street a block away. Jewell and Dina got out.

Charlie leaned out the window. "Why can't I come?"

Jewell answered, "Because if anybody sees you with us they may feel compelled to report it to the police, okay?"

"They're good people in Providence House," the girl protested.

"They also want to preserve the good relations they have with the authorities, I'm sure. And I'd rather not put them in an awkward position. We won't be long." She glanced at Dina. "Ten, fifteen minutes?"

Dina nodded.

"Charlie." Jewell reached in and put her hand over the girl's hand. "Promise me that you'll wait and that you'll be here when we get back."

"Where would I go?" she asked, surly.

"Promise me."

Charlie tossed her head back and blew out a loud, frustrated breath. "*All right.* I promise."

As Jewell and Dina approached Providence House, a gas motor roared to life in back, out of sight. A moment later, Delmar Bell appeared pushing a power mower along the edge of the yard. The lawn still looked wet, and Jewell could see that the wheels picked up a skin of cut grass as they rolled along. She climbed the porch steps with Dina, found the front door locked, and rang the bell. While they waited, Dina stepped back and appraised the structure, the yard, and the handyman with his mower. Jewell had no idea what interested her, but Dina took her notepad from her back pocket and wrote something down.

The door opened and the same woman with whom Jewell had spoken the previous day appeared and eyed them warily. "Yes?" A light came into her eyes. "You were here yesterday. Looking for Charlene Miller."

Jewell said, "May we come in?"

"I can't tell you any more about Charlene than I did yesterday."

"We're not here about Charlene," Dina said. "We'd like to ask you about another client. Sara Wolf."

At the name, the woman's face went ashen. "I can't talk about her."

Dina held out her hand and magically a business card appeared. "My name is Dina Willner. I'm a private investigator from Chicago, and I'm looking into the disappearance of Charlene Miller and the death of Sara Wolf."

"You know about Sara?" the woman asked.

"Yes, we know."

She studied the card, then the faces of her visitors. "Come in," she said at last, and turned back toward the dark inside the house.

She led them to a sitting room full of worn—probably donated—furniture.

"Please sit down."

She took one of the shabby stuffed chairs. Dina and Jewell sat on the old sofa. The angle of the sun kept any direct light from entering the windows, and the room felt gloomy. From outside came the drone of the mower, growing louder whenever Bell approached the house and fading as he moved away. The woman still held Dina's card in her hand.

"You're a private investigator?"

"Yes. And you are?"

"Mary Hilfiker. I'm the director of Providence House. Who hired you?"

"I did," Jewell leaped in. It was close to the truth.

"To look for Charlene?"

"Yes," Jewell said.

"What does Charlene have to do with Sara?"

"If we tell you the whole story, we need to have your promise that you'll keep it to yourself."

Mary Hilfiker weighed her choices and finally replied, "You have it."

"The police have been here?" Dina asked.

She nodded. "An investigator. He left a little while ago."

"That's the first you knew of Sara's death?"

"Yes. What about this story?"

Dina told her about the body in the Copper River, about the kids seeing it, about the search at midnight and the mysterious boat, about Charlie and the attack on her father, and finally about the car that had hit Stuart.

"We think the body the kids saw was Sara. It was carried down the river to the lake, and the storm that night brought it ashore in Bodine."

"How would her body have ended up in the river?"

"We're wondering the same thing. That's why we're here. When was the last time you saw Sara?"

"A week ago last Friday. She left the shelter in the morning to go to school and her job and never came back."

"She was in school and had a job?"

"You're wondering why she'd be in a shelter for homeless youth."

"Frankly, yes."

"A lot of good people have an idea about homeless kids, or the homeless in general, for that matter. That chemical dependency or disability or some inherent weakness in them is responsible for their situation. The truth is, I see mostly kids with great potential struggling against staggering odds. Abuse, broken homes, every kind of family dysfunction imaginable. Sure, some of them are users. And some are chronic liars. And some are schemers. All of these are coping mechanisms to deal with a life they didn't ask for. Removing themselves from that life is often both the best thing they can do—and the scariest. The system fails them, a system overwhelmed and underfunded, and they end up on the street.

"We have programs for those who find their way to Providence House. One of these programs helps kids finish school and get a job. It takes a lot of guts, believe me. They live here on an extended basis, some for as long as two years. So long as they stay in school and show up for work, we give them a bed and food.

"Sara had been with us nearly a year. She'd had a hell of a life, but there was something in her that refused to be beaten down. There was a fire in the way she talked about her future, a very real dedication to change and growth. She had hope. God, hope just flowed right out of her."

"And then she suddenly vanished?"

"Yes."

"Didn't that seem unusual?"

"For many of the kids who come here, this is just a momentary refuge. They stay briefly and are gone—back to their old lives or on to something different. Something better is always my hope. They show up one night, they're gone the next."

"That happens a lot?"

"Yes. I'd love to have the wherewithal to find them, bring them back, keep them on track, but we barely make it as it is. Three-quarters of a million children go missing every year."

"They don't all stay lost?"

"No, but many thousands do, and in my thinking even one is too many."

"You said Sara was in a special long-term program."

"That's no guarantee of anything. We've had kids here I thought would make it, and despite our best efforts, they still end up back on the street."

"So you did nothing when she disappeared?"

"I called the police, which is something I seldom do, but in this case I was concerned."

"Does she have family in the area?"

"She was originally from a reservation in Wisconsin, but she'd been living with an aunt in Clovis. That's a little town south of here. It wasn't a good situation. Her uncle not only abused her, he pimped her. That's why she came here."

"She was Indian?"

"Yes. I don't know what tribal affiliation."

"Any idea where she hung out when she wasn't at Providence House?"

"School and work mostly."

"Where did she go to school?"

"ALC. The Area Learning Center. It's a special program the school district runs for at-risk youth. It's on Baraga."

"And work?"

"Spike's Pizza on Washington Avenue, just a few blocks away. She put in four hours there three afternoons a week."

"How'd she get to school and work?"

"She walked or took a bus."

"Can you think of any reason she would have been in the Bodine area?"

"I can't. But the police . . ." The last words had a bitter edge.

"Go on."

"The police believe she may have gone back to prostitution."

"Why? Once a prostitute, always a prostitute?"

"That's not what they said, but I'm sure that's what they're thinking."

"What do you think?"

"I've been wrong sometimes about kids. I believe they're going to make it and then they just fall apart. But Sara? I was so sure. She was so full of hope. If she was having sex, it wasn't for money."

"Did she have a boyfriend?"

"Not that I knew of."

"Was there anybody Sara was especially close to here at Providence House?"

"All the kids liked her. She was our poster child for self-improvement."

"The uncle who abused her, did he know she was here?"

"No. Absolutely not. We guard the kids' privacy fiercely, and there's no way Sara would have told him. As far as I know, she'd had no contact since she left them. But it's my understanding the police are checking out that possibility right now."

"If she wasn't at school or work, was there anyplace special where she might have hung out?"

"Yes. Muddy Waters. It's a coffeehouse a few blocks from here. Downtown on Main Street. She liked to study there."

"So no reason you can think of for her to be in Bodine?"

"None."

Dina looked at Jewell. "Anything you'd like to ask?"

"How old was she?"

"Just shy of fifteen," Mary Hilfiker replied. "She hadn't even started menstruating."

"Just a kid. My God."

"You think someone killed her and put her body in the Copper River?" the woman asked.

"That's what I think," Dina replied.

"And these same people killed Charlene's father?"

"Yes."

"Are you going to tell the police?"

"Eventually. Right now it's all pure speculation. As soon as we have something solid, we'll go to the authorities."

"I'm guessing you found Charlie. Or she found you. How is she?"

"Safe," Jewell said.

"Keep her that way."

Outside, Delmar Bell was still mowing the lawn. He glanced their way as they descended the steps, and he killed the engine. In the quiet that followed, he sauntered toward them, his shadow sliding before him like a black snake over the cut grass.

"Morning, Jewell."

"Del."

"Any luck finding Charlie, eh?"

"No."

"She'll turn up. Always does."

"It's different this time, Del. Her father's dead."

"You work here?" Dina said.

He looked her up and down. Then up again. His eyes hung too long on the curve of her breasts. He wiped his hands on his oil-stained T-shirt. "Who's asking?"

"My name's Willner. I'm a private investigator."

"A PI? For real?"

171

"For real."

"You're a lot better looking than Rockford, eh."

"Thanks. You're in charge of maintenance here?"

"In charge?" He smiled, his teeth long in need of a good cleaning. "I like the way you put that. Yeah, I'm in charge."

"You get to know the kids pretty well?"

"Not really."

"You know Sara Wolf?"

"Sure. She was around for quite a while."

"But not anymore."

"Haven't seen her for a week, maybe two." He squinted, lines at the corners of his eyes like the tines of a rake. "That what you're doing here? Looking for Sara?"

"If I were, would you be able to help?"

He shook his head. "Like I said, I don't really know any of the kids."

"Not even the ones who are around for quite a while?"

"They pretty much keep to themselves. Look, I got work to do, eh," he said. "Jewell, always good to see you."

He headed back toward the mower.

"You know him," Dina said.

"He's from Bodine. Graduated same year as me, same year as Charlie's father. They were drinking buddies. In fact, he's the one who told Charlie about Providence House and suggested she think about using it when she needed to get away from her father. It was a good suggestion."

"Does he live here?"

"In back. An old carriage house."

Bell yanked the cord, and the mower engine sputtered and shot out a cloud of oil smoke.

"He didn't touch me with anything except his eyes," Dina said. "But I still feel like I need a bath." She started toward the side street where Jewell had parked the Blazer, writing a note in her pad as she walked.

"What now?" Jewell said.

"We find more people, ask more questions."

In the Blazer, Charlie was napping in the backseat, curled in a blanket of sunlight.

"She looks peaceful," Dina said. "She looks like the kid she really is."

"She's had to grow up fast. I'd love to believe the worst is behind her now."

Dina studied Charlie with a soft gaze. "Let's do our best to see that it is."

29

*B*efore she left, Jewell had removed the Penrose drain from Cork's thigh, closed the wound with butterfly bandages, and taped a sterile gauze pad over the site, this at Cork's request. She cautioned him that if he wasn't careful, the wound would open again.

"There's work to do," he'd told her, "and I can't do it with a lot of plumbing hanging out of my leg."

Although he didn't like the idea of being less than a hundred percent lucid, he'd taken a Vicodin to help deal with the pain of what he knew was ahead of him. Now he stood in the lane between the cabins waiting for Ren, who'd gone to fetch the ATV from the equipment shed. The plan was to head along the Copper River Trail as far as they could and look for places that might be likely candidates for dumping a body into the river. It was a pretty nonspecific plan and didn't have a lot of potential for solid payoff, but it had to be done, and Cork and Ren were available.

Cork watched as the boy swung the shed door wide and went inside. At almost the same moment, he heard a vehicle approaching from the main road. He thought maybe it was the women coming back for something they'd forgotten, but he didn't want to risk it and slipped back inside Thor's Lodge. He cracked the curtains and watched as a dusty red pickup came into view. Michigan plates. NMU sticker on the windshield. Locals. Cork pulled the Beretta Tomcat from where he'd snugged it in his belt at the small of his back.

The truck stopped in front of the cabin and two men got out. The driver stood well over six feet, with carrot-colored hair and a long face. The other man was also tall and had a well-trimmed mustache and black-rimmed glasses. He held what appeared to be the plaster cast Ren had made of the cougar print. The men started toward Thor's Lodge, but stopped when they heard the roar of the ATV from the equipment shed. They turned and watched Ren bring the machine up the lane. The boy killed the engine and got down from the seat. He smiled broadly and came forward. Cork moved to the door, which he'd left slightly ajar, so he could hear what was being said.

"Hi, Mr. Taylor."

"Hey there, Ren. I dropped by school. They told me you were home today. Feel all right?"

"Fine, thank you."

"I brought someone who wants very much to ask you a few questions about that cougar of yours. This is John Schenk, a friend from Northern Michigan University. John, this is that remarkable young man I've been telling you about."

Schenk shook the boy's hand. "Ken showed me this cast you made of the track. Nice job."

"Thanks."

"Mind if I ask you about it?"

"That's okay."

"Where did you find it?"

"Over here. I'll show you."

Ren led the man to Cabin 3 and pointed out the track he'd used to make the cast. "This is the one, but there were lots I could have used."

"They were all over?"

"They still are. It's come at least twice, maybe three times."

"Really? When?"

"The night before last, and again last night for sure. But I'm pretty sure it was here yesterday morning as well."

"In the daylight? You saw it?"

"I heard it. Kind of a scream."

That wasn't the truth exactly. He was relating what Cork had told him.

"That's amazing."

"Why?" Ren asked.

"For several reasons. First of all, the preferred hunting technique of cougars is stalk and ambush. It's unusual that a stalking cougar would make its presence known with a scream. Also, they tend to be crepuscular, which means they prefer to hunt at dusk or dawn. And, generally speaking, a cougar in these parts is probably well aware of humans and would tend to avoid them. Ken says you don't have any pets around here. Is that correct?"

"That's right."

Schenk furrowed his brow and said, "Hmph." He looked down at the cast in his hand. "From the size, I'm guessing this is a male. Four and a half inches is about as large a track as you're likely to find. Probably weighs in at well over two hundred pounds, which is good sized for a cougar. There are a couple reasons I can think of that would bring a big cat this close to humans repeatedly. One would be food—a pet, farm animals, that kind of thing."

"We don't have any," Ren said.

"Have you killed a deer or some other animal lately that you've dressed and hung somewhere around here?"

Ren said, "No."

Schenk glanced around. "I thought maybe the smell of blood."

Which made Cork think about the piss-colored Dart behind the shed with his blood soaked into the seat and carpeting.

"Another possibility is that it's been hurt and can't hunt in its usual way and is looking for garbage or anything else that might provide an easy meal."

"It tried our garbage bin," Ren offered, "but we keep the lid closed and locked."

"Sounds like it's definitely hungry, which makes it potentially very dangerous. Like I say, normally it probably wouldn't attack humans, but I wouldn't take any chances."

"How come you know about cougars?" Ren asked.

"I'm a zoologist at the university, but I also consult for the Michigan Wildlife Habitat Foundation," Schenk said. "Cougars are a special interest of mine. Since 1906 the official position of the Department of Natural Resources has been that cougars have been extirpated from Michigan."

"Extirpated?"

"Driven out completely. This despite the fact that every year there are dozens of sightings in both the lower and upper peninsula. A couple of years ago we collected scat from a number of areas around the northern part of the state where sightings had been reported and sent them for DNA testing. Seven of the samples contained cougar DNA."

"What made you think it was cougar scat?" Ren asked. "I mean, out of all the scat you might find."

Schenk laughed. "It's the sniff test. Cougar scat has an unmistakable smell. It's kind of like a housecat's overused litter box, but far more intense. We don't know why. Maybe because they have a short gut and food passes through more quickly so their digestive juices are stronger."

"What should we do? Like maybe notify the DNR?"

Schenk shook his head. "Unfortunately, their general response in a situation like this would be to kill the animal."

"So what do we do?"

"For the time being, take precautions. Don't go out alone, especially when it's dark. And keep that lock on the trash bin. If you do happen to confront the animal, face it. They're reluctant to attack from the front, especially if you stare at them. Generally they'll back down. What I'd like to do is talk to some people I know who'd be interested in tracking and, if possible, sedating the animal. If it is hurt, maybe there's something we can do to help it. I'd sure hate to see a creature this rare around here killed."

"I can handle that," Ren assured him.

"You'd probably like your cast back, wouldn't you?" Ken Taylor said.

Schenk handed it over. "Thanks, son. This is really a good thing you've done."

Ren looked down, as if embarrassed in the face of such praise.

"I'll be in touch," Schenk said. "Come on, Ken, we've got work to do."

In parting, Taylor put a hand on the boy's shoulder. "Ren, you be careful, hear?"

"Sure."

After the two men had driven away, Cork stepped from Thor's Lodge. "Do you have a hunting rifle, Ren?"

The boy looked at him, confused. "You're not going to shoot it?"

"I just want to play it safe. I wouldn't use it unless I absolutely had to. At the moment, all I have is this." He held out the small Beretta. "It might discourage an animal, but it probably wouldn't stop a two-hundred-pound cougar."

Ren said, "There's two of us. Won't that keep us safe? And the sound of the ATV?"

He knew that what the boy was really arguing for was the life of the big cat, and he understood. Ren was probably right. A cougar, even a hungry one, would probably be reluctant to attack two humans, and the sound of the ATV would definitely not be to its liking.

"All right," he said.

They straddled the seat of the ATV, Ren in front, Cork holding on from behind. The engine kicked over and caught. Ren guided the little vehicle through the trees to the Killbelly Marsh Trail, where Cork had found both cougar tracks and those of a man. The boy turned them toward the Copper River, which lay somewhere beyond the trees to the south.

They headed into the woods with no idea of what they would eventually encounter, no idea of the full scope of the horror the Huron Mountains hid.

30

*C*lovis was not much of a town: an old Mobile gas station at a corner of a crossroad, a tavern diagonally opposite, a few houses surrounding them, the whole place situated in a pine barrens of sandy soil and scrub evergreen.

Dina asked at the gas station and got directions.

The house where Sara Wolf had lived with her aunt and uncle was something a good huffing and puffing could have blown right down. It stood back from the road behind a tangle of brush and diseased pines with brown needles brittle as toothpicks. In the front area—it didn't exactly qualify as a yard—a completely rusted-over pickup without wheels sat in sand up to its axles. To the right was a sagging garage with most of the windows broken out. An old cocker spaniel who'd been lying in the weeds beside the front steps roused itself and began barking, a hoarse sound without energy. They all got out and waited a moment beside the Blazer because even an old dog has teeth.

The woman who came to the door to look at them was short and wide. She wore jeans and a dark blue sweater. She shaded her eyes with a plump sandstone-colored hand and stared.

"*Boozhoo*," Jewell called, using the familiar Ojibwe greeting.

"What do you want?" the woman called over the noise of the dog.

"We're looking for Sara's aunt?" Jewell called back.

"What for?"

"We just want to talk to her for a few minutes. About Sara."

"Are you police? 'Cuz somebody already been here."

"No. We're friends."

Under the awning of her hand, the woman's eyes held on them a long time, then she said, "Shut up, Sparky."

The dog seemed grateful not to have to expend any more energy and immediately settled back on its haunches and panted in a tired way as it watched the women approach. When they were close, it eased itself onto all four legs. Its tail began to sweep against the weeds at its back in a friendly way, and it padded forward.

Charlie put her hand out and said, "Hey there, Sparky. How you doing, boy?"

"You knew Sara?" the woman asked.

Jewell indicated the girl. "Charlie here knew her pretty well. I'm Jewell DuBois. This is Dina Willner."

The woman's hair was black and fine and cut carelessly at neck length. Through the open door behind her, the living room was visible in the dim interior light, a cluttered place.

"Could we come in and talk for a few minutes?" Jewell asked.

"No," the woman said. "Frank'll be back anytime. You gotta go before he comes."

"Frank?"

"My husband."

"Sara's uncle?"

"Yeah."

"When was the last time you saw Sara?" Dina asked.

"Cops asked the same thing," she said. "Almost a year ago. She took off one day, never came back."

"Did you notify the police?"

She shook her head. "I was expecting it."

"Why?"

"It wasn't working out here."

"What exactly wasn't working?" Dina asked.

The woman looked at her, her brown eyes hard as hickory nuts, giving away nothing. "Who are you people? Why are you asking about Sara?"

"We live in Bodine, where her body was found. We're trying to understand what she was doing in our town."

She squinted, perplexed, or perhaps just a reaction to the
bright morning sun. "But you're not cops?"

"No."

Charlie spoke up. "We were, you know, friends. I was at
Providence House with her. I liked her."

The woman lowered her gaze and it locked on Charlie.
Something changed in her aspect, a softening. She glanced
toward the road behind them and said, "Come in, but just for a
minute."

They stepped inside, into the stale smell of layered dust and
cigarette smoke and spilled beer and cushions stained dark
with skin oil. She didn't invite them to sit. There was nowhere
that was not covered with some discarded item: clothing,
newspapers, magazines, a couple of pizza boxes. The dog, who
was left outside, whined at the door.

"When she ran away, did you know where she went?" Dina
asked.

"She didn't run away. I told her to go." The woman took a
breath and her wide nostrils flared even more. "Frank." She
said the word as if she were saying *shit*. "She told me what he
done, what he made her do, and I told her she had to go. Not
leave, you know. Get away."

"Did you send her to Providence House?"

She nodded. "A girlfriend told me about it. I thought she'd
be safe there. I hoped."

"Did your husband know where she'd gone?"

"No. I didn't say nuthin'. I told him she run away."

"The police think she might have gone back to prostitution.
What do you think?"

She shook her head firmly. "I don't think so. *Mashkawizii*."

"*Mashka* what?" Dina replied.

"It's Ojibwe," Jewell said. "It means she was strong. She had
inner strength."

The woman looked at her with interest.

"My husband spoke Anishinaabemowin," Jewell explained.

"You Shinnob?"

"Yes," Jewell answered without hesitation.

The woman nodded. "That girl, what life handed her didn't amount to a bucket of spit, but she didn't never give up, you know. I figured if she stuck here either she'd kill Frank or Frank'd kill her. Best thing was to get her someplace safe. That's why I sent her away to that place."

"And you're sure your husband didn't know she was there?" Dina asked.

"I don't know how he could've."

"What does he do? I mean for work."

"Construction, when there's something going."

"Does he ever work in Marquette?"

"Sometimes."

"Is it possible he saw Sara there?"

She thought about it. "He'd've said something."

"What about Bodine? Has he done work up there?"

"I don't think so."

"Have you had any contact with Sara since she left?"

Her eyes flitted away toward the blank television screen. She rubbed her hands, one over the other. "She called me sometimes."

"Here?"

"Yeah. Just to tell me things were going okay." Her head drooped in a tired way. "She kept telling me I should leave him."

Through the open door came the sound of an engine in need of a new muffler and Jewell turned. She watched a gray pickup pull into the drive, skirt her Blazer, and park near the house. A man got out who was like a bone, thin and hard and white. He wore a dirty jean jacket over coveralls, work boots, a ball cap. He checked out the Blazer, glanced at the house, and came toward the door.

"Frank?" Dina asked.

The woman nodded and her eyes had become afraid.

"Have the police talked to him?"

"I don't think so. Not here anyway."

Dina quickly took a card from her purse and gave it to the woman. "Keep that safe somewhere. If you need me, call."

The man's boots beat on the wooden steps like mallets as he came up. He yanked the door open and was inside, glaring.

The woman had retreated behind Jewell and the others. Dina moved forward, taking the lead.

"Who are you?" he said.

"We're here about Sara," Dina said.

"What are you? Social workers?"

"Former Special Agent Dina Willner, FBI," she said. The *former* went by quickly, and Jewell wasn't sure the man even tracked it. Dina's hand shot into her purse. She flashed some kind of ID, then slipped it quickly back where it had come from. "I'd like to ask you a few questions."

"About Sara? She took off a long time ago. Hell, she could be dead for all I know."

"She is, Mr. Durkee."

His eyebrows were thin and blond. There were long hollows in his cheeks, and the skin was rough as if his face had been carved on with a dull knife. His eyes were bright blue and startled. He stared at Dina. "How?"

"When was the last time you saw her?" Dina asked.

She'd taken a notepad from her purse, and she held a pen poised above a clean sheet. The man scowled at the notepad.

"I ain't seen her since she left."

"You've had no contact with her at all?"

"I just said that."

"You haven't talked to her on the phone?"

"No."

"You do construction work, is that correct?"

"Yeah."

"Are you working now?"

"No."

"When did you last work?"

"What does that got to do with Sara?"

"Just answer the question, please. When did you last work?"

"Couple weeks ago, laying some pipe."

"Where?"

"Ishpeming."

"Ever go to Bodine?"

"I've been there."

"When was the last time?"

"Hell, I don't remember."

"Friends there?"

He shifted restlessly, put his hands on hips, stuck out his chin. "No. And I ain't answering any more questions until I know why you're asking."

"We know that you forced Sara into prostitution at one time. Who were the johns?"

"What the hell are you talking about? Who the hell are you, coming into my home like this, accusing me of that kind of shit? I want you out of here." His arm shot out rigidly pointing toward the door. His fingers were long, and the rims of the ragged nails were packed black with dirt and grease.

"I'll just come back with a warrant, Mr. Durkee. You'll have to talk to me then."

"Fine. Bring your goddamn warrant. I got nuthin' to hide."

"That's what your wife said, too. Wouldn't tell me a thing." She gave him a scornful look, then turned and gave the same to the woman. "If I find out you've lied to me, I'll be back, folks, and I guarantee I won't be nice. Step aside, Mr. Durkee."

She stared at him until he moved from the door. She took Charlie's arm and guided her past him. Jewell followed them outside. Returning to the brightness of the morning sun, she found herself a little blind. The cocker spaniel padded aside and let them pass. They trooped to the Blazer in silence, got inside, and Jewell started to back out.

"We're just, like, leaving her?" Charlie asked.

"We're just, like, leaving her," Dina said.

"He might hurt her."

"He might."

"Shit," Charlie said. She crossed her arms and hunched down.

"Exactly," Dina said.

"So what was that all about?" the girl asked. In the rearview mirror, Jewell could see the frown on her face.

"Unless I'm mistaken," Dina said, "Frank Durkee doesn't know anything about Sara. That's important."

"Yeah? Why?"

"Eliminating possibilities, Charlie. It helps us know better where to focus our energy."

"So where do we focus now?"

Dina looked out at the pine barrens. She was quiet for a minute, then she said over her shoulder, "Charlie, do you have any idea where the kids from Providence House hang out when they're not at the shelter?"

31

The Killbelly Marsh Trail connected with the Copper River Trail half a mile south of the cabins. Ren turned the ATV onto the well-worn path that wove among the trees and rocks along the riverbank. The river was thirty yards wide and swift flowing. Near the banks, the water was clear and Ren could see the bottom, which was sand and rock. Toward the middle, the water deepened to a black flow.

Cork, who held on to Ren from behind, called, "Stop a minute."

The boy let the engine idle.

"Bodine's that way?" Cork pointed east, downriver.

Ren nodded. "About a mile."

"What's between here and there?"

"Bunch of cabins on the other side of the river. Summer places. I haven't seen anybody there lately."

While he considered the river as it flowed toward Bodine, Cork gently rubbed the place on his leg where the bullet had exited. "Okay," he finally said. "Let's keep going."

The far bank of the Copper River rose in a steep incline. Occasionally sunlight flashed off the window glass of a hidden cabin. A little farther on, they came to the place where the river funneled between rocky ridges as it curved northwest into the Huron Mountains. Ren glanced up the slope at the thick blackberry bramble that covered the entrance to the old mine where Charlie had hidden. From the river, the mine was impossible to see. He considered pointing it out to Cork, but thought better of it.

Cork tapped his shoulder and called, "Stop for a minute, Ren."

The boy brought the machine to a halt. Cork eased himself from the seat, walked to the river's edge, and scanned the far height.

"Any cabins along there?" Cork asked.

"No. Some new ones are being built near the county road, but that's a couple of miles away. I guess it's too hard to get equipment and stuff all the way to the river."

"What about on this side?"

"Nothing from here to the Hurons."

"Any logging roads, bridges, trestles?"

"Yeah. An old trestle crosses a few miles upriver. No trains run on it anymore."

Cork spent a minute considering the terrain.

It was a warm afternoon and humid as a result of the rain. The blackflies and mosquitoes that often plagued the woods in summer were gone, but the air was still alive with other insects that lazily buzzed past. Ren was aware of the deep tracks the ATV tires left in the wet earth, and he felt bad about it. ATVs weren't allowed on the trail, which was supposed to be only for hiking and snowmobiling.

Cork started back toward the ATV, then stopped and bent close to the ground. Without looking up, he said, "Your cougar's been here."

Ren got off his seat and knelt beside Cork. He saw the print clearly. And he saw something else. "Look. Scat." He walked over to the droppings, bent and sniffed. "Whew! If what Mr. Schenk said is true, that's got to be a cougar."

"I'll take your word for it," Cork said.

"Do you think he's following the river?" Ren asked.

"Maybe. Keeping to the trail because it's easier. Would make sense if he's hurt. Do many people hike here?"

"In summer. In fall, most of the trolls stay on the road and just drive around looking at the color from their cars."

"All right." Cork climbed back onto the ATV. "Let's see that trestle."

They rode for another fifteen minutes. The river rushed past tall cliffs and channeled through narrow cuts. Beside it, the ATV climbed hills and bounced across stony brooks. Ren felt the grip of Cork's hands around his waist, holding tight for balance. It made him feel good—important—to be involved this way. It made him feel as if he were doing something for Stash and Charlie's father and the dead girl. He was thinking that his father might be proud of him, too.

The old trestle loomed into sight, a black spiderweb of posts and beams. Ren stopped beneath it, and once again Cork dismounted and considered the area. This time Ren saw a dark stain on the inside thigh of Cork's jeans.

"You're bleeding," he said.

"I know." Cork didn't even look down. His eyes ran across the trestle from one end to the other. The south side broke from a stand of maples deep red with fall color. The north side disappeared into blue-green spruce. "You said this railroad isn't used anymore?"

"That's right. Not for years, I guess."

"Where does it come from?"

"An old logging camp at the edge of the Copper River Club, maybe five miles north. Like, twenty miles south, it connects with the main line to Marquette."

"The Copper River Club, you said?" He glanced back at the boy.

"Yeah. You know about the Copper River Club, right?"

"Some. But tell me what you know."

The Copper River Club was one of his favorite subjects, a favorite subject of everyone in Bodine, and Ren eagerly filled Cork in.

"There were these really rich guys a long time ago, like a hundred years, see? I mean the richest guys in the whole country. Henry Ford and guys like that. And they didn't want the Huron Mountains to be spoiled by logging the way the rest of Michigan was. So they bought up most of the land and built cabins for themselves and their families, and they won't let anybody in there who's not a member of the Club. They protect the woods and try to keep everything like it always was. Like, once there were plans to build a road from Bodine to L'Anse over on the Keweenaw. These guys kept it from happening. So there aren't roads or anything that go through that part of the U.P. Now movie stars and famous writers and people like that belong or they visit. A couple of years ago I saw Tom Cruise in Bodine. He was stopping for gas on his way up."

Cork nodded and looked impressed. "Tom Cruise? That must've been something."

"It was sweet."

"The river. Where does it go from here?"

"Keeps going northwest. In a few miles it becomes the west boundary of the Copper River Club."

"All right," Cork said. "Let's keep going with the river."

"You're sure? Maybe we should look at your leg."

"I'll be fine, Ren." He limped back to the ATV and climbed on.

Ren revved the engine and they took off.

A while later they came to a creek where the trail seemed to end. Ren killed the engine.

"This is Staples Creek, as far as we can go. Everything on the other side belongs to the Copper River Club."

"So we'd be trespassing?"

"That's right. And they have these guys who patrol looking for trespassers."

"Have you ever trespassed, Ren?"

He had, lots of times. It was a kind of challenge. Because the area was so vast and he never did anything to damage the land, he thought of it as harmless and not really wrong. It wasn't hard to avoid the men who patrolled. More often than not they traveled in pairs and talked, so you could hear them coming.

"Yes," he admitted.

"What's along the river?"

"Nothing. Well, almost nothing. A couple of miles from here there's a cabin that belongs to one of the security guys. I've never really been any farther than that."

"What happens when people get caught trespassing?"

"They just get asked to leave. These people, I guess they don't want a lot of trouble."

Behind him, Ren could feel Cork's eyes steady on the forest ahead of them. Although the Copper River Trail ended, on the far side of the creek was another trail, so faint that unless you knew it existed, you probably wouldn't see it. It was where the security guys walked when they patrolled. Secretly he hoped Cork would say to go on. Given the importance of their mission, and the fact that Cork was a sheriff and all, it seemed okay. Ren figured there was probably some legal right that allowed them to trespass in pursuit of answers to a crime.

Cork said, "Let's see how far we get before we're stopped. What do you say?"

"All right!" Ren lifted his arms as if they'd just scored a touchdown.

He eased the ATV ahead, through the foot-deep water of Staples Creek and onto Copper River Club land.

Before they'd reached the creek, they'd passed a number of "forties," tracts of land forty acres each that had been logged. Ren knew that in the early days Henry Ford himself had walked those woods, handpicking the trees that would be cut and milled for the side panels on his early station wagons. The trees on Copper River Club land had never been cut, and the forest felt different there, sacred in a way. When he'd trespassed on foot, it had been all right because he'd been careful where he walked. Now he was conscious of the destruction the ATV wrought in its passage: the torn underbrush, the ugly tracks, the noise and smell of the engine, which seemed like a desecration in that quiet place. He slowed, stopped, and killed the engine.

"What is it?" Cork asked.

Ren didn't quite know how to say it, and he mumbled.

"I didn't hear," Cork said.

"This doesn't feel right."

"Are we lost?"

"That's not what I mean."

Ren could hear the river to their left, a low steady murmur over stone. The sky was solid blue and out of it came a wind like a long breath exhaled. The trees swayed and the branches rubbed against one another with a sound that reminded him of old men complaining. He smelled the dank of wet earth and rotting leaves and felt the fullness of summer gone and the patient steady tread of winter coming from far beyond the horizon. All this belonged. The machine did not.

Cork was quiet, then said, "I understand. Let's go back. I've probably seen everything I need to anyway."

Before the boy could hit the starter again, a voice to their right commanded, "Hold it right there."

Ren turned and said under his breath, "Oh shit."

The man who'd spoken wore a green billed cap with *Copper River Club* in gold across the crown. He was dressed in a green uniform with a patch that said *CRC Security* on the shoulder of the right sleeve. Above the left breast pocket was stitched *Calvin*. The rifle he carried didn't need a patch or badge or identification. It pretty much spoke for itself.

He came through the trees with the stock of the firearm resting on his hip and the barrel pointing skyward. He walked carefully and didn't take his eyes off Ren and Cork. When he was a dozen feet away he stopped and let the weight of his glare sit on them. He was tall and thin. His pink, bloodless lips reminded Ren of the spongy underside of a mushroom.

"You're trespassing on private property."

"I'm afraid we got a little lost back there," Cork said from behind Ren. "The trail we were on just kind of ended."

"There's a sign where that trail ends tells you to turn around."

"Didn't see it. Must've blown down in the storm last night."

"I'll check on that. Right now you just turn around and go on back the way you came."

Cork nodded toward the rifle. "A Remington 7600?"

"It is."

"That could do a lot of accidental damage."

The man cradled the rifle lovingly in his hands. "Nothing accidental about the damage I intend to do with this baby. We got ourselves a mountain lion skulking around here."

"No kidding?" Cork replied. "A cougar? You sure?"

"Saw it with my own eyes a couple of days ago. Came nosing around my place up the river. I got a shot off, hit it I'm pretty sure, but it didn't go down. Means it's wounded and real pissed off. I was you I'd stay clear of the woods for a while."

"Thanks for the warning," Cork said.

The thin man settled his gaze on Ren and squinted. "You're Jewell DuBois' boy."

"Yeah."

"Then you ought to know better than to be on Copper River Club land. I catch you here again, I'll fry your skinny little ass, understand?"

"Yes, sir."

"And you," he said to Cork. "Next time, the Copper River Club will press charges. Am I making myself clear?"

"Perfectly, Calvin."

Under the security guard's stern scrutiny, Ren made a careful U-turn with the ATV and headed back the way they'd come. When they crossed Staples Creek and were on public land again, Cork tapped his shoulder and called over the sound of the engine, "That guy, his name tag said Calvin. His last name wouldn't happen to be Stokely, would it?"

"It is," Ren said.

"Calvin Stokely." Cork was quiet a moment as if he was thinking. "Your mom told me about him, said he used to scare her when they were kids."

"He still does."

"He's got himself a uniform, a big rifle, and an inflated sense of authority. Ren, I can't think of much that's scarier than that."

Ren laughed.

"You did great back there," Cork told him.

"Really?"

"You kept your cool. Didn't volunteer anything you shouldn't. Not easy when you're facing a man with a rifle. Now, think you can get us back to the cabins before I bleed to death?"

"You bet I can."

Ren smiled to himself with the pleasure that came from fair praise, and he guided them swiftly home.

32

Muddy Waters was on Main Street in downtown Marquette. It was a long, narrow room with high-backed booths like church pews along one side and tables along the other and a counter far at the back. Light came from the front window and from lamps in the ceiling, and there was a dim, intimate feel to the place. It smelled of strong brew and cigarettes.

They found the kid whose name was George but whom Charlie referred to simply as G.

"G hangs at Muddy Waters," she'd said. "He drinks coffee, smokes, writes. He says he's going to write a book just like some other famous guy who bummed around and wrote a book."

"Kerouac?" Jewell had said.

The girl shrugged her shoulders. "Dunno."

G was all arms and legs, lanky, awkward looking, sprawled on one side of a booth toward the back. He wore his hair in dreadlocks that fell like ropes over his face as he bent to scribble in a cheap wire-bound notebook. An empty cardboard coffee cup sat at his elbow. Smoke curled up from a cigarette wedged between the fingers of his left hand. He wrote with his right, using a Bic ballpoint. Jewell pegged him at seventeen, maybe eighteen years old.

"G," Charlie said.

The kid looked up. His eyes were sharp blue, his face the color of coffee full of cream. "Charlie. Whazzup?"

"Can we sit?"

"Who're they?"

"Like, friends."

He took a drag off the cigarette while he considered the two women. He waved his hand toward the high-backed bench on the other side of the table. Dina and Jewell sat there. He took a stuffed backpack off the bench where he sat and dropped it at his feet to make room for Charlie. He slid his notebook aside.

"I'm Dina," Dina said. "This is Jewell."

"Social workers?" G asked.

Dina shook her head. "Like Charlie said, just friends."

G put his right arm across the bench back behind Charlie and turned his blue eyes on her. "Haven't seen you in a while. Things between you and your old man must be okay."

"He's dead."

G took the news without any visible reaction. "Sorry." He considered his cigarette. "On the other hand, maybe not. You okay?"

"Yeah. But they think I did it."

"No shit?" His cigarette hand moved toward his mouth. "Did you?"

Charlie slugged him in the side, not hard enough to hurt. He looked at the women. "Not social workers, huh? Cops?"

"No."

"They're trying to help me," Charlie explained.

"So what are you doing here?" he asked her.

"G, Sara is dead."

That hit him hard. The diffidence he'd affected cracked and as the pieces of that façade fell away the face of a hurt child emerged. "You're lying."

"No. Swear."

"Fuck." He threw his cigarette into the empty cup. "How?"

"Somebody killed her, G."

"Ah shit, no. Jesus." He looked away, toward the empty wall at the end of the booth, and balled his fist as if he were going to hit something, someone. After a moment, he dropped his hand into his lap. "They know who?"

"I don't think so," Charlie said.

"Like they'd even care."

Dina spoke quietly. "I'm a private investigator, G, and I do care. I'd like your help."

He brought his wet blue eyes to bear on her. There was still anger in them. "Yeah? How?"

"When was the last time you saw Sara?"

He stared at her, maybe trying to remember, maybe trying to decide something about Dina. Jewell couldn't tell.

"Week and a half ago," he finally replied. "Just before she disappeared from Providence House. I should've known right away something was wrong."

He reached into his shirt pocket and pulled out a pack of American Spirits. He tapped a cigarette free, jammed it into the corner of his mouth, and lit it with a plastic butane lighter. He blew smoke toward the ceiling.

"Sara, she was on her way, you know? She had a compass, direction. She was going somewhere with her life. Talking with her was always trippy because she was always up. Believe me, that was something, considering all the shit before she came to Providence House."

"She told you?" Dina asked.

"We talked a lot."

"You're a writer," Jewell said, indicating the notebook. "What do you write?"

"My life. And hers." He tipped his head toward Charlie. "And Sara, and all the rest of us, the fucked and forgotten, the trash in the gutters of America's streets." He sucked on his cigarette and shot smoke out his nostrils.

Dina said, "Do you always notice when one of the kids is gone?"

He gave a quick shake of his head. "They come and go. Sometimes they talk, sometimes they keep it to themselves. And I'm not there every night."

Jewell wondered where he stayed other nights. G had money for cigarettes, for coffee. The dreads took time and care. His clothing was clean and decent. She knew that prostitution was a possibility.

"You watch," G said. "The cops'll make a show of trying to get to the bottom of it, but they won't come up with anything, and after a while everyone will forget about it. Who cares about a dead cat beside the road if it's not someone's pet, right?"

"Do you think she went back to prostitution?" Dina asked.

"No way. She was on a ladder and she was looking up." He took a long drag. "Damn."

"Talking to you, did she ever mention any names, anyone she might have been seeing?"

"Like a boyfriend? No. She was focused solid, I mean like a laser, on getting her life in order. She didn't have time for a guy right now."

"How about adults?"

He shook his head faintly. "Maybe at school, I suppose. Or her job. Plenty of adults there. There's the staff at Providence House. But she never said anything, and we talked about everything, I mean deep." He seemed to be wilting. "Look, I need some time with this. Alone, you know? You mind?"

"No, that's okay. Thanks for your help, G."

Jewell stepped from the booth and Dina scooted out after her.

"You go on," Charlie said. "I'll be right there."

They left Muddy Waters and walked into the late morning light. Down the street to the east, Lake Superior filled the gap between high buildings. Above it floated the paler ephemeral blue of the autumn sky.

From her purse, Jewell dug out her pack of Newports. "Cigarette?"

"No, thanks," Dina said. "I quit a long time ago."

"Me, too." Jewell lit up. "So where did that get us?"

"She probably wasn't tricking," Dina replied. "She wasn't involved with anyone. She was putting her life together. So . . ." She looked up at the sun and squinted. "Either what happened to her was completely random or there's a connection we're still missing."

Jewell looked back through her reflection on the front window of the coffee shop. As she did, Charlie leaned to G and they hugged as if they were survivors of a great tragedy. Charlie got up to leave.

"Street kids are tight," Dina said. "They look out for each other. I wish everyone did."

Charlie stepped out the door and Dina put her arm around the girl's shoulders.

"When I was on the streets, I knew a guy like G. He called himself Rimbaud, after a poet."

Charlie eyed her skeptically. "You were on the street?"

"In Chicago. When I was sixteen."

"How long?"

"A few months. It felt like forever. But it was better than home."

Charlie did something that surprised Jewell. She buried her face against Dina, and for a minute she wept.

Jewell reached out, stroked the girl's hair, and whispered, "It'll be okay, Charlie. It'll all be okay."

When she'd cried enough, Charlie pulled away and wiped her eyes with her coat sleeve. Then she walked with the women toward the car, looking less like a kid than a veteran of some long, horrible conflict.

33

*B*y the time Ren brought the ATV to a stop in front of Cabin 3, Cork was exhausted. His leg hurt like hell, and the spot on his jeans where blood had oozed covered most of the inside of his thigh. He eased himself from the seat behind Ren and almost collapsed when he put weight on his leg.

"I need to lie down," he told the boy. "Maybe sleep a little. If I'm not up when your mother and the others get back, come and get me, all right?"

"Sure," Ren said. His eyes dropped to Cork's thigh, and he winced at the big bloodstain. "Maybe I should look at your leg."

"I'll take care of it. Thanks for driving me up the river, Ren."

Cork turned and hobbled up the steps to his cabin. Inside, he took off his boots and gingerly removed his jeans. The jostling of the ATV ride had worked the butterfly bandages loose. Blood smeared everything from his crotch to his knee, and it was still seeping from the opened wound. He washed in the bathroom sink, silently cursing for not asking Ren for more bandaging before he sent the boy away. He was drying himself when he heard a knock at his door.

"Yeah?" he called.

"It's me," Ren said from the other side. "I brought my mom's medical bag. Just in case you needed something."

"Come on in." Cork struggled to his bunk.

Ren scooted a chair next to him, sat down, and bent to examine the wound. He didn't seem upset by what he saw.

"You probably shouldn't have gone," he said.

"Can you fix me, Doc?" Cork asked.

Ren grinned up at him. "Got insurance?"

Cork watched the boy work, his hands moving surely through the ministration. It felt odd, being cared for by one so young, but in a way, he was glad. Through all these unusual circumstances, in the face of enormous challenge, Ren had kept his head. He'd risen to each occasion without confusion or complaint, shown great heart, and Cork couldn't have been more proud of him than if the boy had been his own son.

When a clean gauze pad was in place over the wound, Cork said, "Thanks, Ren."

The boy became intent on putting materials back into the bag. "I just thought, you know, you might need some help. How's the pain?"

"I could use another Vicodin. They're on the sink in the bathroom."

Ren came back with the pill bottle and a yellow plastic tumbler full of water.

"You know, I've been thinking about the hero of your comic book," Cork said, after he'd taken the pill. "White Eagle."

The boy held the tumbler and eyed him uncertainly, waiting for him to go on.

"I don't know much about art, but I've heard the best comes when you tap who you are and what you know. I think you've got everything inside you to create a great hero, Ren."

The boy looked down and for a moment Cork thought maybe he'd trespassed, stepped over a line Ren held sacred.

Ren smiled shyly. "You really think so?"

"I do."

"I don't know. Maybe." He put the tumbler and pill bottle back in the bathroom. "When Mom gets home, I'll let you know she's here."

"And could you ask her for a pair of clean jeans and underwear?"

"Sure."

"Appreciate it." Cork let his head sink deep into his pillow.

Ren paused at the cabin door. "Was it important? You know, what we did, going up the river?"

Cork closed his eyes and tried not to concentrate on the pain. "What do you think we learned?"

Ren was quiet for a while. When Cork opened his eyes, he saw the boy poking a finger thoughtfully into his chin.

"I don't know. She could have got into the river almost anywhere," Ren said.

"When did you spot her?"

"Around sunset."

"And the shelter's not far from the summer cottages, right? So if she'd been dumped in the river somewhere in the vicinity of the summer cottages, it would have been broad daylight."

"Yeah."

"Would that have been smart?"

"I guess not. Someone might have seen them do it."

"Bingo. Upriver, where is there easy access if you were carrying a body?"

"There isn't. Not until you get to the trestle."

"Which connects with an abandoned logging camp on one end and a main line twenty miles away on the other. What would it take to come up that line twenty miles?"

Ren crossed his arms and hunched his shoulders. "I don't know. Something rugged. SUV or ATV maybe."

"Can you think of a reason someone would make that kind of trip into this kind of wilderness only to dump a body into a river that had the potential to deliver it back to civilization?"

Ren shook his head. "That would be stupid."

Cork tried to fight his fatigue, but he could feel himself getting drowsy. He wanted to stay with Ren, to guide the boy to the end of this thinking.

"If it's true these people are trying to get rid of Charlie because she saw the body in the river, then it's the river that's important. Besides the summer cottages and the trestle, where upriver is there easy access?"

Cork had to close his eyes again, he was so tired. He waited. Finally the boy said, "The Copper River Club. You think she came from the Copper River Club."

"You're a smart kid, Ren. Now I need a nap."

He didn't even hear the boy leave, but his sleep was a restless one. At one point he thought he heard a vehicle pull up outside and he thought dreamily, *The women.* He sank immediately back into his slumber and into a dream in which a cougar was chewing on the inside of his thigh.

A knock at his door woke him, and he climbed to a hazy consciousness.

"Yeah?"

"It's me. Ren."

"Your mom home?"

"Can I come in?"

Later, Cork would think how the boy had sounded timid, even a little afraid, but at the moment he was too sleepy to notice.

"Come ahead."

Cork closed his eyes tightly, this time to clear the sleep from them. He worked his neck and shoulders a little, which were sore from fighting to hold himself on the ATV. He let out a deep breath and pushed himself into a sitting position. Then he realized the boy wasn't alone.

34

Cork recognized the man who accompanied Ren into the cabin. He'd been at the old resort the previous day looking for the boy and for Charlie. The newspaperman. Johnson—was that his name?

"I apologize for barging in like this, Sheriff O'Connor," the man said. Despite the barging in, he'd stopped a discreet distance from Cork's bunk. "I explained to Ren the necessity."

"Is it okay?" Ren asked, looking concerned.

"It's okay," Cork said. Then he addressed the man, who once again reminded him of some bulky kitchen appliance with powerful legs attached. "You called me Sheriff. What exactly do you know?"

"Mind if I pull up a chair?"

"Might as well," Cork said. "This feels like it could take a while."

Johnson—Cork remembered his first name now: it was Gary—took a chair from the table, swung it close to the bunk, and sat down. Despite his size, his movements had the fluid grace of an athlete. Ren hovered in the background, still looking as if he were afraid he'd done something wrong.

"I apologize for prying, but it's pretty much the nature of my job, eh." Johnson smiled.

"Just tell me what you know."

"First of all, let me explain that all this is mostly by accident. On the other hand, what I know about reporting is that if you're good, you somehow end up in the right place at the right time. See, I thought Charlie might show up here, so I hiked over early this morning to keep an eye out for her."

"Hiked?" Cork shifted his hurting body and winced. "You came in on the Killbelly Marsh Trail?" He was thinking of the boot tracks.

"That's right." The newspaperman rubbed his hands together, fingers thick as brats. "I set up my stakeout behind the shed. As it got light, I noticed the bullet holes in the car parked back there. I took a good look and discovered blood all over the front seat. Believe me, that struck every reporting nerve in me. I didn't have the patience to wait around hoping for a glimpse of Charlie. I hoofed it back to my office and began making phone calls.

"Sheriff Corcoran O'Connor of Tamarack County, Minnesota, currently suspended from duty for failing to comply with a regulation requiring psychological counseling following involvement in an officer-related shooting."

He paused for a breath.

"Also very recently implicated in the murder in Winnetka, Illinois, of one Benjamin Jacoby, although according to my sources the police don't really consider you a suspect. At the moment, however, they're quite concerned that you've disappeared during the course of their investigation. The car with the bullet holes came from a lot in Kenosha, Wisconsin. Honest John's Quality Used Cars, to be exact, purchased with cash by a man who signed as Liam O'Connell. Three nights ago, police in Kenosha investigated a report of shots fired at the Lake Inn and the disappearance of the man who'd checked into Room 111, a man registered as Liam O'Connell and whose description—medium height, medium weight, thinning red-brown hair—would certainly fit you." He paused, opened his big hands as if expecting something to be delivered into them, and said, "So who tried to kill you in Kenosha, Sheriff?"

"You're a pretty smart guy. Why don't you tell me?"

"Could have been a random act of violence, I suppose. But that would be a pretty big coincidence, eh." Johnson sat back and the joints of the chair creaked. "From what I understand, this man murdered in Winnetka was from a connected family.

The father's a real hard-ass, blames you for his son's death. Nobody would confirm this but I suspect, given the man and his connections, that he's put out a contract on your life."

"Suppose that were true, think all your poking around has helped my situation any?"

Johnson nodded seriously. "I did my best to be discreet, Sheriff."

"You haven't done me any favors, Mr. Johnson."

"Gary. Call me Gary, eh." He leaned toward Cork again, and again the chair complained. "Look at it from my perspective. I see you here yesterday, limping, with a bulge near your crotch that's got nothing to do with anatomy. Then I stumble across that shot-up car of yours. Charlie's missing, her old man's dead. So I'm trying to put together a lot of disparate pieces of information, thinking that the more I know, the clearer the whole picture will become."

"What's going on has nothing to do with that girl's situation."

"I know that now." Johnson nodded toward the bloodied jeans Cork had dropped in a heap on a chair near the table. "You were hit in the Kenosha shootout. You came up here hoping Jewell could fix you. How bad is it?"

"I'll live. These sources you mentioned, who are they?"

"Colleagues."

"Chicago reporters?"

The man only stared at him, but Cork sensed that he'd hit the nail on the head.

"Great," he said. "Now they're down there asking all the wrong questions of all the wrong people."

Cork wanted to get up out of the bunk and slug the man, but he didn't have the strength, and what good would it do now? He heard a vehicle drive up outside. Ren opened the door.

"Mom!" he called.

A minute later the others walked in. Gary Johnson stood up politely in their presence and said, "Hello, Jewell. Ms. Willner. Hey there, Charlie. Come on in and join the party, eh."

35

*R*en stood back, feeling bad, as if he'd failed because he hadn't protected Cork from the newspaperman. Mr. Johnson had surprised him with the things he already knew, and he'd talked in a convincing way about how he needed to see Cork in person so he could help straighten everything out. Ren liked Mr. Johnson but he couldn't help thinking now that the newspaperman had tricked him. Ren didn't believe that he'd been stupid, said anything he shouldn't. Still, he felt lousy.

He leaned against the wall next to the door. Charlie stood beside him. The adults were all clustered near the bunk where Cork lay covered to his waist with a bedsheet.

"Look, Jewell," the newspaper reporter was saying, "some terrible things have happened in Bodine over the last couple of days. I'm just trying to figure them out."

"You have no idea of the trouble you could be causing, Gary."

Ren could tell she was furious.

"I think I do. I also think I could help if you'd let me," Johnson said.

While his mother and Mr. Johnson went back and forth, nobody else said anything. They were old friends, Ren knew, whose relationship went all the way back to when they were kids. He'd seen his mother tear into the man on many occasions when they disagreed over local issues. This was different. This was about family.

"I know the sheriff's situation has nothing to do with Charlie and what happened to Max," Johnson said. "I'd like to hear what she knows about her dad's death." He swiveled and eyed Charlie.

Ren eased closer to her so that their arms touched. Something in the way she looked at him sent a little electric jolt down his body, and he had to avert his eyes.

Mr. Johnson went on: "Three extraordinary events have occurred in town over the last two days. In a place like Bodine it's hard to believe they're not connected, eh. I'll tell you what I see. One"—he held up his index finger—"Max is killed and Charlie runs away. Two: The next day a girl's body is fished out of the lake. Not just any girl but someone with a connection to Providence House where we all know Charlie sometimes hangs out when her father's on a tear. Three: That same evening, Stuart Gullickson is the victim of a hit-and-run that nearly kills him. Stuart is a friend of Charlie's. You see what I see? Charlie's linked to everything."

"I didn't do anything," Charlie snapped at him.

"I didn't say you did," he said calmly. "But I believe you have a pretty good idea of what's going on."

"All we did was see her body, that's all."

"Where?"

Ren saw Cork raise his hand in an attempt to stop Charlie, but it was too late.

"In the Copper River," she said.

Cork sat back, as if what happened now didn't matter.

"In the river?" His large brow formed a puzzled overhang that shadowed his eyes.

"We didn't really," Ren said. "Stash did."

"Stash?"

"Stuart," Charlie clarified. "He saw it. Then Ren and me went looking for it that night and someone else was looking for it, too, on a boat. They saw us."

He nodded slowly, and Ren figured he was putting things together.

"So they were afraid you might say something and went to your father's place looking for you but found him instead. And he wouldn't give you away." He eyed Ren. "But nobody's come after you?"

"They think it was Stash who was with Charlie. That's why they tried to run him over."

The man addressed Jewell. "Do the police know all this?"

"No," she replied. "It sounded pretty far-fetched. We've been trying to get hold of something more solid we could offer them."

"Have you?"

"Not yet. What are you going to do, Gary?"

He shook his head a moment, considering. "This is a lot just to sit on. I can't believe the police haven't put some of this together already."

"The sheriff's investigator probably doesn't know Bodine. He may not realize the connection between Charlie and the dead girl. And there's no way he'd connect Stuart with any of this."

"What about Ned Hodder? He'd know."

"I'm not sure what Ned's told him," Jewell said. "As I understand it, it's not Ned's jurisdiction. Gary, promise me you won't talk to Ned. If anyone says anything to him, it should be us."

"You're asking a lot."

"We could just tie you up and keep you in a closet until all this is finished," Dina offered.

Ren laughed, but no one else did and he shut up quickly.

Mr. Johnson turned to her. "Dina Willner. Don't think I don't know about you."

"Then you know not to mess with me."

Mr. Johnson slowly stood. He towered over Dina. The way the two of them faced off reminded Ren of a sleek cougar confronting a grizzly bear.

"Wolverine two-time all-American defensive tackle," Mr. Johnson said.

"Twenty years and thirty pounds ago," she countered.

Cork laughed. "Gary, if she decides to wrestle you into a closet, believe me, you don't stand a chance."

Mr. Johnson said, "What I do or don't do will be because of Jewell and Ren and Charlie, because they're important to me."

Dina stared at him in a way that, had it been Ren, he'd have melted in a puddle of terrorized flesh.

"Despite your vocation," she finally said, "I believe you're not a bad guy at heart. I suggest you listen to that heart."

"He's on our side, really," Ren's mother offered.

"I'll have to take your word on that," Dina said.

"Tell you what I'll do." Mr. Johnson turned himself so that he spoke, more or less, to all the adults. "No more calls that might jeopardize you, Sheriff."

"I appreciate that."

"And I won't do anything that might expose Charlie or Ren to any more danger than they might be in already. But I want a promise."

"What?" Ren's mother said.

"That in the end this story is mine, Jewell. You don't talk to the *Mining Journal*. You don't talk to *60 Minutes*. You talk to me."

"All right."

Dina said, "You're used to reporting church suppers and town council meetings. What makes you think you can handle a story like this?"

Johnson glanced at Jewell. "You want to tell them?"

"Gary's got a Pulitzer," she said.

Dina looked at him skeptically. "For publishing the *Marquette County Courier*?"

"I returned to Bodine five years ago to take over the paper when my father died. For ten years before that I was a correspondent for the *New York Times*. Covered Desert Storm, then Africa. I've been in more firefights than most combat soldiers, Ms. Willner. Wounded twice. Care to see the scars?"

"I'll pass," she said.

"One more thing."

They all waited. Mr. Johnson swung his eyes toward Ren and Charlie.

"Don't do anything stupid," he said seriously. "I'm pretty fond of you all." He nodded in parting and started toward the door. "If I hear anything I think you ought to know, I'll tell you, okay?"

"Thanks, Gary."

"All this in Bodine." He shook his head.

"Know what this reminds me of?" Ren's mother said as he opened the door. "Tom Messinger."

He stood a moment looking out at the afternoon. "Another

sad chapter in the history of Bodine." He closed the door behind him.

Cork watched until Mr. Johnson drove away, then he turned to Jewell. "A Pulitzer prize? Jesus, did I underestimate him. And who's this Tom Messinger?"

"The boogeyman," Ren said.

"Don't, Ren," Jewell said. "Tom was no monster. He was just a kid who did something . . . incomprehensible."

"What?" Cork asked.

"It was more than twenty years ago," Jewell said. "Ancient history."

"I'd like to hear it."

"A girl was found in Lake Superior just south of town. She turned out to be a runaway. Murdered. For a while it didn't appear that it would be solved. Then Tom Messinger hung himself in his mother's basement. There was a note in his pocket confessing to the murder. It was tough on everybody in Bodine. Tom was a decent kid. We all liked him. He quarterbacked the football team, was looking at a full scholarship to his choice of schools. It was so bizarre."

"How'd it happen? Any idea?"

"It was right after the Bobcats won the championship that year."

"According to the sign at the edge of town, the only year," Dina said.

"So you can imagine it was a big deal around here," Jewell went on. "The Lion's Club threw a team banquet at the Ramada in Marquette. I was supposed to go. I'd been dating Ned, but we broke up. Anyway, after the banquet a bunch of the guys went to a cabin one of the parents owned and they had a party of their own, with alcohol, grass, whatever. As nearly as anyone can figure, when Tom was driving home from the party, he picked up the girl, who was probably hitchhiking. Exactly what happened after that only Tom knew for sure. He killed himself over it. Devastated his mother. The whole town, actually. It was a terrible shock."

Ren said, "If you go to the football field at midnight on Halloween and say his name three times his ghost is supposed to appear."

"Ren," his mother said, casting a cold eye his way.

"That's what everybody says." He suddenly remembered something. "Hey, we know where Sara Wolf's body came from."

Dina looked at Cork. "Is that true?"

He smoothed the sheet over his legs. "I think we have an interesting speculation. Go ahead, Ren. You tell them."

Ren waited, savoring their anticipation. "The Copper River Club." He saw the consternation in their faces. "We figured it's the only place upriver where someone could drop the body easily."

"The Copper River Club?"

It was clear to Ren that Dina had no idea what he was talking about. He explained, "It's a big private area in the Huron Mountains where only really rich people can go. We tried to get up there to have a look but Mr. Stokely stopped us."

"Stokely?" his mother said, scowling. "Isaac or Calvin?"

"Calvin."

"I don't know what the connection might be between the girl and the folks up there," Cork put in, "but I think it's worth checking."

Ren saw a dark dawning on his mother's face.

"I think I know what the connection might be. Delmar Bell."

"Delmar Bell?" Cork asked.

Dina said, "The handyman at Providence House."

"He and Calvin Stokely have been best friends since they were kids," Jewell said. "And for a long time they partnered driving semis cross-country. I've never seen Calvin's place, but I understand he has a cabin on Copper River Club property, right on the river itself."

"I've seen it," Ren said. "It's spooky."

Cork said, "You know these men, Jewell. Think they're capable of doing this kind of thing?"

From the expression on her face, Ren could easily believe his mother was in real pain. "I've never dealt with this kind of thing," she replied. "I would've thought it took a monster, somebody whose face you could look at and see the horror they're capable of. I don't know. I honestly don't know."

Cork turned his attention to Charlie. "You've got to talk to the police now. They need to know."

"No way." She stiffened against the wall. "I'm not talking to anybody."

"What about Constable Hodder?" Ren said. "You know him. He's all right."

She didn't reply.

Ren's mother said, "You won't be alone, Charlie. We'll be there with you the whole way, promise."

Charlie folded her arms across her chest. "They'll put me in juvenile detention. I've been there and I hate it. I hate cops."

"I'm a cop," Cork said.

"You're a gimp," she shot back.

Cork didn't seem to mind. He went on: "Charlie, I know you're scared. But if the guys who did these things—to your father, to Sara Wolf, to your buddy Stuart—are going to be stopped, the police have to know what you know. Do you see that?"

"I don't have to tell 'em," Charlie shot back. "Can't somebody else?"

"It would be best coming from you," he said evenly.

"I won't do it."

"What if . . ." Jewell began.

They all looked at her.

"What if I talked to Ned, told him what we know, and he was the one who took it to the Marquette sheriff's people? If you were the sheriff's investigator, Cork, how would you respond?"

"The first thing I'd want to do is talk to Charlie and Ren myself."

"But if you couldn't?"

"I'd certainly look into things."

"There," Charlie said, satisfied.

Cork didn't seem happy with this, but he finally nodded. "You'll talk to the constable, Jewell?"

"Yes."

"Mind if I go along?" Dina asked. "I might be able to make a few salient suggestions."

"All right," Ren's mother replied. She looked at Cork. "You'll be okay here?"

"Between Ren and me, we can handle Charlie, I think."

He tossed Charlie a kidding smile. In return, she offered him a defiant glare.

36

Jewell was at least six inches taller than Dina Willner. She'd coped with the loss of her husband and was raising her son alone. Generally speaking, she thought of herself as a capable woman. Yet, there was something about being with Dina that made her feel as if they could walk into hell together and have tea with the Devil without breaking a sweat.

"Thanks," she said as she guided the Blazer onto the main road into Bodine.

"What for?" Dina replied.

"Being here. Doing this. A lot more than you bargained for, I know."

"You're welcome."

Jewell glanced at the other woman. "You and Cork, do you go way back?"

"A couple of weeks is all."

"Why are you helping him like this?"

"It's a tangle of personal and professional reasons. Some unfinished business."

Jewell wondered if Cork was the personal or professional part.

"Do you have family back in Chicago?"

"Someone who's waiting for me, you mean? Not even a cat."

"Not even a cat?"

Jewell thought about that, considered what it would be like to come home every night to an empty apartment, to a silence broken only by the soft clatter of her own existence. Some-times at the end of a long day when she walked into the cabin and found that Ren and his friends had left a mess in the kitchen or the living room and she heard the sound of their roughhousing in Ren's room, she would think how pleasant it might be to have the place to herself, as clean and quiet as she'd left it that morning. But that thought always evaporated in Ren's presence when she asked him about his day and he shared with her the precious treasure that was his life.

Dina shook her head. "It's not what you think."

"What?"

"You're thinking, *Lonely life, wasted life,* something like that. Family and children, that's where it's at, right?"

She started to deny it, but Dina had spoken the truth. Jewell said instead, "My life's different, that's all."

"No." Dina looked at her pointedly, green eyes like jade knife blades. "You were thinking *better.*" She turned back to the road ahead. "I could remind you about all the pain you've gone through as a result of the choices you've made—a lost husband, and I'll bet you lose a lot of sleep over Ren—but what would be the point except to defend my own choices. My life is my life, yours is yours. End of discussion."

Jewell offered, "It feels to me like I'm not the one you're trying to convince."

"Look, I like what I do, and what I do requires a particular kind of life. I need to be able to be gone at a moment's notice without worrying about who I'm leaving behind, even if it's only a cat."

They were quiet as they approached the bridge over the Copper River.

"I had a snake once, a constrictor," Dina said in a softer tone. "I got it because if I needed to be gone, I could feed it a mouse and it would be fine for several days."

"What happened?"

"I found that I was coming home to a creature I didn't par-ticularly like, I couldn't talk to, felt cold to my touch, and that I got a rise out of only when it wanted something from me. I realized the snake was just like my ex-husband."

She turned to Jewell and gave a little shrug. They laughed as they crossed the bridge and entered Bodine.

Ned Hodder's office was empty and locked. In the window was a permanent sign giving a number to call if anyone needed assistance. Jewell punched in the number on her cell phone. Ned answered. The signal was weak, his voice choppy.

"Constable Hodder."

Jewell told him where they were and that they needed to talk.

"I'm south of town on the lake, checking on a possible break-in at a summer cottage. But everything looks fine to me. So wait right there. I'll be back in fifteen minutes."

True to his word, he swung his Cherokee onto Harbor Avenue a quarter hour later and opened his office. He walked to his desk, where a cheap wire-bound notebook lay open. He quickly closed it and slipped it into the top desk drawer. Besides his own chair, which was an old wooden affair on wheels that squeaked whenever they rolled, there was only one other chair available. "Wait here." He went through the metal door at his back.

Dina walked around the desk and looked at the drawer where Ned had stowed his notebook. "What was that he put away so quickly? From the guilty look on his face, you'd have thought it was drugs."

"Poetry, probably."

A surprised smile appeared on Dina's lips. "Your constable writes poetry? Is he any good?"

"I don't know. He never lets anybody see it. He thinks we don't know but everybody does."

"That's kind of sweet."

"He's a sweet guy."

Dina sat on the edge of the desk. "Known him long?"

"All my life. We even dated in high school."

"Didn't work out?"

"After graduation we went our own ways. I met my husband, Ned met his wife."

"He's married?"

"A widower."

Dina shook her head. "A sweet guy who writes poetry and is available. What's wrong with this picture?"

Ned returned with a folding chair. He waited until the women were seated, then sat down himself. He crossed his arms on his desktop and leaned toward Jewell, his big brown eyes full of interest.

"What did you want to talk to me about?"

Jewell glanced at Dina who nodded her approval that they proceed.

"We have an idea about how all the horrible things that have been happening here might be connected. Max's death, the girl in the lake, Stuart Gullickson."

Ned sat back with a puzzled look on his face. "Connected? All those things? This I gotta hear."

"I need a promise from you first."

He shrugged. "Run it by me and we'll see."

"Charlie's involved, but she doesn't want to talk to the police."

"Charlie's okay? Thank God."

"We want to keep her out of it as long as we can."

Ned opened his hands, as if accepting the deal. "That's fine by me, but this is really way outside my jurisdiction." His eyes swung from Jewell to Dina. "Why are you telling me? What is it you think I can do?"

Dina said, "You know the investigator. Talk to him, let him know the facts, point him in the right direction."

Ned rubbed a finger across his lips in contemplation. "I can try. So that's the whole deal? I pass the word along to Terry Olafsson but keep Charlie out of it."

"That's the deal."

"You have my word." He leaned forward again, his face full of anticipation. "Talk to me."

Jewell told him what Charlie and Ren had related: Stuart seeing the body in the river; the late-night search along the shoreline of Superior; the encounter with the mystery boat; and Charlie's experience at the trailer when the men killed her father.

Ned interrupted. "But it was Stuart who saw the body, not Charlie or Ren?"

"That's right."

"How do you know anything was really there—that it wasn't just a trick of the light or something?"

"Because the body showed up in the harbor here the next day."

"*A* body did. That doesn't mean it had anything to do with whatever it was that Stuart, who I'm sure was stoned out of his head, may or may not have seen."

"It comes together when you connect all the dots," Dina said.

"Okay." He raised his hands to slow things down a little. "Suppose the kids did see a body in the river—*the* body, why would anyone want them dead for that?"

"Because the river is the key," Dina replied.

Ned looked confused.

Jewell stepped in to help. "They don't want anyone to know that the girl's body came down the river, Ned, because that would point directly to them."

"Directly to who?" he said with a note of exasperation. "There's no one on the river. Outside town, there's almost no way to get to the river except along the trail or farther up at the Copper River Club." As he said those last words, an understanding seemed to dawn in him, and he looked concerned. "You're not saying . . . what? Some rich guys killed that girl and dumped her in the river?"

Jewell said, "The connection's not through money, Ned. The dead girl was living at Providence House."

"In Marquette?"

"That's right. Delmar Bell works at Providence House."

"So?"

"Who's his best friend, Ned?"

"Calvin Stokely." Ned's eyebrows met for a few moments as he put together the information and the insinuation. "Jesus, you're not saying Bell and Stokely did this, are you?"

"All I'm saying at this point is that the only connection we've found so far between the girl, Bodine, and the Copper River runs through Delmar and Calvin."

"Why would they do something like this?"

"We're not accusing them of anything at this point," Dina said, "but the circumstantial connections are certainly there, and at the moment that's all we have. So maybe it's time to start asking this Bell and Stokely some questions."

"Olafsson seemed to think the girl's death might have been suicide," Ned argued.

Jewell shook her head. "We've spent the day talking to people who knew her, Ned. It wasn't suicide."

He locked his hands behind his head, as if his skull were too full now and he was afraid it would split open. "Del and Calvin. Those two have always been creepy. But I can't just walk up to Olafsson and say, 'Take a look at these guys. They're creepy.'"

"It's possible he already has pieces of the puzzle you don't know about and when you give him what we've given you, it may all fit. I think you ought to try, Ned. Please," Jewell added on a softer note.

"Let me see if I can set something up." He picked up his phone and punched speed dial. He waited. Outside, the sky had grown hazy and the light in the room had dimmed a bit. "Terry, it's Ned Hodder. Give me a call when you can. It's important."

He hung up. "Voice mail. Let me try something else." He punched the buttons on the phone and a moment later said, "Yeah, Roberta, it's Ned Hodder in Bodine. How're you doing?" He listened, laughed lightly. "I know. Must be a full moon. Listen, I'm trying to reach Terry Olafsson but only getting his voice mail. Any idea where he might be? Uh-huh . . . uh-huh . . . okay . . . Yeah, I'd appreciate that, thanks." He set the phone in its cradle. "He's in court right now. Roberta'll page him, have him give me a buzz when he can."

Dina put her hand on the desk and Ned looked her way. "This Stokely who has the cabin on the river," she said. "Any chance of seeing his place? Maybe seeing him?"

"Why?"

"Curiosity. Don't you have it?"

The question appeared to catch him off guard and he seemed uncertain whether it had been a jab at his professionalism.

"What did you have in mind?" he asked warily.

"Do you ever have access to this Copper River Club?"

"I get up there maybe once a week."

"So it wouldn't be unusual for you to show up?"

"No. But look, I'm not going to go mucking around in some-one else's investigation."

"Who said anything about mucking? I'd just like to know the lay of the land. Is that possible?"

Ned stared at the phone a long time as if willing it to ring. Finally he looked up at Dina and said, "Why not?"

37

Charlie lay facedown on Ren's bed, sobbing quietly into a pillow. Ren stood near the closed door, hands clenched deep in his pockets, watching with miserable helplessness. He wasn't used to such raw emotion from Charlie unless it was anger, which he knew how to handle. He could rise to her fits of rage. He'd done it all his life. This was different. Charlie was different. She'd seemed to change almost overnight from his best friend into a person of mystifying moods.

"Are you okay?" he ventured.

"No." The pillow muffled the word.

"Do you need anything?"

She shook her head.

"Can I do something?"

She rolled over, wiping at her eyes with her knuckles. She looked fragile, which was a little disconcerting to Ren, who'd always thought of her as tough as a snapping turtle.

"She didn't have anybody, Ren. And neither do I."

"Who, Charlie? Who didn't have anybody?"

"Sara. Nobody to, you know, watch out for her. Nobody to care if she was safe or worry about her being grabbed off the street or whatever. I don't want to be like that, Ren. I want somebody to care about me."

"I care."

"Yeah, right." She rolled back over and returned to her sobbing.

Crying like this was the worst thing she'd ever done to him. He'd rather she'd slug him. In desperation, he went to the closet and pulled out his Nike shoe box. He sat on the bed beside her and opened the box.

"Charlie, look. I've never shown this stuff to anybody."

She lifted her head, saw what he held, considered it while she hiccuped a couple of times, then sat up. "What is it?"

"It's kind of like a treasure chest. I put all the stuff in here that I want to keep forever. Like this, see?" He picked up the stone he'd found on the shore of Lake Superior and cradled it in the palm of his hand. "See the figure there? What's it look like?"

She took it from him and held it near her face. "A wolf?"

"I'm Wolf clan. I just found it. I think I was supposed to find it."

She handed him the stone, and he put it back in the box and reached for something else. "Recognize this?"

"Yeah. That's the cast you made of the cougar track."

"It's pretty awesome, huh?"

Her eyes returned to the box, and Ren saw what she was looking at. He lifted it out.

"Know what that is?" he asked.

"It's just a resin bag. What's it doing in there?"

"Summer before last, you threw it at Skip Hogarth just before you tore into him on the ball field."

She seemed confused. "Why do you have it?"

"I don't know. It was just lying there after everybody walked off, so I picked it up. It reminds me of you, kind of. You really like baseball and you're not afraid to bust somebody's lip who needs to have a lip busted. And . . ."

"Yeah?"

"Well . . . sometimes when I'm alone here and I'm feeling kind of empty and sad, I take it out and hold it and it's like you're here, too, and I feel better, you know?"

"Seriously?"

"Totally. And look here." Ren pulled out a marble, a cat's-eye boulder with an amber-colored heart. "You remember this?"

Charlie stared at it and a smile slowly crossed her lips. "Smackdown."

Ren nodded. "Smackdown. The granddaddy of all boulders. I won it from you three years ago. Man, that was a great game of marbles that day."

"We haven't shot marbles in forever," she said, sounding a little sad.

"You got bored with it, remember? But I kept Smackdown. I think it was the only time I ever beat you at anything." He put the marble back in the box. "Charlie, as long as I'm around, you'll never be alone, I promise."

She looked at him with eyes like warm cocoa. "Really?" she whispered.

"I mean," he said, staring into the box as if suddenly mesmerized by what was there, "you're like my sister or something."

She sat back just a little. "Sister?"

"That's right."

"Sister," she said.

She was still holding the resin bag. The next thing Ren knew it caromed off his face. Charlie bounced from the bed and stomped out of the room, leaving him feeling like a doofus: clueless, stupid, and alone.

Cork was sitting on the sofa giving his leg a rest when the girl came from Ren's room and stormed toward the front door.

"Where are you going?" he asked, hoping he wouldn't have to get up and chase her, because he couldn't.

"Out."

"Not alone you're not." He used his best cop broach-no-dissent voice.

"Bite me," she replied, pulled the door open, and was gone.

Cork struggled to his feet as Ren walked in looking downcast. "What did you say to her?" Cork asked. He hobbled to the front door where he caught sight of Charlie, who'd stopped next to a hemlock tree and was hitting it with the side of her fist as if it had insulted her terribly.

"Nothing." Ren shrugged. "I was just trying to make her feel better. I don't get her."

"She's dealing with some pretty difficult issues right now. She's confused about a lot of things."

"She cries all the time." Ren sidled up beside Cork and looked outside. "She never used to cry."

"Ever?"

"I mean over nothing. Like right now."

"What happened just now?"

Ren took a breath and let out a heavy sigh. "She said she was afraid nobody cared about her. I told her I did. I told her she was just like a sister."

"You didn't."

"What's the big deal?"

Charlie rubbed her fists against her pants—wiping away the pain or wiping off hemlock sap, it was hard to say—stuffed her hands in her pockets, hunched her shoulders, and started walking away, kicking at the ground as she went.

"Let's go out on the porch, Ren, so we can keep an eye on Charlie."

They settled on the top step. It was late afternoon and quiet. A quilt of fallen leaves covered the ground; soft yellow sunlight and long dark shadows overlay everything. It reminded Cork just a little of autumn afternoons in Aurora when he sat on the front porch of his house on Gooseberry Lane and admired the street, the neighborhood, and the town he was happy to call home.

"You're coming right up against a line that all people cross, Ren. Every man, every woman. It's a tough one, so tough in fact that most societies seem to have developed all kinds of complicated rituals to help folks through it. You know, if you were a Shinnob in the old days, you'd have to know how to play a courting flute to get the girl you loved to marry you."

"I like Charlie. We're best friends. But I don't, you know, like her like a girl. I never even thought of her like a girl. I mean, look at her."

Ren's point was well taken. She was slender, breastless, and her head, covered by the dark bristle of her returning hair, looked like a dough ball rolled in iron filings. Her movements were fluid and explosive, and at the moment, kicking viciously at the ground, she resembled more a playground bully than a burgeoning young woman.

"Is there someone you do like that way?" Cork ventured.

Ren seemed totally absorbed in pulling at a wood fragment that was separating from a porch plank. Finally he said, "I guess. Her name's Amber. But I don't want to tell Charlie that."

"I wish I could say there's a right way to go about something like this, Ren, but every situation is different. Mostly I'd advise you to do your best to be honest with Charlie. If you tell her things that aren't true, hoping to spare her feelings, you'll only end up making everything worse in the end."

Ren succeeded in breaking loose the long splinter. He tested the point of it against his thumb. "Why does everything have to change?"

"I don't know the answer to that. I only know it does and that you can't stop it. What you can do is figure how to deal with it."

The boy looked at Charlie, who stood with her back resolutely turned toward them.

"So . . . should I talk to her?"

"What do you think?'

"I guess."

Ren roused himself, descended the steps, and headed toward Charlie.

The exchange with Ren caused Cork to think about his own children, the stumbling of his daughters particularly as they'd made their way across the threshold of adolescence to the worldly realizations that awaited them on the other side. His son was only seven, but he'd make that journey, too, someday. Cork missed them, missed them terribly, and he was suddenly afraid that somehow in his absence—or even because of his absence— horrible things might be happening to them. He wanted desperately to hear the music of their laughter, feel the bump of their hearts against his chest. He wanted to protect them, but it felt to him as if they were on the far side of the sun.

Watching Ren make his awkward way toward Charlie, struggling to find the right words to keep their friendship sealed, Cork understood that at the moment he couldn't do anything about his own children. He could, however, do something about these. And he would. He'd be damned if he'd let any harm come to them.

* * *

Ren's feet crunched on dry leaves. He knew Charlie heard him coming, although she didn't turn around. He stopped a few feet shy of her.

"Charlie, I'm sorry."

He circled so that she had to look at him.

"What do you want?" She glared at him.

"I don't want you mad at me. Well, that's okay really, 'cuz you've been mad at me before. I just don't want you mad because you think . . ."

"What? Think what?"

"I don't know." He felt hopeless, all the right words hiding. "If you were gone, I think I'd die."

"So go die."

"Damn it, Charlie, I mean it. Remember when my dad died, everybody got all weird around me, even my mom. Everybody except you. I could still goof around with you, talk to you like always. That helped more than anything anybody else tried to do for me. I mean, you were just being you, you know. I mean it. If I lost you, I'd be lost, too." He scratched his forehead over his right eye although nothing itched there. "I'm sorry if I hurt you or something. . . ."

"Shut up." She said it quietly, without anger. She stared at her boots. "I don't know what's going on, Ren. Sometimes I want to cry for no reason. Sometimes I feel all this stuff and it scares me because I don't know where it's coming from. I look in the mirror and I hate who I see. This head." She slapped at the dark bristle. "I'm not pretty like Amber Kennedy. I don't have boobs."

"You want boobs?" he asked incredulously.

"I didn't used to but I do now. I don't know what's going on."

"Look, I think it's a heredity thing. Did your mom have big boobs?"

"The pictures I've seen of her, yeah, I guess."

"Well, there you go," he said with a flourish of his hands. "You'll have boobs, too, someday. I'll bet anything. Ask my mom. She knows all about that stuff."

Charlie glanced up, frowning a little. "I should ask Dina Willner. She's the one with the boobs. *You* sure noticed."

"Ah jeez, Charlie. She's, like, pretty and all, but way old. I know that."

"You don't like her?"

"Well . . ." He thought about what Cork had advised. The truth. "I like looking at her and all, but I don't really want to talk to her or anything. I like talking to you."

"You do?"

"Yeah. Way better."

She smiled. "I like talking to you, too."

Ren reached out and rubbed the bristle on her scalp. "I probably shouldn't have helped you shave your head, huh?"

"It's okay. But I'm thinking I'll let it grow for a long time before I cut it again."

Ren shook his head doubtfully. "If it gets too long you'll trip over it when you're running bases."

She punched his arm lightly. "Not that long, dude."

"And listen, if you had boobs you probably couldn't swing a bat."

"Yeah, but I'd have a nice cushion whenever I had to slide into second."

They laughed, and for a little while Ren's world felt right again.

38

The road to the Copper River Club was narrow and not well maintained. Jewell had always suspected that this was because the high-profile members didn't want to broadcast the true nature of the bit of Eden they'd fenced off for themselves at the end of that road. She'd never been past the main gate, although she was acquainted with many in Bodine who had, folks who worked in the compound as cooks or on the grounds crew or doing maintenance or security. And there was Ned. She'd been told that each family had its own lodge, but there was a common dining hall in which truly magnificent meals were served. By the standards of most people of enormous wealth, the accommodations of the compound would be considered rustic. However, the idea at the heart of the Copper River Club, as Jewell understood it, was to preserve forever the virgin beauty of the Huron Mountains and to offer the members a unique escape from their tailored estates and the glass-and-concrete towers from which they oversaw their industries and their fortunes. Which might have made one think a bit of Thoreau and Walden Pond but for the gate across the road, the guard box there, and the firearms carried by the security personnel.

"Afternoon, Wes," Ned said to the guard who leaned in the window of the constable's Cherokee.

Wes Barnes was a resident of Bodine, though not a native. He'd come for the job at the Copper River Club. He was not particularly tall, but he was muscular, with an octopus-shaped scar on his jaw that spread tentacles down his neck. The scar suggested violence, but Jewell hadn't been able to figure exactly what kind. Disfigurement from fire or an explosion was her best guess.

"Ned." Barnes greeted him, then looked at the women. "Jewell, how are you?"

"I'm fine, Wes."

He studied Dina with an eye that seemed to be considering more than just security. "I don't believe I know you."

"Right back at you," Dina said.

"I need to talk to Calvin Stokely," Ned broke in. "Is he around?"

"He went off duty a couple of hours ago," Barnes replied.

"Mind if I drive up to his place, see if I can catch him there?"

"What's the nature of your business?"

"That's pretty much between him and me."

Barnes's eyes crawled like spiders over Jewell and Dina. "And between them, too, apparently." He shook his head. "I can't clear you, Ned, but you want to talk to his brother about it, fine by me. I'll have him come down."

"Appreciate it, Wes."

"No problemo."

Barnes returned to the guard box.

"His brother?" Dina asked.

"Isaac Stokely. Head of security."

"Isaac. He killed their father, right?"

"Right. Protecting his brother and their mother. Still doing his best by Calvin, who's never been able to hold down a job. Got him on the payroll up here, gave him a place to live."

Barnes stuck his head out and called, "He's on his way."

Ned waved a thanks through the open window.

Dina settled back in her seat. "Is this Isaac likely to let us in?"

Ned shrugged. "He's a tough one to read. I make an official visit up here once or twice a week, just to check in on issues of interest to both the Club and the town. I always let Isaac know I'm coming, so getting through the gate's never a problem. Unannounced like this, well . . ." He finished with a shrug.

"What's he like?"

"You'll see for yourself in a few minutes. Left Bodine for a long time, came back."

"A lot of people seem to have done that around here," Dina said. "What's the attraction?"

"Bodine's got its problems, but it's basically a good place to live," he replied.

"A little deadly these days, seems to me."

Ned turned so that he could speak to her over the seat back. "Believe me, this is unusual. In the time I've been constable, I've never dealt with anything much worse than folks who've had a little too much to drink and maybe get a little belligerent, barking dogs, vandalism once in a while, the very occasional break-in. A lot of people in town still don't lock their doors and most don't worry about walking alone at night. It's a good life and folks appreciate that. Heck, it's been a good twenty years since we've had anything like this happen."

Barnes stepped out of the guard box and lit a cigarette in the cup of his hands. A couple of minutes later, a Land Cruiser drove up and stopped on the other side of the gate. Isaac Stokely got out, spoke to Barnes for a minute, then came to the constable's Cherokee.

The dominant characteristic of Stokely's face was a black handlebar mustache, which he took care to keep waxed, so that he greatly resembled the image Jewell held of a lawman of the old Wild West. The pupils of his eyes were small and dark, and whenever she encountered Stokely on the streets in Bodine, those eyes bored right into her. She didn't know him well; he was older by several years. When she entered high school, he'd already left for boot camp to train to be a grunt in Vietnam. After the killing of his father, he returned to duty and remained in the military long after the war was over. When he finally returned to Bodine wearing civilian clothes, he'd become a taciturn man given to intimidation through long, piercing stares. As far as Jewell knew, he never talked about the life he'd lived during his absence from Bodine, but in a small town silence breeds rampant speculation. All kinds of dark, covert deeds had been ascribed to him. In order to have landed the prized position as head of security for the Copper River Club, he probably had contacts in high places.

He put a hand on the top of Ned's Cherokee, as if to hold it there until he was finished with his business. "What's the trouble, Ned?"

"No trouble, Isaac. Just hoping I could talk to your brother."

"What about?"

"Like I told Wes there, it's something I'd rather keep between me and your brother."

"Afternoon, Jewell," Stokely said. He drilled her with his small dark pupils, then did the same to Dina. "I don't believe I know you. I'm Isaac Stokely."

"Donna Walport."

"You ladies a part of whatever it is that concerns Calvin?"

"I'd like them there with me," Ned said.

Stokely squinted at the constable. "Tell you what, Ned. You give me a good idea what this is all about, I might be more inclined to let you through."

"All I can tell you is that it's official business."

"Got a court order of some kind?"

"I'd like to keep it a little friendlier than that if I can, Isaac."

Stokely tapped the top of the vehicle while he considered its passengers. "Got to be honest with you, Ned. I haven't heard anything from you that makes me feel compelled—or even inclined—to open the gate. All a little too vague for my tastes. The folks up here value their privacy highly, and it's a big part of what they pay me for. You understand."

"They won't even know we're here, Isaac. I guarantee it."

"Uh-huh." Stokely stood up straight and pulled a pack of Juicy Fruit from his shirt pocket. He took his time easing out a stick, undoing the silver wrapper, putting the gum into his mouth. He crumpled the wrapper and rolled it around in the middle of his palm.

"Tell you what I'll do. I'll let Calvin know you'd like to talk to him, and I'll suggest he stop by your office. How's that?"

"I'd rather see him right now."

"Take it or leave it, Ned."

"Then I guess it'll have to do."

"Glad you understand. Folks." He put his fingers to his brow in a lazy salute and stepped away.

Ned turned the Cherokee around and started back toward Bodine. "That got us exactly nowhere," he said.

"Is there another way in?" Dina asked.

"Yes," Jewell replied. "The same way Ren and Cork went. Impossible in the dark. What now?"

Ned turned a bend in the road, and when the trees hid them from the gate he pulled to the side. "Let me try Olafsson." He punched in the number, waited, finally said, "It's Ned Hodder again. I've got some information I think you'd like to hear. About the Max Miller killing. Give me a call when you can." He closed the phone. "Voice mail still. Court should be done by now. Maybe he's gone home for the day."

Dina leaned toward them from the backseat. "Back there you said nothing like this has happened for twenty years. You were talking about Tom Messinger, right?"

"You know about Tom?"

"Jewell told me. And it occurs to me that there are similarities here."

Ned glanced at Jewell, then turned back toward Dina, frowning as he worked the comment over in his head. "That was a long time ago. And Tom's dead."

"Humor me, okay? The murder took place after a wild party, is that right?"

"That's always been the theory."

"Maybe Tom Messinger didn't leave the party alone. Maybe he wasn't the only one in the car that night. Do you know if anyone ever bothered to find out?"

Ned shrugged. "He killed himself. He left a written confession. End of story, I suppose."

"Who else was on that championship team?"

"I was," Ned said.

"Besides you."

"A lot of guys."

"Any of them still live around here?"

"Del and Calvin," Jewell leaped in. "They were the star running backs."

"Were you at that after-banquet party, Ned?"

"Yes."

"Were Del and Calvin there?"

"They wouldn't have missed it."

"Is it possible they were with Tom Messinger that night?"

"I suppose it's possible. God, I'd love to ask them."

Dina said, "You can't get to Stokely right now, but Delmar Bell doesn't live behind a gate."

"Way out of my jurisdiction," Ned said.

"So ask as a concerned citizen. Be interesting to see if he squirms."

Ned's cell phone chirped. He lifted it and looked at the LED readout. "It's Olafsson." He answered, "This is Hodder. . . . Yeah, I see. . . . Jesus . . . oh, Jesus . . . No, I'd rather talk to you in person. I'll meet you at my office in half an hour. . . . No, at my office. You won't be sorry when you hear what I have to say." He ended the call and sat a moment staring ahead. "Our deal's off. Let's go get Charlie and Ren. They need to tell Olafsson their story. And we won't be talking to Delmar Bell."

"Why not?" Jewell asked.

"Because this afternoon somebody shot him in his apartment behind Providence House. He's dead."

39

Charlie was sullen the whole way into Bodine. Ren sat beside her, quiet, too. Cork rode up front beside Jewell, who followed Hodder in her Blazer. Dina rode with the constable.

It was evening, daylight almost gone. When they crossed the bridge over the Copper River, Cork looked at the water below; its swift, roiling surface was mostly silver-blue, reflecting the sky. He thought of the river as a living thing. The surface was its skin; the pale streaks where boulders disturbed the flow were scars on that skin. He wondered what the river knew about the girl's death but could not tell. His old friend Henry Meloux, the Ojibwe Mide, might be able to interpret the voice of the river and divine its secrets, but to Cork it spoke not at all.

They parked in front of the constable's office on Harbor Avenue. Hodder unlocked the door, went inside, and turned on the lights. He disappeared through a door at the back where Cork saw the bars of a holding cell. He heard Hodder's boots thumping down wooden stairs, and a moment later the sound of them returning. Hodder brought with him several folding chairs. Cobwebs hung between the legs. He set the chairs against the wall and opened them one by one, brushing at the cobwebs.

"Sorry," he said. "I haven't crowded this many people in here in a long time."

Cork noted the furnishings were spare: a fine old wooden desk, a vintage rolling chair, a couple of tan metal file cabinets. On the wall next to the door was a bulletin board pinned with wanted posters, an emergency evacuation route, assorted flyers related to town events, and a photograph of Hodder standing on a dock holding up a lake salmon and grinning like an idiot. Framed certificates hung on the other walls. Occupying the space directly behind the constable's desk was a print of Renoir's *Luncheon of the Boating Party*. Cork smiled broadly. The same print hung in his own office back in Aurora.

"Anybody want coffee?" Hodder asked. "Be glad to make a pot."

Nobody responded and he let it go. He sat down and one by one the others followed suit. Charlie slumped in her chair with her arms clasped across her chest and a defiant look in her eyes.

"Introductions first," Cork said. "I'm Corcoran O'Connor, Jewell's cousin. I'm sheriff of Tamarack County, Minnesota." He reached across the desk and shook Hodder's hand.

When he'd heard about Bell's murder, Cork knew he couldn't sit on his hands in the shadows any longer. A girl was dead. Another kid was in the hospital. Someone was after Charlie. Ren might even be a target, too. Cork understood the risk of revealing himself to Hodder, but it was what he had to do. He'd find a way to deal with Jacoby; first he had to deal with this.

"Family reunion?" Hodder smiled at Dina.

"Not really, Ned," Dina said. "I'm not related to the family at all. My real name is Dina Willner. I'm a security consultant."

Hodder frowned. "Why the charade? What are you doing up here?"

"That's a long story and doesn't have anything to do with what's going on," Cork said. "But we'd be glad to help in any way we can."

Hodder thought about it. "I guess I appreciate that."

"Why don't we start with Bell's death," Cork offered. "I can't imagine it's a coincidence, him killed just as Jewell and Dina start asking questions."

"If Del was involved in the girl's death, why kill him?" Hodder said. There was a coffee mug on his desk. He wrapped his hands around it and rolled it back and forth between them as if he were trying to sculpt it into a new shape.

"I never liked him," Charlie said. "He was always looking at me."

"At Providence House?" Jewell asked.

"Whenever he was at our place drinking with my dad. At Providence House he was just kind of around. He didn't really talk to us or anything."

"He was the one who told you about the shelter, right?" Dina said.

"Yeah. At first I wasn't sure about it, because I knew he'd be there and I thought he was creepy, but he never bothered me."

"What about the other kids?" Dina asked. "He ever bother them?"

"I don't know."

"Did you ever see him talking to Sara?"

Charlie thought about it. "Maybe, but not like serious or anything."

"You know who Calvin Stokely is, right?"

"Sure."

"Did you ever see him at Providence House?"

"No."

"Look, maybe we're way off here," Jewell said. "Maybe Del and Calvin had nothing to do with this."

"Most murders involve people who know one another. Sara Wolf knew Delmar Bell," Cork said, "and the connection through Stokely to the Copper River is hard to ignore. And we're not trying to convict anybody yet, just looking at possibilities. But you know these guys, Jewell. What do you really think?"

"I hate to think what we're thinking about anybody."

"What about Stokely? Could he have killed Delmar Bell?" Dina said.

"Why would he?" Jewell replied.

"Maybe when Del saw us at Providence House, he panicked and Stokely was afraid he'd talk."

Outside, dark had settled gently over Bodine. The flash of headlights crossed the windows and through the glass came the sigh of engines dying. A minute later Detective Sergeant Olafsson came in followed by a woman, a uniformed sheriff's deputy. He paused and scanned the gathering in Hodder's office.

"What's this," he said, "a town meeting?"

Hodder said, "You know Ren DuBois already. And Ms. Willner."

"I thought it was Walport," Olafsson said.

"Willner, actually," Dina said. She pulled a business card from her pocket and offered it.

Olafsson studied the card. "Security consultant. What's that exactly?"

"Among other things, I do private investigation."

"She was with the FBI," Ren said.

"That so?" Olafsson didn't sound impressed.

"This is Jewell, Ren's mother," Hodder went on. "And Cork O'Connor, Jewell's cousin. Also a sheriff in Minnesota."

"Sheriff." He shook Cork's hand without enthusiasm. "Seems like we got plenty of help, eh?" He didn't sound excited. His stern gaze settled on Charlie and he stepped toward her. "You must be Charlene Miller. I'm Detective Sergeant Olafsson." He extended his hand.

The girl didn't respond, didn't even look up from the spot on the floor where she'd nailed her eyes, just sat with her arms folded across her chest and her lips cemented in a thin line. Olafsson drew back his hand.

Hodder stood up. "Have a seat, Terry."

"Siddown," Olafsson said. "I'm fine. All right, who's going to lay it out for me?" He crossed his arms, as if mimicking Charlie's obstinate gesture, and he stared at her, which did no good since she didn't look at him. "Charlene?"

"I'm not saying anything," she said under her breath.

"That so?" Olafsson swung his gaze to Ren. "How about you?"

The boy glanced at Charlie, who was locked so tight in herself, Cork doubted there was any key that would open her now. Ren looked to his mother, who nodded.

He told it in pieces, chunks of story broken by "mmm's" and "uh's." In the end, however, a fairly complete narrative emerged including even the details that he'd probably rather not have Olafsson know, particularly that the kids were getting high at the old picnic shelter on Copper River when Stash saw the body. Olafsson listened, jotted notes, and stopped the boy only a couple of times to ask a point of clarification. Ren told Charlie's story, too, of what happened at the trailer. Olafsson asked Charlie, "Is that correct?" The girl's only reply was a silent nod.

Hodder stepped in to make the connections: Charlie and Sara Wolf and Providence House, Providence House and Delmar Bell, Bell and Calvin Stokely, Calvin Stokely and the cabin on the Copper River. And finally the speculation about Stokely, Bell, and the dead girl twenty years ago.

The detective put his notepad to his forehead and closed his eyes a moment. "Okay," he said. "If these men killed the Wolf girl, and if they were willing to kill these other kids who saw the body in the river, why dump the body there in the first place? Why not just bury it?"

Cork asked, "Has the autopsy been done? Do you know the cause of death?"

"I haven't had a chance to look at the report." Then Olafsson added defensively, "I've been busy. A lot's been going on."

"Any way you can find out?"

"What difference does it make?"

"Maybe they didn't dump her body. Maybe she wasn't dead when she went into the river," Cork explained.

The blond feathers that were Olafsson's eyebrows dipped toward each other. "You think she went into the river on her own? What, tried to run or something? Drowned?"

"It's a possibility."

"Huh." Olafsson pulled a cell from inside his jacket and punched in a number. "This is Terry Olafsson. Give me Wayne Peterson. . . . page him then. I'll wait." He kept the phone to his ear and eyed Charlie. "One thing nobody's told me is where you went after you found your father dead. Did somebody hide you?"

Charlie stubbornly maintained her silence.

Olafsson spoke to Ren. "Do you know?"

"She didn't tell me," he replied quickly.

"Right," Olafsson said. Then he spoke into the phone. "Yeah, Wayne, it's Terry. Say, I haven't had a chance to look at your preliminary autopsy report on the Wolf girl's death. What's your initial finding for cause of death? Uh-huh. . . . Uh-huh. . . . When will the analysis be complete? Uh-huh. . . . Okay. Thanks, Wayne. 'Preciate it." He ended the call and slipped the phone back into his jacket. "Drowning, he says. Which would be consistent with falling into Lake Superior. We won't know where she died until they've finished analyzing the water in her lungs."

"Jesus, Terry," Hodder said, rising from his chair. "You think all of these odd things are coincidental? Maybe in a city like Marquette, but not up here."

"What do you want me to do?" Olafsson said.

Dina spoke up for the first time. "It would be interesting to talk to Calvin Stokely, don't you think?"

Olafsson lifted his hands as if quieting a restless mob. "Everything you've told me that you believe connects Stokely to the girl's death is pure speculation. I'm more than a little reluctant to barge into the Copper River Club without something a lot stronger."

Olafsson's cell phone rang, the ring tone playing a snippet of a tune vaguely familiar to Cork. As Olafsson pulled his phone from his jacket pocket, Hodder, who'd noticed Cork's slightly furrowed brow, leaned over and whispered, "The Wolverine fight song."

"Yeah?" Olafsson answered. He listened. "I see. I'd be interested in knowing if you find anything that we can trace to Sara Wolf. . . . All right. Keep me posted. Oh, Earl, have you got a TOD on Bell yet?" He looked up at the ceiling. "Killed between three-thirty and four? Thanks." He put the phone away. "State police. I asked them to keep me informed during their investigation of Bell's murder. They've been going through his place. They found Rohypnol. A lot of it."

Rohypnol. The date rape drug.

"All right. I'll go up there, talk to this Stokely." Olafsson pointed to Hodder. "I want you with me." To the deputy who'd come with him he said, "Stay here until I get back, Flo. I'd appreciate you folks sticking around, too. And, Ms. Miller," he said to Charlie, "as of right now, you are in protective custody."

"Meaning?" Jewell said.

"While I'm gone, Deputy Baylor here will make arrangements for Charlene to stay with the juvenile authorities in Marquette."

"Is that really necessary?" Jewell shot back.

"Look, she's a material witness to a murder, Ms. DuBois. In addition, if what you're all telling me is true, then her safety's an issue. What would you do if you were me?"

"I'm not going to juvie," Charlie said.

"Charlene, I'm not giving you a choice here. Flo," he said to the deputy, "she's your responsibility."

"Understood," Baylor responded.

Dina said, "We couldn't get past the front gate at the Copper River Club."

"You didn't have jurisdiction," Olafsson replied.

"They've got money," Dina said. "My experience is that money usually trumps everything but a court order."

"We'll try it friendly first."

Dina shrugged. "Your call."

40

*F*or a little while after that, the constable's office felt like a tomb, with Charlie buried in it.

The look on Charlie's face—a twisting of fear, anger, and betrayal—hurt Jewell deeply. She felt responsible, as if she'd guided the girl unwisely. How could she make Charlie understand that Detective Olafsson was right? Safety was the most important concern, and Charlie was far better off in the custody of the Marquette authorities than open to the threats posed by the dark woods that isolated the old resort. In those woods, anything could hide.

Poor Ren looked pathetic, studying Charlie with such concern. Maybe he felt guilty, too, because he'd been the one who told her story. Maybe he saw that as betraying her to the enemy. But he'd had no choice.

"I'm not going," Charlie said, talking to the floor.

"It would only be for a short time, isn't that right, Officer?" Jewell said.

"I don't know, ma'am."

Charlie lifted her head and pointed her chin at Jewell. "Why can't I stay with you?"

"You wouldn't be safe."

Charlie turned to Dina. "Would you be there?"

"I'd be there," Dina assured her.

"Then I'd be safe."

A warm smile touched Dina's lips. "I'd make sure of it."

Charlie looked at Jewell again, accusing. "See?"

"That may be good enough for us," Cork put in gently. "But I don't think Detective Sergeant Olafsson will see it the same way."

"I didn't want to come here," Charlie said. "I didn't want to tell him anything. I didn't want to tell anybody."

Jewell got up from her chair and knelt beside Charlie. She laid her hand on the girl's shoulder and looked into her stubborn, frightened eyes. Oh, how many times had she seen this look over the years? How many times had she spoken to Charlie like a mother?

"Sometimes we have to do things we don't want to, and we do them because we know they're the right things to do. If you kept quiet and the men who killed Sara walked away free, how would you feel, Charlie? Especially if they're the same men who killed your father?"

Charlie didn't answer, but her eyes glossed with tears, and Jewell held her.

"Are you hungry?" Jewell said quietly. "Sometimes a full stomach can brighten a pretty dour prospect."

The girl nodded.

"I'm hungry, too," Ren said.

Jewell stood up. "Who else?"

"I'd eat," Cork said.

"You don't have to ask me twice," Dina threw in.

"How about a slew of cheeseburgers from Kitty's?" Jewell suggested.

"And fries?" Ren said.

"All right, fries."

"And a milkshake?"

"A milkshake it is. Chocolate?"

"Awesome."

"How about you, Charlie?"

The girl gave her slender shoulders a shrug, then nodded.

"Officer?" Jewell said to the deputy.

The woman Olafsson had referred to as Flo was stocky, with a plain, square face and deep-set suspicious eyes. She'd moved to Hodder's desk and had seated herself in his chair.

"This Kitty's, where is it?"

241

"Right next door."

"They have onion rings?"

"The best."

"Well, then, all right. As long as you're offering. I'll take some rings and a small coffee, black. Here," she said, reaching toward the back pocket of her khaki uniform pants, "let me give you some money."

Jewell waved her off. "Think of it as small-town hospitality."

Cork stood up. "I'll give you a hand."

"Me, too," Dina said.

"Ren?" Jewell looked at her son.

He shook his head, eyeing Charlie. "I'll stay."

"Be right back," Jewell said.

Outside, Harbor Avenue was lit by street lamps. Halloween was approaching, and witches, ghosts, and goblins cavorted among giant orange pumpkins in the windows of the shops along the street. Many of the establishments were already closed for the night. The sidewalks were nearly empty. Once summer ended, there was nothing you would call a nightlife in Bodine except for weekends, when leaf peepers or snowmobilers took over the town. A cool breeze came off the lake, and leaves crawled the street with a scraping sound like crabs across rock.

"The food was a good idea, Jewell," Dina said. "But are we really going to let them take Charlie?"

"You have a better idea?" Cork asked.

"Piece of cake to spring her."

"Don't forget, Dina, I'm trying to keep a low profile here. And the truth is, Charlie's much safer in their hands."

"Did you take a good look at her?" Dina persisted. "Kid looks like she's about to be tortured."

"It won't be a picnic, I'm sure," Jewell said, "but Charlie's a very strong young woman."

"Strong women get scared, too."

"Let it go, Dina," Cork said. "We're not interfering."

She eyed him with obvious disappointment. "This from you? A few days ago in Minnesota, I watched you walk into the wilderness knowing that a crazy man was out there waiting to kill you, and you did it to protect a young woman you didn't even particularly like. But for Charlie you won't cross a crumby hick cop?"

"I'm a crumby hick cop, too, Dina. And I understand where he's coming from."

"Let's stop arguing and get some food," Jewell broke in. "We'll all think better once we've eaten."

Kitty's Café was the place locals gathered for a cozy meal and community. In the morning, it usually bustled with activity, the half dozen tables, the three booths, and the small counter full for two or three hours after the door opened at six A.M. The daily special was chalked on a blackboard beside the malt machine. Tonight the special was Swedish meatballs, mashed potatoes and gravy, peas, and peach pie. It was a quiet night. A couple Jewell didn't recognize sat at a booth, both eating the meatballs. Gordon Ackerson was hunched at the counter, a ball cap on his old head, his arthritic hands working at cutting a fried pork tenderloin while he talked to Marlys Johnson, the waitress.

"Damn, girl, long time," Marlys said when she saw Jewell walk in.

Marlys was a gentle tank of a woman with hennaed hair and folds of fat that hung so pendulously from her arms they seemed like loose white wings.

"Hey, Marlys," Jewell responded. She ambled to the counter and put her hand on the shoulder of the old man there. "Evening, Gordie."

His mouth was full at the moment, and he simply lifted his fork in greeting.

Marlys wiped her plump hands on a dish towel. "Saw you troop into Ned's office a while ago. Thought maybe it was a lynch mob or something. Was that Charlie Miller with you?"

Jewell took a stool. Cork and Dina stood behind her. "Yeah."

"How's she doing, poor kid?"

"Hanging in there."

"I hope they get to the bottom of things pretty quick." Marlys leaned on the counter, the flesh of her arms pooling there. "Lot of nasty rumors floating around."

"About Charlie?"

"Folks look at her shaved head, those piercings, and that's enough for them. Hell, anybody really knows Charlie knows those rumors are a load of crap."

"What are they saying?"

"Heard she took a ball bat to her old man's head," Gordon said. He talked around a big bite of tenderloin and his words were mushy. "Splattered his brains like watermelon, eh."

"Jesus, Gordon." Marlys slapped his arm with her towel.

"What I heard," he said innocently.

Jewell tapped her hand on the counter. "I need to order a few things to go."

"Sure, hon." Marlys drew herself up, pulled the pen from behind her ear and an order pad from her apron. "What'll you have?"

A little rumble of metallic thunder came from the kitchen, followed by a few choice, unprintable epithets.

"Al," Marlys said, rolling her eyes. "The fan on the grill vent's gone out again. Super-mechanic insists he can fix it without calling in an expensive repairman."

"Can you still cook?" Jewell asked.

"Oh, sure."

"In that case, I need five cheeseburgers, a couple orders of fries, two chocolate shakes, an order of onion rings, and a small coffee." She glanced over her shoulder. "You want anything to drink?"

"Diet Coke," Dina said.

Cork said, "Pass."

Marlys finished jotting. "I'll put this right in for you. Ready in fifteen minutes."

"We'll come back," Jewell said.

"I'll have everything sacked and waiting, sweetie. Night, folks," she said to Cork and Dina.

Jewell gave Gordie's back a friendly pat. "Stay out of trouble, hear?"

The old man simply raised his fork in farewell.

They stepped once more into the night. A truck drove by slowly, the street lamps reflecting off the mirror of the dark windows. Jewell couldn't make out the driver, didn't even try, though later she'd think a lot about this moment.

"Okay, food," Dina said. "That's one problem solved. I still think we ought to consider doing something about Charlie."

"If you've got an idea that doesn't involve kidnapping or interfering with a lawful investigation, I'd love to hear it," Cork said.

As they stood on the sidewalk in front of Kitty's, the door to the constable's office banged open and Charlie burst out. She sprinted across the street and dashed into an alley. A moment later the deputy rushed out. She looked at Jewell and the others.

"Did you see her?"

Jewell didn't answer.

"The alley," Cork said, pointing. "But you'll never catch her."

"Gotta try," the deputy said, and gave chase.

In the quiet after, Ren appeared. "Did she make it?"

"At the rate she was going, she's halfway to Chicago by now," Cork replied. He glanced at Dina. "You could have caught her."

"No way was I going to stop that girl," Dina said.

"What happened?" Jewell asked Ren.

He stared toward the dark alley where Charlie had vanished. "The lady was like reading something she found in Constable Hodder's desk. She wasn't paying any attention and Charlie just ran. It was easy."

Cork said, "I'd hate to be in her shoes when Olaffson gets back."

"Should we be worried about Charlie?" Ren asked.

"She did a pretty good job of taking care of herself before," Dina said.

Ren considered that and finally nodded.

"No use standing out here," Jewell said. "Let's get inside."

In Ned's office, she crossed to his desk and found the top drawer pulled out. Lying open inside was the wire-bound notebook. She understood that the deputy had been reading Ned's poetry. Maybe bored or maybe looking for something else, the deputy had opened the drawer and there it was. The handwriting was small, precise. The poem was untitled. Jewell was tempted to read it but hated the thought of trespassing on

Ned's privacy. Although the deputy was ignorant of the importance of the notebook, Jewell understood only too well. She started to close it, but as the pages flipped, her eye caught a title she couldn't let pass:

> *For Jewell*
> *That beauty which to itself is hid—*
> *the sun not risen,*
> *the moon behind a lid*
> *of cloud—*

She shut the notebook without reading further, thinking with a flutter in her stomach, *Beauty? Me?*

She eased the drawer closed.

Less than an hour later, Olafsson returned. Deputy Baylor—Flo—had come back from her pursuit empty-handed and had made the call that clearly she dreaded. She had explained over the phone what happened and it was clear from her silence and her grim face the tone of Olafsson's response. When he strode into the office, he gave her a withering look, but said nothing.

"What happened at the Copper River Club?" Jewell asked.

"Didn't get past the gate," he answered. "No legal reason to compel them. That Stokely, he's one tough son of a bitch."

"I imagine they pay him pretty well for it," Ned said. He sat down and sniffed the white bag on his desk. "Smells good."

"Dinner," Jewell said. "From Kitty's. There's a cheeseburger left in there, and some fries. You're welcome to it."

"Great. I'm hungry. Split it with you, Terry?"

Olafsson dismissed the offer with a surly wave.

"What are you going to do now?" Cork asked.

"Except for his friendship with Delmar Bell," Olafsson said, "nothing I've been told so far connects Calvin Stokely to anything. And except for possibly the Rohypnol, nothing at the moment connects Bell with the girl's death. It's all speculation. Until I have something concrete, there's not much I can do. With those people up at the Copper River Club, I'm going to need to be on real firm legal ground every step of the way." He rubbed the back of his neck and eyed Ren. "You have any idea where Charlene might have gone?"

Ren looked down and shook his head.

Olafsson turned to Jewell. "She was at your place today, right?"

"Yes, but I doubt she'll head back there."

"Hodder, you mind checking that?"

"Sure."

"Flo and I'll have a look at her father's trailer on our way back to Marquette."

Before he left, Olafsson had one last try at Ren. "Son," he said in what sounded like his most officious voice, "if you know where your friend is and you don't tell me, it could be very bad for you."

"Leaning on him awfully hard, aren't you, Detective?" Cork said. "He already told you he didn't know."

He gave them all a parting squint. "I'll see what I can do about talking to this Calvin Stokely tomorrow. In the meantime, you hear from Charlene Miller, I expect to be told. Am I clear?"

When Olafsson and the deputy had gone, Ned said, "He's not a bad guy. And he's dealing with a lot right now."

"Is there any reason to stay?" Jewell asked.

Ned shook his head. "Guess not. I'll come along to your place, check it out for Charlie."

"If she's there, you'll what? Turn her over to Olafsson so he can lock her up in juvenile hall?" Dina said.

"Her safety's the issue," Ned told her.

"If we find her, I guarantee her safety," Dina said.

Ned looked truly apologetic. "I wish I could say that's good enough. Let's go, folks."

He turned the lights out as they went together into the night.

41

Ren didn't sleep. He lay awake thinking, worrying, the weight of so much concern pressing on his chest. There was Stash, almost dead because of him. And Charlie, alone and on the run again. And he'd lied to the Marquette policeman, and later to his mother and Cork and Dina when they'd questioned him about where Charlie might be hiding. He was in trouble—the man named Olafsson had made that clear—and it was only going to get worse.

An hour after he heard his mother go to bed and Dina lie down on the sofa in the living room, where she insisted on sleeping to help protect them, he threw back the covers and dressed in the dark. He folded a blanket and put it in a knapsack he pulled from his closet. From under his bed, he took a package of bologna and what was left of a loaf of bread, which he'd sneaked from the kitchen earlier that night, and he put these in the knapsack, too. It wasn't gourmet but it would keep Charlie from starving. He grabbed a flashlight from his desk drawer and tugged his jacket on. He opened his bedroom door and listened. He could hear Dina making small snoring noises as she slept. As quietly as he'd ever moved, he crept past her, turned the dead bolt, and eased the front door open. A moment later, he'd slipped into the night.

Clouds had rolled in obscuring the moon. The night was tar black. Ren couldn't even see the ground at his feet. He switched the flashlight on and headed toward the Killbelly

Marsh Trail. He moved quickly, afraid that his mother or Dina, if they woke, might look out and see the beam, and understand. He'd lied to them already; if his mother called to him, he didn't want to compound his sin with disobedience, though he would if it came to that. Charlie needed him.

The night wasn't only dark; it was dead still. The crunch of autumn leaves thundered under his boots. Whenever he stepped on a fallen branch, the dry snap was like a gunshot. To anything in the woods that might be interested, his presence was being broadly announced.

Black trees walled the narrow corridor of the trail. Whenever Ren heard a sound and swung the beam right or left, the trunks seemed to leap at him. The sounds, he told himself, were only part of the normal noise of night, the scurrying of small critters for whom sundown meant safety from predators. It was no different from that night after his father died when he'd forced himself to stay in the woods in order to overcome his fear of the dark.

But that night a year ago there had been no hungry, wounded cougar to worry about. Too late, Ren realized he should have brought something along to discourage the big cat if they met. He spent a few minutes scouring the woods near the trail for a broken-off branch suitable to use as a club.

Well before he reached the Copper River he heard the rush of fast water. When he joined the main trail, he turned west toward the Hurons and made his way along the rocky bank. He remembered the scat Cork had found, and the speculation that because the animal was wounded it used the trail.

Please, God, he prayed silently, *don't let it be here.*

He'd been on the Copper River Trail hundreds of times over the years, and if anybody had asked him he would have said he could walk it blindfolded. Stumbling along in the dark with only the thin, wobbly finger of the Coleman beam pointing the way, he realized what a dumb boast that would have been. At night, everything felt different—or this night, anyway, with so much hidden by the dark and with every clumsy step giving him away. He knew deep down how lame the stick in his right hand would be if the cougar caught his scent and was desperate to feed.

What moved him forward step by faltering step was thinking that Charlie had faced the same problems making her way to the one place she believed was safe.

He rounded a bend a quarter mile from the old mine and came alongside a place where the river ran flat and smooth and everything was quiet. From far behind him came the sound of something heavy hitting the ground in a tremendous crackle of the brittle leaves that blanketed the trail. He held his breath. The only sound then was the soft gurgle of the river. He swung around. His flashlight beam created a tunnel thirty or forty yards long in which he saw nothing but empty trail. He flipped the light off and stood another minute, listening intently, focusing all his senses on the enormous circle of black at whose center he stood.

His father had once told him that although an artist might work in images on paper or canvas, good artists were in touch with all their senses and knew how to use them creatively.

Ren focused and tried to touch the skin of the night, to hear the night breathing, to catch its scent. He opened his mouth and let the taste of the night lie on his tongue. What he sensed was that he was not alone. As if to prove the truth of his conclusion, his ears picked up the delicate crumble of desiccated leaves as something again moved toward him on the trail.

He spun, hit the switch on the flashlight, and sprinted upriver. Ahead of him, the beam bounced wildly. Several times he stumbled and almost fell headlong. His footfalls and the noise of his own heavy breathing deafened him to sound at his back, and he ran with the certainty that any moment the cougar would pounce and its razor teeth would slice into his neck. He thought that if he could only make it to the old mine, he could use his club to keep the cougar at bay. Maybe Charlie's presence there would help discourage an attack.

He reached the place along the river below the mine and began to scramble up the steep slope. He was feeding on adrenaline, moving like a mountain goat, using the stick in his right hand to propel himself upward. He reached the wild blackberry thicket that masked the entrance. Falling to his belly, he wormed his way into the small passage that he and

Charlie had fashioned through the bramble. On the other side, he swung the flashlight beam into the mine.

In the light lay a circle of ash and char from a fire, a mound of leaves that had probably served as a bed, several candy bar wrappers, and an empty pint container of Nestlé's chocolate milk. Charlie was nowhere to be seen.

But Ren was not alone. At his back, he heard the rattle of loose stones on the slope. He turned, set the flashlight down with the beam aimed at the opening to the passage. He gripped the club hard with both hands. The blackberry thicket shivered. Ren drew the club back like a batter preparing to receive a fastball. He kept his eyes on the end of the narrow passage, a ragged arch in the thicket. He held his breath and waited.

What emerged was a monster, a creature with huge eyes.

Then Ren realized that the eyes were goggles and the monster was Dina Willner. She put up a hand to block the beam.

"You're blinding me, Ren. Turn the light off for a minute."

He switched off the flashlight. In the dark he heard her silky rustlings.

"Okay," she said. "Give us some light again."

In the illumination, he saw that she'd removed her goggles. She wore camouflage fatigues.

"Where's Charlie?" she asked, peering into the mine.

"I don't know," he replied. "I thought for sure she'd be here."

"This is where she hid before, isn't it?"

She reached into the pocket of her fatigue pants and pulled out a small cyclinder, a mini Maglite. She used it to scan the tunnel back of the entrance.

"Looks completely blocked," she said.

"It is. How did you follow me?"

She dangled the goggles. "Night vision. I'm worried about Charlie, too. I was pretty sure you knew where she was and would go to her. I put these under the sofa and after you left I followed."

"I should have known you weren't really asleep," Ren said. "But I'm glad you're here."

"I almost wasn't. I took a bad spill on the trail back there and you almost got away from me."

"I thought you were the cougar."

"That wasn't smart, leaving at night without protection, Ren, but I understand. I brought this." She reached to her belt under her jacket and drew out a big handgun. Again she swung her Maglite toward the jumble of rock and rotted beam a dozen feet in from the mine entrance that barred further entry. "So if she's not here, where would she be?"

"I don't know," he said honestly.

She knelt and picked up a bit of the ash and char and rubbed it between her fingers. "This is old."

Ren said, "This was the safest place. She should have come here. Unless . . ." He stopped short of speaking his fear.

"Unless someone intercepted her," Dina finished for him. She stood up and put a comforting arm around his shoulders. "You know the *Odyssey*? The story of Odysseus?"

"Yeah," Ren said. He'd read a Classics Illustrated version. He thought the part about the Cyclops especially was way cool.

"Odysseus survived everything the gods threw at him because of his cunning. He was a very smart guy. That's Charlie, Ren. She's very cunning. So I think there's another explanation for why she's not here."

"Really?"

"Absolutely. And when we see her, she'll tell us what it is. Come on. We should both get back."

Dina led the way along the Copper River Trail. Behind her, Ren watched with admiration how gracefully she moved. In that, she reminded him a lot of Charlie.

42

When the cabin door opened, Cork woke up and rolled over in his bunk. Dina walked in carrying a tray covered with a white cloth napkin.

"Breakfast in bed?" Cork said, easing himself upright.

Dina put the tray on the table and pulled away the napkin, revealing a plate of two eggs over easy, four strips of bacon, two slices of very dark toast, a small glass of orange juice, and a cup of black coffee. "Eat hearty," she said. "We've got work to do."

He swung his legs out of the bunk and put his feet on the cold floorboards. He'd slept in a gray T-shirt and gray gym shorts, courtesy of Jewell. Like all the clothing she'd loaned him, they'd once been worn by her husband, Daniel. The night before, she'd also supplied him with a pair of clean jeans, a flannel shirt, boxers, and thick socks, all taken folded from the boxes of clothing stacked in the closet. Cork put on the socks and stood up slowly.

Dina pulled out a chair for herself at the table. "How's the leg this morning?"

"It would be better without holes in it, but I can manage." He limped over and appreciatively eyed the contents of the tray. "Looks like a condemned man's last meal." He sat down, flapped the napkin onto his lap, and took a sip of the juice. "What are we up to today?"

"Trespassing," Dina said.

While he ate, Dina explained about the night's events.

"I've been thinking," she said. "Charlie's a smart kid. Very savvy. I don't really think she was intercepted on her way to the mine, but I'd like to make certain. If there's the slightest chance this Stokely got his hands on her . . ." She didn't complete that thought.

Cork sipped his coffee. "What did you have in mind?"

"We're going to the Copper River Club the same way you and Ren did. We're going to check out Stokely's cabin."

"You and me?"

"That's the plan."

"What about Jewell and Ren?"

"She didn't want him missing any more school, and she needed to go to work."

"They're both gone?"

"Yes."

"What time is it?"

"Seven-thirty. Jewell said we could use the ATV."

"Does she know what you're planning?"

"Not exactly. I thought it best to keep this between you and me."

"How do we find the cabin?" he asked.

"I talked to Ren about that. He said to follow the river from where you two encountered Calvin Stokely yesterday. It's a couple of miles farther on, up a small rise overlooking the river."

Cork picked up the last strip of bacon. "Stokely'll hear us coming."

"He'll hear *you* coming," she said.

"I'm the diversion while you slip into the cabin?"

"You catch on quick. One of the things I like about you."

In half an hour, he was dressed and ready to go. He slipped the Beretta Tomcat into an ankle holster Dina supplied him. Dina took her Glock and a knapsack she said belonged to Ren. The night before, Jewell had put stitches in Cork's opened wound. He wasn't worried about bleeding, but he'd been over the terrain they were about to travel and knew the cost to him in pain. He considered taking a Vicodin but finally decided against it. He needed to be sharp.

The morning was damp and overcast, the temperature in the midforties. There was a dreary feel to the woods, a dismal quiet. Dina drove the ATV; Cork held on behind, shouldering the knapsack. The narrow Killbelly Marsh Trail was a stream of gold leaves wet with dew. At the river, Dina turned west and they went upstream. On this gray morning, the water reflected a slate sky. She stopped a few minutes later and pointed up the hillside to their right.

"The mine where Charlie hid is up there," she said. "Behind all that brush. Wait here."

Dina swung herself off the ATV and hiked quickly up the slope. She disappeared behind a thicket and emerged again a moment later. Back at the ATV she said, "Still empty." She restarted the engine and shot ahead.

In less than fifteen minutes, they reached the creek that marked the boundary of the Copper River Club. Dina stopped again and dismounted.

"Give me the knapsack," she said.

Cork handed it over and she took out a couple of the Motorola walkie-talkies he recognized had come from the resort. She gave one to Cork, kept one herself. She also took out a compact pair of Leitz field glasses in a case with a belt clip.

"Ren said the cabin's a couple miles up the river from here. Give me half an hour," she told Cork. "I'll raise you on the radio when I'm in position and have the place scoped out, then you come roaring in—I mean loud. If you have to, lead him on a merry chase. Just get him away from the cabin."

"Yesterday he had a rifle," Cork reminded her.

"Then keep your head down, cowboy."

She turned and began a steady lope along the river's edge in the direction of Stokely's cabin. She was wearing the camouflage fatigues in autumn color. She quickly blended with the foliage and in a minute he couldn't see her anymore.

He gave her thirty minutes but didn't hear anything on the Motorola. The problem might have been interference, or distance, or a malfunction of the units themselves. He wondered if he should be worried about Dina, but dismissed that concern. He gave her an extra five minutes, then decided it was time to move, regardless. He gunned the ATV and headed onto Copper River Club property.

He followed a faint but definite path that shadowed the river. Cork, a hunter all his life and used to tracking, spotted the thinning of the underbrush that indicated occasional foot traffic. He figured it was the patrol route for the security personnel. After a mile and a half, the trail veered suddenly north away from the river. Cork held up, puzzled. He decided that Stokely was probably the reason: the patrol route steered clear of his cabin to preserve his privacy. He gave the ATV gas and kept heading west, moving carefully through the undergrowth, following the river.

He'd fully expected to be intercepted. Several times he gunned the ATV for no reason other than noise. When he finally broke from the trees into a long clearing, he still hadn't seen a soul. A narrow, rutted dirt road split the clearing. At the south end that overlooked the river stood a small A-frame cabin and three outbuildings. The cabin appeared to be deserted, with no vehicles in sight. In a fenced area between two of the outbuildings, a big dog was barking up a storm.

Cork scanned the woods and saw no sign of Dina, which was what he expected. She was there somewhere, watching. He drove the ATV onto the dirt road and turned toward the cabin. A dozen yards from the front door, he killed the engine, swung his sore leg over the seat, and dismounted. In its high-fenced kennel, the dog, a black and tan German shepherd, was doing everything it could short of pole-vaulting to get at Cork. It dashed back and forth, occasionally hurling itself against the chain links in a frenzy of snapping and snarling. Although the fence looked plenty sturdy, Cork was glad to have the Tomcat strapped to his ankle.

He knocked on the cabin door and waited. He tried to peek in a window but the shades and curtains were tightly drawn. Moving to the garage, he peered through a pane and saw that it was empty inside. He approached the kennel. The German shepherd went into a whole other universe of agitation, sending out a spray of saliva and foam as it slammed into the fence. Cork was a little concerned that it might actually harm itself.

The next building was a wood shop, locked. Through the

window on the door, Cork saw lathes, planes, saws, work-tables, and a floor covered with sawdust and shavings. The last building was a small smokehouse.

He faced the cabin again. It was clear that Stokely was not currently in residence.

He felt a presence at his back.

"Nada?" Dina said.

He shook his head. "No Stokely, no Charlie, no nothing."

"There is something," she said. "Out there in the woods. See what you think."

She led him a short distance into the trees and pointed toward an area of bare ground. Cork saw what interested her. He knelt, grimacing at the pain that shot through his leg, and he carefully studied the prints.

"The cougar," he said.

"The night Stokely wounded it?"

Cork shook his head. "That was a couple of days ago. I'd say these tracks are more recent, within the last twenty-four hours." He reached out and Dina helped him up. He looked from the tracks toward the cabin, barely visible through the foliage. "This close to a barking dog and a man who's already put a bullet in it, that animal has to be crazy or desperately hungry."

"Was it after the dog, maybe?"

"Even if you were hungry, would you think that dog was an easy meal? Maybe it was after garbage."

"I don't see a garbage can out here," she said.

Cork eyed the line of the tracks, which seemed to head toward an opening in the woods a short distance away. He limped in that direction with Dina at his side. They stepped into another clearing, nearly circular and much smaller than the one that held Stokely's buildings. This one was only forty or fifty feet in diameter. It was filled with tall grass and wildflowers gone yellow with the season. The ground was uneven, and the ground cover was unevenly rich, surprisingly thick and lush in places. On the far side, loose soil lay thrown about in scattered splashes, the result of an animal's furious digging. Cork saw a shallow trough scraped in the earth. He crossed the clearing with Dina, and they stood over the hole.

"Oh God," Dina said. "Is that what I think it is?"

Black with rot, ragged from the feeding of the cougar, it was nonetheless clearly a human leg, bare and attached to a body still mostly buried.

Cork turned away, sickened as he understood the reason for the uneven earth and lush undergrowth in that terrible hidden place.

43

At noon the overcast began to break and by two o'clock the sun was nailed to a sky so blue and pure it was almost heartbreaking. The state police working in the tiny clearing cast shadows across the holes they dug and their words to one another were spoken in the hushed tones of men still not quite able to comprehend the brutal enormity before them. There were a dozen vehicles parked along the dirt road leading to Stokely's cabin. Some were state, others county. Ned Hodder's Cherokee was there, and that's where Cork and Dina sat. For too long now, they'd watched the body bags come out of the clearing.

Despite the number of people on the scene, a somber quiet hung over everything. Someone from the sheriff's department had tranquilized the German shepherd in the kennel, who'd gone berserk when all the vehicles rolled up. Hodder said the dog's name was Snatch.

Dina smoked a cigarette she'd bummed from one of the troopers.

"I didn't know you smoked," Cork had said.

"I don't," she'd replied, and they spoke no more about it.

They'd been interviewed separately by the state investigators, had given their statements, and were free to go. Neither of them was ready. Cork still felt stunned, as if he'd been hit between the eyes with a big mallet. He'd seen bad things in his time, but nothing compared to this.

Hodder walked toward them from where he'd been convers-
ing with one of the investigators. He leaned against the side of
the Cherokee, folded his arms across his chest, and stared east
where Bodine lay a few miles on the other side of all those
thick, autumn-fired hardwood trees.

"Children," he said. "They're all children. Fourteen, fifteen
years old. Mostly girls. Some of the graves are several years
old. So far, the most recent looks to be a couple of weeks.
That's the one the cougar messed with." He let his arms fall
uselessly. "God, how did this happen?"

"We abandoned them," Dina said. She threw the butt of her
cigarette onto the road, where it smoldered, white smoke
against dun-colored dirt. "Cats, dogs, we spay or neuter, but
people we let procreate with blithe abandon, people who have
no business bringing children into this world. When those
kids become desperate we don't see them, don't hear them. As
long as they're not haunting our block, staring hopelessly into
our windows, we can pretend they don't exist or worse, that
whatever horror they deal with they've brought on themselves. They're not our children. They're not even like our
children. Believe me, this is something I know about."

Cork rubbed his leg, which was hot and throbbing. He
hadn't done himself any favors that day.

"Sara Wolf was Ojibwe," he said. "Born to The People. It
used to be, in a village everyone watched out for the children.
Blood ties, clans, those things didn't matter. Now . . ." He
looked up at the sky and sighed. "It feels like everything
everywhere is falling apart."

Hodder eyed another body bag being carried from the
woods. "Where did they all come from?"

"Providence House for one," Dina said. "When I talked to
Mary Hilfiker, she told me the kids there came out of nowhere
and vanished the same way, and she had no resources to track
them. She told me that in this country nearly a million go
missing every year. A child abandoned with no one who cares,
that's the perfect prey." She leaned over as if she were going to
be sick. "What I can't understand is why they'd hire someone
like Bell."

"If they did a background check—and they probably did—

they wouldn't find anything. He managed to keep his record clean," Hodder said.

"How do you know?" Dina asked.

He shrugged. "My town. I know things like that."

Terry Olafsson and a state investigator came from the wood shop. Isaac Stokely, head of security for the Copper River Club, was with them. The investigator led Stokely toward the A-frame cabin. Olafsson walked to Hodder's Cherokee. He stood a few paces away and stared down at the cigarette butt Dina had tossed.

"Looks like the wood shop I've got at home," he said. "Smells like it, too. Shavings, sawdust. Always meant good things to me. Not anymore. There's a trapdoor in the floor of Stokely's: leads to a small cellar room, a cinder-block bunker kind of a thing, no bigger than a jail cell. There's a cot, slop bucket, video equipment, some bloody kids' clothes wadded up and thrown in a corner."

He stopped. The line of his mouth went taut. He looked pale.

"The minute you go down there you can feel it. It's like the walls are soaked full of all that horror. It's quiet as a tomb, but Christ, I swear you can hear the screams. I've never felt anything like it."

"What about Isaac Stokely?" Hodder asked. "Was he involved?"

Olafsson shook his head. "Claims he knows nothing about it. He's cooperating. We'll have to wait and see, but I get the feeling he really didn't know anything. He seems just as horrified as the rest of us. He's definitely not protecting his brother."

"It's isolated here," Cork said, indicating the clearing with a wave of his hand. "Controlled access. The security patrols skirt this area. Bringing in a drugged child in a car trunk—"

"Calvin Stokely drives a Dodge Ram with a camper shell," Hodder put in.

"There you go. A perfect setup until one of the children, a kid with a strong will to survive somehow gets herself free and runs. Gets lost maybe or is being chased and stumbles into the river."

"I can't sit here anymore," Dina said. "I've got to do something."

"What?" Hodder asked.

"Find Charlie."

"How?"

"I don't know yet. You coming?" she said to Cork.

"On the ATV?" He winced. "I don't think so."

Hodder moved toward the driver's seat. "I'll give you both a ride. They don't need me here. You can make arrangements to pick up the ATV later."

Olafsson put his hand on the door before Hodder closed it. "It would be a good idea to be available at your office, Ned, in case they decide they want some more information on the locals."

"Will do."

Cork and Dina settled in, slammed doors.

"A BOLO's been issued for Calvin Stokely," Olafsson said through Hodder's open window. "There aren't a lot of roads in this part of the U.P. We'll get him."

He stepped back and Hodder swung the Cherokee around and headed out of the clearing toward the road that would take them to the gate a couple of miles away.

"So Stokely left the Copper River Club yesterday and never came back," Cork said.

"That's how the log at the gate reads," Hodder confirmed. "His dog was hungry, too, which would tend to verify that he didn't return."

"Why stay away?" Cork said. "Nothing had been discovered yet that would incriminate him."

"Probably he killed Bell and panicked."

"And he killed Bell because . . . ?"

Hodder shrugged. "Maybe he thought Bell was ready to break, spill the beans. Maybe they argued. Who knows?"

Dina was quiet in back, staring out the window at the trees that lined the road like a wall of flame.

They stopped at the gate. Hodder spoke to the guard.

"Still pretty quiet, Wes," he observed of the empty road beyond the gate.

"Until the media gets hold of this, then all hell'll break loose," the guard replied.

"What do you think?" Hodder jabbed a thumb back in the direction of all the activity.

Wes leaned against the Cherokee and spoke through the window. "Nobody's asked me yet, but I always got the willies around Calvin. Hell, he wouldn't have the job if it weren't for his brother and we all knew that. We all knew better than to go near his place, too. I mean, the guy freaked. Big duh, huh? Heads are going to roll up here. You want a job as chief of security, there's sure to be an opening, Ned."

"Say, Wes," Cork said. "Mind if I ask you a question?"

"Who's he?" the guard asked Hodder.

"Somebody whose question you should answer," Hodder replied.

The guard said, "Shoot."

"Does it say on your log when Calvin Stokely left yesterday?"

"I'd have to check."

"Check," Hodder said.

Wes went into the guardhouse and came out half a minute later. "He got off duty at three, split from the Club at three-thirty."

"Thanks. One more question," Cork said. "Anybody visit Calvin Stokely on a regular basis?"

"Only one I can think of. A drinking buddy from Marquette. Guy name of Delmar Bell."

"That's it?"

"Believe me, Stokely wasn't the kind who'd have a lot of friends. And anybody who visited would have to come through here, so I'd know."

"Thanks, Wes," Cork said.

The guard stepped back to the box and lifted the gate.

"What was that all about?" Ned asked.

"Just fishing," Cork said. "You never know."

Heading back to the resort, they were quiet. Jewell's Blazer was parked in front of Thor's Lodge, and she came out as Hodder pulled up.

"I thought they needed you at the clinic," Cork said.

"I couldn't concentrate. They called in someone to cover. What's going on?"

"Let's go inside," Cork said.

* * *

She sat stunned, her hand over her mouth as if stifling a scream. Except for "Oh dear God," she'd said nothing as Cork explained what they'd found.

"Charlie," she gasped at last. "Was there any sign of Charlie?"

"No."

"But they still don't know where Stokely is?"

"That's right. They've issued a BOLO."

She stared at him without understanding.

"Be on the lookout."

Ned, who stood awkwardly near the front door, hat in hand, said, "They'll get him, Jewell. As for Charlie, she's a smart kid. I'm sure she's just hunkered down somewhere, waiting this out."

Jewell eyed him hopefully. "You think so? Where?"

He returned her gaze for a moment, then had to look away.

"If Stokely has her," Jewell said, "will he hurt her?"

It was the question they'd probably all been asking themselves, but only Jewell had spoken it. She grabbed for her purse and pulled out her cigarettes. "Damn!" She crumpled the empty pack, stood up, and began pacing. "We have to find her."

"We don't know where to look, Jewell," Hodder said gently. "She could be anywhere."

"The first time she vanished, she was hiding in an old mine she and Ren knew about. But I checked it this morning on the way to Stokely's cabin," Dina told them. "She wasn't there."

Hodder settled his hat on his head. "Look, I need to get back to my office in case the state investigators want to talk to me. On the way, I'll swing by Max's trailer and then I'll check the old lumberyard next to it. I've been thinking it might be a place Charlie would hide. Bunch of abandoned buildings and all."

Jewell nodded. "You'll let us know what you find?"

"I will." He offered a comforting smile before he left.

Jewell stood at the window watching him drive away. "I should have done more," she said to herself.

"You've done everything you could, Jewell," Cork assured her. "What those men did at the Copper River Club nobody could predict."

"The signs must have been there. We just didn't see them. Maybe we didn't want to see them."

Cork hobbled to her and put his arm around her. "Ren will be home from school in a little while. You need to get yourself together for him."

"Do you have tea?" Dina asked.

"In the cupboard to the left of the sink," Jewell replied.

"Jewell, the police are doing everything they can," Cork said.

She pressed a hand to her forehead. "There's got to be something more."

In a few minutes, the kettle began to whistle. As Dina was pouring boiling water into cups, she said, "We could hit the roads ourselves, see if we spot his vehicle. According to Ned, Stokely drives a Dodge Ram pickup with a camper shell. Any idea what color, Jewell?"

A look of horror slowly twisted Jewell's face. "Oh God, no."

"What is it?" Cork said.

"I saw him. I saw him last night. He drove past Ned's office when we were there with Charlie. Why didn't I think of it then?"

Dina came quickly from the kitchen. "When we were there with Charlie, you said? So it was before she ran?"

"Yes. Before."

Dina's mouth settled into a grim line. "This changes things. We'd better let Ned know." She pulled out her cell phone. "What's his number?" Jewell gave it and she punched it in. "Ned? It's Dina Willner." She listened a moment. "Okay. . . . Look. . . ." She explained the situation. "I know, I know. . . . Yeah, we'll be here." She ended the call.

"So?" Cork said.

"He just checked the trailer. Nothing. He's going to call the state police out at the Copper River Club and let them know about Stokely's truck last night, then he'll check the lumber-yard and head back to his office."

"And we'll do what?" Jewell asked. "Just sit here doing nothing? I don't think so."

"I'm right there with you," Dina said.

In his chair, Cork shifted his weight to his right butt cheek, hoping to relieve some of the discomfort in his left leg. "And what is it you intend to do exactly? Where do you start?"

"I don't know," Jewell shot back.

"All right, here's something to think about, something that's been rolling around in my head for a little while," Cork said. "Hodder—and maybe the investigators, too—believe Stokely's a likely suspect for the murder of Delmar Bell. I don't think so."

Dina crossed a leg over her knee and leaned toward him, looking intrigued. "Why?"

"The timing doesn't work. Yesterday I heard Olafsson say the TOD—time of death—on Bell was between three-thirty and four. If the gate log is correct, Stokely left the Copper River Club at three-thirty. It's a good forty-five minutes to Marquette. Unless he flew, Stokely wouldn't have made it in time to kill Bell."

"So Calvin didn't kill Del," Jewell said. "So what?"

"So who did?" Cork said.

"What does it matter?"

"It matters," Dina said. Understanding blossomed in her green eyes. "It matters because it means Bell and Stokely weren't in it alone."

"There are others?" Jewell looked fearful, momentarily defeated. "God, who?"

"That's what we have to figure out," Cork replied. "If Stokely's disappeared, maybe it's because somebody's hiding him."

"Or he's hiding from somebody so they won't take care of him like they took care of Bell," Dina said.

"Or they've already taken care of him like they took care of Bell," Cork added.

"What about Charlie?" Jewell asked.

"I don't know," Cork said. "But if we understand who else is involved, we might stand a better chance of finding her. Let's backtrack a little. You suspected Stokely and Bell in the first place because of the murder of the runaway girl twenty years ago. You told me Ned described a football celebration of some kind, followed by drinking at a cabin somewhere. The kid who confessed to killing her picked her up on the way home. Maybe Bell and Stokely were with him and had a hand in it. That was your thinking, right?"

"Yes," Jewell said.

"So far, it seems pretty reasonable, especially in light of everything that's happened since we started asking questions. But what if there was someone else with them that night?"

"Who?"

"That's what I'm asking you. Let's figure a normal car, big, strapping football players. Four, maybe five could have fit in comfortably. Bell, Stokely, Messinger, and one or two more. Who could the extras have been? Start with an assumption that they were football players on the championship team. Add that it's somebody who still lives in the area. And finally somebody able to come and go at the Copper River Club without raising a lot of suspicion."

Dina said, "That's why you asked the guard at the gate about Stokely's visitors."

"The state police will get around to asking the same question."

"He said Stokely didn't have visitors," Dina pointed out. Then she looked at Jewell. "Was his brother, Isaac, on the team?"

"No, he graduated several years before. He was long gone to the military by then."

Cork asked, "Who else is still around who was on the team?"

Jewell closed her eyes to think, but it was Dina who answered. "Ned Hodder."

"It's not Ned," Jewell said sharply. "I'd know."

"Give me another name, then," Cork told her.

"I can't think," Jewell said a little desperately.

"You have a high school yearbook?" Dina asked.

"Yes."

"Get it. Maybe it'll help."

Jewell went up to her bedroom and came back down carrying a big yearbook that said *Bobcats* in green across the front. She sat on the sofa and flipped through the pages. "Here," she said. "The football team photo."

The photograph was pretty standard yearbook fare: the

whole team suited in their gear and seated on the bleachers of the football field, coaches standing on either side. Jewell's finger went slowly over the list of names below. It went all the way to the end without stopping.

"Well?" Dina said.

"Calvin, Del, and Ned," she said, defeated.

"Hodder visits the Copper River Club regularly. He wouldn't raise a lot of suspicion," Cork pointed out.

"Yesterday when we went to see him, he wasn't at his office," Dina added. "We called him, and he said he was checking on a break-in outside of town. He could have been on his way back from killing Bell."

"Not Ned," Jewell said again, but with less conviction.

"I like the guy, too, Jewell," Cork told her. "And I wouldn't mind being wrong. But for Charlie's sake we need to check it out. Where does he live?"

"His family's always had a place southwest of town, an orchard. Ned lives there alone."

"Dina and I will go."

"I'm going, too," Jewell said. "If it's Ned, I want to know right away."

"What about Ren?" Dina asked. "Won't he be home from school pretty soon?"

"With the hours I work, he almost always comes home to an empty house. I'll leave him a note. He'll be fine."

"What if he's heard about Stokely's secret cemetery?"

"I don't think he has. Gary Johnson wasn't even up there. If our local newsman doesn't know yet, nobody else does."

Cork bent and withdrew the Beretta from the holster still strapped to his ankle. He checked the clip. Dina did the same with her Glock.

"Oh Christ," Jewell said. "You're not going to shoot him."

"Are you with us?" Dina asked.

Jewell took a deep breath. "Yes."

44

*D*ina parked her Pathfinder on the side of the road at the edge of the orchard. They couldn't see the house, which was deep in the trees.

"If Stokely's there," Cork explained, "we don't want him to spot us coming. We'll approach through the trees. Jewell, maybe you should stay here. Things could get tricky."

"I'm going with you," Jewell said.

"Then you need to do exactly as we say."

Jewell nodded. She was scared. The whole situation, all the horrible possibilities, terrified her. But she absolutely didn't want to be left behind.

They closed their doors quietly and crept into the orchard, circling carefully toward the back of the house. Ned's father, who'd been a lawyer, had kept up the orchard as a hobby, and as a teenager Jewell had spent many fall afternoons hired— along with other of Ned's friends—to harvest the fruit, which the Hodders sold from a roadside stand. The apples were Northern Spy and McIntosh, still Jewell's favorite varieties. Ned had often lamented his own inability to keep the orchard in shape, but he was alone in the house and busy with his duties as constable, so the fruit simply fell to the ground. This late in the season, most of the apples had already fallen, and the rotting fruit filled the orchard with a vinegary smell.

As soon as they could see the house, they paused, hidden in the trees.

"I don't see a vehicle anywhere," Dina said.

"Garage?" Cork pointed toward a small structure just east of the house.

Jewell nodded.

He indicated the other outbuilding. "Equipment shed?"

"Ned keeps a tractor in there and other stuff for working in the orchard. Ladders, props, pruning things. He doesn't use them much anymore."

"Let's check the garage first," he said to Dina. "I'd like to know if Calvin Stokely's truck is in there."

"I'll go," she said. "You cover."

Cork took the handgun from his ankle holster, slipped behind an apple tree, and waved Dina forward. Jewell stayed back, thinking how horrible this was, coming at Ned as if he were the enemy. It felt so wrong. Dina dashed across the back-yard to the side of the garage, which couldn't be seen from the house. She edged her way to a window and peeked in. She turned back and gave her head an exaggerated shake. Cork pointed toward the shed. Dina went to the corner of the garage and peered carefully at the house for a full minute, watching, Jewell supposed, for movement at a window, an opening door. Then Dina sprinted for the shed. She stood on tiptoe and peered through a dusty window. Again she gave her head a shake. She pointed toward the house.

"Okay," Cork said over his shoulder to Jewell, "now we check the house. You should stay here."

"Oh, no," Jewell said. "I'm coming with you."

"All right, then. Let's go."

Jewell ran hard, passed Cork, and joined Dina at the side of the house, breathless. Cork was several seconds behind.

"You okay?" Dina asked him in a whisper.

"I know what that wounded cougar must feel like," he said, grimacing.

"Back door or front?" Dina said.

"Back."

They crept there together. Cork opened the screen and tried the door.

"Locked," he whispered.

Dina urged him gently aside, reached into an inside pocket of her jacket, and pulled out a small leather case. She took out a couple of items that looked to Jewell like dentist's tools. She worked on the lock a moment and swung the door open.

Cork put his lips to Jewell's ear. "Stay here," he said softly. "When we're sure it's clear, we'll call you in, okay?"

The house swallowed them without a sound.

Outside, Jewell felt suddenly alone and vulnerable. The idea of being afraid of Ned Hodder was alien, yet that's what she felt. Did she even know Ned anymore? When was the last time they'd had a meaningful conversation? Why had he written a poem about her? How could she have missed so much?

On the road beyond the orchard, a car passed. Jewell heard the sound of the engine mount, plateau, diminish as it sped on.

After that, everything was distressingly quiet. She watched a hawk circle above the orchard, then curve away without a stroke of wing.

Another car approached on the road. This one didn't pass. The sound of the engine simply died.

What did that mean? Jewell wondered in a panic. What should she do? Shout to Cork and Dina? Where were they? They'd been inside too long, she was sure. Something was wrong. She looked toward the empty drive that wound through the orchard, expecting any moment for Ned to appear. She was a sitting duck, she realized.

She turned to run for the orchard and bumped smack into Ned Hodder. He caught her in his arms. She struggled to break free and stumbled back.

"Jewell?" His boyish face held a look of absolute bewilderment. "What are you doing here?"

"We . . . I . . . just . . ." Her eyes bounced toward the house.

Ned followed them. "That's Dina Willner's Pathfinder parked on the road. Is she inside?" He spoke in a deep, menacing tone that Jewell had never heard from him before.

"Ned, listen—" Jewell tried.

He didn't listen. His face had turned an angry red, and he stormed toward the back door just as Dina stepped out.

"What the hell do you think you're doing?" he shouted.

"Looking for Charlie," Dina said calmly.

That stopped him. "Charlie?" He looked at her with the same befuddlement that had been there when he first found Jewell. "Here?"

"Ned, please listen," Jewell said. She put her hand gently on his arm, but he shook it off. "We were thinking," she struggled on, trying for the right words, "that there might be more people involved than just Stokely and Bell."

"And you naturally thought of me," he threw back bitterly. "How flattering."

Cork came into sight now, too. He stepped from the house and stood beside Dina.

"You, too? I should have guessed. Find anything interesting?"

"Stokely didn't kill Bell," Dina explained.

"Hell, I know that," Ned said. "In a few minutes you would have, too."

"What do you mean?" Jewell asked.

"I tore my shirt at the lumberyard," he said, turning so that Jewell saw the rip. "I was coming back here to put on another one and to call you guys. I think I've got a suspect."

"Who?" Cork said.

Ned didn't reply immediately. He turned on Jewell. "You think I had Charlie? How could you believe I'd do something like that, Jewell? And all those kids buried up there? Do you really think I'm capable of that kind of butchery? Jesus, after all these years you don't even know me."

"Ned, I'm sorry. I didn't think . . . all this is so confusing and scary. . . ."

"Am I scary? Is that why you don't talk to me? Don't look at me on the street? Am I some kind of monster to you?"

"No, Ned, no. It's not that. I'm just not ready—"

"Have I pushed you? Have I pressured you?"

"No, no. You've been nothing but sweet."

"Then why this?" He waved toward Cork and Dina and the opened door.

"It was us," Dina answered. "Jewell defended you down the line. We overruled her objections."

"What made you think I might be involved?"

Dina carefully laid out for him their reasoning. At the end, she said, "You're a good cop. I'm betting you'd have done the same."

"I wouldn't break into someone's house."

"Even if you believed you might be saving Charlie?" she asked.

Jewell thought he softened a little, though he still kept his distance from her.

Cork spoke up. "You said you had a suspect."

"Yeah." The late-afternoon sun was in his eyes and he turned so that he didn't have to squint. "I got to thinking after I dropped you all off. Like you, I figured from what Wes said that Stokely probably didn't kill Bell. There might be a lot of reasons someone would put a bullet in him, but for my money it was all about those buried kids. So if Stokely didn't do it, who did? I went back to thinking about twenty years ago, too, thinking like you that if Tommy Messinger and Calvin and Del were all involved in that girl's murder, there was a good chance someone else might have been with them."

Jewell said, "I looked at the team photo, Ned. I couldn't see anyone else still here except for you and Calvin and Del."

"The guy I'm thinking of wasn't on the team, Jewell. At least not that year. Who was Tom Messinger's best friend, do you remember? The same guy who spoke at his funeral and who wrote that long editorial the *Courier* published, pleading for understanding about what Tommy had done and about his suicide. It was very moving and persuasive, as I recall."

Jewell felt as if the sky had suddenly opened. "Gary Johnson."

"Johnson," Ned said. "He couldn't play football that year because he broke his leg in August. He fell from a ladder while he was working for my father here in the orchard, remember?"

"And he was in a cast through most of the season," Jewell added.

"Right."

"I thought he was an all-American at Michigan," Dina said.

"A walk-on," Hodder replied. "He had to prove himself because the scouts had nothing to look at. But he was at every game with the team that year, and he was at the banquet in Marquette and at the private party afterward. If he wasn't in the car with Tom Messinger, I don't know who else it could have been."

Jewell said, "He's been out at the cabins, very interested in Charlie. He said it was because it was news."

"More likely he was desperate to get his hands on Charlie," Dina threw in. "But since he couldn't, and he knew that things were coming apart, I'll bet he decided to get rid of his slimy partners and sever his connection, let it all go down on them."

Jewell said quietly, "This is Gary we're talking about."

Dina gave her a brutally cold stare. "If you have a better idea, let's hear it. If not, we need to move and find Charlie."

"What do we do?" Jewell said.

"We should take all this to Olafsson or the state investigators," Hodder suggested.

"That doesn't help Charlie if Johnson has her," Dina said. "I prefer the direct approach. Where does he live?"

"You tried the direct approach here," Hodder pointed out. "Haven't you trespassed enough?"

"Look, if we're wrong, it's embarrassing and we'll apologize. But what if we're not wrong? What's he doing to her now even as we stand here?"

Jewell said, "Gary's got a home on Lake Superior a few miles south of town."

Hodder nodded. "He's probably there now. I stopped by the *Courier* office yesterday afternoon to talk to him, but they told me he'd gone home sick. I tried again this morning and got the same story."

"Hiding?" Dina suggested.

"Let's find out," Cork said.

45

*I*t had been a hard day for Ren. Although his mother insisted he miss no more school, he wasn't able to concentrate. At lunch when Amber Kennedy dropped her notebook beside the table where he was eating and bent to pick it up giving him a clear view down her blouse, he barely noticed. His worry about Charlie consumed him.

He ditched his afternoon classes and searched for her. He tried her father's trailer, then in a moment of brilliant deduction thought about the abandoned lumberyard next door. She wasn't there, either. He checked the old freight warehouse on the harbor that had most of the windows broken out and pigeon droppings spotting the concrete floor. No Charlie. The only other possibility he could think of was that she'd broken into one of the summer cabins on the lake or along the river, but there were way too many to check them all.

He stopped at the Farber House and Mrs. Taylor let him use the phone to call home. No one answered. He left a message saying he was hanging out in town for a while, and not to worry. He'd be home in time for dinner.

He went to the picnic shelter where he'd got high with Stash and Charlie and where all the trouble had begun. He sat on the table and watched the river sweeping past in striations of white and black water.

Where was Charlie?

He'd been worried before, only to find that she'd taken care of herself just fine. He shouldn't be worried now, he tried to tell himself, but he couldn't shake the unsettled feeling. Everything important in his life seemed to have changed or be changing. His father dead. His mother lost in grieving. Charlie getting weird. Bodine suddenly a scary place. He wished he could go back and stop time, freeze everything in place. He longed for it all to be comfortable and familiar, like the ground under his feet.

He finally got up, followed the Copper River to the old mine, and checked it again. Empty.

It was late when he started home. The Huron Mountains were eating the sun. The woods were full of long shadows. Far to the east, a few feathery clouds were already tinted with the glow of sunset. His mother was probably home from work, making dinner. She'd be worried. Still, he walked slowly, weighted. By the time he reached the Killbelly Marsh Trail, the sun had gone down and the path he followed was a tunnel of cool blue light. He turned off the trail and headed through the trees toward the cabins, past the shot-up car behind the shed. His mother's Blazer was parked in front of Thor's Lodge, but the Pathfinder was gone. Ren stepped inside the cabin and found it empty. The evening light through the windows illuminated the place with a steely grayness. Ren sensed something was wrong and wondered if an emergency had pulled the adults away. He left the door open and hurried to the kitchen, hoping for a note.

He found it on the counter, anchored in place by the toaster:

Ren,
   Gone for a while. Cork and Dina are with me.
   Back soon.

                              Love,
                              Mom

For a moment, he felt relieved.

Then he felt a draft of air on his neck as something moved in the room behind him.

"Hello there, Ren," said a deep, unfriendly voice at his back.

46

*T*hey turned off the highway south of town onto a narrow paved drive that wound through a grove of alders. Sunset was near and they plunged into deep shadows. On a curve still out of sight of Gary Johnson's house, Ned Hodder, who led the way, braked to a slow stop. He got out and waited for the others to join him.

When they all stood together, he said, "It's a couple hundred yards around this curve. A one-story ranch. Attached garage on the north. There's maybe fifty yards of clear ground between the trees and the house on all sides, except for the backyard. That sits on a little cliff that drops straight down into the lake."

"Let's come at it from the north," Cork suggested. "We can use the garage to hide our approach. Check it for Stokely's truck, too."

"We need someone to cover the house while we're doing that," Hodder said. He looked at Dina who had her Glock already out. "You okay with that?"

"If I'm covering from any kind of distance, I'd rather use my rifle."

She opened the tailgate of the Pathfinder, spent half a minute, and returned with a Ruger .44 and the walkie-talkies from the resort. She gave one unit to Cork and kept the other for herself.

"You any good?" Hodder said, indicating the carbine.

"She's good," Cork told him. "Believe me."

Ned went back to his vehicle and lifted a shotgun from the trunk. Cork recognized a Mossberg twelve-gauge, a popular law enforcement firearm. Hodder shook his head. "I can't remember the last time I had to pull this thing out for anything but cleaning."

"If you're not going to use your Glock, Dina, you mind if I do?" Cork said.

She gave it over, along with an extra clip.

"Get yourself in a good position," Hodder instructed Dina— needlessly, Cork knew. "Jewell, you stay close to her, okay?"

"Use that Motorola," Dina said. "Let us know what's going on."

"Will do," Cork replied.

Hodder headed into the alders, Cork right behind him. They walked carefully, conscious of the quiet and everything they did that broke it. They took five minutes to work their way to a place north of the house, where the garage would block any view of their approach. Cork let Dina know they were in position and ready to move.

They could see the whole of the backyard clearly, a neat square of lawn with only a few random autumn leaves lying unraked on the grass. Trees edged the yard to the north and south, but to the east it opened toward the lake, which in the waning light was a stretch of calm water the blue-black color of a new bruise. Above the lake hung a few wisps of pink cloud, scars on the pale blue body of the sky.

"Check the garage first, see if Stokely's truck is there?" Cork said.

Hodder nodded. Together they slipped from the trees and dashed across the yard. Cork's leg was a howl of pain, but it held up and he reached the garage only a moment behind Hodder. He leaned against the side and put his weight on his good leg. The constable crept to the front of the garage and peered through the windows that ran in a row across the broad door. He turned back and gave Cork a thumbs-up. Stokely's truck was there.

"What now?" Hodder said.

"Let's see if we can pinpoint their location inside."

They eased along the wall to the back of the house and

around the corner. They ducked under several windows where the curtains were drawn, then came to one that was clear. Cork could see kitchen cabinets and the glow of a light deeper in the house.

"Ever been inside before?" he whispered to Hodder.

"Couple of times. Kitchen opens onto the dining area. Living room's just beyond that."

Cork hesitated, then risked a peek through the window. The kitchen was dark as was the dining area beyond. In a dim lake of light in the living room, Johnson sat in an easy chair facing the television. The TV set was on, but the screen was an empty blue.

"Johnson," Cork said, "but no Stokely. The curtains on the other dining room wall are open. Maybe I can get a better look from there."

Cork made his way to the far side of the house. The angle through that window was better and he saw most of the living room. He also saw Calvin Stokely.

"Well?" Hodder said when Cork returned.

"Stokely's with him."

"Armed?"

"Dead. He's lying on the living room floor in a pool of blood."

Hodder squinted. "Jesus."

"Johnson's armed. Just sitting there staring at a blank television screen holding a handgun. Your jurisdiction. How do we play it?"

Hodder looked at Cork and at the kitchen window, his uncertainty clear in his face.

"Keep an eye on him," he finally said. "I'll try the back door. If he moves, you've got to let me know."

"Will do."

Hodder took his time with the screen door, which opened without a sound. He turned the knob on the inside door and inched his way into the kitchen. Cork watched him move to a place where he could observe Johnson for himself. Hodder signaled Cork inside and raised his Mossberg to the ready. Cork slipped through the kitchen door, the Glock in the grip of his right hand. The air in the house carried the thick, sweet smell of blood.

Johnson didn't move, didn't seem at all aware of their presence. Still as a stump, he stared at the blue television screen.

Hodder barked, "Police! Drop the weapon, Gary!"

Like a man in a dream, Johnson slowly turned his head. His face was slack, his eyes distant.

"Drop the gun, Gary," Hodder ordered.

Johnson's eyes took a slow stroll from Hodder to the pistol in his own hand. He looked at it without interest.

"Do it now, Gary! Drop it!"

Johnson's fingers gradually opened and the pistol clattered to the hardwood floor. Hodder moved forward and kicked the weapon well out of Johnson's reach. He looked down at Stokely, at the blood gone nearly black around him.

Hodder said, "Keep him covered while I cuff him."

Johnson stood up and lifted his empty hands. "You don't need to do that, Ned. I won't give you any trouble."

"Just turn around, Gary. Put your hands behind your back."

Hodder slipped the cuffs on, pulled a card from his wallet, and went through Johnson's Miranda rights. Cork radioed Dina and Jewell. A minute later, they came in the back door. When they saw the body and blood, they stopped. A small yet audible breath escaped from Jewell, but she didn't turn away.

"What happened, Gary?" Hodder said.

"What it looks like. I killed him. If he sat up right now, I'd kill him again."

Cork checked the rest of the house but found no sign of Charlie. When he came back, Ned was questioning Johnson.

"You say you shot Stokely last night?"

"That's right," Johnson replied.

"You were still holding the gun when we found you."

"Thinking of using it on myself. I was afraid if I put it down, I wouldn't be able to pick it up again." His face was haggard, his eyes deep-set. He looked like a man who'd been through not just a battle but a long, hard war. "Terrible things have happened, Ned, more terrible than you can imagine."

"Try me," Hodder said.

"They killed children. They kidnapped them and raped them and killed them."

"We know. We found graves at Stokely's cabin. How is it that you know?"

Johnson thought a long time before answering, but not, Cork surmised, because he didn't know the answer. It was a difficult thing to talk about.

"The girl in the lake," he finally responded. "I got to thinking about her. When I put it together with what Charlie and Ren told me yesterday, I had a sick feeling I knew what was going on. I left Jewell's place and drove straight to Marquette to confront Bell. He'd been drinking. It didn't take much to get him to admit things. Hell, he was delighted to talk." His face drew taut and his hands made fists. "In Africa, I saw the aftermath of genocide, and I saw that same look on the faces of the men responsible, a grotesque kind of rapture. I knew how to make myself cold and hard so that I could ask the right questions to get the answers I needed. He even showed me a videotape he'd made of what he and Stokely did, and he invited me to join them. He thought I was an animal like him."

"Why would he think that?"

This time Johnson didn't answer. Jewell spoke for him. "You were with him and Stokely and Tom Messinger twenty years ago, the night the runaway girl was killed, weren't you, Gary?"

He stared at her and denied nothing.

"What happened that night?" she asked gently.

His gaze went distant for a while. Static whispered from the television. In the kitchen, the refrigerator motor had kicked on. Dina shifted on her feet and a floorboard squeaked. These were normal, everyday sounds, yet in the terrible quiet of the house, in the repugnant presence of violent death, they seemed macabre and out of place.

"We were coming home," Johnson began. "We'd been drinking, celebrating, feeling good. We stopped for gas just outside Marquette, and she was there. She asked us what was up, where we were going. She said she'd be happy to party with us. We still had beer. Instead of going home, we drove to an old overlook along the lakeshore. One thing led to another and she was willing. We drew straws. Tommy went first. He wasn't used to drinking and he was already almost gone. He went with her to the car. A few minutes later he came back, puked, passed out. Stokely went next, then Bell. Then it was my turn. I don't know what Stokely and Bell did to her, but she was a mess, huddled in the backseat, crying. She didn't want me there."

He paused, tears in his eyes.

"It was my fault. All my fault."

"Why?" Jewell asked.

"I'd spent that autumn on the sidelines with a damn cast on my leg. I missed the whole championship season. Now I was going to miss my turn with that girl. I went back to the other guys, told them. Stokely, Bell, they said like hell. They went to the car, pulled her out, held her down."

Through the big window at the back of the house, Cork could see the light slipping away. At the horizon, the line between lake and sky was hard to distinguish. Dark like a black fog crept into far rooms, and the light from the lamp that lit the dead man seemed to grow brighter.

"I raped her," Johnson finished. A line of tears glistened down both cheeks, but he went on. "I did it and then I left her. I stumbled away. Christ, I was sick at what I was doing, what I'd done. I made my way down to the lakeshore and threw up. I wasn't far enough away that I couldn't hear Stokely and Bell going at her again. I knew I should do something, but it was like I was in the middle of a nightmare and I couldn't move.

"When I got back to the others, the girl was still on the ground. Her eyes were open, but she wasn't moving. I don't know what they did to her, but I knew she was dead. Stokely, Bell, they took her body, threw it in the lake. I didn't even try to stop them. Superior wasn't supposed to give up its dead, except this time it did. Tommy was devastated. He took it all on his shoulders. We killed two people that night. I've spent my life trying to put the memory behind me. I left Bodine thinking if I ran far enough, maybe . . ."

Jewell said, "Africa wasn't far enough?"

"Whenever I closed my eyes, she was there. You can't imagine the sleepless nights."

"Why come back to where it all happened?" Cork asked.

"You're a cop. Don't criminals always return to the scene of the crime?" He looked immeasurably tired. "When my father got sick, he asked me to come home and take over the paper. Running away hadn't done me any good and I thought maybe coming back here and facing the demon might free me." He stared down at Stokely's body. "If I'd been a good person, a strong person, I'd have ended this the night it all began."

"It's ended now," Jewell said softly.

"You think so?" He was a huge man, but he seemed to shrink, to condense into himself, a great balloon deflating. "It never ends."

"What did Bell tell you about him and Stokely?" Cork asked.

"He said for years after that night on the lakeshore they would go over what they'd done to the girl. They fed on the grisly details like ghouls. I'm running all over the world trying to forget, and for them it was the heart of their lives. Bell said they planned other killings but never went through with them—until they began driving trucks cross-country. They came across kids looking for rides everywhere. Tender meat, Bell called them. And so it started. Always kids, always runaways. They brutalized them, killed them, buried them somewhere off the highway where they'd never be found.

"When they had to give up trucking, Bell looked for another source of prey. He found it in Providence House." He shook his head bitterly. "Providence. Hell of a name, when you think about it. Provided him and Stokely with God only knows how many victims. He said they chose kids no one would miss, and there were a lot of those. He told me he'd been eyeing Sara Wolf for a long time. Finally he couldn't stand it anymore, so he waited for her one day after school, pretended to be passing by, offered her a ride. He gave her a Pepsi he'd laced with Rohypnol and brought her up to Calvin's cabin. But she fought them and damned if she didn't beat them. Got away from Stokely and his dog, Bell said, and threw herself off a cliff into the Copper River. He was disappointed because he still had a lot of ideas about what he could do to her.

"Since I came back, I'd exchanged no more than a couple of dozen words with Bell and Stokely. I purposely avoided them.

But there he is, spilling his guts to me, telling me these things because in his sick thinking he really believes that night twenty years ago made me just like him. So I killed him. Blew his heart right out of his chest. I came back to Bodine and called Calvin. When he got here, I started the video Bell had given me." Johnson nodded at the blue screen. "I asked him, was he a part of this? He was smarter than Bell. He understood exactly what I thought of him. He stared at me and said, 'You won't say anything. Because if you do, I'll tell everyone what kind of man we both know you really are.' He grinned, grinned at me like he had me cornered. I shot him where he stood. All the hours since, I've had that gun in my hand, thinking I might as well kill myself while I'm at it."

"Why didn't you just go to the police, Gary?" Hodder said.

"Because everyone would know what I am. A monster just like Bell and Stokely."

"You're no monster, Gary." Jewell tried to move toward him, to reach out and comfort him, but Hodder kept her back.

Johnson stood slumped over, his enormous shoulders rounded in shame. "I don't feel human, Jewell. Not anymore. Maybe never since that night. Tommy had the right idea. I thought I could do what he did, only it turns out I don't have the courage. I've been sitting here for hours. I couldn't bring myself to do it."

Cork asked, "Did either of them talk about Isaac Stokely being involved?"

"Just them."

"Did they say anything about Charlie?" Dina asked.

"Bell did. Said they went looking for her at Max's place. They killed him when he wouldn't tell them where she was. Bell said he had a lot of ideas about what he'd do to Charlie when he got hold of her."

"He didn't get hold of her?"

"Didn't sound like it. Why? She's with you, isn't she?"

"She ran away last night. Nobody's seen her since," Dina replied. "What time did Calvin Stokely get here?"

He thought about it. "Maybe eight o'clock or nine. He took his time getting here after I called. I figured he'd been drinking in a bar somewhere, eh. I could smell it on him."

"And he didn't say anything about Charlie?"

He shook his head. "Our exchange was brief, then I shot him. I just kept pulling the trigger, I wanted him dead so bad."

Hodder laid a hand on his shoulder. "We're going back to my office, Gary. I'm going to hold you there and call the Marquette Sheriff's Department."

Johnson nodded and let himself be taken.

Cork said, "I'll meet you guys outside. I want to check Stokely's truck." He didn't have to add that he was looking for Charlie's body.

He went through the door between the kitchen and the garage and turned on the light. The place was neat. Johnson's dusty Jeep was parked next to Stokely's big Dodge Ram. He found Stokely's keys in the ignition. He unlocked the tailgate but hesitated before lifting the rear window of the camper shell.

When he stepped from the house, the others were waiting, their shadowed faces tensed for the worst.

"Nothing," he said, to their great relief. "No Charlie."

As they walked to their vehicles, Cork breathed deeply the autumn-scented air, cool off the lake, cleansing his nose and mouth and throat of the death smell that filled the house. He thought about Charlie and believed there was still plenty of room for hope.

Hodder put Johnson in the back of his Cherokee, and the newspaperman sat there, bent forward a little like a wilted plant.

"I've got to take care of this," the constable told the others. "One possibility with Charlie is that she's broken into a summer cabin and is hiding. After I turn Gary over, I'll make a swing and check all the ones I think are likely. Terry Olafsson's going to want to talk to you, so make yourselves available."

"Ned." Jewell moved close to him. "I'm sorry."

"It's okay. This is all so crazy, Jewell."

"When things are settled, I'd love to sit down over dinner and talk."

"I'd like that, too."

He smiled briefly, then turned to his duty.

"Good man, that," Cork noted as the Cherokee pulled away.

"I know," Jewell said. She let out a deep breath. "Ren's probably worried. We should get home. Who knows, maybe Charlie's showed up."

Dina's cell phone chirped. She pulled it from the purse she'd left in the Pathfinder.

"Willner," she answered. While she listened, her face darkened. "Okay, Kenny. Thanks." She looked at Cork. "Lou Jacoby's passed a message to you through my people. He says, 'Eye for an eye. Son for a son.'"

For a long, stunned moment, Cork couldn't breathe. "He's going after Stevie," he finally said. "The bastard's going after my son. Give me that phone."

Cork punched in the number for Rose and Mal at the duplex in Evanston. Jo answered.

"Cork?" she said. Her voice was flooded with relief. "You're all right."

"Jo, where's Stevie? Is he there with you?"

"He went with Rose and the girls to a movie. I hoped it might get their minds off worrying about you for a while. Why?"

"Which movie? Where?"

"Cork, what's going on?"

"Do you know which movie theater, Jo?"

"Yes."

"Get him out and get him home. Then you and the kids lock yourselves in Rose's place until I get there. Do you understand?"

"What is it?"

"Lou Jacoby might try to hurt Stevie because he can't get to me."

"Oh God."

"Find him, and when you're back at the duplex, call me." He gave her Dina's cell phone number. "Get our son, Jo."

He ended the call.

"What's Jacoby's number?" he asked Dina, who would know because she'd worked for Jacoby in the past. He punched in the number she gave him. An old, modulated voice answered, which Cork recognized as Evers, the houseman.

"Give me Jacoby," Cork said.

"Mr. Jacoby is unavailable."

"Tell him it's O'Connor. He'll make himself available."

"I'm sorry, sir—"

"Tell him, Evers. Tell him I'm coming and I'm going to kill him. And if you don't tell him, I'm going to kill you, too."

"Cork, let me." Dina spoke firmly and held out her hand. "Evers will listen to me."

He slapped the phone into her palm.

"Evers, it's Dina Willner. Lou will want to talk to us." She listened a moment. "Thank you." She gave Cork the cell phone.

He waited, a fire raging in his gut, climbing into his chest, burning his throat. Then Jacoby spoke at the other end. "I'm listening."

"Listen good, you son of a bitch. You touch my son, I'll not only kill you, I'll kill everything you ever loved."

"Everything I love is already dead, O'Connor. You saw to that."

"It wasn't me, you blind fuck. It was your daughter-in-law and Salguero. The cops are ready to cuff them both. Leave my son out of this."

"You can make that happen. You know what I want."

"I'm on my way, all right. I'm coming down from Marquette, Michigan. Give me that time and I'll give you me. I swear it."

The line went silent, but Cork knew Jacoby was still there.

"You have until morning," Jacoby said. He hung up.

Cork made one more call, this one to Boomer Grabowski, a friend and ex-cop in Chicago, a guy as tough as they came. Boomer told him no sweat. He'd get up to Evanston right away, stay with the family until Cork got there. Did Cork want any help dealing with Jacoby?

"Thanks, Boomer. I'll take care of him myself."

"What's the plan?" Dina asked.

"Jacoby gave me until morning," Cork said. "We get Jewell back to the cabins, then I'm leaving."

"I'm sorry, Cork," Jewell said.

"Let's just go."

He limped to the Pathfinder, saying a silent prayer. At the same time, he imagined himself pumping round after round into Lou Jacoby until that withered old body lay good and dead in a lake of its own warm blood.

47

Ren hung by his arms from a tree branch. His wrists had been duct-taped together, then he'd been lifted and hung up like a side of beef. A strip of tape sealed his mouth.

"Insurance," the man had said in the cabin. He tried to sound friendly and he smiled a lot, but the gun in his hand spoke differently to Ren.

"Where's O'Connor gone?" he'd asked.

Ren told him he didn't know.

"Any idea when he'll be back?"

Ren shook his head.

That was when the man produced the roll of duct tape. "Relax, kid, you're just my insurance if things go south."

He'd marched Ren outside into the trees, hung him up, and sealed his mouth. He had already set up a scoped rifle on a tripod low to the ground, the barrel pointed toward the cabins. He lay down, checked the scope, and made an adjustment. Then he sat up and looked no more at Ren.

He wasn't anything like Ren had imagined a hit man to be. He had a bald spot on the top of his head over which he'd combed a few strands of mouse-brown hair. He wore wire-rimmed spectacles that he slipped to the top of his head whenever he sighted through the scope. He was dressed in a brown corduroy sport coat with a tan turtleneck beneath, blue jeans, white sneakers. From a stained white paper bag near his feet came the smell of barbecued meat.

It was twilight now. Through the branches directly above him stripped half bare by the storm the night before, Ren saw the faint gleam of an emerging star. The woods were a murk of tree trunks and low brush gone gray or black in the failing light, still and indistinct as images in an underdeveloped photograph.

Ren's shoulders and arms ached from the hanging weight of his body, but he tried to ignore the pain and think if there was some way to warn Cork and the others. Because there was nothing else he could do, he tried kicking, hoping to break free of the branch. His legs struck at empty air and the effort only made his shoulders hurt even more. He considered the quiet of the evening, the dreadful calm, and thought hopelessly how easy it was going to be to hear the cars coming up the lane. Occasionally from the woods around them came the rustling of a squirrel scampering among the fallen leaves beneath the undergrowth. At first the sounds had startled the man, but he quickly learned to ignore them.

In a while came the distant whir of a vehicle on the main road, the engine winding down. Someone was coming. The man moved to a prone position, his eye to the rifle scope. Ren tried to think what he could do. He decided when the others drove up, he'd make the loudest sound he could behind the seal of the tape and maybe, just maybe, they would hear and be warned. The man would probably get mad and do something horrible to Ren, but he'd take that chance.

Amid the stillness all around him, he suddenly saw movement out of the corner of his eye. Had he been looking straight on in the dim light, he might have missed it. He swung his gaze left. For a few moments he didn't see anything. Had he been mistaken? Then he spotted the soundless slide of something large, pale, and horizontal against the vertical darkness of a tree trunk. Only a second of motion, then nothing. Ren strained to see clearly, but the mottled shading in the woods made it difficult to distinguish anything.

Motion again, a brief creeping movement, and now Ren recognized the stalking behavior of a cat. He discerned the outline of the cougar moving stealthily—creep, pause, creep—toward the man, whose attention was on the cabin and who had no idea of the danger at his back.

What Ren understood from the reading he'd done after he first discovered the animal's tracks was that cougars preferred to attack from behind, allowing their prey to pass where they crouched before pouncing. Attacking a man was unusual, but this was a desperate beast, hungry, maybe half-crazed because it had been wounded by Calvin Stokely.

Then Ren had another thought. Maybe the cat wasn't coming for the man. Maybe the cat was interested in the easy meal hanging from the tree.

He held his breath, felt the terrible ache of his shoulders, the kicking of his heart. He hung directly between the beast and the man, and Ren couldn't tell which of them was the prey. He wanted to close his eyes to keep from seeing what he couldn't stop—the long claws, the deadly teeth—but he couldn't force his eyelids closed. He hung there powerless, damned to see the end as it came.

48

Dina turned the Pathfinder onto the rutted lane leading to the cabins. Ahead was a long stretch of gray growing dimmer as the daylight faded. She switched on her headlights, and immediately a figure leaped from the trees.

Dina braked and said, "Charlie?"

The girl rushed to the vehicle. Dina opened the door.

"Ren," Charlie gasped. "He's got Ren."

"Who's got Ren?" Jewell said from the passenger side.

Charlie caught her breath. "I don't know. A stranger. A dude. He came after you guys left. He was, like, hiding in the woods."

"How do you know that?" Dina asked.

"I was hiding, too, watching for Ren to come home. After you left, this dude comes out of the trees. He's got a gun. He's all, like, creeping around, checking everything out. He looks in Thor's Lodge, then Cork's cabin. Then he checks out the car behind the shed with all the bullet holes in it. Finally he goes back to the trees and waits and when Ren comes home he follows him, brings him out, and hangs him up in the woods."

Jewell leaned across Dina. "Is Ren okay?"

"Yeah, when I sneaked away he was. But we have to get him back."

"You don't know this guy?" Dina said.

"No."

Dina looked confused. "Gary didn't say anything about anybody else."

"Maybe this isn't about the kids," Cork said from the back-seat. "Maybe this is about me."

"The hit?" Dina thought it over and nodded.

Jewell stared desperately down the lane. "Ren," she said fearfully.

Cork swung his door open and clambered out. "Jewell, get on your cell phone and call Hodder. Tell him the situation. Charlie, can you show us where this man has Ren?"

"Sure."

Dina was out, too, and checking her carbine.

"I'm coming," Jewell said, climbing out her side.

Cork took her by the shoulders firmly. "You have to stay here, Jewell. When Hodder shows up, or anybody else, they need to understand the situation. They can't come barreling in. Dina's going to give you one of the Motorolas. When we know what's going on, we'll contact you. You have to do this. You have to do it for Ren."

"I can't just wait here."

"I know how hard that is, but you have to. Dina and I do this for a living. We're good at it. We'll get Ren back safely, Jewell, I promise you."

He could see how torn she was and he understood completely. Finally she nodded and said, "All right."

She reached for her cell phone. He reached for the Glock Dina had given him earlier.

Cork and Dina followed Charlie. They cut through the woods west of the lane until they came to the Killbelly Marsh Trail. Charlie moved quickly—too quickly for safety, Cork thought. Dina must have thought so, too, because she touched the girl's shoulder and spoke close to her ear. After that, Charlie led the way more cautiously.

A quarter mile up the trail, she stopped and pointed toward the trees that hid the cabins. "A hundred yards in," she whispered.

Dina nodded and whispered back, "We'll take it from here."

Charlie shook her head vigorously and started ahead. Cork reached out to stop her but was too late. Dina held up her hands in frustration, which was all she could do, because any verbal objection now, any undue disturbance, might alert the man who'd taken Ren. There was nothing but to follow Charlie.

Cork brought up the rear, his wounded leg ready to buckle. He concentrated all his efforts on moving the leg forward, carrying him carefully and quietly toward Ren. They had no plan, which was a problem, but there was no time for planning. The light was fading and dark was the worst enemy of all. They had to rely on Charlie to guide them, and then they would have to improvise. In this, he trusted Dina. At that moment, there was no one he would rather have as a partner.

Charlie raised her hand and stopped. Her head turned slowly right, then left. Had she made an error? Were they off track? Charlie turned to them, a pained expression on her face. She was uncertain.

They were near where the trees edged the old resort. If the man's plan had been to shoot Cork, then he'd probably set himself up just inside the tree line. This was a delicate moment. They were close enough to give themselves away easily, but still not certain of the exact location of Ren.

He touched Dina's shoulder and pointed for her to move right. He indicated he would go left. She nodded and signaled for Charlie to come with her. They separated and crept away twenty yards, then waited. Cork slipped left the same distance. On his signal, they moved forward again. With luck, he hoped Ren and his captor would be caught somewhere between them. Cork walked on the outside of his soles, an old stalking technique he'd learned hunting that allowed him to move silently. All his senses were focused on the woods around him as he sought to pick up anything out of place. A trickle of sweat crawled down his face like a spider. Suddenly he walked into the unmistakable aroma of barbecued meat. There was almost no wind, just enough to carry the tangy scent. From which direction? He bent and cracked open a milkweed pod, plucked a piece of fluff from inside, let it go. The fluff drifted lazily northwest. The man and his barbecue were somewhere southeast. Cork adjusted his line and crept ahead.

Ten seconds later the silence around him was shattered by a scream that was followed by a thrashing in the underbrush and the grunting of a desperate struggle. Cork abandoned stealth and rushed ahead, afraid for Ren.

In the dim evening light, Cork stumbled onto a nightmarish scene. On the ground a man wrestled to free himself from the grip of a cougar, whose powerful jaws were locked on the back of his neck. The man flailed and screamed, but the cougar, larger and heavier, held tight. A few yards away Ren hung from the branch of a tree, his wrists high above his head, his feet just inches off the ground, his eyes wide as he watched the horror of the attack.

Cork swung the Glock toward the struggle on the ground, but the two figures were so tightly enmeshed, he couldn't risk a shot.

Dina and Charlie appeared beside Ren. Dina sighted down the barrel of her carbine but didn't fire.

The cougar, intent on its kill, hadn't seen the others arrive. Cork raised his Glock and fired into the air, hoping to distract the beast, to startle it into breaking off its attack. The cougar spun, teeth bared.

Cork, Dina, and Charlie all held dead still, but at the sound of the gun, Ren had begun to kick his legs wildly, crying out through the tape over his mouth a muffled "No!" It was a plea, Cork understood, not to kill the animal.

All that movement, which Ren meant to save the wild cat, in the end spelled its doom. The cougar, confused and threatened, focused on Ren and his wild legs. The animal's ears lay back. As it gathered on it haunches, Dina moved instantly between Ren and the cat.

The animal launched itself and Cork fired twice.

The cougar cried out like a kicked housecat, turning awkwardly in midair as if its internal gyroscope had been destroyed. It fell far short of Dina and Ren and lay on the ground, stunned. After a moment, it tried to struggle to its feet but, failing, became still. For a minute, the quiet of that small circle of woods was broken only by the animal's labored breathing.

The man groaned and rolled onto his back. "Help me," he rasped.

"Keep him covered," Dina told Cork.

She wrapped her arms around Ren and lifted him free of the branch. Charlie already had her pocketknife out and she cut the tape from his wrists. He pulled the strip off his mouth and the first thing he said was "We've gotta save the cougar."

"I'm hurt," the man on the ground pleaded.

"Cover me," Cork said to Dina. "I'll pat him down."

"Fucking gun's in my belt," the man said. "Take it. Just get me to a hospital."

Cork pulled the gun, a nine-millimeter Ruger, from the man's belt and ejected the clip. He went over the rest of his body but found no other weapon and stepped back.

"The cougar," Ren repeated, edging near the downed animal.

"Stay back," Dina said firmly.

"But it's going to die."

Dina put the Motorola to her lips. "Jewell, do you read me?"

"I'm here. What's going on? What were those shots?"

"Ren's safe, but we need you up here and bring your medical kit."

"It's not Ren?"

"No. A couple of wounded animals. A cougar and a rat."

"Ned's here. He's coming with me."

"I'll meet you at the cabins and guide you over." She lowered the walkie-talkie.

"I'll go," Charlie offered. "I'm faster."

"All right," Dina said. "And, Charlie? You did a good job today."

The girl flashed a big smile and was gone, bounding swiftly and gracefully toward the distant cabins.

"You okay, Ren?" Cork put his arm around the boy's shoulders.

"Yeah, I guess." He sounded distracted, his attention focused on the wounded wild cat.

Dina walked to the man on the ground, looked down at him, and shook her head. "Vernon Mann."

"You know him?" Cork asked.

"'The Mann who would be king,' we used to call him when I was with the feds. He was DEA back then, full of delusions of grandeur. Went private like me. Not nearly as good or as principled, however. Still overachieving, Vern? You're way outside your comfort level here, schmuck, but I bet for five hundred thousand dollars you'd slit your own grandmother's throat."

"I don't know what you're talking about," Mann said.

"On second thought, you'd probably do it for a lot less. Who clued you in, Vern?"

Vernon Mann didn't answer. Dina bent down, drew him up roughly into a sitting position.

"Let me take a look at those cougar wounds," she said.

Mann leaned forward slightly.

"A couple dozen well-placed stitches and you'll be fine, Vern."

Cork couldn't see exactly what Dina was doing, but Mann suddenly arched his back and screamed in pain.

"So how 'bout it, Vern? How'd you find us?"

"All right, all right," he cried. "I got a buddy at the *Sun-Times*. Somebody called him from up here looking for information about O'Connor. He called me. I did some digging, came up with a relative, Jewell DuBois."

They heard the vehicles rumbling up the lane to the cabins. Through the trees, Cork saw the Pathfinder and Hodder's Cherokee stop where Charlie waited. Jewell jumped out, ran to her Blazer, and grabbed her medical bag from inside. Hodder joined her. They spoke briefly with Charlie, then followed her at a jog toward the trees.

The moment she saw Ren, Jewell wrapped him in her arms. The boy didn't pull away from his mother's public display of affection.

"Can you save it, Mom?" he asked, nodding toward the downed cougar.

"Hell, what about me?" whined Vernon Mann.

"Relax," Dina told him. "You'll live. And, Vern, I heard Michigan prison food isn't all that bad."

Ren started toward the cougar, but his mother put her hand on his shoulder. "I'm going to try to sedate him. Then we'll see."

As Jewell opened her bag, the cougar's rasping breathing ceased and a terrible moment of quiet followed.

"No," Ren cried. He tried to move toward the animal, but Dina held him back.

"Don't go near him, Ren," his mother ordered. "Don't anybody go near him. Let me check him first."

Cork watched Jewell approach carefully. He still had the Glock trained on the animal. It was a beautiful creature of sand-colored fur and strong muscle. Its eyes were open. Cork, who'd hunted all his life, knew the dead look in them, but he found himself hoping he was wrong, that Jewell would discover some sign of life.

She stayed clear of the big paws and the long teeth and gingerly touched the animal's side near its haunch. Her hand drifted slowly up the sleek body, pausing here and there to feel. She drew a stethoscope from her bag, slipped it under the front leg, and pressed it to the cougar's chest.

Cork glanced at Ren. The boy stood rigid, waiting. His eyes, which had already seen so much horror, were half-closed in anticipation of the truth.

"He's dead," Jewell pronounced at last.

The boy broke.

It wasn't just the cougar, Cork told himself. It was the strain of all that had gone before. Ren knelt and sobbed bitterly over an animal he'd never seen before.

"You killed it," he accused, his dark eyes attacking Cork. "You murdered it."

Cork lowered the gun that had been trained on the cougar. "I'm sorry, Ren."

"It's not right," Ren insisted. "It's not right."

"He didn't have a choice," Jewell said.

"Dude," Charlie jumped in, "that thing was going after you and Dina. I don't care how beautiful it was, I'd rather have you alive any day, dork."

Ren gently stroked the still, tawny body. "It's so beautiful." He shook his head. "Everything dies." It sounded like a hopeless truth.

"You didn't," Charlie told him. "And here I am."

Ren stood up, tears trailing down his cheeks. He turned away and ran toward the cabins.

"Ren," Charlie called.

"Let him go," Jewell said. "He'll be all right."

Cork watched him stumble away. "Jesus, I feel like a murderer."

Jewell put her hand on his arm. "Give him some time. He'll understand."

Ned Hodder said to Charlie, "Where were you hiding?"

"In one of the summer homes on the river. I broke in. I guess I'm in trouble, huh?"

Hodder gave it almost no thought at all. "Under the circumstances, I think we can square things pretty easily."

Jewell closed her medical kit. "Ned, would you call DNR and let them know what we've got here. Have them pick up the cougar's body."

"And how about getting a fucking ambulance for me?" Vernon Mann cried.

Cork's leg finally gave out. He sat down with his back against the tree where Ren had hung. Dina sat beside him.

"I guess we're even," she said.

"Even?"

"I saved your life, now you've saved mine."

Cork heard sirens coming from the direction of the Copper River Club: the state police responding to Hodder's call.

"We're not done yet," he said.

Dina closed her eyes and tilted her head as if listening to a distant song. "I know."

49

By 9:00 P.M. the authorities were gone. The state police had taken custody of Gary Johnson. They also took Vernon Mann to be treated for his wounds from the cougar attack, then to be booked. Olafsson headed back to his office in Marquette looking weary at the prospect of the paperwork ahead of him but buoyed by his understanding of how all the tragic events in his jurisdiction were tied together. He'd even agreed to allow Charlie, for the moment, to stay with Jewell while things got sorted out legally. Two officers from the Department of Natural Resources had taken the dead cougar away. Ned Hodder stuck around.

Jo had called to let Cork know she and the kids were safe. They were all at the duplex with Rose and Mal. Boomer Grabowski was there, too. He was just as big as she remembered him.

"What are you going to do?" she'd asked. "You're not going to just hand yourself over to Lou Jacoby?"

"I don't know yet, Jo."

"The police can help, can't they?"

"If Jacoby wants me dead or my son or the pope for that matter, he's got the money to make it happen despite the police. At this point, there's only one way to deal with Jacoby."

"Cork, I know you're angry, but listen to me a moment." She was struggling to remain calm, he could tell. Probably she was fighting back tears. "The Jacobys have hurt us enough. I can live with the rape and everything else that's happened. I can't live without you. Come home, sweetheart. We'll think of something together."

"I can't do that, Jo."

"Is Dina there?"

"Yeah."

"Let me talk to her, okay?"

He gave Dina the phone. She listened and nodded. "That makes two of us. Don't worry, Jo. He's sometimes a little too noble, but he's not dumb. We'll see you in the morning, I promise."

She handed the phone back to Cork.

"I love you," Jo said. "I miss you."

"I know. Same here."

"Then come home."

"Kiss the kids for me," he said.

He had hung up before Jo could say more. For a while after that, he didn't talk to anyone.

Charlie had disappeared into Ren's bedroom, and the sound of their voices occasionally drifted through the cabin. They knew about the horror at Calvin Stokely's cabin and were processing it, Cork guessed. He drank strong black coffee from a mug, preparing himself for the long drive ahead. Dina sat on the floor, hugging her knees to her chest, the firelight etching shadows across her face. Ned and Jewell sat on the sofa, almost touching.

"It's time," Cork said at last. He took a final gulp of coffee and set the mug on the table.

"I'm going with you," Dina said.

"We'll be walking into a real mess."

"Like we haven't already?"

"Thanks," he said.

"You're leaving?" Charlie stood near the kitchen. Cork hadn't heard her come in. She was staring at Dina, looking worried. "For good?"

Dina got up slowly. "For a while."

"But you'll come back?"

"You want that?" Dina asked.

Charlie looked down at her hands and spoke softly. "Yeah."

"When this business down in Illinois is finished, I'll come back."

Charlie raised her eyes, hopeful. "Promise?"

"Cross my heart."

"How's Ren?" Cork asked.

Charlie shrugged. "You know."

Jewell stood up. "Let me have one last look at that leg, Cork. In the bedroom."

She got her medical bag and Cork followed her to the guest room. She closed the door. He dropped his pants and sat on the edge of the bed. She knelt and examined his wounds.

"The new stitches are holding," she said. "No infection. Let me clean them again, then promise me that when you get to Chicago you'll see a physician." She opened her bag.

"I'm sorry, Jewell. I was wrong coming here," Cork said. "I thought it would keep my family safe and wouldn't threaten you and Ren. I couldn't have been more wrong."

"I don't mind how it's worked out."

"We were lucky."

She looked up into his eyes. "I don't think so. I believe we were guided by a wiser hand than we realized."

He winced as she took a cotton ball soaked in hydrogen peroxide and wiped away ooze that had crusted over the line of stitches. "I've got a friend, an old Ojibwe Mide named Henry Meloux," he said.

"Meloux? My mother used to talk about him. Fondly."

"A wise man. He told me once every falling leaf comes to rest where it was always meant to."

"You haven't come to rest yet." She finished with his wounds and laid her hand against his cheek. "You'll be careful?"

"Of course. And I won't be alone."

"Dina." She seemed comforted by that. "When it's done, let me know that you're safe. And, Cork, let's be family again."

"We never stopped."

She closed her bag. Cork hiked his pants up and they returned to the main room.

Ren was waiting. "I didn't mean to be, like, such a . . . you know."

"It's okay," Cork told him. "I feel bad about killing the cougar, but I'd do it again in a heartbeat if it meant saving you."

The boy thought about it. "I guess that's being a man, huh?"

"I don't know about that. It's what I'd do, is all."

"If it was you, I guess I'd do the same."

Cork put his hand on Ren's shoulder. "I'm sorry my situation got you in serious trouble. I made a mistake, a pretty big one."

Ren waved off the apology. "It's okay. I just wish you didn't have to go."

"But you understand?"

"Yeah."

"I'll be back. A lot, I promise."

Ren tried to smile. "You want to see something?"

"Sure."

He led Cork to his bedroom and picked up the big drawing pad from his desk. Cork studied the fine line sketch of Ren's hero White Eagle swooping out of the sky over a rocky shoreline that was clearly a Lake Superior landscape. He was pleasantly surprised by the figure of White Eagle, whose face now very much resembled Daniel DuBois, Ren's father.

"He would have liked this," Cork said.

The boy held the drawing in his hands and nodded. "I know."

When the Pathfinder was loaded, they gathered on the porch of Thor's Lodge.

Ren stood next to Dina, eyeing her shyly.

"I've got something for you," he said. He handed her a rolled page from his sketchbook.

Looking over her shoulder, Cork saw that it was the drawing Ren had done of a cougar with Dina's face. The boy had managed to make her seem mythic, a creature both wild and lovely. Cork thought Ren had captured her spirit beautifully.

Dina looked down and her face grew soft in a way Cork had not seen before. "It's the nicest gift anyone's ever given me, Ren."

Charlie, who was standing beside Ren, said, "Most of the time he's pretty lame. But once in a while he gets it right."

Dina kissed his cheek. "Thank you."

"Oh Jesus. Now he's never going to wash his face." Charlie laughed and playfully punched Ren's arm.

Cork signaled Hodder away from the others and spoke to him quietly. "Ned, I'm worried about someone else showing up before I've taken care of Jacoby. Also, this place will be crawling with reporters by tomorrow."

"Until I get the word from you that things are squared, I'm not leaving here," Hodder replied. "I may not carry a hand-gun, but I'm good with a rifle, believe me. And I've got a part-time deputy constable I'll call in to help. We'll keep things covered, and I'll give Jewell a hand dealing with reporters."

"Thanks."

Hodder offered him an easy smile. "I'm not doing this for your peace of mind."

"That makes it even better." They shook hands.

Cork spent a few final moments in the porch light with Jewell and Ren. Their three shadows stretched away and merged into one form just this side of the dark.

"You have a long way to go," she said, and hugged him. "I'll be praying."

Cork turned to Ren and laid his hand the young man's shoulder. "Take care of yourself."

"You, too."

Cork got into the Pathfinder. Dina drove down the bumpy lane and turned onto the main road. The moon was up, the sleepless eye of night. As they crossed the bridge over the Copper River, Cork stared at the water, a long sweep of silver that ran to the great lake. The river had carried the body of the dead girl far, carried it right under the noses of Ren and his friends. An accident? There was spirit in all things, Cork believed, knowledge in every molecule of creation. Nothing ever went truly unnoticed, from the fall of a single leaf to the death of a child.

"Long night ahead," Dina observed.

"God willing, we'll find daylight at the end," Cork replied.

He settled back and closed his eyes to rest and to plan.

50

*T*he call came when they were south of Green Bay, in the dead of night. It was Captain Ed Larson calling from Aurora, Minnesota. Dina gave the phone to Cork. Larson told him that Gabriella Jacoby, Lou Jacoby's daughter-in-law, had been picked up by the Winnetka police and questioned about the death of her husband. They had a lot on her and she'd rolled over and given them her brother, Tony Salguero. She claimed he planned the whole thing and that he was the one who killed Jacoby's other son, Ben. The Winnetka police were looking for Salguero. He'd disappeared.

"Anybody tell Lou Jacoby this?"

"He knows."

"Thanks, Ed."

Cork ended the call.

"So," Dina said, "that's it?" She looked straight ahead, eyeing the highway, black and empty in the headlights. Nothing in her voice gave away what she might be thinking.

"No, that's not it." Cork tossed the cell phone into the Pathfinder's glove box. "I want to see Lou Jacoby. I want to get right up in his face."

Dina shot him a look that might have been approval. "Whatever you say."

A little before seven A.M., they stopped a hundred yards south of Jacoby's estate on the shoreline in the exclusive community of Lake Forest. The predawn sky above Lake Michigan

was streaked with veins of angry red. They got out and began
to walk. The air was cool and still and smelled of autumn and
the lake. Their shoes crunched on the loose gravel at the edge
of the road with a sound like someone chewing ice. They
passed through the front gate onto the circular drive. Jacoby's
house looked like an Italian villa. The windows were dark.

"Motion sensors?" Cork asked quietly.

Dina shook her head. "Not outside. Security system is all
internal."

She led the way to the rear corner, where Cork could see the
back lawn, big as a polo field, stretching down to a tall hedge.
Beyond the hedge lay Lake Michigan reflecting the red dawn.
Dina stopped at a door on the side of the house and took from
her jacket the pouch with her picklocks.

"Will you trip the alarm?" Cork asked.

"Relax. I designed the system for him."

They were inside quickly, staring at a large kitchen hung
with enough pots and pans and shiny cooking utensils that it
could have served a fine restaurant. Dina tapped a code into
the alarm box beside the door. She signaled for Cork to follow
her.

They crept down a labyrinth of hallways and rooms and up
a narrow set of stairs at the far end of the house, and came out
onto a long corridor with doors opening off either side. Dina
moved to the first door on the left. She reached down and
carefully turned the knob. The door slid open silently. She
stepped in.

They found themselves in an anteroom that opened onto an
enormous bedroom. The place smelled heavily of cigar smoke.
The drapes in the anteroom were drawn against the dawn, but
the bedroom was lit with the fire of a sun about to rise. Dina
stepped silently through the far door. She turned to her right
and spoke. "Up early, Lou."

Cork heard Jacoby reply without surprise, "No, Dina. I'm
just not sleeping these days. I thought you were with . . ." He
paused as Cork limped into the room. ". . . O'Connor."

Lou Jacoby stood framed against the window. He wore a
dressing gown and slippers, and smoke rose from a lit cigar in
his right hand. He was nearing eighty. In the light through the

window—the only light in the room—he looked pale and hard, more like the plaster cast of a man.

"Our business is finished," the old man said.

"You put a contract out on me," Cork replied.

Jacoby waved it off. "That's been taken care of."

"An eye for an eye, you said. You threatened my boy. Another kid I'm fond of was kidnapped by someone looking to collect on that half-million-dollar bounty you put on my head. A lot of other innocent people stood to get hurt."

Jacoby looked unimpressed. "And you're here to what?"

"Maybe start by beating the living shit out of you," Cork said.

"Bloody an old man?" Jacoby opened his arms in invitation.

"I told you it wasn't me who killed your son," Cork spit out.

Jacoby almost laughed. "And I was supposed to take your word for it? Hell, I know my garbageman better than I know you."

"How does it feel having to accept that it was family killing family—your family? And by the way, Salguero's disappeared. Doesn't that leave your coffer of vengeance a little empty?"

Jacoby lifted his cigar, took a draw, and said through the smoke, "Does it?"

Dina gave a short, hollow laugh. "They'll never find Tony Salguero, will they, Lou? You had him taken care of."

"I don't know what you're talking about," Jacoby said.

"There's still Gabriella," Cork pointed out. "With a good lawyer—"

"She'll use the lawyer I pay for," Jacoby said. "And he'll make sure she rots in prison."

Jacoby moved away from the window to the side of the great bed. He reached out and pressed a button on the wall.

"And her two boys?" Dina looked at the old man with a kind of sickened awe. "You'll take them from her, won't you, Lou?"

"I'll raise my grandsons to be the men my sons never were."

Cork went for Jacoby and grabbed a handful of his soft robe. Somebody needed to take this son of a bitch down. Jacoby dropped his cigar and looked startled, then afraid.

Cork pinned him to the wall. The old man seemed flimsy as cardboard.

Cork felt Dina's hand on his arm, gently restraining. She moved up beside him. He looked into her eyes and their calm brought him back to his senses. It would be easy enough to beat the old man to a pulp, and probably not hard to go further. But to what end? His own family was safe. Giving in to anger would only start the trouble all over again.

Sometimes a man had to swallow hard and accept what he could not change.

He nodded to Dina, and she dropped her hand. He let go of his grip on Jacoby and stepped back. The old man smoothed his robe and bent to retrieve his cigar.

Shuffling came from the hallway. A moment later, Evers, the houseman, appeared at the bedroom door. He was almost as old as Jacoby and, like his employer, wore a robe and slippers. His white hair was mussed from sleep. He looked at Dina and Cork with surprise but said nothing.

"See them out," Jacoby said.

"Yes, sir."

"And tell Mrs. Portman I'm hungry. I'd like breakfast."

"Very good, sir." Evers stood aside so that Cork and Dina could go before him.

They drove to Evanston, to the duplex that belonged to Cork's sister-in-law and her husband. He'd used Dina's cell phone to call ahead and let them know he was coming. Dina parked on the street in front but left the motor running.

"I guess this is it," she said.

"What are you going to do now?"

"Go home, get a little sleep, then head back to Bodine."

"Charlie?" he asked.

"Charlie," she answered.

"You've only known her a couple of days, Dina."

She shook her head. "Her, I've known my whole life."

"Back there at Jacoby's, I was ready to kill him. Thanks for stopping me."

"You were about to make a mistake I knew you'd regret. And I'd hate to lose you to the Illinois state penal system. It's a harsh world, and men like Lou Jacoby will always be in it. What keeps things balanced is men like you."

"Yeah?" He turned to her. Her face in the rising light of morning was soft and bright. "Seems to me not long ago you accused me of being a lot of things that aren't good. What was that all about?"

She reached out and cupped his cheek with her hand. "Mostly this: You always struggle so hard to do the right thing. Nobody always does the right thing, Cork, not even you. Be easy on people when they disappoint you. And be a little easier on yourself while you're at it."

She leaned to him and kissed his cheek.

"Go on." She nudged him gently. "Time for you to go."

He got out, walked around the car, and leaned in her window. One last time he looked into her eyes, which were as green as new leaves.

"Let me know how it goes with Charlie, okay?" he said.

"The truth is I'm a little scared."

"You? That's a first."

"Good-bye, Cork."

She slipped the car into gear and drove away. He watched until she turned the corner and was gone.

He stood on the sidewalk of a street still deep in the quiet of early morning. Behind closed curtains, men and women shared their beds, their fortunes, their lives, and their dreams, and their children were the sum of all these things made flesh. To rise in the morning and watch his sons and daughters stumble sleepy-eyed into the day, to send them out into the world on wings of love, to lie down at night and draw over himself the comforting quilt of the memories he shared with them—batting practice on a softball field or wrestling in the living room after dinner—what more could a man ask for or want?

Cork looked up and a seven-year-old boy appeared in the upstairs window of the duplex. Stevie's face lit up as if the sun had just risen after a very long, dark night. He smiled beautifully and his lips formed a single word that Cork could not hear but understood absolutely.

Daddy.

Krueger, William
Kent.

Copper River.

$24.00

		DATE	

BAKER & TAYLOR